BARBARA B]

MW00595581

Oberon

Originally published as

HOMECOMING

Other Books by Barbara Bickmore

In print & eBooks

East of The Sun 1988
The Moon Below 1990
Distant Star 1993
The Back of Beyond 1994
Homecoming 1995
Deep in the Heart 1996
Beyond the Promise 1997
Stairway to the Stars
West of the Moon

Books available in electronic format for Kindle, Nook & iBook

Oberon
Barbara Bickmore
eBook Copyright © 2011 Barbara Bickmore
Copyright © 2012 Barbara Bickmore
Original printing "Homecoming" Copyright © 1990 Barbara Bickmore

Published by Armchair ePublishing.
www.armchair-epublishing.weebly.com
Anacortes, WA 98221

www.barbarabickmore.com
Facebook: Barbara-Bickmore
Twitter: BarbaraBickmore
Email: Barbara@barbarabickmore.com

DEDICATED TO:

My beloved Mexican friends, friendships that have stood the test of time:

These are two of the wonderful friends I met during the 7 happiest years of my life, while living in the little village of Ajijic, in the mountains of Mexico.

Moreen (Binkie) Chater, British delight whom I met in Agustin's computer class in 1992 and still cherish and whom I'm able to Skype all the time.

Agustin Velarde, my Spanish teacher, computer guru, and dear friend, who shared the happiest and most exciting years of my life.

and to the memory of **Mark Clapp,** my son; No children should have to die before their parents.

and to

Walt Davis, whose friendship remains invaluable.

Barbara Bickmore

PROLOGUE

Aside from high mountain forests or national parkland, it may be one of the very few places in America that is pretty much as it was three hundred years ago.

Three hundred years ago there was already a great manor house and outbuildings that housed servants, a blacksmith and farrier, a windmill. There has not been a new building added in that three hundred years, unless you count the east and west wings of the house.

The square central section of the impressive brick house was started shortly after Martha Hamilton gave birth to the first child born on Oberon in 1672. The east wing was added over a hundred years later, in 1793, after there was a United States of America. The west wing came in the 1840s, though it burned down in 1908 and was rebuilt in the two years following that.

Oberon is one of the most beautiful places in America. It is an eighteen hundred acre island, lying one mile off the eastern shore of Maryland in the Chesapeake Bay. It contains marshlands on the north where thousands of birds winter: it has forests, three lakes, and a river which springs from the ground and divides the island nearly in half, creating an inviting cove in which many sailors, victims of the bay's unexpected summer storms, have found a haven.

There's not much that stirs a soul more than sitting in a rowboat, the mist rising from the water, and, as the dawn breaks, hearing the thunder of a hundred thousand pairs of wings beating the air, the honkings of the geese and watching the glorious birds blacken the sky.

It has been going on every year since the beginning of time. These giant birds fly thousands of miles from their northern breeding grounds in Canada, over the barren reaches and lakes, honking across the stony land of what is now called New England and New York, following the Susquehanna four hundred miles south from its origin in upstate New York to the largest estuary in North America, to the Chesapeake Bay.

It's a low-lying island with stately trees rising high into the air. Towering pines and oaks, maples red in autumn, sweetgum, birch and chestnut, with the shining green of holly sprinkled throughout the forests. Azaleas, rhododendrons, and dogwood dot the woods all up and down the Atlantic seaboard, and in the spring their blazing color quickens the heart.

Deer are prolific on the island, since no hunting has ever been permitted, except for the first twenty years when killing a deer could be a matter of life and death in the harsh winters before the great house afforded protection. The ducklings and geese served on the baronial sideboard came from the rivers of the mainland, the Miles and Choptank Rivers that meandered for miles. Every Hamilton assured the waterfowl that they were safe on Oberon. It was sacred ground.

It can be just as soul-stirring-in fact, it can make the heart thump-to sit in that same rowboat at dawn, the bay like a mirror, and watch the eastern sky streak pink like jagged fingers, observing fish jumping and seeing the less dramatic birds-the orioles and mourning doves, the thrushes and finches, the bluebirds and quail, and the warblers.

It can be silent shortly after dawn, when the sun's rays begin to warm the land and the water. The bay is shallow, despite the billions of gallons ejected from the rivers that feed it from the west: the mighty Susquehanna, the Patuxent, the Potomac, the Rappahannock, York and James Rivers, all of great historic significance. And on the eastern shore, the more slowly moving rivers-the Choptank, the Miles, the Chester-flow gently into it. Along the riverbanks are loblolly pines, hickories, beeches, poplars, oaks, and willows.

It is a flat land of great beauty and tranquility, except when there are summer storms that churn the waters into monstrous waves and darken the skies with thunder let loose by the gods. Its earth has nursed-tobacco farms for over three hundred years. It was some of the earliest land to be settled in the New World, having been discovered through an exploratory cruise by the same Captain John Smith who had helped to found Jamestown a year earlier, in 1607.

From a land grant with which the Crown endowed Lord Baltimore, parcels of which he sold, the first home was built along here in 1658. It was built by indentured servants and slaves who had been introduced into the land of freedom from its founding. By 1662 there were a number of manor houses, where lands had been cleared; they still stand, having raised tobacco for England over the years.

Since everything moved by ship, the first settlements were along the Bay or the rivers, and in 1671 it was to the Chesapeake Bay area that Samuel and Martha Hamilton headed. Newly arrived from Surrey, Samuel vowed to carve out a fiefdom larger than the estate his older brother would inherit. He needed a wife to help him, not one of the landed aristocracy that he would have married at home, but a rugged woman who could stand the hardships of living and working in the wilds, someone who could bear his children and weave their clothes and cook their food and help him with the work, for at first there were only the two of them, no servants. And never any slaves.

They left Jamestown on their wedding eve, the last day of April 1671. Martha had been born in Jamestown, and her father, the blacksmith, tried not to weep at her going. Her mother did not control her bawling, and yet she envied her daughter, starting an adventure with a man as handsome as Samuel, and obviously so well-born. The thought that the blood of nobility would run in her grandchildren's veins gave her some consolation, but she was afraid she would never see her daughter again.

By the time, four, months later, that Martha and Samuel found the spit of land that Samuel fancied, their arms were muscled from rowing, their hands calloused and rough, and Samuel, to his great surprise, had fallen in love with the sturdy woman he'd married.

Together they built a house that lacked even one true right angle on land that was bounded on one side by the Miles River and on the other by the vast expanse of Chesapeake Bay. On clear days one could see the western shore, whose low forests glistened darkly. Martha thought there was no prettier place in the world.

Samuel knew that come spring they would have to return to Jamestown to restock, but he thought they had enough stores to last the winter.

On a beautiful August afternoon they went berrying, taking time enough to make love under a spreading oak tree, untouched by the Puritanism of their New England cousins. When they returned to their cottage in the late afternoon all that remained were burning coals and smoke-filled air.

Their stores for the year had gone up in flames. The only thing that remained was the boat, which had been hidden in high reeds in a cove nearby. In the boat were a knife, a hammer, and a bucket, along with seeds left over from their planting in May, not that they would do much good at this time of year. Though his pistol was nowhere to be found, his musket was in the boat.

"We'll have to return to Jamestown," Samuel said, and thought maybe the pain in his chest was his heart breaking.

"Is it Indians?" Martha asked, though she knew the answer before he nodded. She was frightened, envisioning her scalp ripped from her head and, later, her skull on the end of a long stick.

They headed for the boat, and Samuel began rowing not up or down the coast but out into the bay, toward the patch of green closer than the opposite shore. It turned out to be an island, though he did not know that for a long time.

They stayed there the first night. Martha was so frightened she vomited in the morning, and could eat none of the berries Samuel collected. He was careful not to build a fire, so that no Indians could discover them.

Martha was ill for days, lying in a bed of tree boughs that Samuel rigged up for her, until it finally dawned on her that she was with child. She vomited constantly. Samuel boiled bark and leaves from trees for her. He felt desperate. This woman he had come to love so much, who was bearing his child, could not die on him. He had to save her, but she was too ill to travel.

He shot a buck, and they had meat for weeks. He needed salt, though, if he was to preserve meat.

There must be other homesteads around, on the mainland, he thought. With great misgiving and fear in his heart, he set out to find his nearest neighbors.

When he rowed back, two weeks later, with flour and coffee and other stores which he hoped would last long enough to transport his ailing wife to the little village of six houses which he had discovered, Martha met him, smiling, with the carcass of a wild boar and greens she had gathered in the woods. She told him she would not think of leaving. She wanted to have their child on this island, which she had circumnavigated, and hoped he could find some way to buy it, because it was here that he was going to found his dynasty. It was the most beautiful place in the world, with meadows and forests and ponds and marshes.

They argued.

Samuel returned to the village and bought saws and hammers and nails. And in February, in the midst of an ice storm, the first Hamilton born in the New World arrived, with his father delivering him in a protected thicket of forest surrounding a little lake. Martha never loved any of the feather down beds she would have in the remaining years of her life as much as she did the soft and aromatic bed of pine needles where her first son was born.

Two years later, when they met up with their first minister, they had him christened John. John Jay Hamilton.

By then, there was a second to name also, Talbot Raleigh Hamilton.

And they christened the island, too.

"Oberon," said Samuel.

"That's a fanciful-sounding name. I never heard it before," said Martha.

"He was the King of the Fairies in a Shakespeare play."

Martha had never heard of the playwright who had died only fifty-six years before. Martha could write her name, and read a bit, but a playwright was beyond her.

"And our boat shall be called The Titania."

Martha looked at their little skiff and smiled. A highfaluting name for such a humble boat, but she was perfectly willing to humor her husband.

By the time Samuel died, in 1717 at the age of seventy, the central portion of the manor house at the southern tip of the island had been built, as had all the outbuildings and the windmill that would last for well over three hundred years. The house itself would be added onto by succeeding generations, for in 1717 there were no great east and west wings. But the magnificent square house that would eventually be the central portion of the mansion rose regally from lawns that were green and mowed, surrounded by gardens that, if not reminiscent of English gardens, were at least spectacular. Twenty-five people lived on the island, including Samuel and Martha, who outlived him by seven years.

The oldest son, John, and his wife, Merry, had three children, only one of whom stayed on Oberon, the others wending their way west. Talbot, their second son, and his wife had but one daughter, and she died when six years old. Charity, Samuel and Martha's daughter, came to visit for Christmas and each summer. She married a man who owned an Annapolis shipyard, which was now run by their grandson.

During the 1740s, the Bay was infested with Spanish pirates. Jamestown had, unfortunately, been settled in the mosquito ridden area that was to cause so much death to the founders, mainly because the British did not want to be near the open sea where Spanish buccaneers could pillage and plunder them. No one ever said it aloud, but when another Hamilton daughter, Alice, quickly married the man who had courted her for years and whom everyone knew bored her to extinction, people wondered. And when the child arrived, barely seven months after the wedding, eyebrows were raised at the swarthiness of the skin, the blackness of the hair and eyes.

And people remembered, silently, that pirate ships had been seen sailing up the coasts, but had never been discovered in hiding or near any cannons. Her own father wondered if any of those ships could have lain in anchor in the coves at Oberon, where tall trees hid the entrances to deep creeks.

Alice and her husband moved to Baltimore, and thence to Philadelphia.

By the time of the Revolution, in which three Hamilton men fought, Oberon was a renowned estate, famous as far away as Washington. Hamilton men had much to say about the running of the new county and in the state government after the Revolution.

In the middle 1800s, surrounded by estates that used slave labor, Hamiltons swore they would never deny another person freedom. Thomas Hamilton often hid runaway slaves on their way to freedom. If he believed in anything, and he did, it was that the United States was a land of freedom for all, not just for whites. Black men knew that if they could somehow get this far north, and get a boat and row to that island a mile offshore, they would be taken care of. They could count on being fed, having clean clothes and shoes. And they would be sent to safety and freedom, with perhaps a few pieces of silver in their pockets.

Oberon. The word echoed through the Underground Railroad. It represented safety.

Maryland itself was divided on the issue of slavery. Though most of the large estates profited from slave labor and the manners and mores of Maryland were closely allied to the South, it voted to stay in the Union and to abolish slavery. The fact that it voted against its pocketbook was admirable.

By the late 1800s, most Hamiltons had left the island for greener pastures and more exciting cities. They became explorers of the West, bankers scattered throughout the East Coast, builders of empires through construction and the China trade, founders of tobacco companies. Later they spread out into the new automotive industry and into steel, but by then most of them were no longer named Hamilton or even knew of each other.

There were only two pieces of land that had been held longer than Oberon by one family since the founding of the country.

By 1949, the only Hamilton who was a direct linear descendant of the original founders, who had spent vacations and Christmas holidays at Oberon, and who had visited his grandparents there, was Oliver Wendell Hamilton. And he was the first Hamilton not to entertain a president there. From the time of General Washington until Herbert Hoover, every President of the United States had been entertained at Oberon.

In fact, while President Taft was visiting, the west wing caught fire thanks to one of the guests, who fell asleep with a lighted cigar. Oliver's father spent a fortune rebuilding and refurnishing it much as it had been for well over a hundred years.

No one had lived full-time at Oberon since the late 1880s, but it was beloved land, held in trust not only for future Hamiltons but for future wildfowl, whose ancestors had been coming as long as birds had used the Atlantic Flyway. It was a haven. No bird could be shot on Oberon. Blackwater Wildlife Refuge, to the south, protected them too. But Oberon was private land and the owners had always and ever felt that it was their duty to help preserve the future of the world.

Which is why Oliver Hamilton did not invite Franklin Delano Roosevelt to dinner. He was sure FDR was leading the United States down the path of destruction. And Harry Truman followed in his footsteps.

By 1949, there wasn't a Hamilton born who didn't love that island more than they loved any other place in the world. Who wouldn't have fought to keep it American? Who wouldn't fight to preserve it as it had been preserved for two hundred and seventy-seven years of belonging to Hamiltons and one hundred and seventy-three years of being part of the United States of America? Oliver Hamilton was one of America's most influential men. And though he was one of its wealthiest, very few people outside of New York City had ever heard of him. He did not have the wealth of the Rockefellers or the Fords or the Mellons or a hundred other families, many of whom the public had never heard of. No one, including Oliver himself, knew exactly what he was worth. But no one in his family ever had to ask the price of anything. His family had never had a scandal, not once in all those years. Or if they had, it was someone whose name was no longer Hamilton, and whose connection with Oliver was vague or tenuous at the very least. No Hamilton ever caused a ripple in society. And although they were one of the oldest families in the United States, they did not participate in the New York social scene. Though they had a penthouse on Park Avenue, their profile was low indeed. Their names were seldom in the papers, other than contributing a library to a university now and then or, by the 1930s, in Republican politics, though no Hamilton would ever run for office. Oliver worked behind the scenes and through his mouthpiece, <u>The New</u> <u>York Chronicle</u>, which he bought in 1925, the same year he married the beautiful Silvie Templeton Holister of Oyster Bay, the year he was twenty-seven.

One

The coincidence was not lost on either of them.

It was the year that Walter Kerr's review of the smash hit musical *South Pacific* was headlined, "Pearls, Pure Pearls." Ezio Pinza made "Some Enchanted Evening" famous... *Across a crowded room*

And Sydney first saw Jordan Eliot across a crowded room from her vantage point atop a piano, where she was dancing. He was leaning with his back against the wall, smoking a long cigarette, the only man not in a white dinner jacket or a tuxedo. His dark brown hair was too short to curl, but the tendency to do so was obvious. He must have been six-two, broad-shouldered, with a narrow waist. He wore a navy blue blazer and a blue silk patterned ascot instead of a tie. He was staring at her, laughter filling his eyes. He was the most beautiful man she'd ever seen.

Jordan had been watching her ever since she'd clambered onto the piano and begun to weave her hands through the air, shimmying with abandon. She was the classiest looking girl he'd ever seen. Straight-cut, honey-gold hair just brushing her shoulders, high cheekbones, a finely chiseled aristocratic nose, a wide, generous mouth. But she wasn't pretty. He realized that instantly. She was skinnier than the women he usually liked, though that red dress promised a great body. She was certainly stunning, but not pretty, he told himself again. People wouldn't turn around to look at her twice, yet he could not take his eyes from her. It was, he decided, her sense of joy that attracted him.

When their eyes met he began to thread his way through the throng of dancers until, when the song ended, he was standing in the curve of the baby grand.

She knelt down and slid to a sitting position on the edge of the piano. His first words to her were, "You've got dynamite legs."

"And you're the handsomest man with the bluest eyes I've ever seen."

"You embarrass me," he said.

"And you embarrass me when you introduce yourself with a remark about my legs."

He bowed slightly, his eyes flickering with amusement. "Touché," he said. "Understand I shall not make the same mistake twice."

Sydney slid off the piano and leaned down to pick up her shoes, reaching out to hold on to Jordan's arm as she wriggled her foot into one shoe and then the other. "In that case, let's find me a drink. I'm dying of thirst."

"I'd think so, after those gyrations."

"You're not from New York, I can tell by your non-accent."

"Elk Park, Indiana," he admitted. "I hope you don't hold that against me."

She looked at him with a sidelong glance. "When I hold something against you, it won't be that you're from Indiana."

That took him back for a minute. "Well, your accent doesn't sound it, but I'll bet a million to one you *are* from here. No one but New Yorkers talk so outrageously or dance on pianos. I thought that went out with the Charleston."

They arrived at the bar. "A Coke," Sydney said.

"Beer," he said.

"Come on." She took hold of his arm. "The terrace is this way. I need some fresh air."

They parted the billowing silk drapes and the soft air of New York in spring filtered over them. From their lofty vantage point, the city sparkled like diamonds.

"I'm Jordan Eliot."

She leaned her elbows and her back against the parapet and, holding her glass in both hands, faced him. "Sydney Hamilton," she said, "Sydney with a 'y.' "

"I've never met a girl named Sydney."

"My parents conceived me while there on their honeymoon."

"Imagine that," he murmured, looking out over the city, "honeymooning in Australia."

They were silent for a minute, he studying the city, she studying him. "You're not even self-conscious about being the only man not in formal attire."

He looked at her again. "I don't come from a place where they wear it. We didn't even wear it to dances at Northwestern. I figure if people judge me by those standards, they're not people I particularly want to know."

"Northwestern," she said. "Let me guess. You've come to the big city to make your fortune in corporate law."

He laughed. "That was half my classmates. Not me."

"You're interning at New York Hospital."

"That's for Cornell, not Northwestern."

"Hmm," she said, "I'm usually pretty good at this. Let's see. Ah, Wall Street."

"Perish the thought," he said. "All that sounds so repugnant. Well, not medicine, but that's not for me."

"You can't be a physicist. Physicists don't look like you."

"Is it necessary to wear glasses, squint, and be humorless to be a physicist?"

"I don't know." Sydney smiled at him. "I've never seen one outside of the movies. Okay, how do you earn your living?"

His look was serious. "How I earn my living and what my profession is are two different things."

Sydney turned to look out over the city. "Explain the difference."

"It couldn't possibly interest you."

"Ah, trying to hide what you do. A jail bird, then?"

He shook his head. "You don't seem like the kind of girl who hangs around with waiters."

She jerked her head to look at him again. "Go on! I don't believe it. A Northwestern graduate who looks like a business intern, a waiter?"

"I majored," he said, "in Drama."

"Oh, Lord, a would-be actor."

"There, you've nailed it. Now, what about you? You're a secretary waiting until the right man comes along, and you're going to help him rise up the corporate ladder and get rich."

But he already knew that was wrong. If he'd ever met someone who came from money, who had class and breeding, someone who had never had to worry about money, it was this Sydney.

"To quote someone I've just met, and think I like despite some limitations, perish the thought."

"How about a professional party goer?"

"Actually, I'm not really fond of parties or any large gatherings." She stared at him, tossing her head back so that her straw-colored hair swung out and her golden earrings shimmered. "I'm a senior at Wellesley."

"Ah, Boston. I've never been there." He leaned his elbows on the railing and looked at her as she looked down at the sparkling lights. "But, you're really a native New Yorker? I didn't know there was such an animal."

"You're partly right. Though I've lived here all my life, I was born in Maryland."

"Home for the weekend?"

"Mm-hmm. I'm catching the six a.m. train back to school. I graduate in three weeks."

He glanced at his watch. "Five and a half hours. We either part now without ever getting to know each other or we go take the Staten Island Ferry and get a romantic view of New York and then have breakfast at the Automat and I'll get you to Grand Central in time for your train and we find out what this is."

"What this is? Ten minutes of conversation is an *it?*"

He nodded.

Sydney laughed. "I've lived in New York City nearly twenty-one years and I've never done either of those things."

"Do you have a coat?" he asked. "Where is it?"

He grabbed her hand and she led him to the coat room.

"We don't have to say goodbye," she said. "The hosts don't even know who's here."

"I don't even know who the hosts are."

She took his arm. "That's New York for you."

The evening was warm enough that Sydney only had to toss her coat over her shoulders. Since there was only a very slight breeze, she wondered why gooseflesh swept over her. She took hold of his arm and had to skip a bit to keep up with his long strides.

"How do we get to the ferry?" he asked.

"You invited me. I don't know. I've never been to Staten Island."

"Never?"

"What in the world would I go there for?"

He laughed. "I don't know. The movies make it sound like it's a sentimental thing to do."

"That's because ferries are romantic, I imagine. So, let's go find it." She raised her hand and rushed to the curb as a taxi rounded the corner. Its brakes screeched as it halted. "The cabbie will know where to go."

. On the way downtown she discovered Jordan's father owned the hardware store in Elk Park, Indiana. That his father's father had moved there from Friendship, Maine, after discovering his grandmother, whose family had lived in Elk Park since the mid-1880s. No one in the family understood why Jordan would want to become an actor, but he'd known since he was a junior in high school that that's what he wanted to do. Another alumnus from Northwestern, a year ahead of him in school, was Charlton Heston, who was already getting breaks in the theater. Several years ahead of them, Patricia Neal had gone the other way, west, and broken into movies, starring with Gary Cooper in *The Fountainhead*.

"Northwestern's got a good reputation for drama," Jordan said, reaching for Sydney's hand, "but I don't want to follow in Pat's footsteps and be in movies. The money may be there, but Broadway's the real place. Hollywood's just a bastard child of Broadway. But, look, I don't want to talk any more about me. Let's talk…"

"About me? I've been to Europe three times. The rest of my life has been spent here and in Maryland. I'm going to grad school in Philadelphia."

"University of Pennsylvania?"

Sydney nodded.

"I'm impressed. Not an easy school to get into."

The cabbie twisted around and practically shouted. "Here ya are."

They were in luck. A ferry was leaving the slip within ten minutes. There were hardly any passengers at this hour, and Sydney and Jordan, without any verbal agreement, walked up the iron stairway to the upper deck. From a loudspeaker someplace music sifted through the night. They had the place to themselves.

They leaned against the railing as the horn announced the departure by blaring loudly, and the ferry slowly moved forward, out into the open. Moonlight danced on the water.

"I always think I can see across to Europe," Sydney said.

"Nope. You're looking toward South America."

She cocked her head and looked at him. "How come you know more about my part of the world than I do?"

It wasn't Ezio Pinza but Frank Sinatra, who began to sing Some enchanted evening across a crowded room someday you'll see her...

Jordan turned and held out his arms. Sydney walked into them, moving to the slow rhythm of the muted music. She liked the feel of his arms around her, guiding her expertly. She didn't even have to concentrate to follow him. He pulled her close as Sinatra crooned, *"It's just one of those things...*

"One of those crazy things... " Jordan sang into her hair.

"A *trip to the moon on gossamer wings,"* she murmured, closing her eyes and thinking Jordan smelled good. It was probably just his after-shave; nevertheless, she liked it. He might be a hick, she thought, but there was an edge to him.

She stopped dancing and he looked at her quizzically. Untying the arms of her coat that she'd wound around her neck, Sydney threw it on one of the benches. It wasn't that she was too warm. It was that she wanted to be close to him, feel him as they danced, feel his heartbeat next to hers, feel his leg move against hers.

Reaching for her hand, he twirled her around. They danced as though they'd moved together before, for a long time before, knowing what steps each would make. There was no one to see them. Only a gentle breeze followed them around the upper deck. They did not stop dancing even when Sinatra's voice faded away. They danced with the lapping of the sea against the boat their only rhythm, their bodies melding close, touching each other before he spun her around again.

The ferry's horn blasted as they approached Staten Island, and as Jordan drew Sydney to him, his arms wound around her and his lips crushed down upon hers. She closed her eyes as her arms twined around his neck, as her mouth opened for him and felt the warmth, his soft lips urgent, tasting her. Her mind blanked as she felt that for perhaps the first time she was being truly kissed.

When the ferry bumped into the piles, they looked at each other, and hand in hand ran down the stairs onto the wooden pier and rushed into the ticket stall. Jordan shoved a dollar at the tired looking, uniformed man trying to look like a naval officer, and they ran back, never stopping to walk, running up the stairs again until they were out of breath. Then they laughed, leaning against the railing. Voices floated up the stairs, but that did not stop Jordan from pulling her close.

The hard urgency of his kiss belied the softness of his lips and, when they pulled apart, Sydney said in a low voice,

"Whatever they teach you out in Elk Park, I like."

Jordan's arms were still around her as they gathered up her coat. "Well, girls in Elk Park haven't kissed like that, or anyplace else, for that matter."

A group of four young men and two girls in their teens burst through the door, talking loudly.

Sydney and Jordan didn't speak, staring out onto the brightly lit Staten Island dock, leaning against the railing with their arms around each other. When the ferry again pulled out of the slip they did look at each other, grinning, and Sydney leaned her head against his shoulder.

"I don't even know you," he said as they were nearing the Manhattan dock. "Yet I know I've never known anyone like you."

"I don't think I'm all that different, though all my life people have been telling me so. I don't quite understand."

"Maybe not according to your lights. Don't you think our grandchildren will be delighted to hear how I first saw you, dancing on top of a piano?"

She raised her face to his. "Kiss me again. I like what your kisses do to me."

He leaned down and met her mouth, his tongue moving along her lips. The group at the other end of the deck paid no attention to them. Jordan turned so he could pull Sydney into his arms and she sighed, thinking she'd never felt quite this way when she'd been kissed before. His arms made her feel safe; at the same time, his kisses made her yearn to cast safety to the winds.

The ship jolted against the dock, and they broke apart. Jordan looked at his watch. "Just enough time for an Automat breakfast. You were pulling my leg, weren't you, when you said you've never eaten there?"

"I really haven't."

"I know where one is up near Grand Central," he said, "but you've got a choice of either walking all that way or paying for the cab. I don't have enough money for a taxi *ana* a breakfast."

"I'll opt for the cab," Sydney said. Several were waiting on the street as they came out of the ferry station. "I want you to treat me to my first Automat experience."

"Actually, this isn't the time of day when they're at their best," he said as the cab driver drove north through empty streets: "Their baked beans are the greatest."

"Baked beans?"

She paid the driver as he stopped in front of Horn & Hardart's, realizing this was the first time she'd ever paid for a cab, or anything else, when a man was with her. She looked up at Jordan as he reached to help her out of the cab. Well, if looks were all that mattered, he was worth it. No one she'd ever met looked like he did. Why weren't people stopping on the street and staring at him? she wondered.

As they entered the nearly empty Automat, people did turn to look at him, and Sydney could understand why. And the way he kissed. Well, the cab was certainly worth it.

Jordan nodded toward the audience of onlookers. "See? They're all looking at you. Are you always the center of attention?"

Sydney laughed loudly. "Just goes to show you. I thought they were staring at you."

"Am I wearing a red dress that looks like I've been poured into it with cleavage that nearly reaches my navel?" He took her hand to lead her over to the food dispensers. "How much time do we have? I mean, you have to go get a bag and change your clothes, don't you?"

Sydney was fascinated by the little glass windows that contained such a variety of foods. "I never bring a bag when I come home. And I can wear this on the train."

He raised his eyebrows. "In the middle of the day?"

"Sure. No one knows me. And if they do, they won't be surprised. Come on, where are these baked beans?"

"At five in the morning?"

She shrugged, peering into each glass door. "Ah, look, here they are. Now what do I do?"

"Wait a minute. I forgot to get my dollar changed into nickels."

His dollar? But she saw him give the woman at the counter two-dollar bills and receive a handful of nickels.

He slid five nickels into the slot and the glass clicked open. She pulled out the savory smelling beans. "I don't even like baked beans."

"Why in the world are you getting them?"

"You told me they're good."

"So's the brown bread. Get some orange juice to ward off scurvy."

"I need coffee if I'm going to stay awake. I have to study for a test this afternoon once I get on the train."

"Study what?" he asked as they sat down at the marble topped table.

She pulled a book out of her coat pocket. "This."

He glanced at it. "What're you majoring in?"

"Oh, God, who knows? I started out as an English major because I've spent my life reading and writing. But then I switched to political science. And now I'm graduating with a double major. History and poli sci."

"What are you going to do with it?"

She shrugged. "These beans *are* delicious. Divine." She buttered the brown bread and took a swallow of coffee. "I don't know."

"What am I going to-do about seeing you again?"

She leaned toward him, an elbow on the table, a cup of coffee in the other hand. "Kiss me again," she said. "I like the way you kiss."

He glanced around the large, nearly vacant room and reached over to brush his lips against hers. "Well, that's not quite what I had in mind, but it'll do for now."

He smiled at her. "How am I to see you again?"

"Write to me at Wellesley."

"Will you answer?"

"How persuasively can you write?"

"How can I look you up in the Manhattan phone book?"

"We have an unlisted number."

"You're not being terribly cooperative."

"When I come back to the city, after graduation, if I stop in New York on my way to Oberon I'll come dine at Giorgio's."

"Not Tuesday or Wednesday. They're my nights off. Otherwise, I work from four until closing."

Sydney leaned back in her chair and studied him. "Are you really a good actor?"

Jordan put a hand over hers. "I've got to think so, don't I? When I get a part I'll let you know and you can come see me and decide for' yourself. Yeah, I think someday the name Jordan Eliot is going to blaze above a theater."

He held out a pack of cigarettes. Sydney shook her head. "One of the habits I've never taken up."

"Do you mind if I do?"

"Not if you're not going to kiss me afterward."

He raised an eyebrow, looked at her, and put the pack back in his shirt pocket. "Okay, I'll wait."

She nodded. "Thanks, I hate the taste of cigarettes. And the smell of smoke."

"I can't say I haven't been warned. You have all sorts of strong likes and dislikes?"

"Mm. All sorts."

He pushed his chair back. He wanted to kiss her again. And again. "If we go over and wait for your train we can kiss each other in front of all the trains that are departing, and people won't pay any attention to us."

Sydney flashed a smile. "That's a great idea. Even a little better, but barely, than coming here and having baked beans and dancing across to Staten Island."

Holding hands, they walked down the block to Grand Central. Before entering the cavernous station, Jordan turned and put his arms around her, kissing her slowly, a lingering kiss. Sydney sighed.

He led her up the steps and looked around. "We still have half an hour. Come on." They found a gate where people were pouring through, and he put his arms around her again' and brought his mouth down to hers. No one took any notice.

They walked around the entire perimeter of the large waiting room, stopping to kiss in front of every open gate.

"God," said Sydney, "who would ever dream the most erotic place in the world is Grand Central Station?"

"You're right," Jordan agreed. "What I want to do right now is throw you down on the floor and make mad love."

"Sounds like a great idea," she whispered. "Impossible, but great."

"Shit," he said. "Let's go find a dark corner and really kiss." They did, clinging to each other, straining through their clothes to feel each other's closeness.

"Christ," he murmured. "I feel like I'm in a corny movie," Sydney said. "I mean, this is silly. We're acting like kids."

"What I feel isn't like a kid," he said. "But I can't stand it. Come on, let's go find your train."

It was already boarding, steam hissing from the engine. "Do you have something to write with?" Sydney asked.

"Nope."

"Neither do I. So it's no sense giving you my phone number."

"I'll find you," he said. "If I don't, find me at Giorgio's. What date do you graduate?"

"June eighth."

"Giorgio's on the ninth. I'll be there."

As she' started to mount the steps to the train, he grabbed her, kissing her as though he might never let her go.

"Have we figured out what 'it' is?" Sydney smiled at him.

"I can't answer for you," he said, holding on to her hand as she climbed up the first step. "But I have."

"All aboard," sang the conductor.

She waved to Jordan Eliot, a last glance through the dusty, spattered window as the train began to chug out of the dark terminal. Several people stared at her, so she pulled her coat around her, trying to hide within it. She closed her eyes and leaned back in the seat, hugging herself. Oh, God, she felt good.

Jordan Eliot.

Sydney Eliot.

Her eyelids flashed open. What the hell was she thinking of?

Mrs. Jordan Eliot? The wife of a waiter? A would-be actor?

Someone she hadn't even known six hours ago. Her parents would have a shitfit.

And then she laughed out loud. A romantic night, dancing, a man who really knew how to kiss. *Really.* And she was ready to bind her life to his? She must be nuts.

She shook her head as though to clear it. Animal magnetism, that was all. He was handsome, he danced divinely, he had a nice sense of humor, and his kisses lit a fire within her. That was all.

She closed her eyes, slept all the way to Boston, and got an "A" on her test anyway.

Two

"You musta scored," said Monday Pearson, standing in the bathroom doorway watching Jordan shave. "I got home about five and you weren't back yet." His eyes were bloodshot even at three-thirty in the afternoon. He drank tomato juice as he watched Jordan's reflection in the mirror.

Monday was also a waiter at Giorgio's and Jordan's roommate at their two-room flat on Bleecker Street. He was from Falfurias, Texas, and you could cut his accent with a knife despite his four years at Stanford. Jordan was constantly impressed with Monday's intellect, which he hid under a bushel barrel most of the time. Equally impressive was his sense of humor, the part of him he showed to the world.

Jordan glanced at his watch. They had to be at work in half an hour. They'd left work after eleven last night and gone to the party, people whom Monday had met someplace or other. Monday was always meeting people and dragging Jordan along after work. But, unless there was casting for a new play Jordan could sleep until after noon. Monday was sitting at his typewriter by nine every day. He wouldn't budge from it until he had five pages written.

"Whether it's shit or not, I make myself write five," he always said. He threw away over half of what he wrote and rewrote all of what he wrote, sometimes seven and eight times.

Jordan wondered why Monday felt he had to live in New York to make it as a writer. He thought Monday would get farther if he lived in the woods or the mountains where there weren't as many distractions. But Monday said he needed New York, for which Jordan was glad. Monday was easy to room with, and Monday gave him a social life. He liked the nights after work when they didn't go out, when they sat around drinking beer and solving the world's puzzles. Someday, Monday promised Jordan, he'd write a Pulitzer Prize-winning play in which Jordan could star.

In the meantime, he wrote mornings, worked evenings, and played nights.

"I met a girl."

Monday cocked his head to the side and studied Jordan as he put away his shaving gear. Monday balled girls several times a week, but he knew Jordan hadn't stayed out all night since they'd begun to share this flat nine months ago.

"Get laid?"

"Better than that."

"Nothin's better'n that."

"Can you remember the names of all the girls you've laid this past month?"

Monday shook his head. "I can't even remember the name of the one two nights ago."

"Sydney Hamilton." Jordan rolled the name off his tongue. He repeated it. "I shall remember her name for a long time. A class act."

"Now I get it. Class acts don't let you lay them."

"Monday, good friend, you are narrow-minded, and you are not yet a success as a writer because you deal only with the more crass emotions. You do not deal with matters of the heart."

"Matters of the heart are what sell books and movies but screw up life."

"They also make life worthwhile."

"You just need to get screwed, Jordie boy. Don't confuse your glands with emotions."

Jordan was not confused at all. He knew that he wanted to see Sydney again. And again. He whistled as he tied the black bow tie that Giorgio's demanded, and still whistled as he and Monday walked down the four flights of stairs into the warm sunshine of a late May afternoon in Greenwich Village. "New York is the most beautiful place in the world," he said.

"Oh, Christ." Monday slapped him on the back.

Sydney was furious with herself. In the midst of whatever she was doing — studying for a test, playing tennis or bridge, reading, walking across campus with a friend, Jordan, Eliot popped into her vision. She'd be talking to someone, or starting to hit the tennis ball, and, instead, saw the face of Jordan Eliot.

She'd go to bed at night and as soon as she closed her eyes she remembered how his kisses felt.

She'd never dated anyone who hadn't gone to a prep school. The only male she knew who wasn't an Ivy Leaguer was her brother, Evan, who simply didn't have the marks and didn't care. All the males she knew were destined for a life like the one she'd always known. They'd become lawyers or doctors or stockbrokers or head their own, or their father's, businesses. Or they'd do nothing. Sail around the world in yachts. Summers on sailboats, winters on skis. They'd wear expensive suits with white shirts, perhaps pale blue for the more daring. They would be just like each other, just like their fathers.

They would not come to a von Damien party in a blazer and an ascot. They would not dine in an Automat, even for breakfast. Like her, they would never even have entered an Automat. They would not think riding the Staten Island Ferry the height of romance.

They would dine at, not be a waiter in, Giorgio's.

Sydney wondered if Jordan might ever have waited on her. She never noticed waiters.

No man she knew would ever think of becoming an actor. Wasn't that rather effete? Yet look at the men who were tops in that field. Clark Gable might have passed his prime but no one could ever call him anything but masculine. Gary Cooper. Cary Grant. Elegant.

But acting wasn't what serious men did. It was make-believe, not part of the real world.

What real world? Maybe she had no idea what the "real" world was. She'd led a sheltered life, she knew that. Did she have any right to judge what was real and what wasn't? And how many of those prep school clones that she'd known all her life had kissed her as Jordan had, had made her blood run hot, as he had? How many had seemed as genuine as he did, whether he opted for a world of make-believe or not?

She closed her eyes and remembered dancing across the deck of the ferry like Fred and Ginger in a romantic movie. Nothing she'd ever known had touched her the way he did, the way that whole evening did from the moment she saw him staring at her with that look of amusement on his gorgeous face.

And it was a gorgeous face. Was she acting like men acted, falling in love with a face rather than a person? Love? My God. That's nonsense. Why had she even thought the word love? She didn't even know Jordan Eliot. Yet she could not erase his face or his kisses or how she felt when she was in his arms.

The whole week was spent with him. Wherever she went and whatever she did, he accompanied her.

So, she was not surprised to see him standing in the dorm lobby when she went down to breakfast Saturday morning. He was across the room, just as he had been at the party Sunday night, leaning against the wall, but this time he wasn't smoking a cigarette. Since he'd been in every room with her, all week, she didn't even nod to him, but kept on going, until his voice stopped her. "Aren't you even going to say hello?"

She froze. Had her mind gone or had he really come to her? She turned slowly, knowing he would vanish if she looked hard enough.

But he didn't.

He stood there smiling, in cotton twill pants and a striped shirt, a sweater slung across his shoulders.

"You found me."

"It was easy. But even if it hadn't been, I would have."

They looked at each other for a minute. And then she walked into his arms. He kissed her, and kept kissing her even as other students walked past them, giggling.

"I figured," he finally said, "that if you have to study this close to finals it won't make that much difference, and besides, you're not going to flunk at this late date. I traded days with someone, and you've got me until Monday morning."

"I have a date tonight."

"Break it."

She broke into laughter, feeling exorbitantly happy as she reached out to take his hand. "Have you had breakfast?"

"I didn't even have dinner last night."

He wolfed down a breakfast of eggs, bacon, pancakes, orange juice, and three cups of coffee. "This is what I used to eat after I'd spent an hour shoveling snow before breakfast," he grinned

"I've been right," Sydney smiled, sipping her coffee.

"About what?"

"I thought everyone beyond a thirty-mile radius of New York City was a hick."

"New Yorkers are so damned insular," he said. "You don't think life exists beyond a thirty-mile radius. You're the limited ones. You'll see. You're young. You have growing to do."

He was baiting her. "What are you? Twenty-four, five, Mr. Experience?"

"Five. I came to New York last June, the week after graduation. Before college, I spent three years in the Navy. In the South Pacific, then Japan for a year after the war. I expected New Yorkers to be so sophisticated I'd be tongue-tied. Instead, I've found them very limited, quite amusing, and I'm aiming to spend the rest of my life there."

He lit a cigarette, then looked at her, remembered, crushed it out. "I don't care about getting rich really. I just want to act."

"Do you yearn to be a star?" Sydney was ashamed to realize her smile was condescending. All of Middle America, it seemed, wanted to be a movie star. Or write the great American novel. The hinterland was filled with dreamers.

He shook his head, pushing his chair back from the table. "Well, I don't want to be in movies. Except if a movie now and then would give me enough money to live nicely. The Broadway stage doesn't too often do that."

"Oh, you're a purist? Acting as art." He raised his eyebrows. "Doesn't sound like you approve of me." He stood up.

She said, "Let me get the check, unless you're the kind of man who won't let a woman pay."

"What kind of man is that? And, besides, I spent all my money to get up here."

She threw a five on the table and picked up the check.

"Boy, are you an extravagant lady. Five bucks for a breakfast tip in a place like this?"

"I'd think, as a waiter, you'd find it one of my charming traits."

"It sounds like we've begun to argue."

"I hope not. I look forward to more of your kisses."

They walked out into the May sunshine. "Do you want to see Boston?" she asked.

Jordan shook his head. "I don't want to have to concentrate on anything but you today. Let's just walk around. And wasn't that a lake I saw? Do they rent boats, or can we just sit someplace in the sun and stare into each other's eyes?"

"God, you're a romantic," she said, placing a hand on his arm. "Keep it up. I love it."

They walked through the campus to Lake Waban. He took her hand and she ran to keep up with his long strides as he led her down one of the paths through the trees.

When they were out of sight of buildings and people he stopped and turned, putting his arms around her. "All week long, I've thought about you. I've closed my eyes and remembered your kisses."

She giggled. "I thought I was the only nutty one."

"You are nutty. I've never met anyone like you. You're so carefree, and you don't care what people think."

"Not quite true," she said, loving the feel of his arms around her. "I just don't care what people I don't know think about me. But you'll be glad to hear I did feel a bit self-conscious in that red gown on the train."

"Aw, shucks," he said, imitating James Stewart. "I'm disillusioned." He kissed her again and she melted. In the middle of the day, in bright shining light.

"Want me to come to your graduation?"

"Oh, God, no." She leaned back to look at him in mock horror, running a hand through her hair to keep it out of her face. "I've only just met you. I wouldn't wish that on anyone."

"If it's important to you, I want to come."

"Well, it's not. Ceremonious things never are. Even my parents won't get that much of a kick out of it. After all, everyone in my family for God knows how far back has graduated from college. No big thing. The end of something, the beginning of something else."

"Philadelphia," he said, sitting under a tree on a patch of grass that overlooked the pretty lake. "When are you going there?"

"I'm not going until fall," she said. "And then it's just a couple of hours to New York, you know." Her smile teased him. "Close enough for me to come see you on opening night."

"Well, at least you'll be in the city all summer."

She shook her head and her hair swung across her face. "No one, but no one, stays in New York in summer. You can fry eggs on the pavement. The humidity is terrible."

He reached up to take her hand and pull her down next to him. "What do you do? Are you one of those who goes to Bar Harbor or Newport?"

"No."

He breathed a sigh of relief.

"I go to Oberon."

He pulled her close. "Oberon?"

"It's an island in Chesapeake Bay."

He was silent for a minute, staring at the sun sparkling on the water. Then he said, "Oberon is the King of the Fairies in <u>A Midsummer Night's Dream</u>."

Sydney nodded and smiled. "That, too. Oberon is the most magical place in the world. It is a fairyland."

"You have a summer cottage there or what?"

She turned away so he couldn't see her smile. "You might say that. Sometimes we go down for Christmas, too. Daddy always goes in the fall to hunt geese and ducks."

"More waterfowl winter in the Chesapeake delta than anyplace else in the world," Jordan said, as though that were a fact he'd long ago memorized for a geography quiz, and she realized how much she liked his voice. It didn't sound theatrical, though. She couldn't imagine his voice projecting to the back of a theater. But there was smoothness to it, a Middle America-ness, an indefinable something that made him sound trustworthy. An ingenuousness, that's what it was. No fakery about him at all, and she'd thought people in the theater reeked of phoniness and egotism. But Jordan wasn't like that.

Sydney said aloud, "You're not like most actors. You're not vain hut you seem to have great faith in yourself."

"Hope, more than faith. I've given myself three years. I either get a break in the next two years or I figure something else to do. Teach, maybe. My dad did. He taught history before he realized he could make a lot more money running a hardware store."

"Then why would you think of teaching?"

"Good question," Jordan answered. "My sister's a teacher. And do you know how much money she earns? Twenty-four hundred dollars. Two thousand, four hundred dollars a year. I make more than that in tips alone at Giorgio's."

Sydney started to say her allowance was more than that, but thought better of it.

"Well, money's not what it's all about," he said. "But it would be nice not to have my whole life dependent on whether I can afford a taxi or a train trip to Boston. I've no desire to make a fortune. I may have what you call faith in myself but I'm never going to be in the category of Tracy or Cooper or Gable or any of those guys. No one in the Broadway theater is that rich. I'll be satisfied to be comfortable. My wife doesn't need fur coats."

Sydney was amused at the thought of taking Jordan home to meet her father. They were poles apart. Suddenly she said, "I bet you liked Roosevelt, didn't you?"

He looked at her quizzically. "He was a hero. Truman's pretty good, too."

Sydney waved her hand in the air as if to dismiss him. "Truman might, just might, mind you, make a nice mayor of a small town. But President of the United States?"

"You'll see," Jordan shook his head. "History will be kind to our President some day."

"As for Roosevelt, I was brought up to think that after Hitler and Stalin, and maybe John L. Lewis, Roosevelt was the most evil man in the universe."

Jordan laughed. "You're pulling my leg, aren't you?"

Sydney shook her head and gave him a wry smile. "Not in the least. The country's going to the dogs with these Democratic administrations."

He looked at her a minute and reached out to pull her close, her head on his shoulder. "Sydney, let's not talk politics. I want to get to know each other, but let's not start with the things we don't agree on. Let's talk about things that have to do with us, not with the world. Let politics and religion and morality and philosophy wait, okay?"

"Where did morality come into this?"

"Politics is morality."

She thought a moment, and decided if they continued to know each other they could argue about that in the future. He was right. At this point they should stay away from dangerous topics.

"Jordan Eliot, you may possibly be more interesting than any other guy I've gone out with."

"We haven't even gone out yet."

"Kiss me again."

Gently he pushed her down on the ground, and the sun dappled across her face, through the greengold leaves of spring. "You have the most expressive mouth in the world," he said. "I love to look at it and I love to touch it, and I may kiss you until the end of time." His hand caressed her left breast. She closed her eyes.

She wanted him to kiss her there, she wanted to feel his tongue against her skin, but he went no farther. Later, he said, "Let's walk or do something. I can't stand what you do to me."

"I can't invite you up to my dorm room."

"It's a damned good thing," he said, his arm around her as they walked back toward the campus.

* * * *

When he left on the seven-twenty train Monday morning, he said, "I can't afford to come up next weekend."

She had her arms around his neck. "I don't want to see you until after I graduate. It's just two more weeks. I couldn't face my family if I flunked out of here now. Can you get a week's vacation?"

"No pay? I can't afford that."

"Work something out and drive down to Oberon with me when I'm through here. Spend a week in paradise with me."

"Who else will be there?"

"Big Mommy, my grandmother, will already be there. She usually goes down about Memorial Day. The caretakers live there year-round. Let me show you the place I love most in the world."

"Now, that," he said, kissing her eyelids, "is worth losing my job for."

"Well," Sydney said, not wanting to let go of his hands, "where will I pick you up on-oh, what's the date?"

"I don't have a phone. Call me at Giorgio's."

"All aboard," shouted the conductor. Jordan broke away from Sydney and walked up the metal steps. She watched as he strode down the aisle, choosing a seat next to the window, trying in vain to open it, his eyes locked with hers.

She threw him a kiss as the train began to move slowly. He craned his neck to look at her as the distance between them lengthened, waving until they could see each other no more.

"I've done it," she said aloud, still watching as the train snaked out of view. She'd vowed to be the first of her crowd not to fall in love while in college. She was going to show everyone that just because it was the time everyone thought you should fall in love, she hadn't. She hadn't even tried very hard. No one, of all the dozens of boys she'd dated in the last four years, had touched her heart. And now, within the space of one week she had completely lost it to the unlikeliest man she'd ever met.

"Jordan Eliot," she said as she walked out of the station into the cool early morning. "Mrs. Jordan Eliot."

She knew, as certainly as she had ever known anything, that that's who she was going to be. Sydney Hamilton Eliot, wife of a struggling actor. Wife of a waiter.

She laughed until it verged on hysteria. That's what was such fun about life. You never knew what was going to happen.

It was certainly worth waking up for.

She turned a cartwheel in the middle of the street and when a couple smiled and pointed at her, she cried to them, waving her hands in the air, "I'm in love!"

Three

In her four years at Wellesley, Oliver had not once visited Sydney. Her mother had come twice, once on her way to Kennebunkport. But then Sydney had gone to New York at least once a month. Silvie, her mother, made it clear, however, that her father was coming to her graduation. Sydney took for granted they would fly, because Oliver never drove when he could get someplace more quickly.

But Silvie phoned four days before graduation to say they would arrive early Saturday evening, and they would be driving. They hoped she would drive back with them on Sunday. Oliver could not wait until Monday morning to return to the city; they would leave after the graduation ceremonies Sunday afternoon, and Sydney could arrange to ship her baggage.

That suited Sydney fine. If they arrived back in New York Sunday night, she would have time on Monday to pack for the summer at Oberon, and take-off Tuesday. She called Jordan, who had phoned her twice a week since she'd last seen him.

"You going to come away with me?"

"Will you love me if I'm jobless?"

"Who said anything about love?" Well, he'd at least mentioned the word. "If you're coming with me, and you'd be a fool not to, I'll pick you up at your flat, or whatever it is you live in, about eight next Tuesday morning."

He gave her an address on Bleecker Street. "The village? I should have known."

"Then I just have to roll out of bed to get to work."

Of course, he was only a block or two from Giorgio's. That and Mama Leone's were New York's most famous Italian restaurants, and both were in Greenwich Village. "Everybody went to Mama Leone's, for it was famous far beyond Manhattan's boundaries. But only a distinguished clientele was welcomed at Giorgio's.

"Make it seven," she said. "It takes about six hours or so to drive there."

When her parents arrived, her father was driving a fire engine-red Packard convertible, so unlike him that Sydney had to laugh.

"Why, Daddy, what's happened to you?"

"Change of life," said her mother. Silvie Hamilton always looked as though she'd walked off the cover of *Vogue*. Even when she sunned herself at Oberon or on their twenty-sixth floor Park Avenue terrace she looked as though she was expecting the Queen at any moment. No, Sydney amended, she looked like the Queen herself, except she had a flair for fashion. American royalty. Which, Sydney supposed, is what they were, to some extent. Sydney had never seen her mother tousled. Even when, as a little girl, she crawled into her parents' bed early in the morning, her mother always looked ready for an audience. Sydney wondered, not for the first time, how it was that Evan, and not she, had inherited her mother's looks and her elegant ways.

As she was growing up, Sydney tried to be a lady like her mother.

"Be your own self," Silvie had urged. "You don't have to be like me or anyone else. There's not a person in the world you have to impress. Be who and what you want to be.'"

So her mother had seldom disapproved of the zany antics Sydney had been involved with and which had gotten her pictures in the papers. Never the *Chronicle*, of course. It never printed pictures of that ilk, anyhow. It didn't even have a gossip column. No Walter Winchell. No Earl Wilson. No Dorothy Kilgallen. Sydney wondered if that had to do with its lack of circulation, even if it was up there with the *Times* as one of the nation's most respected, albeit least read, newspapers.

Actually, Oliver had never admonished her, either. He'd look at the *News-he* did subscribe to all the other New York papers and glanced through the pile at breakfast, reading them more thoroughly in his limousine on the way to work-and it wasn't Sydney's antics that made him shake his head but the fact that the *News* found Sydney jumping into Senator Morton's swimming pool With all her clothes on more of a news splash than anything political.

Or when the crown prince of-heavens, she couldn't even remember what country, drank champagne from her shoe.

But poor Evan, when he did anything outrageous, and the *News* or another tabloid carried his picture and commented on the antics of society's rich and decadent, then Oliver did have a tizzy.

"But Daddy," Sydney would say, trying to defend Evan. She'd been at the same party, and Evan hadn't really done anything shameful. "You don't have a fit when I do the same thing."

"Oh, that's different," Oliver mumbled.

"Why?"

"Because, dear," Silvie said as she reached across the breakfast table to put a hand -over Sydney's, her eyes on Oliver, "you're a girl, and girls are allowed to be frivolous."

"I don't think I'm so frivolous," Sydney objected. "I have all A's in school."

Oliver looked over the top of the paper. "Why can't Evan emulate you in that way?"

Poor Evan. He never seemed able to win. He'd even flunked out of Colgate, despite Oliver's offering them a sizable donation. Oliver had sent him to Europe, hoping he'd acquire some civilizing influence. He'd sent Mother's younger brother with him. Uncle Billy was only twelve years older than Evan, and had never worked a day. But he came in handy now and then, and accompanying Evan to Europe was one of those times. Everyone loved Uncle Billy, including Oliver, who willingly supported him in a lifestyle that pleased his brother-in-law.

Mother and Uncle Billy's father had lost everything in 1929 and had never recovered. They used to visit him in the sanitarium out in Yaphank when they were little and Grandpa was still alive. For as long as Sydney could remember, Uncle Billy had lived with them in the big bedroom at the end of the upstairs hall, with a terrace that overlooked the city he loved so much.

He left once, to marry some rich lady and live with her a couple of years, but he came back. Even his ex-wife loved Billy. The only time Sydney ever saw him, though, was at the dinner table a couple of times a week. She didn't know where he spent most of his time. He didn't enjoy coming to Oberon.

"God, the country!" he'd say, slapping his forehead, as though he couldn't imagine a worse fate. He did come for Christmas the year after Grandpa died, but he thought living outside New York City was decidedly barbaric.

Sydney and Evan had spent all their summers with their other grandparents, Oliver's mother and father. Big Daddy and Big Mommy. Big Daddy had never really done anything in the line of work. He'd never had to. He could sit on his verandah at Oberon and by the time he arose from the chaise longue two hours later he'd have earned another hundred thousand. He and Big Mommy actually moved to Oberon from New York City when they were in their sixties and Sydney and Evan could hardly wait for summer to come, and Christmas vacations. Christmas was the most joyous time of the year to the Hamiltons, and Big Daddy always saw that they cut down the largest pine on the island. Until Sydney was nine she thought Santa decorated it, for when she went to bed Christmas Eve there was no sign of a tree. Now, when she looked back on those times, she imagined how hard all the adults had had to work to trim the tree and how late they must have stayed up so it could be such a wonderful surprise for the children.

Big Daddy had been dead three years now, and living alone out in the midst of the bay wasn't the safest thing in the world, so Big Mommy moved to the Park Avenue apartment, too. She and Uncle Billy-no relation, of course-would sit up playing canasta or double solitaire until long after Evan came home in the wee hours of the morning. They could be heard laughing together until nearly dawn. Neither of them was visible, then, until well after noon.

The Saturday of graduation was the first day of the year the temperature reached into the nineties. Sydney hadn't warned Silvie and Oliver, hoping they would find it a nice surprise, but she knew where they were sitting in the audience. When she stood to make the valedictory speech, she was pleased to see the look of surprise, the round "0" of Silvie's mouth, Oliver's raised eyebrows.

When the ceremony was over and the graduates and their parents were finding each other, Sydney saw her mother's arm waving high above the crowd. Sylvie was dressed in a white silk suit with a navy polka dot scarf wound around her neck. Her pearl teardrop earrings accentuated the few strands of gray at her left temple. Sydney thought her mother aged gracefully, as she did everything else. How old would she be now? Forty-six.

"Darling, we're so proud of you!"

"Well, you were salutatorian of your class right here. Did you graduate in this very place?"

"In this very place." Silvie smiled, putting an arm around her daughter. "It's a poor daughter who can't do better than her mother." -

But you haven't done anything with all your smarts, Sydney thought. You married Daddy and had Evan and me and haven't done anything with all your wonderful brains.

Two hours later, after Sydney had stowed what baggage would fit into the convertible's trunk, they were ready to take off. Oliver tossed the keys across the car to her. "Want to drive?"

Sydney smiled at the thought. "You trust me?"

"Doesn't matter," he grinned. "It's yours."

She squealed "Oh, Daddy, how perfectly lovely," and ran around the car to kiss him.

"It was your mother's idea," he said as he nodded toward Silvie. .

Sydney kissed her, too. "So that's why you drove up?"

"Of course you're going to keep the top down, aren't you, and my hairdo is going to be completely ruined."

"Mother, you're going to the hairdresser tomorrow anyway." Silvie went to Pierre's every Monday and Friday and had for as long as Sydney could remember.

The car purred as it ate up the miles.

"Mama," which was what Silvie called Big Mommy, "can't wait 'til you get to Oberon. When are you leaving? I suppose I won't get to see you at all."

Sydney turned to look at her mother. Oliver was trying to sleep in the backseat. "I plan to go down Tuesday."

Silvie sighed. "Well, I'll be down by the end of the month. I guess our togetherness will have to wait until then."

Sydney reached over and put a hand on her mother's arm.

They smiled at each other. "When's Evan coming home?"

Silvie shrugged. "Whatever your father suggests, Evan seems bound to do the opposite."

"I should have suggested he flunk out of college," Oliver shouted into the wind that hit him full in the face.

"He's never been a student," Silvie said.

"He's bright enough," Sydney said, defending him.

"He's bright enough to get whatever he wants without working," Oliver boomed. "He gets what he wants."

"Not if it takes discipline," Silvie said. "Besides, you know, he and Sydney don't always have to do the same things. When they do, Evan always comes out second best."

"Billy doesn't work, but you don't seem to resent that," Sydney said.

"If Evan were half as amusing as Billy, maybe I wouldn't mind. But he lacks a sense of humor."

It was true. Evan lacked charm, though he had an intensity despite his laziness.

Some part of Sydney recognized that her home was not an average home; nevertheless, she took it for granted. The elevator went only to the penthouse. No one else was permitted to use it. And on the twenty-sixth floor it opened into a small lobby where fresh flowers in a tall vase always greeted visitors.

The intricately carved wooden door led to the living room, which was only half the size of the lobby at Penn Station. As children, Sydney and Evan had skated around it, played marbles over its expanse, had birthday parties, and listened to their mother read them bedtime stories. It looked, however, as though a child had never disturbed it, as though everything in it-all the oversized dark walnut furniture-was always in place. There was never a speck of dust, never magazines or newspapers out of order.

It looked as though it were waiting to be photographed for *Better Homes & Gardens*. And, indeed, it had been featured in nearly every home magazine in the country and one in France. Despite its impeccable condition and because of the obvious taste used in decorating it, it was warm, a room that Sydney loved, though not as much as she loved the library with its wood-paneled wainscoting, a perfect backdrop to Oliver's collection of Renaissance masters. All winter long, whenever Sydney entered that room, a fire glowed in the fireplace.

They dined nightly in the formal dining room, even when there were no guests. There had been parties where not only the dining room but the enormous living room had been set with candle-lit tables with a uniformed waiter for each group of six. There was always, it seemed, someone extra for dinner. When Sydney and Evan were growing up their friends were always welcome, though Evan had gone away to Groton when he was thirteen. Oliver had hoped it would knock some discipline into him, improve his marks. But it didn't. Sydney had gone to Chapin.

Now there was always Big Mommy, and often Uncle Billy was around for dinner. Sometimes he didn't go out on the town until nine or ten. But just as often he didn't show. There was frequently some visiting dignitary whom Oliver brought home for dinner. Then he and his guest would disappear into his study, the odor of cigars permeating the whole lower floor.

When there were no guests, Oliver and Silvie would sit in the library, reading. Silvie usually had a novel and Oliver studied newspapers from around the world. He seemed to have an antenna that made him know exactly when to turn on the radio and listen to Gabriel Heatter deliver the news in his doomsday voice. Two or three evenings a week they dined out.

Big Mommy, on the other hand, had a card game going three nights a week in the library. There were different people each night. For Monday night bridge, there were two tables of women like herself, widows, women who had known each other for close to fifty years. They had gone to school together and had married into the circle and were now alone. The grande dames of New York. Tuesdays there were three men and five women. The laughter was not as robust as Mondays, for this was more serious. Friday nights it was a poker game, one that had been going on for years. Included on Friday was Carlos, Big Mommy's chauffeur, who had been with her for over twenty years and had attended these poker games for that long, too. They had a running tab. At the end of the year if Carlos owed Big Mommy money, he took her out to dinner, bringing her a corsage. When she owed him money, she sent him on a vacation. In this way he'd visited Barbados, Greece, Spain, Mexico, and Majorca. Their poker games filled Friday nights with laughter. Unlike the consistent members of the bridge groups, there were usually different players Friday nights. But there was always Carlos.

Big Mommy wished aloud that Oliver had inherited some of her egalitarianism. Oliver would not think of playing cards with his chauffeur.

But the room where everyone congregated at some time or other during the day or evening was the informal breakfast room. Breakfast and lunch were served here, though luncheon was always buffet and whoever was around came and ate when they wanted. Sometimes no one appeared, but the buffet was always ready. It was the sunshine room, Big Mommy said, lemon yellow with flowers painted on the walls. Chessie, the retriever, spent most of his time in this room, where people tripped on his rug. He was allowed any place in the apartment, welcome in all sixteen rooms, but he knew that sooner or later everyone would pet him if he stayed here. The butler, Warren, gave him scraps and took him for walks three times a day, finding him a helpful aid to meeting young women who strolled through the park too. Warren had been with the family longer than Sydney had, but he still looked like he was still in his thirties. Sydney imagined he had to be closer to forty-five, maybe even fifty. He served as Oliver's valet, too, and sometimes seemed to know what Oliver was going to do or say before Oliver thought of doing or saying anything. Warren's politics were exactly the same as Oliver's, and he took Oliver's pronouncements as word from on high. Only in religion did he diverge from Oliver's thinking, having been brought up a Catholic, and never having found any sound reason to defect. When Oliver railed at Catholicism, Warren's face froze into place, and some years' earlier Silvie had suggested that Oliver's tirades against the Pope were not particularly diplomatic in front of Warren.

Oliver had looked surprised, but from then on kept his ideas of Warren's religion to himself. Warren was grateful. As far as Sydney could tell, Warren had only one vice, and that was horse racing. He spent an hour in the mornings poring over the racing sheet and talking on the phone about afternoon races. But Sydney had never noticed any disappointment when his horse lost or any joy when he won. Warren was the great stone face, yet she and Evan had always been fond of him. He had told them bedtime stories when they were children and Silvie was gone for the evening. On Saturdays he had taken them to the Museum of Natural History, the Planetarium, the Zoo, or' Radio City Music Hall and had never seemed to resent being with them. He would tell them wildly amusing stories and make them behave with never a harsh word.

Oliver would say, "I wish I knew what you do. They're never that well-behaved when you're not here."

"It's a secret, sir," Warren answered.

Sydney had never fathomed the secret. She just always felt like behaving when Warren was around. Her reward would be climbing onto his lap after the movie and having hot chocolate while he sipped a beer from the bottle. Once in a while he even took Evan on his lap, despite the fact that Oliver had made it quite clear that little boys needn't be cuddled. He, himself, always shook hands with his son, though Silvie would hug him and call him her darling rascal. Upstairs, on the second floor, at the top of the long staircase, were the bedrooms. Uncle Billy's at the end of the hall, and then Evan's, and then Sydney's, and across the hall what came to be Big Mommy's. At the other end of the hall Oliver and Silvie had their enormous bedroom and two dressing rooms, almost the size of the three big bathrooms that lined the hall. Nearly as large was the nursery, where Evan and Sydney had spent many rainy afternoons as children. Sydney had dabbled with painting in oils while Evan splattered watercolors around. Neither of them was talented in the art department. Evan took to the piano, but Sydney barely got through the scales. Evan could play anything he heard without a lesson. He rebelled at being taught, refused to practice, and stopped playing the jazz he loved until Silvie abandoned the idea of lessons. Once the music professor disappeared, Evan returned to playing the piano again, with gusto. Sydney used to sit afternoons, curled up in one of the big armchairs, and listen to Evan improvise. Sometimes he sang along and she thought he had a great voice. But he never sang in front of anyone but her. She thought Evan the handsomest boy in the world, even though he seldom smiled. Handsomest, that is, until Jordan Eliot.

A staff of three took care of the apartment. Three, aside from Warren and the two chauffeurs. Sydney seldom saw them; they were invisible. Evan left his socks and underwear wherever he stepped out of them, but Sydney was neat as a pin, putting her laundry in the bathroom hamper and hanging up her clothes each evening. She had tried for years to talk Chessie into coming upstairs and sleeping with her, but Chessie chose to remain on her rug in the breakfast room. Sydney looked around at the only home she'd ever known, and realized if she married Jordan Eliot she'd never live in a place like this again. Yet she'd lived here all her life and nothing about it made the blood course through her veins like the sound of Jordan's voice or Jordan's kisses. In three short weeks it was almost as though nothing else really mattered except this would-be actor who eked out a living waiting on tables in an Italian restaurant.

Four

Dressed in charcoal gray gabardine slacks, a pale gray silk blouse that clung to her which she wore not only because it did but also because it made her eyes look grayer–and silver sandals that were nothing more than thin straps, Sydney rang the bell of the brownstone.

Jordan's unmistakable voice came through the intercom. "That you, Sydney?"

"No other."

"When the buzzer sounds, come up to the fourth floor."

The hallway was dark, the carpet threadbare as she walked up, holding onto the railing. Jordan stood at the top of the stairs, smiling down at her. She hadn't seen him in over two weeks and at the sight of him her knees went weak. She stopped in mid-flight, her hand grasping the railing, her legs wobbly. Is this what love was? She began to mount the steps again, slowly.

When she reached the top he took her into his arms and kissed her.

"Good morning."

"Mm," she answered. "I've missed you," he whispered. "I've thought of you every minute."

She closed her eyes as his mouth met hers again. Then he said, "Come on in. I'm packed and ready. Want coffee before we take off."

"I thought we could eat on the way. I know a great little restaurant about an hour into Jersey."

She followed him into a sparsely furnished but extremely tidy flat. She heard water running and, as Jordan disappeared into the bedroom to pick up his bag, another young man stuck his head out of the bathroom. He had a toothbrush in his hand and said, "Absolutely the only thing in the world that would get me up at this hour is to see what the most exciting woman in the world looks like."

"Don't judge by the outside." Sydney grinned at him. "It's all inside."

"Not all," said the nice looking young man with a crew cut. "I'm Monday. Monday Pearson."

"Monday?" Must be a stage name, she thought. "Another actor?"

"No. Waiter."

"Ah, Giorgio's."

"Right the first time. Make sure he's back a week from tomorrow."

"Or else?"

"Or else."

"Okay, I promise."

Jordan came out of his room, a sweater slung over his shoulder, a bag in his left hand. "Let's go," he said, taking her hand. When Sydney headed to the red Packard, Jordan stopped a minute and whistled.

"Graduation present," Sydney said. "If you're really nice to me, I'll let you drive it later."

As he slid into the passenger seat, Jordan said, "What does your father do, anyhow?"

Sydney slipped into first gear and pulled smoothly out into the street. Carts already jammed the street, their shouting owners hawking wares at the top of their lungs.'

"He's in the newspaper business."

"Well, he's more than just a reporter if he gave you this for graduation."

Traffic wasn't bad out of the Holland Tunnel. It was all coming the other way, into the city. Nor was the Pulaski Skyway crowded, going south. As always, that part of New Jersey smelled to high heaven.

Sydney reached into the glove compartment and brought out a bottle. "Suntan lotion," she said, handing it to Jordan. "You'll be red as a lobster by the time we get there if you don't use some."

"So," he said, "tell me something about this sacred shrine."

She shook her head, and hair flew in front of her eyes. "No, not yet."

They stopped at Borden's, the little roadside restaurant where Sydney liked to have breakfast. As he wolfed down buttermilk waffles topped with fresh strawberries Jordan said, "You know, except for that weekend in Boston, I haven't seen any of the East Coast. I hardly know a thing about Chesapeake Bay."

"Along with the Yangtze, it's the largest estuary in the world." '

He looked at her and burst into laughter. "Now, that's not the kind of information I was expecting. What's an estuary? Where a river dumps into an ocean?"

She nodded. "I guess that's an 'okay description, even though woefully inadequate."

"Well, educate me."

"Let's go if you're finished." She tossed two dollars on the table. She hoped her paying the bills wasn't going to upset him.

As they exited into the June sun, already warm at nine-thirty, she tossed the car keys at him. "Want to drive my new toy?"

He slid into the roadster and started the motor. Before taking off he grinned at her. "A honey."

"Me or it?"

"Yeah." He gunned the motor and took off.

They didn't talk much as they sped through New Jersey. By early afternoon they'd passed through Philadelphia and Wilmington and were headed into the rich, brown farm country of Maryland.

Jordan reached for Sydney's hand and held it as he drove along the highway.

"You're going to think you've moved to another country," Sydney warned. "The Bay separates everything along the eastern shore from the rest of the country. On weekends crowds of people take the ferries over from Baltimore and Annapolis. "

"What do they go over for?"

"The beaches at Ocean City and Rehoboth. They're starting construction of a bridge across the narrows, and I imagine that'll change the face of the whole eastern shore. I don't think I'll like it."

"Pretty country," Jordan observed. "What kind of farming do they do?"

"Tobacco. Soy beans. That sort of stuff. Those who live by the water make their living from it. Oysters. Crabs. You haven't lived until you've had a Bay crab cake."

"I think I'm just beginning to live anyhow," he said, raising her hand to his lips. Her whole being seemed to dissolve as she sighed contentedly. "My happiest times have been at Oberon," she said. "I'm glad you decided to come."

"The houses around here, the little towns, they look so old."

"They are," she leaned her head back against the leather upholstery. "The Chesapeake has been settled, sort of, since 1608."

Jordan laughed. "Your history is off. The Pilgrims didn't land until-what was it, about 1619?"

"No," Sydney said, sitting up straight. "Jamestown was begun in 1607, and John Smith began exploring the Chesapeake in 1608. The *real* first Thanksgiving wasn't at Plymouth Rock. It was in Virginia, along the James River."

Jordan raised his eyebrows and grinned at her. "You a history buff?"

"Sort of," Sydney nodded. "At least about this part of the world."

"Okay," he said, "educate me some more."

She shook her head. "I don't want to bore you."

"You're not. I want to know."

She thought a minute. "It's a fascinating part of the world. Maryland sided with the North during the Civil War, yet there was a period when they had slaves yet Oberon was a headquarters for the underground railway."

"Wait. Wait. On Oberon? How big *is* this island?"

"Eighteen hundred acres."

He digested that. "What is it, a colony of summer homes? Or do fishermen live on it, too?"

"You have to wait until we get there."

"How do we get out there?"

"In a boat, silly. How else does one get to islands?"

"You sail?"

She nodded. "Of course. I've spent every summer of my life here. But we don't sail to get there. It's not that far from shore, just a mile and a half."

"I've never been on a ship."

"Ships are big. We just have boats. Ships sail across the ocean. Well, I guess some boats do, too. But none of our boats is big enough to be a ship. Not that we own a skipjack, but none of our boats is any bigger than that."

"None of your boats? A skipjack?"

"Skipjacks are oyster boats. They're beautiful. They drag the bottom of the bay. More oysters are gathered here than any place else in the world. You'll see them. The *Titania* is about as big as one of those. That's our sailboat."

"Titania. Of course: She was the queen when Oberon was king."

Sydney smiled. "There has always been a *Titania* anchored at Oberon, ever since 1682."

"You're pulling my leg."

"No, it's true. My family has owned the island since then."

Jordan didn't say anything, but slowed down as they came to Chestertown. "Looks like this town has been here that long too."

"Isn't it lovely? Look at all these old colonial houses. I don't imagine it's changed much since Revolutionary times."

"How much farther?"

"About an hour. The boat will be out of winter dry dock and waiting. I let Walter know we'd be here today."

They drove along in silence, the sun beating down on them, though with the convertible top down a soft breeze cooled them off.

"So you're American as far back as that."

"As far back as that."

"Your family has owned one plot of land for two hundred and fifty years?"

Sydney nodded.

"That's phenomenal. What the hell *does* your father do?"

"He owns *The New York Chronicle*, but he doesn't make money at it. He's always pouring money into it."

Jordan slapped his forehead, "He's the publisher of that conservative paper? My God!" He turned to look at Sydney with a new expression on his face. "Ah, *those* Hamiltons."

Sydney asked, "Can't it just be you and me for a week?"

In answer, he reached out an arm and put it around her shoulder, pulling her close, leaning over to kiss her hair. They drove that way until Sydney said, "Turn right," at the sign that said "St. Michael's."

St. Michael's was a waterfront village of two hundred and twenty-four souls, with a pier, along which were docked dozens of boats of all sizes. "The fleet's back by this time in the afternoon. They go out at dawn. Here, pull into that boatyard."

She pointed. A weather beaten sign, with fading paint, indicated this was "Walt's Marina."

As soon as Jordan put on the brake, Sydney skipped out of the car. "We'll leave the car here."

A tall, broad-shouldered man opened the door of the shanty that served as his office and grinned at Sydney. "No longer my little girl, are you?"

Sydney ran into his bear hug. The man looked at Jordan and said, "I've known her since before she was born."

Walt had readied the boat the Hamiltons used to ferry across to their island, a sleek white cruiser with blue awnings and trim. Jordan imagined it could easily sleep six.

"They're expectin' you, all right. Martin came over to stock up on groceries this week." Walt kept his eyes on Jordan.

Sydney introduced them.

" 'Bout time you brought a man with you. I been waitin' for this for years now." He leaned over and whispered in Sydney's ear. "Must be someone special." His voice was filled with the eastern-shore twang. No one, else in America spoke in quite the same manner.

Sydney's smile revealed that Walt had guessed correctly. She jumped over the side of the boat with grace and nodded her head at Jordan. "Come on. It takes about half an hour."

"To go a mile and a half?"

"Sometimes twenty minutes. Looks like today might be one of those."

The water was calm, not the mirror stillness of twilight, but there was no breeze. It was hot. Hot and humid.

"Come on. Let's get these suitcases on board." She could hardly wait for Jordan to see Oberon.

Jordan sat in the canvas chair Sydney had indicated as she stood behind the wheel, chugging the motor into life. Walt threw them the rope that had tied the boat to the dock, and Jordan caught it. Rather than observing his new surroundings, he studied Sydney, who was intent on maneuvering the boat out of the marina.

Looking up, Jordan saw that the riverbanks were studded with enormous, elegant colonial houses. The boat moved slowly as Sydney studied the river.

"We go downriver about half a mile before heading into open water. Not that it's like the ocean. The bay averages just twenty feet deep, though there are some stupendous storms."

Jordan turned his attention to the landscape, awed at the size of the gracious homes and the acres surrounding them.

Money. Old money, he gathered. Charm. He hoped Oberon was not like this, not so ostentatious. He wouldn't know how to behave with the kind of people who must own this impressive real estate.

So Sydney was one of those Hamiltons who'd been part of New York society forever. Part of it? Led it, wrote the rules, he bet, though one didn't read much about them. A hazy picture sifted into his memory. A couple of years ago, her photograph was in Life -she'd jumped into someone's pool with her clothes on and created quite a splash. So, she was *that* Sydney Hamilton.

Now that they were speeding across open water, a wind cut into them. Gulls circled overhead, crying, following the boat. Jordan couldn't hear what Sydney was shouting, so he moved from the chair, walking over to stand beside her. She was pointing.

"There. That's Oberon."

Ahead of them trees seemed to rise out of the water. "Over there, to the right, that's our woods. We call it Martha's Forest–over a thousand acres of oaks. Timber's never been cut. There are a couple of little lakes in there. It's primeval."

"Who's Martha?"

"You'll see her grave. She and her husband were the first Hamiltons here. They canoed over to escape Indians. She was pregnant and gave birth there, in Martha's Forest. Later, they bought the island. Well, really, it was a land grant. That's how we got it, in 1682."

Sydney steered the boat to the left of the island. Jordan heard himself gasp as she began to head toward shore. Sitting on the southern point was an immense brick three-story house, six tall white pillars fronting the main section while wings spread out gracefully on either side. A long front lawn sloped down to the dock. Dogwoods and towering trees lent shade to the lush grass that surrounded the house. Beyond the house were other brick buildings.

Sydney watched Jordan's reaction. "I love Oberon more than any place on earth."

He could see why. "Holy shit!"

"Well, holy, anyhow," she said with a laugh.

Like a phantom, a woman in a flowing white robe was running slowly from the house toward the dock.

"That's Big Mommy," said Sydney with obvious pleasure.

"One of the world's wonderful people. She's my father's mother."

Jordan turned to look at Sydney. He could see her palpable excitement. Her eyes shone with happiness.

"She lives with us in New York during the winter. Memorial Day marks the beginning of her summer and she heads here." Sydney had a wistful tone to her voice. "My brother and I have always come down as soon as school's out. This is the first summer Evan hasn't been here. I miss him already."

"Younger or older?"

Sydney expertly maneuvered the boat alongside the dock. "Two years younger. He and Uncle Billy are in Italy. Or maybe France. In Europe, anyhow."

"Doing what?"

Sydney cut the motor after she'd slid next to the pier. She made it look like the easiest thing in the world. "Oh, I don't know, just seeing Europe."

Big Mommy was standing at the end of the dock, waiting for Sydney and Jordan. Jordan stared at her. Her white gown was ankle length and around her white hair she wore a loosely knotted white chiffon scarf. The strangest thing about her was her makeup. Her face was chalk white, and with her dark brown eyes she had a cartoon-like appearance.

Sydney leapt from the boat and ran along the narrow wooden pier, her arms outstretched. Grandmother and granddaughter hugged as though they hadn't seen each other in ages. Actually, Sydney had seen Big Mommy when she was home the weekend she'd met Jordan.

"I brought a surprise," she whispered into her grandmother's ear.

"I see."

Sydney turned around and stretched out an arm toward Jordan, who was approaching them, trying to balance on the thin wooden slats so he wouldn't fall into the water, shallow as it was. 'Jordan Eliot, Big Mommy."

Jordan reached out his hand to the pale apparition. Her heavily made-up eyes accentuated her eccentric looks. "I don't suppose you play poker, do you?"

He shook his head.

"I was afraid not. Well, then, I guess you're stuck with Sydney."

"Stuck?" squealed her granddaughter. "Well, maybe you are." She reached for Jordan's hand, and the three of them began to walk up the sloping lawn toward the great house.

"Want me to get the bags?" he asked.

"No. Martin will take care of everything. God, it's hot. Well, maybe we better get your bag. You did bring a bathing suit, didn't you?"

He nodded and, letting go of her hand, turned around to walk back to the boat. "You don't even have to tell me," said Big Mommy. "You're in love. Both of you."

"I'm not sure," Sydney said. "That's why I brought him here. I only met him last month, and I want to see how I feel about him here before I'm sure whether or not to go on."

Big Mommy laughed. "You talk like the head has something to do with the heart. Forget it, my dear. I suspect it's already too late for you. Probably was within the first ten minutes of meeting him. You can tell me all about it later. He has the bluest eyes I've ever seen."

He also had the most beautiful body Sydney had ever looked at. She hadn't' thought male bodies were beautiful until she watched him walk out on the diving board wearing a bathing suit that hid nothing. She wished she could see him naked. She was surprised. She'd never thought that of a man before, never wanted to rip off a man's bathing suit and touch him. Stare at him. Fondle him. Kiss him. She wanted his body against hers.

He jackknifed into the air and disappeared into the water. When he surfaced he was next to her. "Am I here on approval?"

"I've never needed approval for anything I do or anyone I like. No. You're here because I want to be with you."

"Your grandmother is ... different."

Sydney laughed and lay on her back, floating. "She's worn white, nothing but white, forever. She's not conventional in any way. Now, my father is. And so's my mother, pretty much.

"Yet Mother and Big Mommy get along famously. Big Daddy and Big Mommy were as different as could be. He never cared about what he wore. He was pretty aloof, except with Big Mommy. He didn't like people around. They moved here about ten years ago and just stayed all year long, until he died. Our family burial plot is here. Hamiltons for the last 268 years. Martha's second baby was stillborn and is buried here. I'll show it all to you tomorrow."

Martin appeared on the terrace with a silver tray holding glasses and a shaker. He set it down on the table under the umbrella. "Shall I pour, Miss Sydney?"

She looked at Jordan. "You like daiquiris?"

"Right now I'd like anything."

Martin heard and poured two drinks, walking over to the edge of the pool and handing a glass to Sydney. Jordan swam over to Martin, who handed him the other glass and left them.

"Mm," Jordan said, sipping. "Tell me about Martha."

"Ah," Sydney said, placing her glass on the pool's edge and hoisting herself out of the water to sit beside the glass. Her legs dangling in the water, she said, "So, you want me to start at the beginning.

"Well, they were hiding out from Indians who had burned the cabin they lived in, and it was in 1672..."

By the time she'd finished, an hour and a half had passed. The sun was low in the sky and they'd drunk the pitcher of daiquiris.

Jordan was still stretched lazily on the chaise, and Sydney was curled next to him.

"Is this all true?" he asked.

Sydney shrugged. "The family Bible lists the births and deaths and marriages of all the Hamiltons, but I don't know about the details. We know Martha and her husband rowed over to the island to escape marauding Indians and hid deep in the forest where Martha gave birth. In the family archives we have the original papers showing they petitioned Lord Baltimore for the land and he sold it to them for just a little more than the Dutch paid for Manhattan. "

"The year 1685 is carved into one of the pillars. Amazing, isn't it, to have these bricks and those pillars all brought over by boat?"

"I don't even know anything of my family beyond my grandparents," Jordan said. "They trekked to Illinois from Pennsylvania in the 1880s or 1890s, but I've no idea before that. Indians? Am I German, French, English? It's amazing that you can trace yours so directly."

"I've always felt special because of it," Sydney admitted.

"You are special," Jordan murmured as he leaned over to kiss her. "The most special person in my universe."

"Tomorrow," Sydney said, "I'll show it to you.""

"I'm looking forward to that," Jordan said as the housekeeper announced dinner would be served in ten minutes.

"Better get dressed." Sydney said as she stood up. "Nothing formal, but something other than our bathing suits."

"They're dry. So, why not?"

"Not at Oberon," she smiled. Actually, she wouldn't have minded if they hadn't worn anything.

Five

"I haven't been on a horse since I was a kid and visited my Uncle Andrew's farm in Iowa," Jordan said, though Sydney thought he sat nicely on Chester and handled his reins well.

"It's like bicycling," she said, "it comes back to you. We're just going to walk along, maybe trot a bit, but nothing serious."

"That's a relief," he said with a grin.

They rode along a path, north behind the outbuildings and the lawns. Sydney pointed. "That was the blacksmith's shop– forge, bellows, and anvil. Over there is where the carpenter worked." It was a trim-looking little building, with a high window the only light. "It's one of the oldest buildings in the whole United States," she said, pride evident in her voice.

Jordan was impressed. There were enough outbuildings to seem like a small village.

"That's where indentured servants lived," Sydney went on, nodding to a well-kept, two-story building.

"Indentured?"

"You know," Sydney said, looking at him as though he must have forgotten his history. "People emigrated here, signing on to be servants for seven years to pay off their passage."

Jordan nodded. He guessed somewhere in his elementary education he had learned that, but certainly he'd forgotten. "Another form of slavery," he mused.

Sydney nodded. "At least we didn't use prisoners, as so many did." '

Jordan looked surprised.

"Well, up until the Revolution; we took all those criminals England had no room for. Thousands of British prisoners were sent here as laborers for plantation owners. After the Revolution they were sent to Australia. Over there," She pointed to the far end of what was now a field of hay. "Those were the cabins."

As they rode through the meadow toward the towering trees that offered shade, Jordan pointed ahead. "My God, look at that windmill! It's immense."

Sydney smiled. "It was built in the early 1700s," she said proudly. "It's still in use."

"Why so big?"

"So it could be seen from the mainland. See, when not in use it forms an 'X.' In the 1700s this whole bay was rife with pirates. Here on the island, we had a clear view south of the bay and would be the first to see foreign ships coming north. We'd send a servant out to change the 'X' on the windmill to a cross, which was a signal to those on the mainland that pirates were coming: Danger, put away 'valuables."

Jordan grinned at Sydney. "How do you know all this?"

She shrugged. "Stories handed down over the years. Bits of history in the family Bible. Old newspaper clippings."

"Newspapers?"

"Certainly. They were quite civilized around here."

A family of wild turkeys waddled across the path, scattering when they observed the horses approaching, then disappearing into the underbrush.

Sydney and Jordan rode along in silence for a few minutes.

"Your grandmother is something."

Sydney nodded. "She is that. I suppose you're wondering why she wears that unique…"

"Unique is the right word."

Sydney laughed, filled with a happiness she could not control. "The story goes that Big Daddy told her he fell in love with her the minute he saw her dressed in white, holding a pale pink rose. He sent her pink roses every Saturday of their lives, and since the day she married, she's never worn anything other than white. As for the ghost-like makeup with those kohl rimmed eyes, I don't know. She's never had to answer to anyone for her looks, and by now no one would recognize her in any other garb or makeup. Big Daddy told her, I bet it was every day of their marriage, that she was beautiful."

"She is."

"She was a senator's daughter. Her father was the senator from Virginia, and she met Big Daddy when he was a senior at the University of Virginia, at a dance in Charlottesville, where Big Mommy lived. She was just seventeen."

They came to the edge of the trees and followed the path as it wound through dogwoods, azaleas, rhododendrons, all past their blooming season. But little lavender and yellow flowers dotted the ground cover.

"This has to be Martha's Forest," Jordan said.

"The fringes. Where she gave birth and where they built their first cabin is a little ways on, by the pond. That's where I learned to swim. I spent the summer after eleventh grade trying to make friends with the fish and catch them in my hands like Thoreau did at Walden. That fascinated me."

"I didn't go that far," Jordan said with a grin; "but he's one of my heroes."

A deer leapt across the path in front of them. Sydney reined in her horse and Jordan followed suit, his horse halting beside Sydney's. A few seconds later a fawn, awkward on its spindly legs flew through the air behind its mother. The sight never failed to thrill Sydney.

The woods were filled with stands of oak, dripping mistletoe high in their branches, locust, hickory, all fragrant the way primeval earth smells. The sun dappled through the leaves high above, sending narrow shafts of golden light through the forest.

Jordan leaned over to kiss Sydney's ear. Their horses bumped. Sydney turned her head and their lips met.

"Mmm," she sighed.

"I'm glad you're not coy," he said. "So many girls play games, tease you and make you chase after them. You're honest. It's one of your nicest virtues. Among many, I may add. Especially your legs. They're another asset."

Her legs were covered up in tan twill breeches and black boots.

"Jordan Eliot, I bet you never had to chase a girl in your life. Who would run away from you?"

He just continued to smile. "Come on, I want to see Martha's place."

Sydney urged her horse into a trot, wondering if Jordan would know what to do. She glanced over her shoulder to see if he was about to fall off, but he was managing quite well. Within a few minutes, the reflection of sun shining on water shimmered through the trees. Sydney brought her horse to a halt and slid from the saddle.

"You make that look easy," commented Jordan.

"Want help?" she asked, her eyes teasing. He jumped off, if not quite as gracefully, at least not awkwardly, looking not at Sydney but at the pond ahead of them. He walked toward it, ahead of Sydney, leading his horse. When he arrived at the bank he just stood, gazing at the water and the cobalt of the sky reflected in its clarity. "This must be the most tranquil place in the world," he said

Sydney sat down, looping her horse's reins over her wrist, then pulling her knees up and hugging them. "This is where I learned to swim," she said. "This is where Martha and Samuel drank, where they watered their garden. It's what I think of as pure. Maybe that's what Oberon is to me. Purity. Even in these hectic times, it's a retreat for me, away from the maddening world, a place that remains constant, innocent. None of the world's vices are here."

Jordan pulled his horse around, slid the reins over its neck, then sat down beside Sydney and took her hand. "A fairyland?"

"Not quite," 'Sydney said, gazing out across the pond. "Big Mommy says if we live our lives well enough now, the future will take care of itself. We have to tend the now if the next is to have any meaning, to show we haven't lived our lives in vain. But we're the ones entrusted with the future and we must live purely now, or what comes next will be the chaos that we, ourselves, have created."

Jordan thought a minute and nodded. "I like that. If Oberon, as a microcosm of the world, is tended properly or, as you say, with purity, then the future won't be polluted. Does she mean the environment or the inner man?"

Sydney looked over at him and knew, with no doubt at all, that she would love him forever. "Maybe they go together."

"Cast away greed," Jordan decided.

Five minutes passed before he asked, "So most of the island is this forest?"

"Oh, no. At the northern end there are over three hundred acres of marsh. That's where the birds winter. A few stray ones always stay over the summer, too, for reasons that no one quite understands. Daddy, and Big Daddy before him, always plants corn on the fields around the marsh, probably another couple of hundred acres, to feed the birds. Wait till you see. More ducks and geese than you could ever believe.

"Daddy comes down to hunt every fall, but he motors over to the mainland. He won't allow hunting at Oberon. Hunting clubs have tried for years to lease the marshland during duck season. I don't quite understand how Daddy can hunt when he won't allow hunting on his own land."

"A mystery, isn't it?" Jordan agreed.

"When I was young, oh, sometime in junior high, Daddy taught Evan and me to shoot one summer. We both got so good we always hit the bull's-eye. We thought it was a big deal that he brought us down here at Thanksgiving, when he was going duck shooting, and outfitted both of us and took us with him. We thought we were quite adult. Mother had a fit. She was sure we were going to shoot each other by mistake, or another hunter would get us. But Daddy had us wear red caps just like he wore. I was surprised he taught me to shoot and took me along because he has such narrow ideas of what's proper for girls. But I guess enough women skeet shoot that he thought it was okay to take me. Evan and I couldn't think of anything else for weeks."

Sydney was quiet for a minute, and Jordan waited expectantly. It seemed to him that the recounting of that time was difficult for her. He wondered if she was going to cry.

"We rose long before dark-it must have been around three—and stopped over in St. Michael's for Walt, who was going to guide us to the best place. It was up the river quite a ways, and when we turned a bend in the river it was the most beautiful sight I ever saw. There were waterfowl by the thousands. Beautiful Canadian geese, so big as to be unbelievable.

"And ducks ... I thought since I'd spent summers here all my life, watching birds flying around, I was familiar with ducks. But God, there were thousands. Their noise was so loud you couldn't hear another person shouting. We went into a duck blind and didn't even sit for very long. I remember having to be so quiet. And then the most traumatic thing I can ever remember. These beautiful birds, mallards with their fantastic coloring, the males anyhow, the females are sort of blah-looking ... and the mergansers. Have you ever seen-red breasted or hooded mergansers?"

Jordan had never even heard of such birds.

"I didn't want to shoot them, I wanted to paint them. But Daddy was showing us what to do and Evan was hitting them as they flew directly into the air from the water, shooting them as though they were bull's-eyes at target practice, and Daddy said, 'Come on, honey, take aim.' But I couldn't. My gun just lay on my lap, until Daddy leaned over and picked it up, put his arms around me and the gun and thrust it into my hands, forcing-though I think he thought he was encouraging-me to take aim. That part was easy. And oh, how beautiful that bird looked. I wanted to fly to it, become part of it, but Daddy kept whispering to me, telling me to pull the trigger. I hit it with my first shot, watching that great beautiful bird fall out of the sky, twirling down onto the brown dried leaves, so dead it could never lend beauty to the world anymore. And I began to cry.

"Daddy was disgusted with me, but Walt reached out his arms and I crawled into them and burrowed my head in his jacket. He held me close and he let me cry, smoothing his fingers through my hair, whispering, 'I understand, baby. I really do'."

There were tears glistening in her eyes, even so many years later, and Jordan reached out an arm to pull her to him, holding his arm around her shoulders, holding her against his chest, just as Walt must have. The horses moved, restlessly, beside them.

"I've never held a gun again. I couldn't even eat the turkey we had for Thanksgiving that year." She looked up at Jordan to see if he understood.

Jordan pulled her closer and kissed her eyelids, kissed her nose, moved his mouth onto hers. "In case I haven't mentioned it before," he said, "I've fallen in love with you. You must know that."

"Oh, Jordan," Sydney's voice was but a whisper, "I think it happened the first night we met, by the end of the ferry ride. Do such things really happen so quickly?"

In answer, he kissed her again. Then he stood up and pulled her along with him. "Come on. Show me the rest of the island. Show me the house Martha and Samuel built with their own hands."

They remounted and guided the horses along a quiet woodland path. "There are only remains, over here," she said, as they rode through the woods. About fifty feet back from the pond, sheltered by a grove of oaks, were the ruins of the first Hamilton abode on Oberon. Gray stones, varying in height from one to three and four feet, outlined a space about nine by twelve. A small space for a family to have lived in as long as they did.

"Imagine being able to look at a place where you know your family had its roots hundreds of years ago."

"Two hundred and sixty-seven years ago, to be specific."

"I'm impressed," he said with a grin. "In fact, I think what I really am is out of my league."

"Please don't let it deter you."

"Nothing and no one is strong enough for that."

Sydney laughed. "It doesn't seem to me you've had to pursue me very strenuously. You haven't seen me running, have you?" She moved her horse closer to his, reached out a hand to him.

"You know what I want to do this minute? Toss you on this ground, maybe in that house your ancestors built, and make mad, passionate love to you."

"Funny, I've been feeling those same urges."

Jordan sighed. "It's not time."

"No?" Disappointment drew out the syllable.

"Not yet," he said. "Not yet. But when the time comes, we're going to light up the sky, Sydney."

'Is that a promise?"

"That's a promise. The aurora borealis is going to be tame compared to us."

They didn't speak again as the horses plodded slowly back through the woods, along the shore of the pond, and back to the stables. Anyone could tell that magic was in the air.

Six

Sydney swam across the pond with strong strokes, flipping to float on her back, letting the sun bum onto her fair skin, which would be golden in another two weeks. She didn't know if she'd ever felt happier. Back for another summer at Oberon. Jordan. She sighed contentedly and opened her eyes, turning to swim back to the shore, with Jordan beside her.

"I like looking at you," he said. "You belong here, don't you?"

"I'll race you back to shore."

"No," he countered, shaking his head. "I'm not doing anything in a hurry this week. I'm savoring every minute and hope it lasts forever."

They began to swim together—long, slow strokes, hardly making ripples in the water. When it was shallow enough for them to stand, he reached out and took her hand, turning her to him, leaning down to kiss her. Her breasts strained against his chest. His leg parted hers. He picked her up and carried her to the shore, laying her down in the shade of a tree whose leaves didn't move in the heat of the late afternoon.

He looked into her eyes and then slid down the slender straps of her bathing suit, rolling them back so that her breasts were exposed. He leaned over and circled her right nipple with his mouth and she moaned softly. One of his hands feathered along the inside of her thighs.

"You're all I think of," he whispered, his tongue circling her nipple, his teeth gently biting her.

She moved, arching her back, her buttocks tightening as she raised herself. He looked at her, into her, his eyes locked on hers before his mouth crushed hers again. Then he pulled his head back and smiled.

She wound her arms around his neck and pulled him back to her, kissing him, loving the taste of him, the smell of him. "You sure know how to kiss," she said. "Most men don't."

He cocked his head, raising his eyebrows. "Have you kissed most men?'

She smiled. "Enough to know you're incomparable."

His hand cradled her left breast, and he kissed her eyelids, her ear, feathering down to her neck.

"In case you're wondering," she said, "I want you to make love to me."

"I know you do," he said. "You're wonderfully responsive. But I'm not going to, not all the way."

Her arms around him, she asked, "you don't want to?"

"Don't be silly. Look at me. You know I'm ready. Physically, anyhow. No, not yet."

"Sometime?" She was disappointed.

"For Christ's sake," Jordan said, standing up and walking over to stand in the water. "Sydney, your father would kill me. A waiter ravishing his daughter. Look at all this," he said, waving his arm in an arc. "I'm not in your league, Sydney. I'm so in love with you I thought I couldn't think straight. And now, I see this—Oberon—and realize what it means ... more money than I've ever even dreamed about."

She laughed, but it was not a happy laugh. "It's so ironic. Ever since I was fourteen guys have been trying to get me in bed and the first one I want to say yes to says no to me."

"I'd have made love to you the first night we met, or up at Wellesley. I've dreamed of making love to you every night and about thirty-two times each day since we met. But I didn't know you came attached to this."

"In other words, if Oberon weren't my family's ... oh, this is good. I brought you here for an idyllic weekend and instead it turns you off. You don't have to marry me, you know. Making love with me has no strings attached."

He turned to face her. "You're twenty-one years old and we're supposed to make love and then I walk away into the sunset and everything would be fine?"

"No," she shook her head. "I don't think your walking away into the sunset would be fine."

"Have you even mentioned me to your parents? Do they have any idea I'm here with you this week? That I've even entered your life?"

"No," she admitted.

Jordan walked over and sat down next to her, taking her hand in his. "I have entered your life, haven't I?"

"And how!" Sydney smiled at him. "Answer a question. Have you written home about me?"

It was his turn to smile. "Nope."

"Do you want my parents' written permission to make love to me?"

"Maybe this whole bit has unbalanced me," he said. "I thought we were coming to a beach cottage, not a whole island with a mansion on it."

"So, in other words, I should wait to let some man with as much money and prestige as my family has claim my maidenhead? If I go do that next week, will you come back and make love to me?"

"You're impossible," Jordan leaned over to graze her lips with his. "You just can't even begin to comprehend..."

* * * *

"Because one's expertise in measuring the wind's direction and velocity is so vital, your first step in learning to sail is to try to be sensitive and conscious of the wind."

"How do I do that?"

"You *feel* it," Sydney said. "If you concentrate you can feel it. You can look at the water and see the ripples. They're produced at ninety degrees to the wind. You can feel it in your face."

Jordan watched Sydney as she expertly handled the little sailboat.

"It's easier to launch it here, off the dock, than it would be if we were on a beach. Look, I'm pointing the bow into the wind. I want to avoid the windward side when launching."

"The windward side?"

"Yeah, the side the wind blows upon."

He shook his head.

"Now, we'll hoist the sails. I think we'll put the mainsail last so the swinging boom won't impede the movement. Here, pull up the jib halyard."

"The what?"

"Those ropes. We hoist the sails with them, there, now, fine. Pull up tightly and cleat it securely."

Jordan wondered how Sydney seemed to be doing six things at once when it was all he could do to concentrate on the job she'd given him.

"Once these sails are up we'll get going so that, hopefully, there won't be any extreme flapping."

After a few minutes Jordan said, "It feels great, casting off all bonds of earth, sort of."

Sydney glanced over at him and grinned. "I won't bore you with all the terms and such things your first ride. Just relax and enjoy it. It's a perfect day for sailing. We'll get sunburn and you can see how beautiful this part of the world is. You can have the Rockies..."

"Have you ever seen them?"

She admitted she had not. "Nevertheless, to me this is the most beautiful place in the world."

"Can we go swimming?"

"Nope. Jellyfish at this time of year. "

Jordan stretched out on the deck, his hands pillowing his head, and watched Sydney at work. Six weeks ago he could not have imagined himself sailing across Chesapeake Bay with the woman he knew he wanted to spend his life with.

"What," he thought aloud, "makes one person fall in love with another?"

Sydney swept her hair out of her eyes and didn't look over at him. "Sex?"

"Nope. That's only part of it, but you know what? We come from such different worlds, but when I'm with you I feel I've come home. Not the home in which I grew up, but the place where I feel fulfilled, where the other half of me has been waiting to make me whole."

Sydney looked over at him and stretched a toe out to touch his arm, since her hands were on the tiller. "Why, Jordan, that's lovely. So, I do that to you, do I?"

"Among other things."

"Later, I'll show you some of those other things."

"Promises, promises," he said, kissing her toe.

"I approve of you, Jordan Eliot," said Big Mommy, "not that that probably matters."

"Of course it does," Sydney said.

They were having coffee and blueberry pie after a Virginia baked ham dinner.

"It shouldn't," said her grandmother. "I think it's rather nice that I do, but if you really love each other it shouldn't matter what anyone thinks."

Sydney wondered if Big Mommy was trying to tell her something. "I never knew my own grandmother," Jordan said, "but if I have a choice in the matter, how about adopting me."

"There may be other ways to accomplish the same thing," she said, standing up. "Now, it's time for bed. I have to give myself time to read. I can't fall asleep without a book in my hands. I used to be able to, but ever since your grandfather died…"

Jordan stood up and leaned down to kiss her cheek.

"Your head's screwed on right," said the old lady. "You have a sense of humor the men in my family lack, except my husband. He had one. I think it's the most important element of character. I've enjoyed laughing with you all this week, and I hope I'll see you again. I may not be up by the time you have to leave in the morning, but, come again. Even if she doesn't want you to. Come visit me. I'm not too old to appreciate a good-looking young man who has such nice manners, too."

It was after three before Jordan and Sydney went to bed. They sat on the dock until almost midnight, holding hands and kissing each other, watching lights on the water. They talked of everything they felt they hadn't yet covered. God. Music. They were delighted to discover that they both yawned through opera and the ballet, but loved musical comedy and thought Marlon Brando the most dynamic new actor on the American stage. Sydney was more drawn to art and museums than Jordan was, but then he'd never been exposed to them. She promised to take him to the Metropolitan and the Museum of Modem Art.

Their differences—their politics for instance—they brushed aside. Their differences didn't matter. It was what they shared that joined them together.

And they were joined together, they thought, in all ways but the ultimate one, though each was filled with longing for that.

At midnight they swam in the pool, and Sydney teased him. "I'm not going to my room to get my suit, and I'll let you decide whether or not you like my body."

She stood at the edge of the lighted pool and disrobed, trying to feel unself-conscious, hoping Jordan would like what he saw. She had never tried to seduce someone before.

She did not succeed, though they touched each other, and kissed under water, and he kissed her breasts while her legs were wrapped around his torso, and Sydney said, "I'm wild with desire, damn you."

They did everything but.

When he left in the morning, Sydney watched as he disappeared into the early morning fog. She had driven him to the Easton bus and, as she drove slowly back to St. Michael's, she realized her life had taken a new direction. She wondered where this path was going to lead her.

Although she had not seen him act, she knew with absolute certainty that he was going to succeed. She wondered if he knew that she was going along on the ride and speculated how it would be being Mrs. Jordan Eliot.

A smile lit her face as she left the car at Walt's and motored across the bay to Oberon.

The summer settled into routine. Oberon was the only place where Sydney tolerated that. Maybe because, except for the dinner hour, the routine at Oberon was based on lack of routine. Dinner was always at seven-thirty, and it would have taken an earthquake to break Nettie's routine in this matter.

She always had enough breakfast to feed an army, and if one got up at six-thirty or ten, it was warm on the long sideboard in the dining room that could easily seat thirty. Grits, hash browns, scrambled eggs with chives, fried onions, biscuits, homemade strawberry jam or raspberry preserves. On Sundays cinnamon rolls and German apple pancakes were added to the buffet. Whether Sydney was there alone or they had company of twenty, there was enough left over to feed several families. The leftovers were always given to Brandy and Sherry, the two brown-and-white Chesapeake Bay retrievers that had been part of Oberon since Sydney was eleven.

Oliver had trained them and though he came but seldom they always remembered him, wagging their tails as soon as they heard his voice at the dock. In the fall, it was as if a certain scent in the air promised hunting, or else it was the honking of the thousands of geese that flew in V-formation to the feeding grounds.

Sydney spent more time than ever with Big Mommy that summer. Big Mommy was one of the grande dames of New York society, but that had never mattered to her. She wasn't interested in art or museums. She'd rather write a check to a charity than attend one of its dress-up balls. Big Daddy had always told her, "You don't have to impress anyone. We've owned land in this country since before it was a country. There's been a Hamilton's name on land deeds here longer than nearly anyone else in the country. Hell, I married you because you don't like parties." He was only half joking. Everyone who knew them knew that Big Mommy and Big Daddy had a love match that had lasted as long as they'd known each other. Sydney remembered when she'd been eighteen and Big Mommy would have been, what? Sixty-eight. She'd never had the nerve to talk about sex with her parents so she asked Big Mommy, "At what age do you lose interest in sex?"

After a sharp look, Big Mommy smiled like a Cheshire cat and said, "I'll let you know."

Sydney thought it was the most wonderful answer in the world.

Big Mommy spent her summers at Oberon on the verandah out front, sitting in a rocking chair older than she was, reading. Her summer varied from looking down at the words, in the book to gazing out over the sun-dappled water. She loved it when there were storms. Then she sat in the upstairs observatory and watched the waves crash against the dock and the trees bend in the wind, feeling a pit in her stomach when boats bounced up and down, caught unprepared for the storm.

Sydney and her grandmother were sitting on the back verandah, overlooking the pool.

"I like the idea of your going to graduate school. You're such a pleasure," said her grandmother. "Always coming up with ideas your mother and I'd never have the guts to do."

"Why, I thought you and Mother have always had wonderful lives. Haven't you been happy?"

Big Mommy nodded. "As happy as any woman in my generation could be, I guess. But I've spent my life, like your mother, literally or figuratively in rocking chairs, watching. Your grandfather and I had a happy marriage because I went along with whatever he wanted. I reacted. That's how I've spent my life. Your mother, too. We react. Oh, I think she's been happy, too. But, happy is not the same as fulfilled."

Sydney sat down at the edge of the pool and took her sandals off, flinging her legs in the water, leaning back on her elbows.

"The height of my life, aside from having children, has been keeping up this house. Not much to brag about for a lifetime of living, is it?"

"How can you talk that way? This is the most beautiful house in the world, thanks to you. You and Big Daddy traveled all over the world..."

"Sydney, I went along. But I've done very little on my own. Your grandfather would have had a hemorrhage."

Sydney stared over her shoulder at her grandmother.

"I want to live awhile longer, see what you're going to make of your life."

"Why, I imagine I'll do the same as you and Mother have done."

Big Mommy brushed her hand through the air as though to ward off that idea. "Maybe you'll do what we've done, but you'll do something besides. The world is changing for women. The war started it. The riveters haven't been content to go back to dishes, not earning their own money or making decisions. You'll see. Pretty soon women will begin to live different lives, and that's going to upset men a lot. Go to graduate school, darling. Do something with your brains and education."

"Are you telling me not to get married?"

"Of course not, but do things your mother and I never had the intestinal fortitude to do."

"But I want children and marriage. I want what you've had."

Big Mommy nodded. "That's fine, but you'll have more, too. I want to stay around to see it. Both your mother and I are college graduates, and what have we done with it? But you, you're going to graduate school."

"Big Mommy," Sydney said as she stood up and went over and kicked her feet in the water, "I hate to disillusion you, but..."

Big Mommy was silent a moment, then she said, "I know."

"I'm insanely in love." Sydney raised her hands in the air, stretching as far all she could.

Her grandmother sighed "I could tell he feels the same way. He couldn't keep his eyes off you."

Sydney couldn't see the expression on her grandmother's face. She turned around to face her.

Big Mommy smiled "Well, at least he's refreshingly different for this family. But tell me, do you have to rush into marriage and forget graduate school?"

"I've only known him a month. He may not even be thinking marriage. He hasn't a dime."

"Your father will have a conniption."

Sydney nodded in agreement and slid into the pool.

"That he's impoverished has certain charms, you know. At least he's educated. And from the Middle West! I like him. More than that, I found him delightful. Refreshing after all those young men who've flitted in and out of the apartment over the years. I don't mind your being in love with

Jordan Eliot. I just hope you'll go on with your education. Women are going to need more education for the same jobs…"

"If I marry him I'll probably be our main support." Sydney dunked her head underwater. When she surfaced, she, said, "Actually, he'd never heard of us. You have to admit we're not household words, thank heavens. Not like the Vanderbilts and the Rockefellers. Of course, they're far richer and much splashier."

"They've had to prove who they are. We've never had to."

"We? Big Mommy, you weren't a Hamilton."

Big Mommy shook her head, her dark brown eyes smiling. "And I didn't know who *the* Hamilton's were until after I was in love with your grandfather. Grover Cleveland was President the second time, and Big Daddy's daddy threw a party for him. His father invited us to come to the party, and my papa, as you know, was senator from Virginia, so we came sailing over here on the most beautiful Saturday afternoon in June. Standing on the dock, below a flag blowing in the wind, stood your grandfather. My heart began to beat faster before we even docked. I'd no idea when I'd met him the previous winter that he had this kind of money. He didn't look like he'd be the son of the owner of such a place as this. His pants and jacket were wrinkled, just as they were the rest of his life. Clothes were never a priority with George."

Sydney remembered. Big Daddy had ·always looked like he'd just rolled out of bed.

"But he stood there, the· breeze blowing his hair and that darling mustache … in over fifty years I never saw what he'd look like without that mustache. And when he took my hand to help me out of the boat and looked at me with those sea-colored eyes and smiled … we stood there looking at each other as if nobody else in the world existed and you know, from then on no one did. Not for either of us. But I certainly hadn't known who *the* Hamiltons were, and I didn't care. I think the first one who's cared is your father, and it's not the money or the social status he cares about. It's being powerful and influential. That's why he bought that paper. He wants to convert the world to his ideas.

"He's the one who stopped inviting Presidents here, isn't he?" Big Mommy shook her head. "Well, we're not known for being egalitarians, Sydney. He thought, and rightly so, that Roosevelt was leading us into economic chaos."

"Big Mommy, it seems to me he led us *out* of economic chaos, out of the Depression."

"Only because war came along. He thought government should help people rather than letting people help themselves. Well, that's neither here nor there." Big Mommy always said that when she wanted a political discussion to come to an end.

"Maybe it is, though," Sydney said. "Jordan says politics is about morality."

Big Mommy thought about that and then grinned. "I thought morality was wanting to sleep with someone and not doing it."

"Maybe that's politics," Sydney said wistfully.

Seven

The gunmetal gray sky reflected Sydney's mood.

As she walked across the campus-so different from the serenity and beauty of Wellesley–she wondered why she was here, in Philadelphia.

Nothing about studying for any of her courses interested her. She used to love learning; she had always dreamed of being someone important someday, accomplishing something. But now all she could think of was Jordan, one hundred miles away.

She glanced at her watch as a bunched-up, empty cigarette package swirled at her ankles. Dirty city. Ten of eleven. If Jordan and Monday had been out partying, he was probably still asleep. Or maybe he was at a casting call.

As she walked quickly to keep herself warm, a scarf wrapped around her neck and her camel's hair coat clutched tightly against her, she knew that someday, she hoped soon, Jordan would get a break. And when he did it would make him famous. She'd never even seen him act, yet she knew he'd be marvelous.

The gunmetal gray sky reflected Sydney's mood.

As she walked across the campus-so different from the serenity and beauty of Wellesley–she wondered why she was here, in Philadelphia.

Nothing about studying for any of her courses interested her.

She used to love learning; she had always dreamed of being someone important someday, accomplishing something. But now all she could think of was Jordan, one hundred miles away.

She glanced at her watch as a bunched-up, empty cigarette package swirled at her ankles. Dirty city. Ten of eleven. If Jordan and Monday had been out partying, he was probably still asleep. Or maybe he was at a casting call.

As she walked quickly to keep herself warm, a scarf wrapped around her neck and her camel's hair coat clutched tightly against her, she knew that someday, she hoped soon, Jordan would get a break. And when he did it would make him famous. She'd never even seen him act, yet she knew he'd be marvelous.

He worried that he was living in a dream world, but Sydney knew that someday his name would be up in lights, above the play's title. People wouldn't be coming just to see a play, but to see Jordan Eliot.

But, she thought, what if he had to settle for something less, something that would earn money, that would support not only himself but a family. Would she still want him, still want to be Mrs. Jordan Eliot?

He was giving himself another year and a half. She should have her master's by then, and could get a good job and support them and they'd get married and—and, what?

Her parents would have a fit. Even if he didn't make it and decided to settle for being a banker or any of the other things he could do. A banker with a Drama major? Well, something else then. A teacher? Oh, God, her father would never condone something like that. What did teachers earn? Forty-eight hundred max? What did ordinary people *do*? What did all these people who lived in apartments around the campus, who lived in salt box houses in Boston, who lived in brownstones in New York what did they all do?

Well, she couldn't decide for Jordan what he'd have to settle for if he was forced to give up his dream. She had to ask herself if she could live like that-in a little house with no maid, doing the dishes every night and washing diapers, wondering if they had enough money to take in a movie.

She pulled open the heavy door and walked into the heat of the lecture hall. Most of her classes were seminars, but this one was in the auditorium. She was glad. It meant she wouldn't have to participate, wouldn't even have to think and be alert.

Would she? Would she settle for Jordan with nothing else? Mightn't it be fun to live in an apartment for a while, live like she guessed the rest of the world did? Like she was doing in the little flat she now had? She'd insisted on that. No, Daddy, no maid; thanks. Just a little two-room apartment, close to the campus. Let me try it on my own.

It seemed a game, like playing house when she was a child. She'd bought a *Fanny Farmer Cookbook* and was teaching herself to cook, something no woman in her family had done in her memory. It was enjoyable deciding what she'd eat every evening. She enjoyed shopping at the little Italian grocery down the block. She'd never been in a grocery store before.

She didn't much like vacuuming and dusting, however. Or defrosting the refrigerator, which she'd finally had to do last week.

She'd furnished the apartment herself, with no advice from anyone. Not that anyone had asked her, but she thought it had a bit of charm. Might not make it into Better Homes and Gardens, but it gave her a sense of pride.

She wished she'd gear herself up to invite a couple of her classmates to dinner, just something simple like spaghetti and a salad with red wine and Italian bread.

Though she had met several compatible students, once she got home all she seemed to want to do was sit and dream of Jordan. She didn't want to get dinner for anyone, didn't want to have her thoughts interrupted. She wanted to close her eyes and see the blueness of his eyes, wanted to feel his lips on hers, his arms around her.

Since she was late, Sydney was forced to' sit in a front-row seat in the crowded lecture room. The professor was already talking, and she heard students laugh as he said something provocative. She hardly heard his voice.

Big Mommy had said, "Go to bed with him before you marry him." Her defense was that sex was an important part of marriage and if it wasn't good before marriage it certainly wouldn't be afterward.

"No," she smiled, that hadn't been her problem. She and Big Daddy had been very compatible that way. But she'd heard … in fact, she couldn't imagine her son being a thoughtful, ardent lover. She'd often wondered if Silvie-well, never mind.

Sydney wondered if she and Jordan had gone to *bea* together if she'd be thinking about him so much. Wouldn't that tension, at least, have dwindled? When she was with Jordan, she wanted to rip off her clothes and make love. She wondered if he'd like her body, if he'd think she was beautiful without clothes on. She knew what he looked like. She'd seen him in those bathing trunks. .

Would her breasts be large enough to please him? Would she know what to do? Did he already have experience, and how would she compare to other women he might have had? Would he be patient? Oh, God.

She looked down at her notebook and saw that she'd doodled "Jordan Jordan" all over the page, like a silly junior high school girl.

Maybe she should just quit and go home to New York, where she could see him every day. She wasn't getting anything out of school now. Thank goodness Christmas vacation was only two and a half weeks away. Even though Jordan had come down for his days off three weeks ago, she felt she'd die if she didn't spend time with him soon. They'd visited the Liberty Bell, and driven out to Valley Forge, and kissed each other constantly.

No, he wasn't going back to Elk Park for Christmas. That was a busy time at Giorgio's. He and Monday were toying with having a Christmas party. He'd like her to meet some of their friends.

She'd told him, "Evan and Uncle Billy will be home for Christmas. Will you spend it with us? They'll both be crazy about you, I know. And I want you to meet them so much. We sit around and open presents all morning, and have eggnog and ooh and ah for hours. Promise me you'll come spend Christmas with us."

"Hadn't you better check with your parents?"

She laughed. "Of course not. I love you, so they'll be happy to have you there. Please, say you'll come."

He was well aware that her parents had not reacted enthusiastically to him when she'd brought him home for dinner after her summer spent on Oberon. She waited until Big Mommy had returned to New York so she and Jordan would have an ally.

After dinner, when Jordan had left, through thin lips her father said, "Elk Park?" in a derogatory· tone. "The Middle West?"

"His father owns a hardware store?" Silvie had smiled through clenched teeth. "How nice."

Probably neither of them had ever set foot in a hardware store, or in a town like Elk Park.

But he was going to marry Sydney. Christ! He'd never wanted anyone so much in his life. He wanted her in his arms, he wanted her in his bed. He wanted to watch her awaken, he wanted to kiss her breasts, he wanted ... he wanted all of her.

But could he ask her to live in a cold-water flat, like his on Bleecker Street? Ask her to act like any other young woman and be a wife and keep house? She'd probably never even made a bed in her life. Shit. Why did she have to come from -money, and so much of it? Well, maybe one of the casting calls he'd attended last week would come through.

At noon the following day, November 28, 1949, as Sydney came in from classes, her phone was ringing. Jordan's voice was excited. "I'm catching the two o'clock train," he said. She could tell he was smiling. "I'll be there in time for one of your home-cooked dinners." It was his night off.

"One of my home-cooked dinners, huh? You must be desperate."

"That spaghetti we had a couple of weeks ago was great. Not even Giorgio's is better."

She'd have to rush out and buy Roma tomatoes, more onions and garlic, let it simmer all afternoon. Get some Chianti and a loaf of Italian bread and Parmesan cheese. So, she wouldn't make it to her four o'clock seminar.

Sydney spent the afternoon cooking, taking a leisurely bath in lilac salts, and trying on dress after dress. Finally she settled on a pair of gray flannel slacks and a white cashmere sweater. She brushed her hair until it shone. The only makeup she usually wore was lipstick, but she added a bit of rouge. Not for the first time she wished she was beautiful. When she was with Jordan he made her feel beautiful. He told her she was.

He appeared at her door with a small bouquet of violets and a bottle of champagne.

She looked at him? His face lit with a smile, his hair long enough that a curl fell over his forehead, his sapphire eyes smiling at her, lighting up the room and her heart. He wore a hand-knit blue sweater over an open-necked shirt. He was holding his coat over his arm, brushing snowflakes from it.

He walked into the room, throwing his coat across a chair, offering her the violets in his left hand as he gathered her and the champagne into his right arm, leaning down to kiss her.

"You smell good," he murmured into her hair.

"You kiss good," she said, reaching for the, violets. "This is an unexpected delight. I'm not used to mid-week spontaneity."

"It's not just to see you," he said as he stood back from her. "I have a purpose."

"I don't care what the reason is so long as you're here."

"You will care what the reason is," he said, "but first, let's open the champagne."

"I'm no good at that. You open it while I get glasses." She went to the kitchen and heard the cork pop as she found two wineglasses. So, Daddy and Mother would have tulip glasses. They'd never use wine glasses for champagne. The smell of tomato sauce permeated the small room.

She offered the glasses to Jordan, who poured champagne into each before setting the bottle on the table. Then he got down on one knee, raised his glass in the air, and, grinning, said, "Beloved, I am here to ask you to marry me."

"Jordan! You got a part."

His smile covered his face, leapt out of his eyes, and he reached out to pull her to him. "Come on, yes or no. Are you going to drive me any more crazy than you already do?"

She knelt down on the floor, facing him. "Tell me every detail."

He kissed her, spilling champagne as he did so. "Hey, drink up. This was not inexpensive."

"Tell me."

"We open in New Haven in six weeks. The star — are you ready — Is Leonard Matisse and I'm to play his son. It's a story about a father and son."

"Oh my," Sydney gulped "You must be important."

"Matisse chose me himself," Jordan seemed about to burst with pride. "It's a wonderful play."

"I'll marry you. Of course, I'll marry you. I'd marry you even if you didn't have a part."

"What I thought was we could plan it for June, when you're through here. By then things should have settled down so I'll have time for us. Until it opens I'm keeping my job at Giorgio's. I can continue to work in the restaurant from six till closing. I earn more there than I will in the play. But I'm on my way, darling. *We're* on our way."

He stood up, placing his glass on a table, and reached down to pull her up, swinging her around. "I want you on this trip with me. I need you by my side, in my life. I want to share it all with you."

"Oh, Jordan, it's marvelous."

"I know. I just found out at eleven. I rushed home to tell Monday and phone you. God, Sydney, I can hardly think straight."

It was wonderful to see him so elated. But suddenly he stopped smiling. "Your parents aren't going to like this, are they?"

"Jordan, if I'm happy, I'm sure they'll be happy. Daddy measures who I should marry by money and old New York families, not by who I love. He'll get over it. Mother, well, we'll see. But no matter how anyone else in the world feels, I'm going to marry you. I'm going to spend my life with you.'"

He grabbed her and hugged her to him. "I don't know if I can wait until June."

"You know what Big Mommy told me?" '

He raised an eyebrow and asked, "What?"

"That I should sleep with you before marrying you."

He stood back from her and crinkled his eyes in a smile.

"She said that, huh?"

"I told her that once I tried to seduce you, but you wouldn't. As long as we're getting married, what difference should a little piece of paper make?"

He burst into laughter. "Feed me first. I haven't eaten all day. And then maybe we can discuss this ... advice."

The fuchsia neon light kept flashing into the darkened room. Jordan stood in the doorway, one arm leaning against it.

"I don't know why you're embarrassed. You have the most beautiful body in the world."

Sydney self-consciously turned to face him, her clothes scattered on the floor around her. She'd wanted the light off and he'd wanted to watch her undress. They'd compromised this way.

He stood spread-eagled, still in the doorway, and began removing his clothes. Sydney had never seen a naked man before. Oh, sure, Evan, when they were kids. Pre-teens. But 'none since then. Now, they stood facing each other across the room. Jordan walked slowly over to her, reaching out to cup her breasts in his hands.

"That feels good," she whispered.

"It does that," he agreed, pulling her to him, his mouth meeting hers. She could feel his nakedness, his hardness. His tongue meshed with hers, gently exploring as his left hand rubbed her breast.

Picking her up, he walked over to the bed and laid her down. The flickering light from outside danced across her body as Jordan lowered himself to lie beside her, leaning on his elbow as he danced his hand over her. "God, you're smooth." He leaned over to kiss her breast.

"I've never done this before," she whispered.

"I know that," he said, his tongue running across her nipples before he took her breast into his mouth. Sydney felt stirrings between her legs and Jordan's hand slid down to touch her there as he gently bit her breast. Sydney moaned. .

He moved on top of her, and she jackknifed her legs, spreading them wide apart. The neon lights outside the window blinked their fuchsias, chartreuses, milky blues.

"It may not be the aurora borealis," Jordan murmured, "but it'll do for now."

"It'll do forever," Sydney whispered as he entered her and she thought, I don't ever need any more than this.

Eight

"Daddy, do you know what you're saying?"

Oliver jerked his head back and looked at Sydney.

"You're saying the only reason a man could love me is your money. Daddy, look at me. I'm not unattractive!" Her voice sounded as though she was close to tears.

Oliver's hands unclenched and he walked over to put them on Sydney's shoulders.

"Honey, that's not what I mean at all But you won't have any doubt if you marry someone from our class."

"Our class! Daddy, for heaven's sake, this is America."

Oliver shook his head and walked away from Sydney, back to his favorite leather couch before the fireplace in his study.

"An actor, Sydney. My God. How unreliable. How impractical. He'll never be able to support you in the style…"

"The style to which I've become accustomed? Daddy, don't you think I have any fiber? I don't have to have money to be happy."

Oliver interrupted with a sharp laugh. "It helps."

"Maybe it does. But look at the millions of Americans, of people all over the world, who live with so much less than we do. I'm willing to try it, Daddy."

"Sydney, sit down a minute. Try to calm down and let's talk rationally." Sydney's heart was pumping so fast she didn't think she'd ever calm down.

"Now, let's talk practicalities."

Sydney sighed.

"Ninety-nine chances out of a hundred-no, nine hundred and ninety-nine out of a thousand, that's what this young man's chances of succeeding are, of earning enough to support a family. Someday, unless he expects you to work to support him, he'll have to face up to reality and settle for earning a living. What? Go back to Indiana and work in his father's hardware store? Could you take that, my dear? A small town in Middle America?"

The thought did not appeal to Sydney. Like most New Yorkers, she thought that anything outside a twenty-five mile radius of Manhattan was the boonies, that there was no culture, that it was all baseball games and lodge picnics and small town gossip. What did one do without museums and the theater and the kind of dinner parties to which New Yorkers were partial? The kind of stimulating conversation, about politics and world problems and the economy?

No, Sydney couldn't imagine herself in a small town. Especially the way Jordan painted it. "He doesn't want to return to a small town, Daddy. Look, he's an educated guy. Northwestern, graduated with honors."

"In what, English? How the hell can he earn a living with that kind of degree?"

"You hire people with English degrees all the time."

Oliver nodded. "And not one of them could support you."

Sydney shook her head as though her father were a hopeless case. "Daddy, why is it that fathers always seem more interested in how their daughters will fare financially in a marriage than the emotional aspect?"

"Sydney, you're so young. You don't even realize how much one has to do with the other."

"Maybe so, Daddy, but would you rather have me marry someone whose father and grandfather made their millions and who are themselves dodos"

Oliver laughed. "Dodos? That's a new one. I gather that's the male version of a dumb blonde. Certainly Evan has had enough of those, but at least he hasn't married one of them. He's got more sense."

"Would you prefer I just sleep with Jordan? Go live with him and wait until someone with class, that's your word, and money comes along and then give Jordan up? Daddy, I know you don't mean that. Please, please think of my happiness. I'm twenty-one years old and I've never been in love before. I know Jordan's right for me. I know I'll never in my whole life love anyone like I do Jordan."

Oliver shook his head again and his lips tightened, "Glands get in the way of common sense at your, age."

Sydney stared at her father. "Your mother loves him, too."

"My mother," Oliver said, "has never had a practical thought in her life."

"Whose fault is that?"

"Well, you won't need to, either, if you'll marry a man who can take care of you."

Sydney thought she might just possibly scream.

"I'll tell you what. Send your young man to talk with me at the office. Let's see," he glanced at the calendar on his desk. "How about Thursday? The day after tomorrow."

"He has rehearsal then. The only time he's free during the day is Saturday. He works at Giorgio's evenings."

"A waiter," Oliver said, with derision.

"He could come here to lunch on Saturday, couldn't he?"

"No, Sydney. I want to talk to him without you around."

Sydney laughed. "You going to try to buy him like you do Evan's girls?"

"That's a thought."

"Don't tell me you haven't already thought of it Well, Daddy, if he can be bought off, you'll have cured me of loving him. I think he's much better than that. I also think he loves me a lot more than any amount of money. If that's all you're going to try to do, I feel safe. He thinks money is low on the list of priorities for happiness."

Oliver leaned forward, his elbows on his desk. "And what are his priorities?"

"Oh, Daddy, he's so fine. He won't deny that money's important for security and freedom. But he thinks loving your work and feeling that you're contributing to society are important."

"How does society benefit from actors?'

"Don't sound like that. First of all, look at all the people who love the theater and the movies. Actors bring pleasure to people, Daddy, and you know it. But that's not all he means. He'd like to make enough money to be able to contribute to society or to the world in some way that will make a difference. He's interested in ecology."

"The what?"

"The environment. He thinks we're polluting ourselves off the face of the earth."

Oliver laughed. "A nut – I thought so."

Sydney stood her stance filled-with tension. "Oh, Daddy, you can be so infuriating. But, you'll see. I'll ask him to meet you on Saturday."

"My office will be fine."

A place where he could intimidate Jordan, or any young man brave enough to ask for Sydney's hand.

"Okay, we'll go through the archaic ritual of letting him ask for my hand, as if you're so all-powerful you can grant my hand to whomever you want? No, Daddy, you can meet with him, but approve of him or not, I'm going to marry Jordan Eliot."

Oliver never did take Jordan to lunch. Jordan walked out before it got to that stage.

Oliver wasted no time getting to the point. "A hundred thousand's not enough? How about five hundred thousand, a cool half-million?"

Jordan stared at the aristocratic-looking man who would be his father-in-law. "You know, sir, I thought this happened only in Grade-B movies. I didn't know fathers really did things like this. Let me make it clear. Your daughter's financial situation did make me hesitate. I know I can never give her what she's been used to. Do you think Sydney can't adjust to living like the average American? I think she can, sir. I think Sydney can do whatever she sets her mind to. I'd be willing to bet on it."

"That may be, but love dies in cold-water flats."

"We're not talking cold-water flats for long, sir. Maybe a year at the most. If I haven't made enough so that Sydney can stop working."

"Sydney working?"

"Yes, sir. She doesn't want her education to go to waste,; and she's perfectly willing to help support us until I'm able to. I've promised only another year to see if I can make it big in the theater, sir."

Oliver laughed, not a pretty sound. "And then what?"

Jordan hesitated. "I haven't allowed myself to consider the possibilities, Mr. Hamilton. But, I do have a deadline. And if I'm not making a living in the theater by then, I won't make Sydney suffer for that. I'll do something."

"Like what?" Oliver continued to pressure.

Jordan shook his head, his eyes not leaving the older man's. "I don't know, yet. But if I'm not successful, at least by my standards, by January 1, 1952, I'll quit, sir, and hope I won't look back."

"That's almost two years from now. What will you do then? Go back to Indiana?"

"God forbid. No, I don't know. Something here in New York, preferably, if you're afraid of Sydney's moving away. I like cities, sir."

"Do you know how much it costs to live in New York with what I imagine you'd call an average job?"

Jordan leaned forward. "Average is a word I never apply to myself, Mr. Hamilton. If it were, your daughter and I wouldn't be in love. Nothing about us is average, sir. My income may only be average according to your standards; but my life will never be average, whether I have that kind of money or not.

"I'm going to marry your daughter, sir, and since we'll be in-laws, I hope you can live with that."

Oliver shook his head. "I can't. And I shall do everything in my power to thwart this marriage. I shall cut her off without a cent, Mr. Eliot."

Jordan laughed. "I don't think that's enough to deter either Sydney or me. I never expected a woman to bring money to a marriage."

"She'll be cut out of my will, and she'll have nothing. Your children will have nothing. And I'll be no part of a wedding ceremony."

But someone had more power than Oliver. Silvie told him that any daughter of hers would have a whale of a wedding, and he would give her away. They had the biggest fight of their twenty-three years together.

"She won't get a cent."

"That's up to you," Silvie said. "But the wedding's up to me."

So, without a smile on his face, with a rigid body and erect stance, Oliver went through the formalities of handing Sydney over to Jordan on June 28, 1950, in what the tabloids called "the wedding of the year, if not the decade."

Jordan was overwhelmed, and his parents, his sister and brother-in-law, and their three children were awed. As were his two aunts on his father's side and their husbands and his mother's sisters and their families, including half a dozen children under twelve.

Silvie insisted on putting them up at the Plaza and footing the bill. She never asked Oliver for the money, but Big Mommy willingly came through. Sometimes Big Mommy thought Silvie was her daughter and Oliver her son-in-law.

"Well," Big Mommy told Silvie after the wedding when they were at Oberon together. "I'll leave my money to Sydney."

Silvie laughed. "Don't tell her that. Let it be a surprise. Right now they think love is triumphing over money and they feel quite superior. I like him. Oliver's going to be surprised. Jordan's going to make it.'"

She and Big Mommy had both attended the opening night of the play and had both been impressed. Besides, Big Mommy thought he was delightful.

"He's got his head screwed on right, even if he is an actor," she said, over and over again. Besides, he'd never once acted as though her makeup or her clothes were out of the ordinary.

"I'll see Oliver leaves half of this island to her, or I'll just skip him in my will," Big Mommy said and grinned wickedly. But both women agreed to keep this a secret between them. "Sydney's worth ten of Evan," her grandmother said. "And I happen to know that Oliver's spent over a million on that wastrel son of yours already."

Silvie looked up. "A million? Oh, Mama, You must be wrong. Evan's just gotten into a couple of little scrapes. A million? You can't be right."

Big Mommy nodded. "Some day someone should teach that young man about wearing rubbers."

Silvie looked up, startled. No one had ever said that word aloud to her before, and she certainly never expected her mother-in-law to do so.

"Grow up, my dear," Big Mommy told her daughter-in-law, but kindly. "Oliver's like so many men. Thinks women shouldn't know the sordid facts of life. What do they think we are, anyhow? Porcelain dolls? I don't know where he gets it, certainly not from his father. Oliver has too much virtue for his own good. And Evan, too little. Funny, isn't it? He'll let his son do anything, and bail him out of any scrape. But his daughter; who's never done anything but make him proud of her, can't be allowed to marry the man she wants."

Silvie nodded. Oliver was not the easiest man in the world to live with. But she'd married him because her father stood in the way of her marrying the man she thought she loved, the local doctor in Bar Harbor, where her family spent their summers.

She guessed she'd grown to love Oliver over the years, but he was so rigid that sometimes it was more than she could take. At those moments she took off and went to Oberon to stay by herself or enjoy Big Mommy's company if it were sometime between Memorial Day and Halloween.

Where did people go without an Oberon? Where did people escape what seemed so often inescapable? Where did they go to feed their souls, to find solitude and parts of themselves? To find the courage to go on?

"I think," she'd once said to Big Mommy, "that there's so much crime in big cities because people don't have enough room. They're crowded, and there's no space to refuel."

"Refuel?" Big Mommy asked.

"Replenish their spirits, come to terms with the problems of life. See beauty, see the sky and trees, hear birds. Look to the horizon. If people could do that, maybe there'd be less crime."

Big Mommy thought that sounded too simple, but she thought Silvie had a valid point, nevertheless.

"A place where what the world thinks doesn't matter a damn," Silvie said.

"You mean the world doesn't matter at all?"

"Oh, no," Silvie responded, "the world matters a lot. But what the people in it think of you doesn't matter. Certainly, the world matters. And maybe it's at such a place as Oberon that one comes to terms with the world. If you can't save it from itself, come to terms with that, too."

They sat in their rocking chairs on the front porch, gazing south over the water, the sun reflecting so brightly that Big Mommy closed her eyes.

"Silvie, I am blessed having you for a daughter."

Silvie was very aware her mother-in-law had not said "daughter-in-law."

She reached over and put a hand on Big Mommy's arm, her other hand shading the sun from glaring as she watched a sailboat in the distance, skimming across the mirror-like bay that protected her from the rest of the world.

"Someday," she said, "Sydney and Jordan are going to show Oliver how wrong he is."

"Well, he'll never admit it, I'm sure," said his mother. "He's such a hard ass."

Silvie's hand flew to her chest, and she sat up straight. Big Mommy opened her eyes, which were smiling.

Silvie laughed aloud.

"Tell me," Big Mommy said, "not that it's any of my business. But I don't imagine Oliver's ever laughed while in the midst of making love, has he?"

Silvie was shocked. No, of course he hadn't. Laugh while making love?

Nine

Uncle Billy – William Seabright Holister – and Evan Hamilton were an odd couple in some ways. In other Ways, they were not. Neither had ever worked for a living or could even imagine doing so.

They were snobs. Billy was not a snob in the way that Evan was, though he couldn't understand people who had no money or who lived outside the pale of Manhattan Island. He couldn't understand people who did not feel their souls elevated at the opera, did not enjoy the Broadway theater, did not read the latest best-sellers, or who did not spend summers in the Hamptons or Newport, or who did not trek to Europe annually. The season in London was a must for Uncle Billy.

He grew up with a cultivated manner of speaking, wore the most expensive clothes, tailored just for him, and always looked as though he might be the wealthiest and most arrogant man alive.

He was neither. He treated servants with great respect, even having a before-bed nip with them in the kitchen, or coffee on a winter afternoon. Though he expected, and invariably received, service from them, he did not treat them as though they were less than human. In fact, he was known to play cards with them, and even listened to the opera on Saturday afternoons with Warren, when he was not at the Met, that is.

Servants loved Uncle Billy. He always told the cook, whether it was true or not, that the meal was excellent. If he was alone in the apartment late at night he was known to invite Warren to watch the new television with him. They drank Scotch and smoked Pall Malls...

He never was without a cigarette, waving it around in a long cigarette holder that was even longer than FDR's.

Billy and his sister Silvie-older by a dozen years-had had golden childhoods, even though not at the same time. They had grown up in Oyster Bay, and Billy attended Amherst. He aced classes with little study, a maximum social life, and a general attitude of good humor toward everything and almost everyone. The only thing he had ever studied assiduously was the piano, for which he had a passion. Early on he realized he would never play Beethoven and Mozart except by rote, so he set out to be the life of the party by playing Cole Porter even better than Cole Porter could. If you arrived at a New York party and heard "Night and Day" or "Begin the Beguine" in the background, you knew Billy Holister was already there.

No one ever called him Bill. He had the ability to make people smile. When Billy Holister was in the room, everyone was happy. He was witty and clever and thoughtful, too. His humor was never at another's expense.

He was very average looking, about five-feet-ten with sandy hair and a rather thin face but with the prominent cheekbones for which the Holisters were famous. His thin lips were usually curved in a smile, which never–not ever–seemed fake. For all his dramatic gestures, all his snobbishness, Billy never seemed insincere. And when you talked with him he looked at you with rapt attention, as though nothing else in the world mattered.

He remembered names and faces.

Though he dated women all the time, he only became intimately involved once. Usually he remained friends with women he'd gone to bed with. When the 1929 crash hit, Billy was only fourteen. He remained virtually untouched by it, wondering why his father, who lost everything, including the home at Oyster Bay, sank into a depression that eventually rendered him dysfunctional. In fact, his parents sent Billy to live with his sister, Silvie, and her husband, and their two-year-old daughter, in the Park Avenue apartment in which he would remain for the rest of his life.

Silvie became a second mother rather than an older sister, and Oliver was a mixture of older brother and the father Billy's own father could no longer be. Billy adored Oliver; He made Oliver laugh. He made Oliver proud of him as he breezed through Amherst, and Oliver never for a second minded the fact that Billy didn't go to work.

The only thing for which Billy ever evidenced passion, aside from the piano, was his family. He loved Oliver and Silvie and Sydney and Evan as much as he was capable of loving. He hated hunting, but he learned how to use a gun so he could accompany Oliver to Oberon and sit in duck blinds and shiver. For no one else in the world would he have made himself so uncomfortable.

When Sydney had an attack of appendicitis at age thirteen, Uncle Billy was twenty-five. He sat at the hospital all day and all night for the first two nights she was there. When Evan was kicked out of school, it was Billy who went to bring him home, who never once censured him, and who laughed with him. Not about flunking out of school, but about someone they knew, or some joke. Billy's jokes were never off-color, so everyone could find them amusing. They were never corny, but always rather witty.

Billy's pants were always pressed with a razor-like crease. He was one of the first to wear pastel shirts, and then, later on, stripes. His suits were of silk, even in winter, and in summer they were always white. From Memorial Day to Labor Day, Billy wore white. White ducks, white shirt, white jacket, white socks, white shoes, and a navy blue tie.

Billy did not like to be uncomfortable, but for his family, including his brother-in-law, he would have walked on hot coals. In return, Oliver gave him a handsome-annual allowance, never forcing Billy to ask for money, but on Christmas handing him a check, which he could spend as he saw fit throughout the year. It was a princely sum.

His nephew, Evan, and he shared some of the same traits, yet they were polar opposites.

Evan wore his arrogance prominently. Most people felt he literally looked down his nose at them. He did, but this was partially caused by his myopia. From the age of eight Evan had had to wear glasses, and this infuriated the hell out of him. Yet no one, not once, ever called him "four eyes." A glance from Evan Hamilton could wither. He was a bully. He beat up kids who were smaller than he, younger than he, not as wealthy as he. He was not a large person, but he liked to fight, and the only subject in which he excelled in his various schools was wrestling. , He liked other sports and was good at them, too, sports like polo, horseback riding, and skiing. He was the only one in the family who could sail a boat better than Sydney. He drove cars as fast as a car can go. The year he was seventeen, he accrued traffic tickets in the amount of four thousand, six hundred and seventy-five dollars. Oliver had a fit. He took Evan's license away and refused to let him drive any of the family cars, thinking that would teach him a lesson.

Servants disliked Evan. He seemed to think they were scarcely human. He treated them with contempt if whatever he wanted wasn't ready the minute he wanted it. He spent hours preening in front of mirrors, buying clothes, trying to look as elegant as Uncle Billy. He nearly achieved this, but he lacked Uncle Billy's endearing qualities.

Evan wasn't kind, and he had absolutely no sense of humor. Not about anything, and particularly not about himself. His short fuse was set off often, but never more so than when he gambled and lost. And he loved gambling. Any kind. Horses, baseball, cards. When he and Billy arrived in Monaco they were both happy. They liked the lifestyle and Evan liked the tension.

He also liked the women who gambled because he discovered they usually went to bed indiscriminately with any good-looking, rich man. And if there was anything Evan liked better than gambling it was being in bed with a woman.

When Evan was fifteen, Oliver paid a twenty-one year old woman a hundred thousand dollars to get an abortion. At seventeen Evan told his father he had to get married and introduced him to Lurlene, whom he'd met at the Copacabana. Lurlene told him she was pregnant, and Evan knew the minute Oliver met her that he'd buy her off. Lurlene wouldn't make a Hamilton.

After the third such experience, Oliver bought Evan a dozen condoms and asked Billy if he'd go with Evan to Europe, so Evan could sow his wild oats over there. "For God's sake, keep him supplied with condoms. Doesn't that boy have any sense? And introduce him to some women of our class, will you, Billy?"

"They won't go to bed with him."

Oliver rolled his eyes and sighed. "Where does he get this? Not from me."

"Don't look at me that way. Not my side of the family, either."

They both knew the truth of that. Neither of them would have gone to bed with the women Evan favored. "Find some blue bloods over there," Oliver said.

A sexy blue blood, royalty who needs money, Billy thought. He imagined that was what Oliver thought, too. At least some woman they wouldn't be ashamed to have as a Hamilton.

"He'll gamble," Billy told his brother-in-law.

"I know. Try to keep it to a minimum, will you?"

They sailed over on the Queen Elizabeth, and Billy seldom saw Evan, except when he awoke mornings and Evan was asleep in the other bed. Evan slept until the middle of the afternoon. Billy didn't rise much before noon, but Evan was never there when he turned in sometime after two in the morning.

Evan did not treat Billy as though he were a chaperone, and indeed, Billy was too bent on his own pleasure to pay much attention to his nephew. But his pleasures were not at the gaming tables or in someone's bed-they came from mingling in first class, dining at the captain's table, and the captain found him so delightful that he invited him three nights in a row. Billy joined the orchestra and improvised on the piano, and the dancers loved his little arpeggios, so unexpected and so perfect. There wasn't a song written that Billy couldn't improve upon.

But, despite all Billy's charm and Evan's arrogance, it was Evan who attracted the women. They draped their arms around Billy's shoulders, smiled at him and bantered with him, but were enticed by the brooding countenance of Evan Hamilton, even without knowing he was one of *the* Hamiltons. His eyes seldom smiled. He looked removed and distant yet at the same time predatory, like a lion stalking a mate. His golden hair and blue eyes belied the danger lurking beneath his boyish exterior. The kind of women to whom he was attracted sensed the challenge he offered, deciding it would show their mettle if they could tame him. For they knew he was wild.

He didn't stop for any of them. He went through women like fire through forests. That is, he didn't stop until Monte Carlo.

He and Billy both loved the Riviera. Billy loved the beaches and the hotels and the kind of people who stayed in the hotels. He ran into three people he knew the first day.

Evan loved the gaming tables and the bars.

They both loved the parties and the dancing. They were invited to costume balls and picnics. Being a Hamilton had distinct advantages.

And it was here that Evan at last stopped for a woman.

Veronique Beauchamp was the most stunning girl Uncle Billy had ever seen. He'd been around class all his life, and he knew it when he saw it. But Veronique had much more than that. She had a figure that turned every male head in the room, and she looked like she'd been poured into the white dress that clung to her sculptured body. The dazzling whiteness accentuated the gold of her skin. Like Evan, she had golden hair, and she wore it in a smooth chignon with flowers twined through it. Her eyes were a mirror of Evan's. Blue. Steel blue. Her wide, generous mouth, covered with too-red lipstick, had been made for kissing, Evan observed to Billy.

"A hundred to one she's that color all over," Uncle Billy said as he lit a cigarette.

"Who is she?" Evan couldn't take his eyes from her.

"Want me to find out?"

Evan nodded and Uncle Billy stood up, reaching for his straw hat.

Evan could only see her back, bare bronze against her white dress. Another woman reached across the table to light her cigarette. Evan was sure he saw heat waves shimmer above her head.

He didn't even try to seduce her. He was told her attention was not easy to attract and that she didn't need the Hamilton money.

She wore low-cut gowns that showed her firm, full-rounded breasts. She wore no bra and when her dresses clung, they outlined her nipples. She laughed as seldom as Evan did.

Her mother was British and her father had died as a guerilla fighter in the war. Her stepfather was the one with a title, the count. Of course, there had been no real royalty in France since Napoleon, but those who claimed such ancestry kept up the facade. The Comte de, or the Duc de…

Evan didn't care where her family came from. To him, she was a princess. He slowed down for Veronique. He took his time.

Barbara Bickmore

Ten

What fascinated Veronique was that the brooding young American paid absolutely no attention to her. He was too young for her, actually, she knew that. He couldn't be any older than she was. But she was not used to being ignored by men that age, or any age, for that matter.

He wasn't gay, she was pretty sure of that, but he paid her no heed whatsoever. He concentrated on his gambling, and he won rather consistently the night she first noticed him. The next night he lost, but gracefully. It didn't seem to bother him a bit. She liked that.

He hardly smiled. His eyes flitted aimlessly around the room, not resting on her, though for a flicker of a second their eyes met. He wasn't handsome, but he was terribly attractive. He looked, she thought, as though he should have dark hair, swarthy skin, and a pencil-thin mustache, instead of being such a golden-boy. She wondered if he'd ever had a woman. She wondered what his kisses were like.

Usually she had to fight men off. This one looked right through her.

Every other man, and nearly every woman, too, turned to gaze at her because her eyes flashed like sapphires, and when she did laugh it rippled across the room. Evan noticed that it did not reach her eyes.

Her sequined red chiffon bodice clung to her, and she wore no jewelry, except for diamond earrings. Her glorious neck and arms were bare. Only blood-red nail polish adorned her hands.

Evan sent Billy to stand next to Veronique at *chemin de fer*, and in his usual charming manner, Billy began to converse with her. Now here, she thought, is the man I should go for.

He's got to be in his early thirties—elegant, urbane, debonair. He looked born to the manor, and was someone her parents would approve of, she was sure of that. But he did not flirt with her, either. He simply made idle chatter. But when he moved away from the table she knew that the golden boy was incredibly wealthy, that his father owned one of New York's most prestigious newspapers, that he was sailing tomorrow on Countess Schiaparelli's yacht.

Within an hour she, too, had an invitation.

What a boring day! He had never shown up. To Veronique, the people on the yacht were ancient, gossiping about people old enough to be her parents, and she had to fight off passes from old men of at least forty.

Bored to extinction, Veronique decided to dine alone at El Meson's, where she would not have to dress up. Her hair was awry, she knew, her skin dry from the day in the sun, her temper short. She would not go to the gaming tables. She would dine and retreat to her room and do her nails, take a long luxurious oil bath and rejuvenate herself.

As she sipped her wine, the man who had stood next to her and the golden boy entered, standing by the maitre d's desk, waiting for a table. The older man pointed at her, nodded, and threaded his way across the room.

Oh, shit, thought Veronique. And me looking like this.

The young man, apparently bored, followed him to her table.

"How pleasant to see you again. I never did get your name. Permit me," Billy said, introducing himself. "And this is my nephew, Evan Hamilton."

Evan thought he had never seen a more beautiful woman.

He liked the poutiness of her sensual lips, the slash of bright red lipstick, her hair wantonly cascading in tendrils down her neck. She looked the way she should look just after making love.

"May we join you?" Billy asked, already pulling out a chair.

"Of course," Veronique answered. "I was just feeling sorry for myself, all alone."

"It must be by choice," Billy said, gazing at her with frank admiration but no hint of awkwardness.

"It is." Veronique turned to look at Evan, who was lighting a cigarette and paying no attention to her at all. His eyes skirted the restaurant.

"Your English is excellent," he said, still not looking at her.

"I'm half English," she said. "I spent my school years in England; hating every one of them."

Billy and Evan ordered drinks, and Evan finally began to turn his attention to the woman across the table. "Didn't I see you last evening?" he asked. He'd seen her every evening since they'd arrived.

"Could be," she said, a tenseness flitting across her chest.

She'd never felt so forcefully attracted. "I met your friend here last night."

"Billy," said Billy.

As Evan looked at her, Veronique felt as though she'd been stripped of her clothing, as though she sat across from him naked, yet his eyes had not lowered themselves to her cleavage.

They had not left her eyes and her mouth.

They talked very little, Billy carrying the burden of conversation. He saw very well what was happening, and after the chateaubriand he excused himself, saying he had arranged to meet someone at the gaming tables.

Veronique and Evan stared at each other. His leg brushed hers, but barely, under the table and she wondered if it were deliberate.

"Dancing or gambling?" he asked.

"How about a stroll on the beach? There's moonlight."

He followed her out of the restaurant, and they walked down the boulevard to the beach.

"Your first time in Europe?" she asked, feeling her skin peeling away from her body, totally exposed in front of this man.

"You've looked at me all week. I've seen you," Evan said.

"I didn't think you'd even noticed me."

"Where are you staying?"

He stood gazing into her eyes, which seemed bottomless in the moonlight. Then he reached out and ran his fingers down her arm. That was all.

She waited for him to kiss her. When he didn't, she felt sorry she hadn't opted for dancing so she could feel his arms around her. They stood staring at each other and then he turned, gazing out into the darkness, over the water. "Shall I walk you home?"

When he opened her door with the key she handed him, he bowed slightly and said, "Until tomorrow. Or perhaps the next day?" Turning, he left.

She stood open-mouthed and astonished. He knew he could have had her. Every man who'd had her before had wanted her insatiably. Had he not even desired her? There was no way to tell what he was thinking, him and those blue eyes as cold as the northern sea.

For the next three days she searched for him. She dined in a different·restaurant each evening. She went to a different casino each night. She wandered through the hotel bars. She hated herself.

The fourth night, there he was, at the twenty-one table. He glanced up at her and smiled, but barely. She used all her willpower not to cross the room.

Billy was not in sight.

Evan looked across the room at her. Her shoulders were bare, the curve of her breasts apparent in her clinging lilac chiffon.

They drove to Paris in her silver Karmann Ghia, with Billy in the backseat. He enjoyed the scenery. Evan and Veronique had eyes only for each other. .

"Mon Dieu!" exclaimed her father, when told they wanted to get married. "He's an *enfant.*"

But Veronique would not be dissuaded. Nor would she and Evan wait. Oliver and Silvie flew over for the ceremony, and Oliver breathed a sigh of relief. He gave them a generous check as a wedding present, and Evan said he guessed he'd stay in Europe awhile longer. That was all right with his parents. He'd settle down now that he was married, even if he was barely of age.

He'd turned twenty-one three days before the wedding. Certainly Veronique was beautiful, but Silvie found her arrogant and heedless of others, including her new in-laws.

"What kind of woman did you expect Evan to choose?" Oliver asked. Veronique and her parents were a great improvement over the girls he'd bought off, Oliver thought silently.

Billy came back to New York. He'd had a grand time, hadn't lost any money gambling, but then gambling was not his thing. He had just enjoyed the experience and the people he'd met. They'd all been his kind of people.

Evan knew without ever asking Veronique that she wasn't a virgin. The thought excited him. She'd have something to offer him, her wildness had already been tapped He listened to the shower running, and lit a cigarette.

She'd have bought a splendid nightgown, he imagined, one that was supposed to titillate and excite him, as though he needed it. He'd never been with a woman twenty-four hours a day. He'd bet they could stay in bed twenty-four hours. Could make love, honest-to-God love. He'd never done that. Not once.

The shower stopped. .

Should he put on the gray silk robe he'd bought for the occasion or were the navy pajamas all right? What would Veronique expect?

The bed was turned down. Burgundy satin sheets. He laughed aloud. Well, the honeymoon suite, after all. His body tingled at the thought. He'd let her get in bed first. He hoped she wouldn't insist on darkness. He wanted to see that body, see if she was tanned all over, wanted to stare at those firmly shaped breasts, run his tongue over them, take them into his mouth. But he'd go slowly.

The door to the bathroom opened. He crushed out his cigarette and turned. Veronique stood in the doorway, legs spread apart, hands on her hips.

"Christ," he said. He'd never seen such a beautiful body.

No white nightgown. No nothing.

She cupped her hands under her breasts and, smiling invitingly, slowly crossed the room, her eyes never leaving his. He, however, let his eyes roam over her body. She *was* gold all over.

He picked her up and moved to the bed, ripping off his pajamas, his lips meeting hers. God, she tasted good. Love. She mesmerized him. Her fingers feathered along his back as she pulled him against her. His mouth encircled her left breast, his tongue tasting sweetness.

"Don't hurry," she whispered.

He had no intention of doing so.

She's mine, he kept thinking. All this is mine. Something he'd gotten all on his own. Something-someone-who loved him. The most beautiful woman in the world, and he felt her nails clawing into his shoulders, felt her legs winding around, felt her mouth against his.

Slow, he reminded, himself, you've got the rest of your life;

When, finally, he could tell she was on the verge, when he thrust into her, his eyes closed, he said, "Shit!" Whether aloud or not, he never knew.

In that instant, as with all the other girls at that moment of entry, it was Sydney's face he saw, Sydney's low moans he heard.

He began to move in frenzy, opening his eyes to look at the beautiful woman who was his wife, far more beautiful than his sister could ever be, more beautiful than any woman, anyplace. He saw the beads of perspiration on her upper lip, felt her arch her back, grinding rhythmically with him, moving together, and he suddenly wanted to hurt her. She had not erased that image, after all.

He thrust deep inside her until her eyes flew open and he saw the surprise reflected there. But it was too late to stop, and her eyes glazed over as he kept up the thrusting, timing himself so it was like a pulse beating. When he felt her tighten around him and heard her ecstatic cry, he let himself come.

A flood. A goddamned flood.

Afterwards, he reached for a cigarette and lay, his left arm under his head, smoking, staring at the ceiling.

Veronique curled into the hollow of his arm and tossed her leg over his. She purred. After a few minutes he said, "Want to go down to the tables?"

Her murmur was negative. "After this? It's two in the morning."

He fought the urge to get up, put on his clothes, and walk out of the room to the broad stairway to the gaming tables where he could order a drink. Several drinks.

Yet he knew that going alone would not be acceptable on his wedding night.

He blew a smoke ring, letting it curl and vaporize into the air, wondering what Sydney's wedding night had been like. At least Jordan could never have looked at her, underneath him, and known she was the most beautiful woman in the world.

Had they hit the sack before they'd married? Had Sydney trembled? Had she worn a white silk nightgown, with lace molded against her breasts? That was another thing Jordan had missed out on. Sydney's breasts sure couldn't compare with Veronique's.

Three weeks later, at midnight, after he and Veronique had made love for the third time that day, he told her he was going downstairs for a quick game of twenty-one. Her muffled, "Fine," told him she was on the edge of sleep.

Before he reached the tables, he detoured to the bar for one fast drink. On the barstool next to him was nineteen-year-old Giselle something-or-other who had already appeared in a walk-on role in Fellini's latest movie, still unreleased. Her dark, liquid eyes ran over Evan.

He never got to the gaming tables.

When Veronique awoke at seven she murmured, "you're up awfully early."

He was fully dressed. She didn't realize they were the same clothes he'd worn when he'd left the room seven hours before.

He smiled. He imagined not many men had gotten it up as often as he had the past twenty-four hours. At least he hadn't seen Sydney once. Not once.

But then, he hadn't let himself close his eyes.

Eleven

Although Jordan and Sydney found a small apartment on Christopher Street, leaving Monday alone at the Bleecker Street flat, they all managed to eat together. Usually it was near midnight, after Jordan's show closed.

Sydney walked around feeling tired all the time. She arrived at the apartment close to six, just as Jordan was readying himself for the subway ride to the theater. They did have half an hour most evenings to share the day's events. Not that Sydney had much to report concerning her job at Bonwit's. The manager of her department had noticed her flair for fashion and steered Sydney into work that, while it didn't challenge or excite her, didn't bore her. But she found nothing fascinating enough to tell Jordan. Certainly he wasn't interested in what women wore or all the small talk. She left her work at the door of the Fifth Avenue building and rushed home to hear Jordan's always-amusing stories about the noonday crowd at Giorgio's, and how madly in love with each other they were.

As soon as Jordan left for the theater, Sydney fell asleep by seven. The alarm awakened her at ten, when she'd take the subway uptown and meet Jordan at the St. James, just off Broadway. She'd never been backstage before and each evening, as Tim, the doorman, greeted her, she felt drawn into a magical orbit.

They and most members of the cast and, more often than not, Monday, who loved hanging out with actors, would head to late-night bistros or Sardi's. If they'd just been paid, they'd gorge themselves and sit, often until after two, laughing and enjoying the camaraderie. The stars of the show even joined them once in a while.

Nightly, Sydney and Jordan made love. Jordan could sleep until nearly noon, of course, but the alarm woke a begrudging Sydney at seven. Sometimes she could barely open her eyes.

But weekends, ah, weekends. Grand, glorious weekends, even with Saturday matinees. They would roam the streets of the city, breakfasting in delis on bagels and lox, delights heretofore unknown to Jordan. They would stroll through Central Park or downtown through Battery Park, even in winter when the raw, damp wind off the Atlantic chilled them to the bone.

They often spent Sunday afternoons in the art theaters, watching avant-garde foreign films, spending hours dissecting them as they consumed Nathan's hot dogs. Monday usually accompanied them. Afterward the three of them would head back to Christopher Street where Sydney would mull wine or make hot chocolate, and the men would pop corn.

Sometimes, on hot summer Sundays, they'd pack a picnic lunch and the three of them would take off for a day at Jones Beach, a place Sydney had never been, despite having lived twenty-five miles from it all her life. But then, she'd never spent summers in New York. She did feel nostalgia for the long, slow, lazy days at Oberon, and one weekend she did go down to visit Big Mommy. Though she could only stay overnight, she and her grandmother had a wonderful weekend.

Monday had the sense and sensitivity to leave by nine Sunday evenings, sometimes earlier. Then Jordan and Sydney would take a bath in the enormous, four-legged, claw-footed bathtub, which would lead to other earthly delights.

Evan brought his family home for Christmas. He and Veronique had a son, Peter, and she was expecting again, though she didn't yet show it. In the last year and a half, while Veronique was awaiting the birth of their son, Evan had had eleven women, one of them twenty-eight years older than he.

The high living they led appealed to them both. They enjoyed gambling in Monte Carlo, usually at least breaking even. They liked skiing in Gstaad, and Veronique was furious when the doctor told her it was not safe to ski while pregnant. They came to New York for both the Christmas and theater season.

Sydney was excited when she heard Evan was coming home with his wife and son. They were visiting for six weeks, and would stay with Oliver and Silvie. Despite Evan's failings, Sydney told Jordan, he had been the most important person in her youth. Though he was two years younger, they had learned to ride together in Central Park, and though Sydney was a better sailor, Evan was the better rider. They had been a closed corporation, with Warren the only other person able to penetrate their shield. When they spent Saturdays with him at Radio City Music Hall or the Roxy, or skating at Rockefeller Center, or at the Museum of Natural History, Warren's personal favorite, the, three of them giggled together at secrets no one else fathomed.

In the darkness of the museum, Warren would tread like the stick figures from the Egyptian tombs, and they would all double over in laughter. They would walk down the streets, gusty winds swirling cigarette wrappers around their ankles, holding hands, Warren in the middle, and use private hand signals. Two squeezes meant look to the right, three meant the left. They could not stop giggling. There were women in saris and men dressed as women, and hookers in provocative dresses. In fact, it was from Warren that they learned what they knew about sex, before hearing more lurid details from their classmates.

Summers, without Warren, they were left on their own. They spent long, lazy afternoons on their little Star sailboat, Windsong, which skimmed lightly across the water. They lay at anchor in coves, and while swimming was not safe in the bay in the hottest months, thanks to the jelly fish, they would lie, their hands pillowed under their heads, and look up at the tall trees, at the white puffs that skittered across the sky, and talk of a thousand and one things, exploring the universe together.

"When storm clouds gathered," Sydney told Jordan, "Evan and I would kneel at the windows in Big Mommy's bedroom and watch the sky darken and the water boil. I remember one particular storm, when I was fifteen. Evan must have been thirteen … it was a hot day, so humid we could hardly move. It was sultry and oppressive as days there are in the summer. Evan and I had been swimming and then I'd sat reading in my room when he rushed in and said, 'Syd, come on. Come see the clouds.'

"I looked out my window and couldn't see anything but blue sky. 'Come on,' he said, grabbing my hand. 'Let's go down to the dock for this one'."

"As we ran across the lawn we saw a young deer skittering along the shore, running inland into the forest. Birds cluttered the air, flying across the bay toward the eastern shore. A charging bank of rolling clouds blackened the sky to the southeast. It rushed toward us at an incredible speed.

" 'Maybe it's a tornado,' Evan cried. I told him we didn't get tornadoes in that part of the country. Besides, there was no funnel.

"As we watched, sitting on the dock, our legs dangling in the air, the water on the western shore began to churn. What had been placid water now tossed like ocean waves. White foam lashed into the air and, as we watched a small boat capsized. The waves crested and leapt into the air.

"The black, rolling clouds marched across the bay toward us, and we didn't even move. The bay's waters beat the shore of the island and sprayed into our faces. Evan's hand reached out to grasp mine, but his eyes were alight with the thrill of it.

"In moments, the clouds crossed the bay and struck full force. We were pummeled by sheets of rain. The leaves in the trees whistled and the bushes shook, bending with the force of the gale. Majestic flashes of lightning followed roaring thunder that seemed to shake the heavens. Still we didn't move but held hands tightly.

"The storm rushed with fury toward the western shore, but neither of us could see for it was like the world was drowned in rain that ripped along with such force we couldn't have stood up even if we'd tried.

"It didn't last long, though the dock shook as the waves lashed it with driving impact.

"When it passed we looked across the bay and all we could see was a gray cloud of rain. We were soaked and began to laugh, dancing like Indians in the soft, falling rain that followed the storm.

"We were alone in the universe that afternoon, and both of us knew it."

When, Sydney wondered, had they begun to grow apart? Evan had never even written to her once in the four years he'd been in Europe. She wondered what kind of woman was this wife who'd kept him abroad all these years. When she met Veronique, she understood. Veronique was the most beautiful woman Sydney had ever seen. But her eyes were hooded and Sydney felt she could not get behind them to the woman. She dressed with elegance. People stopped to stare at her. Her eyes followed Evan wherever he moved, but they hardly spoke to each other. Neither of them paid any attention to Peter. His nanny did that. Evan and Veronique did attend the theater, and they did the nightclub route, always making the gossip columns.

Evan came down to Sydney's apartment, without Veronique, and after one look never came back. He might have been a stranger for all the closeness Sydney could experience with him. However, he and Jordan did not clash, as she feared they might.

It was the first Christmas Sydney didn't go to Oberon. Big Mommy, Silvie, and even Oliver all knew that Christmas was not the same. Some of the joy was gone from it. All day Big Mommy and Silvie wondered what Sydney was doing, how she was spending the holiday, if she'd enjoyed the one hundred presents Silvie and Big Mommy had so carefully shopped for.

If she wasn't at Oberon, at least their spirit would be with her. Jordan nearly fainted to see a hundred presents! Sydney didn't enjoy any of them, for there were only two for Jordan, one from Big Mommy and one from Silvie, aside from the few his family had sent. She felt self-conscious and spoiled the entire time. On the other hand, deep inside she understood why her mother and grandmother were doing this.

Separately, she and her mother and grandmother all vowed to themselves that next Christmas they would see that a truce had been declared, and they would spend Christmas at Oberon, Oliver notwithstanding. Nobody felt at ease with Evan and his family, who only stayed at Oberon three days before returning to the liveliness of Manhattan.

Sydney had become so fond of the cast members in Jordan's play that she felt a pang of disappointment when, the following summer, Jordan won a much larger role in a play being directed by George Abbott, which just about assured its success. Jordan was on top of the world.

In the six weeks of rehearsals there were no late-night get togethers, which Sydney missed, and normalcy briefly entered their lives. She and Jordan returned to the apartment about the same time each evening. They took turns cooking dinner and Sydney felt for all the world as though she were playing house.

She learned to whip up soufflés and crepes and stuffed pork chops, while Jordan concentrated on lasagna, and a spaghetti sauce he'd start before leaving for rehearsal, letting it simmer all day.

Once a week they went over to Monday's, where he always had a Chinese meal sent in. Sydney hated Chinese food but didn't have the heart to tell him.

When the play opened in New Haven before heading to Boston, Philadelphia, and Baltimore, Sydney had ten days to

Herself. Evenings, she went over to the Park Avenue apartment for dinner.

Her mother had not scolded her for refusing to come to Oberon for Christmas, for Oliver was still unbending. Silvie and Big Mommy had climbed all four flights to visit Sydney shortly after she'd moved into the Christopher Street apartment, but had not volunteered another visit.

When Sydney did dine at her parents' home, Oliver acted as though she had never left, was still unmarried, arid there was no Jordan Eliot in her life. He never asked her about her life or her work or her husband. He talked of politics.

"Time," said Big Mommy when Sydney mentioned how awkward she felt around her father. '

'Big Mommy took off for Oberon in late May, two days after Sydney discovered she was two months pregnant.

She was afraid to tell Jordan. What would they do without her paycheck? She didn't know how she could be pregnant. She'd put her diaphragm in every single time. Except, well, maybe it was that one night she'd drunk too much and fallen in to a deep sleep, only to have Jordan awaken her somewhere before dawn and make love to her while she was still half asleep. Oh, dear, just careless once.

But Jordan was thrilled. Silvie offered to rent an apartment for them that had an elevator and hot water, no matter how upset that might make Oliver. Or, on the other hand, Big Mommy would be willing to do it and Oliver would never even know. But Sydney and Jordan refused. They wanted to do it on their own.

Silvie did have her way, however, by insisting that Sydney go to Dr. Beckwith, and she'd foot that bill. No nonsense about not having the best of care for her only daughter and grandchild.

What Silvie did, she never divulged, but on opening night, November fourth, Oliver accompanied Sydney and Big Mommy and Monday to the opening of the play, which won rapturous applause from the first night audience and kudos from the critics. By November fifth, Jordan was the darling of New York. Sydney was so proud she could have burst. And she looked big enough to, even though the baby wasn't due until the end of December or even early January.

Oliver made no comment about either the play or Jordan's role, but Big Mommy just shook her head as if to say, "See? Time. I told you so. Give him a little more. A grandchild, that sort of thing."

Oliver announced his pleasure when Sydney quit work and "started acting-like a woman," waiting for the birth of her baby.

Jordan felt sure enough now of a long run in the play that he and Sydney began to look for a decent apartment in the Village, which they enjoyed so much.

The Monday after Thanksgiving, Jordan's' agent, Michael Cross, phoned to tell him that Metro wanted him to take a screen test.

"No way, "Jordan laughed.

"C'mon, Jordy." Aside from Monday, he was the only one to call Jordan that. "It won't hurt. It can go on file for future reference. The head of the whole shebang, Millard Watson, saw your show the other night and thinks you might be just right for that blockbuster novel, *Bent Willows*, he's turning into the picture of the century, if you can believe the rumors."

Jordan hesitated a moment. "What part?"

Mike laughed. He had a hook into him. And Jesus, Hollywood paid much more than Broadway. "Nicholas."

Nicholas? Despite his feeling that the silver screen was but a bastard child of the "real" theater, Jordan found his heart skipping a beat. "Well, I suppose it wouldn't hurt."

"Wouldn't hurt!"

"Hey, Mike, my cup runneth over right now."

"I know, I know. The toast of Broadway, aren't you?"

Jordan's face was on half the weeklies in the city, and was slated for the nationals in January. What the media loved about him was that he looked the way a leading man should look. He had that indefinable something that made women melt. But the critics didn't even mention his looks. They admired the talent that leapt across the footlights, the voice that caressed even the last row of the theater.

"Okay," Mike continued, "it won't take more than a couple of hours. You don't even have to fly to the coast for it. Just go over to a warehouse in Jersey where they'll do the filming. Watson says Felicia Mountebank's in town; in fact, saw your play with him and his wife the other night and she might be willing to play opposite you for the test. Can't get much better than that, even if she is old enough to be your mother. Well, your aunt, anyhow. Thursday at … wait, here's the address."

But Jordan was so caught up in his role and the audience response each evening that he almost forgot to go over to the warehouse in Jersey. He even neglected to tell Sydney and only told her after the fact, when they were dining with Monday that evening after the play.

No one made much of it, even though they knew that the lead in *Bent Willows* was a star in anyone's firmament. Putting it in perspective for them all, Monday said, "For God's sake, Jordan, you're not thinking of moving out among the lotus eaters, are you?"

"No," Jordan replied firmly.

None of them could imagine living anyplace but Manhattan, center of the world, where all that was worth having in life was crammed into one small island that, to them, was the whole universe.

"I know Jordan will feel awkward, but his spirit is so big. I mean, so much bigger than Daddy's," Silvie said to Sydney, her arm around her daughter's shoulder as they lunched together. "For your sake, for the sake of the family, surely you're going to have this baby at Oberon."

Sydney hated the thought of breaking such a tradition. Evan already had his two children born in Europe. "When I brought it up to Jordan he said he thought I really should have it in a hospital. What if there were complications?"

Silvie nodded. "I know, darling. All of us who've given birth on the island have wondered that. But no one knows better than Dr. Beckwith, and at the first sign of any complication, Daddy said he'd have a helicopter waiting to fly in specialists. But I talked with Dr. Beckwith and he says you're strong as a horse, everything seems fine, and he's willing to come to Oberon for the birth, just as he did when I had you and Evan."

Sydney sighed.

"Oh, Mother, if only there weren't this thing between Daddy and Jordan. Can't Daddy see how happy I am? Doesn't that matter at all? And look how far Jordan's come in the last year and a half."

Silvie reached over to put her hand over her daughter's.

"Honey, I do think he sees. He just has such damnable difficulty admitting he's ever wrong. Even to himself. Maybe when Jordan is the father of his grandchild..." Her voice trailed off. "You just have to have this baby on Oberon. This can't be the first generation to break the tradition. Bad enough Evan's children are French!"

"Oh, Mother, I want to! Let me talk to Jordan about it. And then, of course," Sydney's face lit in a smile, "we'll just have to spend Christmas there, because it's due so close to then." Since she knew the exact minute of conception, she knew the baby was due December twenty-eighth, though Beckwith had warned her that didn't always mean anything.

"Are you going to call it Holly if it's a girl?" Silvie asked.

Sydney made a face. "I doubt it. We're still debating. I think it'll be Christopher if it's a boy."

"For Christopher Street?"

Sydney nodded. They'd been so happy in their first apartment.

Jordan graciously gave in even though there was tension every minute he and Oliver were in a room together. Oliver acted as though Jordan were invisible. Sydney asked her mother and Big Mommy not to give her so many gifts, no more than they gave Jordan. In fact, she suggested they make them all for the baby. Jordan had to leave Christmas afternoon, taking the ferry to Baltimore and flying to the city just in time for the evening performance. So, he missed the birth of their daughter, Ashley Hamilton Eliot, born at 1:33 A.M., December twenty-sixth even before Dr. Beckwith could get there. Oliver motored over to Walt's, and together they raced into Easton and found the obstetrician. He wanted to bring Sydney over to the hospital, but could not stand up to Oliver.

Sydney was only in labor three and half hours, and the delivery was easy, occurring about thirteen minutes after Dr. Clarke landed on Oberon.

By the time Jordan arrived that afternoon he had other news.

"I'm leaving for Hollywood January third," he announced, holding his new daughter. .

"January third!" Sydney blinked her eyes.

"I haven't even told them I'm quitting the play this week."

He kissed the top of Ashley's head, the soft fuzz making him grin. "I don't know how they'll find a replacement this quickly."

"Leaving New York? Jordan, you can't do that! You've just made it to the big time. New York loves you."

"It'll only be for six months, Syd. I'll tell them I'll come back to the play then. God, this play is going to run forever. But I can't turn down the part of Nicholas, and besides, they're going to pay me three hundred thousand dollars! Do you know how long it'd take to earn that on Broadway? A third of a million dollars for six months work!"

He brought Ashley to the bed and cradled her in Sydney's arms. "As soon as you can travel you and the baby come on out. Look, I know, hon, it's not what I want either, but it's the way to fame and fortune." He laughed. It was happening so much faster than he'd imagined it might. "It'll just be for a few months. An adventure. You've never been to California, either. Something new and exciting!"

He went over to his suitcase and removed a camera. He knelt down and adjusted the viewfinder, then snapped thirty-six pictures. "The women in my life, on film for posterity. Me, a father! Oh, what a year 1951 has been!"

He came over and sat next to Sydney, his eyes filled with tenderness. "Can you possibly know the happiness you've given me? I may love this daughter of ours more than life itself as I get to know her, but nothing, ever, can equal what I feel for you."

Sydney raised her face for his kiss. "I wonder if we can ever be as happy as we've been," she said.

"It's only the beginning," he whispered into her hair.

****

None of them was surprised when Evan phoned to announce he and Veronique were divorcing.

Two days after his divorce became final, the *Daily News* carried a photograph of Evan with a hatcheck girl he'd met in a nightclub in Zurich. She couldn't compare to Veronique physically, she had no money, but she smiled a lot and had a great shape. But then, so had Veronique. She just hadn't smiled a lot.

Evan cavorted around France and Italy for three months with Deirdre before leaving her in a hotel in Vienna early one snowy morning.

Twelve

Holding Ashley tightly against her, Sydney stepped off the plane into the February sunshine. Palm trees swayed in the gentle breeze. She looked around for Jordan.

Monday waved as he ran toward her. As he approached them, he threw his arms around her and Ashley and said, "Jordan's on the set today, so he sent me." Sydney's heart sank, though she was glad to see Monday. He looked, as usual, as though he'd slept in his clothes and his hair was awry. He did not look like a summa cum laude Stanford graduate and budding playwright. He'd already been out here two weeks, Jordan having arranged for his job at the studio. "It's not a great job," Monday told her as he guided her to baggage pickup, "and not that I really do anything creative yet, but it pays more and the climate's better than Giorgio's."

When Sydney pointed to her bags, Monday lunged forward and grabbed them. "Come on," he said, "the car's not too ar."

The car was a lemon yellow Oldsmobile convertible. "Jordie and I bought it together, since neither of us could afford one. Isn't she a beauty?"

Jordan had never mentioned buying a car.

"Wait'll you see where we live. A pool, palm trees, bougainvillea, hibiscus."

"We?" Sydney asked as Ashley opened her eyes' and began to fuss.

"No, I don't live with you," Monday grinned. "But I do have an apartment-just a studio, mind you, across the pool from you. It's lotus land, by golly. Even those of us who are poor peons can live among the flowers. God, Sydney, why would anyone live back East in the cold winters and humid summers?"

Sydney had to admit it was a lovely change from New York in February. As they drove along, she observed the stucco houses painted in every shade of the rainbow. Gardens burst with flowers she had never seen before. "LA doesn't seem cityish like New York."

"No. It goes out, rather than up. Very few skyscrapers, and then they're hardly worth the name. It stretches out for miles and miles, though. Look, orange trees, lemons. Sydney, it's great out here."

He drew up before a long, low apartment complex surrounded by lush lawns and eucalyptus trees. Ashley began to cry.

"I have to nurse her," Sydney said.

"Well, we're here," Monday said, turning into a slot between two apartments. "Don't need a garage out here, so we park in the carport. That, on the left, is where you live. Furniture's not great, but other things make up for it."

That the furniture wasn't great was an understatement, Sydney thought after Monday left so she could nurse Ashley in privacy. As the baby sucked noisily at her breast, Sydney looked around. Avocado green carpeting, but at least the drapes and walls were off-white. The couch and an overstuffed chair were both gold. Not what she'd choose, but she could live with it awhile. They'd only be here a few months.

There was the small living room plus a kitchen/dining area with a Formica table and chairs and an avocado refrigerator. There were two bedrooms. Jordan had already set up a crib in the smaller, darker one that also held a twin bed and a high, narrow bird's-eye maple chest of drawers. It would be adequate for Ashley for the time they'd be here.

Their bedroom contained twin beds, which Jordan had pushed together. Twin beds? How could they make love? How could she sleep in his arms? Well, maybe they could splurge on a double bed. A queen size, perhaps.

She laid Ashley down in the crib and walked over to her suitcases. Monday had suggested she come out to the pool when Ashley napped. "Learn to live like the sybarites do."

She stripped off her winter clothes and slid into her swimsuit. How pale she looked. She'd better ask Monday for some suntan lotion or she'd be red as a beet in no time.

She grabbed a towel, checked on Ashley, and went out to the pool, where Monday, in scarlet trunks, was waiting for her with a Tom Collins.

He eyed her appreciatively. "Motherhood seems to agree with you."

She knew her breasts were fuller, and she'd almost regained her waist. She hoped Jordan would notice. They hadn't made love since a month before Ashley was born. He'd left for Hollywood before Ashley was ten days old. "You've got great legs, Sydney."

She smiled. "Those were about the first words Jordan ever said to me."

"I can see why." But he wasn't looking at her legs. His eyes met hers. "Jordan's one lucky duck."

"You sound like a character out of the thirties."

"Hollywood does that to me." "Aren't you supposed to be at work, too?"

"Naw. It's after three. Writers don't write after three. Besides, if truth be told, I'm not really doing anything yet. I go to my office at nine and sharpen pencils and smile at people and walk to the water cooler and hope someone remembers my name and go back to my office and tell a secretary to get me coffee, and put my lined yellow pads in order and wait."

"Wait for what?"

"I don't know yet. If nothing else comes along, I keep looking over all the secretaries."

"You know, there's more to women than their looks."

Monday screwed up his face. "So you keep telling me. So my mother told me. That's what women like to think. But I look at a woman from the neck down and then if I like what I see, I look above. And they've both gotta be, well, zoom!"

"I wonder why I like you, Monday. You're so crass and insensitive for a would-be writer."

"What do you mean would-be?"

"Well, what have you written since I've known you?"

"Touché! Well, want to jump in? I'll race you to the end of the pool."

"Let me get used to it first. Then I'll race you." There were two young women at the end of the pool, sitting under an umbrella and talking. "In the evening, when people come home from work, then it's crowded. The social place to be."

Sydney walked over to the edge of the pool and dunked her toe in. Not as warm as one might think. She looked over her shoulder and saw Monday observing her. "What time does Jordan get home?"

He shrugged. "Depends on how many takes of how many scenes. He has to be at work by six for makeup. He's been getting home anywhere between six-thirty and nine."

Sydney looked out, over the pool, beyond the roofs of the single-story apartment into the tall trees that blocked off the sound of the traffic. What kind of life would this be, married to a movie actor? Not quite the same as the regular Broadway hours when they'd had time on weekends to walk in the park or take in a movie. True, it hadn't been terrific with her working all day and his going to the theater at night. Well, maybe she could rearrange her schedule so she'd be sparkling evenings. They'd at least have dinner together and weekends free. So what if they dined late? While she was growing up they had never dined before eight. She closed her eyes and dove into the water. It was cool and invigorating. How much nicer than the dirty, snowy grime of New York streets. When she surfaced she thought a whale must have jumped into the pool, but it was only Monday, who had leapt in feet first. When they did race, he beat her hands down. Not even close. She'd have to get in shape.

By seven she'd nursed Ashley again, showered, put on her new pale green silk dress and the shoes she'd had dyed to match. Her hazel eyes were as green as her gown.

She felt as excited as a teenager getting ready for the prom. She hadn't seen her husband in thirty-two days.

When he did walk through the door, at eight-thirty, it was so good to see him, even if he did look tired. His hand still on the doorknob, he grinned at her. "You're a sight for sore eyes," he said before crossing the room and gathering her in his arms, kissing her, smearing her lipstick. His hands wound through her hair and he pulled her close.

Without saying more, he picked her up and carried her to the bedroom. So much, she thought, for these lovely clothes. Within two minutes, she was out of them.

They smiled, naked, reaching out to touch each other, kissing.

"God, the feel of your body against mine. There's no better feeling in the world."

"Wanna bet?" she said, laughing as she lay down on the bed, pulling him on top of her.. He leaned over to kiss her breast, his tongue kindling fire within her, as it always did. His right hand parted her legs, fondled her, before he leaned down to kiss the inside of her thighs. "It's heaven," she whispered, her body undulating as he caressed her.

Electricity charged through her as his kisses feathered over her body. It had been too long. Time enough for leisurely lovemaking later. She wanted him now.

He knelt above her, his eyes locked on hers. She looked up at him and said, "Come to me."

Slowly, he touched her, drew back, entered her, drew back, and then thrust himself within her as she arched her back, raising herself to meet him, wanting him in her as deep as possible, feeling him become part of her. Then she cried, "Don't stop!" and he plunged one final time. The warm, wonderful sensation swept over her. "Oh, don't stop," she whispered again and she heard him moan, knew he had come, too.

He lay on top of her, their breathing ragged. After a few minutes, he rolled her over with him so that they lay on their sides, facing each other, legs entwined. She closed her eyes. He kissed her eyelids.

"Not even acting can compare with this," he said, running his hand across her breast, putting his arms around her and touching her buttocks. "I've missed you. When you're not with me it's like the light is gone."

"It's sunnier here than any place."

"That may be, and now that you're here it's even brighter."

Ashley's mewling cry could be heard. Jordan jumped and, getting out of bed, ran naked to the other bedroom. He was back in a minute, carrying his daughter. "She's beautiful," he exclaimed. "Looks just like you."

It was true. Maybe not just like Sydney, but her coloring was the same and the shape of her face and her bone structure. She was definitely Sydney's daughter. A Hamilton.

"Here," Jordan said as he held the baby toward Sydney. "Nurse her."

"She just ate less than three hours ago."

"I don't care. She's awake. And I want to see you nurse her. I haven't had that pleasure, you know."

Sydney held the baby to her left breast, and the little girl began to suck noisily.

Jordan sat on the end of the bed and grinned. "And you're mine. You're both mine. I wish I were a painter. I've never seen anything more beautiful." He ran his hand up Sydney's leg.

There was a knock at the door.

"Oh, Christ! That's Monday. He and someone he just met were going to bring Chinese food over. I'll get dressed. Take your time."

Monday's girlfriend, Linda something, was ravishingly beautiful. She had dark hair and doe-brown eyes that reminded Sydney of Bambi. Her figure was enough to make men turn and stare down the street after her. Her beige linen dress clung to her as though she'd been poured into it. Her tanned legs were bare and she wore sandals with plastic flowers on the toes.

Sydney thought her dull. She giggled a lot, but her conversation was nil unless they talked of movies, and then she seemed to have a Ph.D. in trivia. With her long, red fingernails, she ate the Chinese food out of a carton, eschewing a fork or the chopsticks Monday had brought. Sydney, Jordan, and Monday struggled with the chopsticks and laughed themselves silly.

"I can tell you two guys have been practicing," Sydney said.

"We live on Chinese and pizza," Jordan said.

"It's all we can afford," Monday chimed in.

"Monday and Jordan chatted about the studio and drank beer. Jordan held Sydney's hand and grinned at her every few minutes. Finally, he said. "I have to get up at five."

Monday took the hint, pulling Linda up from her chair. "Okay, hasta manana. I'll be back from work about three-thirty or four," he told Sydney, "in case you need to do some errands. Jordan'll take the' car to work, then I'll take the bus later and bring it home."

They looked in on Ashley before going to bed, and despite the fact that Jordan had to get up in six hours, they made love again, slowly, with a passion that built up to a steady heat. They touched every part of each other, until holding back became excruciating, until they were wet with sweat and the frenzied rhythm of their passion nearly consumed them.

They lay next to each other, on their backs, exhausted. They fell asleep that way, not having said good night. When Jordan arose at five, he covered Sydney with a sheet, but not before leaning over to kiss her breasts. She did not stir.

For the first few weeks Sydney busied herself with Ashley and cooking. She bought a carriage and walked three blocks to a grocery store each morning, buying fresh fruits and vegetables. She spent an inordinate amount of time each day planning recipes. Monday came to dinner every night, insisting on bringing the wine arid French bread.

Sydney hardly participated in the conversations. It wasn't like the old New York days, when the three of them discussed politics, and whether or not the President's economic policies were viable. Jordan and Monday discussed movies and the studio and people about whom she had never heard.

They did not stay up late evenings, for Jordan really needed eight hours of sleep if he was going to 'look good on camera. And after dinner he always had to spend time learning his lines for the next day.

They had no social life. Sydney met none of the people about whom the men talked. In the afternoons, when Ashley napped, Sydney sat by the pool acquiring a golden tan and streaked, bleached hair, an effect she quite liked. She discovered a library ten blocks away, and, with Ashley in the carriage, she strolled over there once a week and loaded up with new books. She thought she was reading her life away. Well, it was just until Jordan finished the picture. No later than June, he'd said.

One afternoon Evan phoned her. "I'm heading to Hawaii tomorrow, but thought I'd stay overnight in LA and see you out there in fairyland."

"Oh, that'll be wonderful."

"Make reservations at some good place for dinner."

She didn't even know of a good place. "I won't leave Ashley alone," she said. "You'll have to try my cooking."

He laughed. "I can't even envision that, but I'm game. It won't be just me. I'll have someone with me."

"A new woman?"

"What else? Of course. Don't bother to meet the plane. I have reservations at the Beverly Hilton. We'll get a cab from there. See you about seven."

"Wonderful. Tell me, though, are you happy?"

"Christ, Syd, what's happiness? I want to get out of New York, away from the family. They drive me bonkers."

Sydney labored all afternoon over the dinner. Her biggest problem with cooking was having everything ready at the same time. She hadn't yet mastered the art of being able to sit around drinking for an hour before serving dinner, but decided if she tried lasagna it could be baking while they chatted. She hoped Jordan would be home early.

She could tell by the look in Evan's eyes when she opened the door that he thought she was slumming. His gaze skirted the apartment quickly and then he said, "You've got to be kidding."

Behind him stood a very young blonde who had a smile on her face, a perpetual smile, Sydney decided before the evening was over. When Evan introduced them the blonde said, "Charmed."

This was not a woman he was going to marry, Sydney decided. This was a Hawaiian vacation. Maybe she was part of the therapy one needed after divorce.

It still rankled that Oliver hadn't objected to Evan's marrying anyone, or paying well over half a million to some French woman, but had practically disowned Sydney for marrying an actor., a nice, wholesome, well-educated American who was working hard and refused to take a cent from Oliver, even if he should offer.

"It's only temporary," Sydney started to say and then decided she had no need to apologize. This was the life she'd chosen and she didn't regret it.

Evan looked around "You're looking for a drink," Sydney said. "Come on out to the kitchen."

Evan poured drinks for himself and whatever her name was-Linda? No, that was Monday's girlfriend. Louise. That was it.

"I've never been to Hollywood before," Louise said, sticking her finger in her drink. "Or Hawaii, either."

"You look great," Evan told his sister.

"I'm happy," Sydney said. "I like being a mother."

She brought Ashley from her crib and insisted Evan hold the baby. It was not a role he was comfortable with, despite having two children of his own. "Do you ever see Peter and Dianne?"·

He shook his head. "I haven't been back to Europe since we separated." He looked into his drink. "Veronique's remarried."

Sydney looked at him. It was impossible to know what he was feeling. It had always been so.

Just then Monday and Jordan drove up in front of the apartment. Jordan burst through the door, extending his hand to shake Evan's, throwing an arm around his shoulder, acting for all the world as though they'd always been friends. He said to Louise, "Evan's always had a penchant for beautiful women."

"Penchant?" she asked, but no one enlightened her.

Monday peered into the kitchen. "Ah, the table's set for five. I wasn't sure. Let me go change."

He disappeared.

"So, you're in the movies," Evan said as he sat down on the couch and patted the spot next to him. Louise sat there and crossed her legs, her drink in one hand, caressing her smooth leg with the other. Evan put his hand on her knee, but paid no other attention to her.

Sydney studied her brother as he and Jordan talked. He was so thin, and his patrician face had an edge of arrogance to it. It always had, even when they were children. Evan was so sure of himself. They'd both been, but she hoped she didn't have that imperious air about her. And lately, out here in Hollywood, she didn't have that same sense of self-assurance. She felt isolated. She'd talked with a couple of other young wives who lived in the apartment complex, but they seemed to have nothing in common. Much as she loved Ashley, she didn't enjoy sitting around talking about diapers and formulas, or about who the gossip columnists suggested was sleeping with whom. Evan was talking of deep-sea fishing, which he'd just done off the Florida coast. He was anxious for the polo season to start and thought he'd participate this year, now that he was back in the good old United States of America. He was heading for the big island of Hawaii to get in on the marlin fishing. They were getting the Lurline tomorrow and he hadn't decided whether to take the ship back or fly. He'd make up his mind when the time came. He had reservations both ways, but then if he got bored he'd leave earlier than planned.

He wasn't eager to go back to New York City. "Dad keeps trying to make me learn the newspaper business." In which he had no interest at all. Sydney recalled her mother saying that if it required self-discipline, it was not to Evan's taste.

Later, after Evan and Louise had left, Monday said, "Well, I don't blame Evan. If I didn't have to work, I wouldn't."

"You'd sit and write all day. That's work."

"Not to me it isn't."

"So, you have to dislike it for it to be work?"

Jordan interrupted. "I work all day and love it. I don't ever want to have to do anything else."

With that he went to bed. "I'll study my lines in the morning. I'm too tired now." It was after midnight.

When he came home the next evening, tired as he was, he was excited. "My agent called me today. I'm being offered the lead in a movie, based on our dailies."

Sydney threw her arms around hill. "How wonderful." But, she thought, that means staying out here.

"If it goes through," he said, grabbing a beer from the refrigerator, "I know how you hate apartment living. How about our buying a house? Why don't you keep the car one of these days and go out looking when we find out for sure."

Well, that would make it more acceptable.

"You do the groundwork and then Sundays we can look over what you like. I'll be able to swing a nice down payment if this deal goes through."

"What kind of part is it?" Sydney asked, curling next to him on the couch.

"Not my cup of tea, actually. It's an action-adventure film. Mike said he'd get a script over to me tomorrow. He thought I'd like it, even though it's not a drama. He likes the money. Agents are always more interested in the bottom line than anything else;"

The bottom line was so terrific they could afford a seven-room house in a tract of homes that had once been an orange grove. It already had streets lined with trees.

Thirteen

Within two years they had left that house, and Sydney was hoping to be pregnant again. .

Jordan had made one film after another, until he'd become one of the more bankable Hollywood film stars. Only after the last one did he take a vacation, insisting he was "pooped" and needed a break.

They flew to Hawaii and that's where Sydney became pregnant. There were just the three of them and though they couldn't walk down the street or breakfast on the Royal Hawaiian's patio without a crowd gathering to stare 'at Jordan, they were away from the maddening, crowded life they lived in Hollywood.

When they returned, they moved into a house that reminded him, in size if not style, of those he had seen along the river in Maryland that first day Sydney had taken him to Oberon. Not as stately as Oberon, not as immense, but their new house had a dozen rooms, and that didn't include the five bathrooms. Sydney insisted on doing the decorating herself, claiming it relieved her boredom. Jordan left for work before dawn and was often not home until after dark.

They dined, whenever he arrived home, on the patio by the pool. Monday was often there, too, with what seemed to be a different girl every month. Always striking, sometimes intelligent, but more often just giggly.

Jordan, when he was home, was what Sydney thought the perfect father must be. He was never too tired to play with Ashley, to sing to her, cuddle her, take her for rides on the pony he'd bought her for Christmas. He was also a loving and considerate husband. Whenever he walked into the house, boredom fled and excitement permeated the atmosphere.

Sydney spent months decorating the house, room by room, and her thoughtfulness, patience, and taste resulted in a house that was at once stunning and homey. She loved it. And she loved no longer having to dust and vacuum and iron. She still did most of the cooking, for the dinner hour was unpredictable.

After the decorating was completed, she found herself at loose ends again. Much as she adored Ashley, one could be preoccupied just so many hours a day with a young child. Jordan urged her to play tennis at the club. She did. She enjoyed the exercise, but the conversation was generally about who got ' what roles, who was sleeping with whom, who was "in" and who was "out," and this drove Sydney wild. This was not what made life worth living. Her days were busy, but her mind longed for challenge.

Sydney found she'd slipped into the very role she had accused her mother and grandmother of playing, letting her education go to waste. She felt she had to relinquish her dreams of doing something herself, of accomplishing anything more than being a wife and mother. She tried not to resent Jordan's exciting work, while she was relegated to housewifely duties and playing tennis and golf.

Whatever picture he was in, his co-workers were his intimates for the time being. At Sunday brunches, they would entertain his co-star and whoever was her man of the moment, as well as other friends he'd acquired. Sydney would look at the woman, always beautiful, and wonder about their love scenes. Had they been kissing each other this week? Had it meant anything?

Sundays were always filled with laughter, and there was always a champagne brunch by the pool. In the year they'd lived in Beverly Hills there hadn't been a Sunday when Jordan hadn't wanted to entertain. But Sydney found herself invisible. Just like the leading lady's man, she was an appendage in a movie star's life.

Certainly Jordan's co-workers were pleasant to Sydney, but they never asked her a single question about herself. They never included her in their conversations and since they always talked about things that occurred at work, she couldn't join the conversation.

Monday fit right in, even though he was not part of whatever picture Jordan was in, and he enjoyed the brunches. He always talked with her, even though she saw him seven days a week, and he seemed to sense her feelings of not belonging.

The only time she felt really close to Jordan was when they made love, which they did with continued passion, inventiveness, and abandon. Sometimes he would wake her while it was still dark, before he left for the studio, and gather her into his arms. Often he would arrive home from work and say, "Before dinner, I have to make love to you." Her body began to tingle when she knew he would soon be home. She would awaken Sunday mornings and look at him as he lay sleeping, throwing back the covers so she could look at his naked body, touching him, kissing him awake, tantalizing him until their coupling could have lit fireworks in the sky.

She knew that millions of American women dreamed of him, and she knew he was as sexy as they imagined, even more so. She loved him with a wildness that sometimes she could scarcely contain.

When they vacationed in Hawaii, she had asked, "Is it okay with you if I don't take my diaphragm along?"

He grinned. "I think we can easily afford another child. Would you like that?"

"Ashley's two. I think it's time."

That will solve her restlessness, he told himself. He couldn't understand it. Within five years of their marriage they had moved from a fourth-floor, cold-water, Manhattan flat to one of Beverly Hills' large estates. Sydney could pretty much live the life she'd been accustomed to. She could do what she wanted. He enjoyed the fact that he couldn't walk down a street or enter a store or restaurant without a crowd gathering, but he missed the privacy of anonymity. However, all in all, he still could hardly believe how quickly and easily this had all come to him. First, Sydney. Then Ashley. Success and fame and riches. He was the luckiest man in the world.

If only the restlessness he sensed in Sydney could be alleviated. Maybe a second child would do it. Yet she was a perfect mother and wife. Those came before anything else. What she filled the rest of her life with was just that-filler. She lived her real life through him and Ashley.

Their sexual wildness and passion was like nothing he'd even dreamt of. No one, upon meeting her, would imagine that part of her even existed. She always looked and acted so regal, so cool, not that she didn't generate her own excitement, except she did that far less often out here than she had in New York. She looked like she would never be mussed, and he had to smile at that, for when he thought of her being mussed, he went on to think of her, with no clothes on, and the very thought titillated him. Five years together and she could still do that to him. There had been no lessening of desire. The best of all possible lives, and he knew it. Why didn't Sydney feel this way? He didn't take any of this for granted, appreciating every minute of his charmed life. Why wasn't she as charmed by it as he was? She no longer had to apologize to her parents for the man she married, not that she had ever apologized. She'd been wonderful the 'way she stood up to them. And Jordan had noticed them softening lately, urging them to come to Oberon for Christmas;

He thought maybe that had been hardest on her, Christmas away from Oberon. She'd only flown back East once since they'd been out here, to spend last summer at Oberon with her grandmother.

It had seemed like forever to him, with Ashley gone, too. Joy returned to his life when they came back at the end of September. He realized that no matter how much temporary passion and rapport was engendered with whatever actress he was playing opposite, no one could compare to Sydney and his love for her and Ashley.

But her restlessness confused and sometimes irritated him.

What did she want? It didn't have to do with money-he sensed that. She said she felt useless, hut it seemed to him she was busy all the time. golf, tennis. The opening nights they attended. Certainly their life was filled with glamour. He had to admit he got a kick out of those opening nights. He loved looking up at marquees and seeing *Jordan Eliot.*

He knew that Sydney took vicarious pride in that, too. He relished each day of his work. He even enjoyed the dangerous stunts, though he had always envisioned himself a serious actor. He certainly had never planned on staying in Hollywood. '

He was disappointed when Sydney said that she was going back to Oberon for the birth of this next child.

"I'm going to be in the middle of a picture," he said. At last, a serious one. "I can't get back East for the birth."

But Sydney was adamant. "Every Hamilton has been born there since the beginning of time."

"Evan's wife didn't have theirs there. And besides, our babies aren't Hamiltons," he argued.

Sydney shook her head. "Someday our children will own Oberon. They're Hamiltons."

"Your father said he cut you out of his will." -

Sydney shook her head. She knew the island would be passed on to hers and Evan's children, if not to her and Evan themselves.

"Syd, there's not even a hospital there. The one in Easton can't compare to any we have out here. What if something goes wrong?"

"Mother and Daddy will send Dr. Beckwith down. His father delivered Evan and me there. He delivered Ashley."

"He's not even an obstetrician."

Sydney looked at her husband. "Do you really think my family would have anything less than the very best doctor available?"

No, he didn't think so.

"I'm healthy as a horse. Look at the easy time I had with Ashley. Dr. Jacobs doesn't foresee any complications at all."

Jordan reached out for her' hand. "Are you going to rob me of being with you? Take that away from me?"

She'd thought about it. "I guess so. I just have to have my children on the island. We've always done it. It's tradition."

He knew that. This was the penalty for marrying into one of the oldest families in the country. Tradition left him cold. Tradition for tradition's sake meant nothing to him. Ritual meant little, but he wanted to be with his wife when their baby was born, not three thousand miles away. He wanted to feel part of the birth.

"Shit," he muttered.

Sydney looked over at him sitting on their king size bed. She walked over to the closet, which took up the whole wall. She opened the door and studied her evening clothes. She wasn't so pregnant she had to wear maternity clothes yet, but she needed something loose-fitting. They were going to a party Monday was throwing at Romanoff's. His first play would open on Broadway in November, and he was returning to New York City, so he had decided to throw himself a going-away party for a few friends.· ,

The few friends turned out to be close to a hundred. When he danced with Sydney, Monday said, "Lacey Stafford's agreed to play the leading role. Can you believe it?"

Sydney was delighted for him. "Maybe you can take a weekend off and come down to Oberon this summer."

"So, you're going, despite how Jordie feels?"

She nodded. She'd be damned if she'd let herself feel guilty. She was going to lie in a bed that looked out at the trees in Martha's Forest, where the first Hamilton had been born, and give birth to her second child, just as she had with Ashley. And if it was a boy she hoped Jordan would let her name it Hamilton. Hamilton Eliot. That wasn't such a bad name. And if it was a girl ... well, she hoped for a boy. One boy and one girl. "I envy you, going back to New York," she said to Monday. "Sure, the hot humidity of the summer, the cold, dead snow of winter. The rain and dampness. Sure you do."

"I do. The energy and excitement. The change of seasons."

"You're not that happy out here, are you? Not like Jordie and I've been?"

She shook her head, and they stopped dancing as the music ceased. "I'm not important out here. Hardly anybody even knows me. I'm Jordan's wife-that's my only identity. And the other day at tennis I overheard two women saying· they wonder how long he'll stay married to me when he works with such glamorous actresses every day. That knocked me for a loop. I went home and looked in the mirror, and for the first time I had doubts about me."

"Oh, God, Sydney, looks aren't everything!"

She looked at him, aghast. "You've never even dated a woman who's not beautiful."

"Yeah, but when I first met you I might not have thought you were a knockout, but within five minutes of talking with you I saw an inner beauty. It shone like a beacon."

"So, then, what's happened to me? Ever since I overheard that conversation, I've felt mousy."

When she repeated the conversation to Jordan, later that night, he said, "you just don't have the joie de vivre you had back East. You were always up then, always filled with ideas and fun. Here, you act like you're waiting, on the sidelines, not quite a part of life. You don't carry an inner light around with you anymore."

Jordan grabbed her in his arms and twirled her around, his eyes shining, she knew Monday's description of her was right. She recognized herself. She was on the sidelines, and she didn't like it.

Well, maybe she could try to do something about it after the baby was born.

Fourteen

Jordan burst through the door, his eyes filled with excitement. There were just two more weeks of shooting on *Desert Stars*. Sydney had been hoping there would be a month's break—or longer, if she was lucky between pictures. Jordan had been turning down offers, saying the scripts didn't appeal to him, Maybe they could go back East. New York or Oberon, it didn't matter. Someplace where there would be a chill in the air, clouds in the sky. Someplace that would invigorate her.

"I've been offered the damnedest, most beautiful script in the world," he shouted. "And not only that, they're going to shoot it on location."

He gathered her in his arms and swirled around. "We're going to Africa!"

"We?" She knew he didn't mean her. He meant the location crew. The people involved. '

"We. You and me. At least, I hope you'll come. It's going to be shot in the Congo and we'll be over there anywhere from four to six months. My God, Africa! Can you believe that?" Jordan was practically singing. He ran *over* to the hall table and began beating it, trying to imitate a bongo drum.

Sydney watched him, a mixture of amusement and dismay in her heart. His enthusiasms were boyish, one of his charms.

"Come along, Syd. I told them I wouldn't go unless they included you. It'll be the experience of a lifetime, and the script, my God, it's a dream. And you know who's going to play opposite me? Lili Davidson. I mean this picture can't miss with a script like that and Kirk O'Malley as the director." He grabbed and kissed her as he began dancing around the room.

"I can't go," Sydney said, "and you know it."

He stopped with one foot poised midair. "What do you mean *I know it?* I don't see any reason you can't come."

"I'm not going to take the children over there, where they could get all sorts of diseases."

"No, no, of course not," he grinned. "I know that. I thought we might ask my mother if she'd like to take care of them while we're gone."

Leave the girls for over four months? Maybe half the year? "Leave them when Juliet is just beginning to walk? When Ashley needs me? Oh, I can't. I won't even think of it."

"You can't let motherhood circumscribe your love, hon. We have to remain open to adventure. Besides, I told them I won't go unless you come. I'm not about to be without you for that length of time."

"And I'm not about to be without the girls for that length of time."

He sat, down on the sofa and grabbed her hand. "My mother will love the chance to get to know them. I know she will. You'll be making her happy. And I need you, maybe more than they do. I won't go unless you come."

Sydney pulled her hand away. "That's blackmail."

Jordan got up and walked over to her, drawing her into his arms, looking down at her. "Do you know you've lost a sparkle, a zest for life that you used to have? You need a change of pace. I think tying yourself to the girls and not doing anything else is pulling you down. *We* need an adventure, something different. Come with me, be part of my work, get involved with my life. Understand what I do and why I feel the way I do about it."

"I understand why love your work. I think it's wonderful that you do."

"But you're not part of it. Even when we have my friends over here, you never seem to enter into it. Come with me, Syd. Please." His arms tightened around her. "I love you. I want you to be part of everything."

When she didn't say anything, he added, "you can fly home anytime you can't stand being away from the girls."

She sighed. "Well, then, how can I say no?"

"You can't," he said, kissing her So that she knew she couldn't bear to be away from him for half a year.

He knew that she'd go anywhere to be with him, even if it meant giving up watching Juliet learn to walk. She had yearned for the New York days, when they were the center of each other's lives. Now, the center of his life was the studio and she knew it. She and the girls were the frosting.

When he came home from work about seven he had trouble turning off the character he'd become all day, but he threw himself into playing piggyback with Ashley, into crooning to Juliet. They were his first priorities at home. He made sure they never went to bed without playing with him. Ashley had gotten old enough, at three and a half that she loved being read to, and Jordan read her to sleep every night before he and Sydney sat down to dinner.

By the time their dinner, and thus their togetherness for the day, was over, it was nine and Jordan had to learn his lines for the next day. He never appeared on a set unprepared.

Saturdays they took the girls to the beach or the zoo or Jordan would take Ashley and Juliet to a Disney movie. He always devoted that day to the family, and seemed to derive pleasure from it. Why not, Sydney thought, once a week? Sundays were stilt brunch days. Invitations to the Eliots' Sunday brunches were sought after, and Sydney suspected some of those at the country club played tennis or golf with her hoping to be invited. Sydney had acquired the knack of entertaining sumptuously, though she remained in the background, so unlike the days of her youth.

And she knew something, she wasn't sure what, was missing from her life, and she didn't like it. She loved Jordan wildly, insanely, completely. She adored her daughters and received intense pleasure from them. She delighted in their house and the way she had decorated it. She forced herself to play golf and actually enjoyed tennis. But Jordan was right. She wasn't involved with the main part of his life. Jordan was always the center of attention.

She had seen herself referred to in a gossip column. Reporting an opening night gala, one of the columnists wrote, "The handsome Jordan Eliot, and his always impeccably dressed, elegant wife…" So, someone had at least noticed her, just hadn't remembered her name. She was Mrs. Jordan Eliot. No one ever referred to the fact that she was a Hamilton. What was important in Hollywood was who was making a movie and how big it was and how successful the last one was. Jordan was on top. In just five years Jordan was up there, perhaps not quite Spencer Tracy, not quite Jimmy Stewart, but he'd taken over the kind of roles Gable had done when he was young.

****

They had merely passed through Heathrow, not even staying in London overnight. But they had three days in Rome, and Jordan loved it as much as Sydney had when she'd visited as a teenager.

"Let's face it," he said, ogling everything, "you're a city girl, a big-city girl."

She loved Oberon, but she *was* a city girl. Rome brought her to life again, and she skipped as they toured the city, trying to cram as much in as they could in their brief time there.

"The sun's different here," Jordan said, excited at his first time on European soil.

The sun was different in Africa, too. They stayed four nights in Nairobi, long enough to outfit themselves with necessities they'd need in the Congo. Jordan was disappointed. "I thought it'd be-oh, you know, African. Instead, it's a city. Look at all the cars and tall buildings."

"You're in love with the *noble savage* idea, I think," Sydney said. It was fine with her that Nairobi was as citified as it was. But it lacked luxuries to which she was accustomed, though they had a passable steak and really good wine.

"Certainly the Congo's not going to be this." He waved his arm around. "It's too civilized." Jordan's eyes took on a dream-like quality. "Now, the Congo. Gorillas. Elephants. Are there lions there or is it too jungly?"

The Congo. Sydney had visions of leeches and brown, sluggish rivers, trees dripping snakes along their branches, of monkeys and black, glistening bodies. She loaded up with insect spray and suntan lotion.

The next day the hotel began to fill up with their crewmembers. The cameraman and his crew were already on location, but everyone else who would be working on the film congregated in the hotel bar. Lili Davidson was the only one who hadn't arrived by nightfall.

"Leave it to Lili," muttered Kirk O'Malley, the director. "I was told I'd rue the day I chose her."

"Why did you?" Jordan asked. He had never met Lili.

Kirk looked at him, one eyebrow raised. "You've read the script. Can you imagine anyone better?"

Sydney had never met Kirk O'Malley, and she was charmed the moment she set eyes on him. He was short and squat, with a build like a gorilla himself, but he had the most engaging smile she'd ever seen. He never stopped chewing on cigars, which he never lit. His thick black mustache drooped onto his wide, sensuous looking lips.

"He's about as sexy-looking as men get," she told Jordan as they were getting ready for bed.

Jordan hooted. "Sexy? Kirk? Why, he's downright ugly. No wonder you like my looks."

Sydney took off her mauve linen dress, already wrinkled, and hung it up ill the closet. She kicked her shoes off and let them lie where they fell.

"I didn't say he was handsome. I said he was sexy looking. He just looks so male. When he talks to you he zeroes right in on you as though you're the only person in the world. He's very good for one's ego. I bet he's fantastic in bed."

"My God," Jordan said as he lay down, waiting for Sydney to finish removing her makeup. "You've got the hots for him, I do believe."

"Nope." Sydney threw the tissue into the wastebasket and turned to her husband, who no longer cared about anything concerning his director. "I just made a gut-level statement. Just because some man looks sexy doesn't mean I yearn for him. You're all the man I need in my life." She put her hands on her hips and walked slowly over to him.

Jordan grinned.

She straddled him and brought his hands up to cup her breasts.

"When I'm through with you tonight," he said as his hands caressed her, "you won't even think of another man, ever."

"I never think of other, men that way, anyhow," Sydney said, as she began to grind herself against him.

He rose to meet her.

Lili Davidson was not beautiful. This surprised Sydney, for on screen, Lili radiated beauty.

Lili Davidson was self-assured without being arrogant. Her clothes were so expensive that they simply looked casual, as though they would have been proper to wear anyplace. Even in a tailored white silk shirt and trim beige slacks, one could see that her body was one of the world's all-time female figures. She wore no stockings on her tanned legs and her sandals were thin strips of Gucci leather. Her hands, which she used often, waving them dramatically when she talked, were flawless and graceful.

Sydney wondered if her teeth were real, so perfect were they. She had never seen eyes like Lili's. They went from blue to green in the flick of an eyelash.

Even people who didn't know who she was turned to stare at her. She seemed not to notice. Her husky voice, which was familiar to over a hundred and fifty million Americans, mesmerized her audience.

Kirk O'Malley, obviously as hypnotized by her as Sydney was, made the introductions. Lili nodded at each person as Kirk mentioned their names. Her gaze was solemn and serious.

"Okay," said Kirk when he was finished. "I've heard you can remember the name of everyone I've introduced you to. All..." he said as he turned and rapidly counted the people in the large dining room, "forty four. Is that true?"

Lili laughed, a low, deep sound like a bass fiddle. She looked at the first people introduced to her, a makeup man and the wardrobe mistress. "LeVar Hailey, Sally Thompkins ..."She went around the room, never faltering nor hesitating. When her eyes met Jordan's she smiled. "Well, you look just like you do in the movies."

But when she came to Sydney, she frowned. "My God, this must be a Freudian slip. You're his wife, I know, but I'll be damned if I can remember your first name. I must have *craft.*"

"That a new disease?" someone said, laughing.

"An acronym for can't remember a fucking thing," Lili said.

Jordan grinned. "My wife's name is Sydney."

Lili studied her. "I shall not forget again. Forgive me."

And Sydney sensed trouble.

But the trouble never was what she suspected it would be.

* * * *

A twin-engine plane flew them to Stanleyville in the Congo. From there they drove south as far as roads could take them, and then over roadless terrain before resorting to boats. The Congo, the great, wide, fast-moving river of renown, was neither wide nor fast-moving here, so far from the ocean, so near its source.

The humid air was suffocating. Sydney felt hemmed in, the tall trees creating a canopy above them. They were able to see only patches of milky blue through the lacy leaves that always hung over them.

Monkeys screeched and swung from tree to tree, following them up the river that wound like a snake through the dark green jungle. When they finally arrived at the location site, it was a relief. The jungle thinned out and a cobalt sky appeared. A village of thatched huts had already been created for the filming.

They were to live in the huts which, unlike real African huts, had windows for cross-ventilation. Sydney began to think it would be fairly comfortable after all. She was tired of living out of suitcases, tired of bumping along on rutted roads, tired of being so far from civilization. What if the girls got sick? They were completely out of touch with the world.

Jordan thought that was fascinating. He found everything engrossing and exciting. He studied it all, filled with wonder. The jungle astounded him. Being paddled upriver by blacks with fan-shaped oars, he watched the banks with delight. Storks nested in eddies, crocodiles raised their ugly heads as they slithered into the muddy water. They nearly bumped into a hippopotamus that just looked at them with great drooping eyes. Birds cawed loudly. It was never silent.

"I think it's their way of letting other animals know that strangers are present," Jordan said. Sydney wondered how he knew.

Once they arrived at their more or less permanent camp-permanent for the next four months, anyhow-Sydney began to relax. Camp cots had been set up in each of the huts, and she guessed it must be like camping out back home, something she had never done. But she was determined to be a good sport, to let herself participate as fully as possible so that she could become part of Jordan's life. Become part of what she guessed was the most important aspect of his life.

"If you're going to put on shorts," the assistant director told them, "put on insect repellent." He'd been here over two weeks, setting up the camp.

How in the world had anyone found this remote corner of the world? Sydney wondered.

Enervated by the humidity, the first thing she did was take a nap. When she awakened, Jordan was nowhere around. She splashed water from a bucket onto her face and neck and wondered what to wear for dinner. If insects were profuse, she guessed it might be smarter not to wear shorts. She decided on khaki pants and the matching cotton blouse she'd bought at Abercrombie and Fitch. They had assured her this was *de rigueur* in Africa.

It was barely six, yet darkness was descending. In the tropics there is no slow, spectacular setting of the sun. Night simply begins. Day ends, all in the flash of a few minutes. And night is as long as day. There is no seasonal variety, no differences in the length of days. A little after six in the evening, darkness descends. But it was still dusk when Sydney emerged from the tent and walked over to where most of the crew was sitting in camp chairs, smoking and sipping from tall glasses. Jordan patted the canvas chair next to him and called, "I've been saving this for you."

He was talking with his co-star, who was saying she thought shooting on location was so exhilarating.

"I said yes when I knew where we'd be shooting even before I read the script. That, and knowing Kirk would be directing. He's the most innovative director around. I'd never even met him until two weeks ago. The fact that you were going to be in it, too, was frosting on the cake. I've long been an admirer of your work." Without a pause for breath, Lili leaned forward and smiled across Jordan. "Good evening, Sydney."

They looked at each other. Each was wearing the identical outfit. "I admire your taste in clothes as well as in men," Lili laughed. "Obviously we came well prepared. You must have stopped in New York, too, so you'd be dressed comfortably? You look quite smashing."

Sydney smiled, unable to resist her friendliness. "I must say the same for you."

"Isn't this thrilling?" Lili's husky voice drew attention whenever she talked. She waved her arm in an arc. "When I was growing up in Webster, New York, I certainly never dreamed I'd be sitting in the jungles of Africa. Where's another drink?"

"What do you want to drink, Syd?" Jordan asked as a black man with shorts and an impeccable white jacket appeared. She gave the man her order, and here, in the heart of this dark continent, he returned with gin and tonic with a squeeze of lime.

For dinner, which was offered buffet style from a long table laid out with white linen, there was meat that had been simmered for hours, tiny sweet onions, tender carrots, and a root vegetable that Sydney couldn't identify but which was tart and sweet at the same time. '

"Have you ever worked for Kirk before?" Lili asked Jordan.

He shook his head. "I hear he improvises as we go along. The movie people will eventually see in theaters won't be the movie we start shooting. He's ' genius, of course. He's afraid of you, you know."

This didn't seem to surprise Lili. "Everyone is before they meet me. Are you?" She batted her long, black' eyelashes at him. Sydney had an idea she wasn't going to like Lili. Of course, stars of the stature which she and Jordan had become were catered to. Everything in their lives centered around them. Maybe that's what had gone wrong with her relationship. For the first time, she admitted to herself, something was wrong with her marriage. She and Jordan were going different ways. No, that wasn't quite accurate. Jordan was going one way and Sydney wasn't going anywhere. Jordan laughed in response to Lili's question. "If I was intimidated, I am no longer."

Lili touched the back of his hand briefly. "Good. I have a feeling we're going to make magic together. This bodes very well for this picture."

Just then Kirk O'Malley came over. He looked around and jerked his head at the man sitting next to Lili. The man jumped up and offered his chair to Kirk, who immediately pulled it so he was sitting opposite Lili and Jordan.

"Okay, let's talk about tomorrow. I want to shoot that first kiss while you still don't know each other so you'll still feel awkward, and hope some of it'll rub off and audiences will be caught up in it."

Jordan and Lili looked at each other.

Later, as Sydney and Jordan settled into their camp cots, mosquito netting surrounding them, Jordan said, "Well, we're off. What do you think about Kirk and Lili?"

"I don't know." She didn't like, sleeping on a narrow cot, with Jordan on the other side of the hut, even if it was only a few yards away.

"You don't know? My God, they're giants."

Sydney wondered how she was going to feel tomorrow morning, watching her husband kiss this woman he so admired.

Fifteen

Lili was right. She and Jordan did create cinema magic, and no one even had to wait to see the rushes to sense that.

But Lili could turn it off the second the camera stopped rolling. Then Jordan became her friend, her confidante, and she reached out to include Sydney. She would hold Sydney's arm as they walked around. She walked to dinner with Sydney. She sat next to Sydney at breakfast. Sydney got the idea she was being wooed, and she liked it. Lili was the only person who acted as though Sydney was important, too.

Lili treated the cameramen, the wardrobe mistress, the makeup man, the crewmembers with camaraderie they were unused to from celebrities. She was never temperamental. She knew her lines as well as Jordan did. They were both professionals. She took direction well; she spoke up when she disagreed with Kirk, but did so in a conversational rather than a confrontational manner. In spite of herself, Sydney liked her. A lot.

Because of Lili's attitude, Sydney dared not gripe aloud about the humidity or the insects. Lili acted as though it was all a wonderful adventure. Everyone fell in love with her, including Kirk O'Malley. Sydney watched it happen right before their eyes.

However, Sydney thought she'd scream if she had to watch one more scene being reshot. She couldn't understand how all those involved were willing to do a scene over and over, couldn't understand their waiting between takes and studying their lines or laughing together. But she sat in a canvas chair and watched, and she did not take gracefully to living on the side-lines, experiencing emotions vicariously. She chafed at the bit.

And began to drink.

Everyone headed to the bar, set up in a tent under an okuame tree, as soon as the day's shooting was over. They drank into the evening. They drank for many hours. Yet early in the morning there were no hangovers, no bloodshot eyes. At first Sydney wondered how they did it, but after a few weeks she found herself one of them, in this respect at least. Pretty soon, she was wandering over to the bar in the middle of the afternoon, pouring herself a stiff drink. Then she'd wander to their hut and lie down on her cot. Before she knew it, Jordan was awakening her, telling her it was time for drinks before dinner.

She wrote to the children weekly, trying to think of amusing things to report, knowing that Juliet was too young to understand and that Ashley wouldn't quite comprehend where her mother and father were. She tried to describe the trees, the crocs that slithered along the banks, the hippos who reared their ugly heads from the middle of the river. She described Lili and Kirk and Arthur, the cameraman who limped. She described the runners and baggage handlers, the black man who poured their drinks, and the two chefs whom Kirk had brought along, who wore tall white hats even in the midst of the jungle.

One night after dinner as they sat around a campfire designed to ward off insects, Lili plumped herself into a camp chair next to Sydney's and said, "It's none of my business but..."

Sydney cocked her head and looked at the famous woman.

"You're drinking too much." She didn't mince words.

Sydney looked away from her, into the fire.

"You're bored," Lili went on. "I understand. I couldn't stand to just sit around day after day, doing nothing, not participating, watching. It would drive me crazy. So, let's think of something to occupy you. Not just your time, but your mind."

Instead of resenting Lili's intrusion, Sydney felt warmth. Someone noticed her. Someone cared. "I miss my children," she said.

"I would, too, if I had any. But what we have to do is find you something to do. You're watching us all working and then all we do evenings is either learn our lines for the next day or sit around talking movies. I'd think it would be hard on your marriage. I've sworn I'm never going to marry. Being an actor takes too much of oneself away from others. It's a very self-centered occupation. You don't have much left over to give to anyone else."

"Not marry? Lili, you don't know what you'll miss."

Lili shook her head. "I didn't say I wouldn't have any liaisons. I can't imagine living without a man now and then. I like sex. I like the passion and excitement of new relationships. But I've been in this business long enough to know that when I'm making a movie the people working with me are my family. And a year from now I won't remember most of their names. Any passion I feel now will dissipate when this picture's over.

"Right now, Kirk is about the best lover I've ever known, but next year?"

Sydney raised her eyebrows, though she tried not to show she was shocked that Lili should tell her this.

"Are you in love with him?"

Lili laughed. "As much as I allow myself to feel love. In feeling too much for someone, I don't have anything left over to project onto the screen."

Sydney smiled. "You sound hard as nails, but you're not, you know."

Lili nodded. "Of course I know. I'm really very involved with people and I care about them. It's just that the people I care about now aren't necessarily the people I'll care about next year. But once this filming is over, so are Kirk and I. He'll go on to his next star and I'll see what happens."

"Does he get involved with all his stars?"

"No, I wasn't being fair to him, was I? No, he doesn't have that reputation: And I do find him fascinating. He's so erratic, so impulsive. I've never worked for anyone like him before. He makes me feel emotions I didn't know I had. And as for Jordan, God, he's fantastic. He's one of those few actors who make me want to be better, make me rise to his heights. Now, understand, Sydney, I'm not in love with him, but I am when I'm acting with him. Does that make any sense at all?"

Sydney wasn't sure.

"When we're in the midst of a scene, I feel" myself rising. I know I'm good. And I know he's not concentrating, like Cary Grant always does, mainly on how he looks. He's into the scene, too. Does he become the characters he plays? Does he bring that part of him home?"

Sydney nodded. "I'm glad you understand. Yes, he doesn't just throw off the character when he leaves work. It's sometimes tough."

"Deliver me from marrying an actor! I refuse even to have affairs with them. I'd rather go to bed with a cameraman than an actor. Anybody but an actor."

Sydney looked at her. How come she felt so subservient and meek in Jordan's world? Her energy was sapped, and she knew it wasn't just the jungle heat. Her only real role was being a mother, and she didn't even have that to hang onto here. Much as she loved motherhood, that wasn't enough.

Being here with Jordan, so far from her children, did not bring her into his world, despite sitting all day, every day and watching him and the people with whom he worked. If anything, she felt farther from him than before. She was only an observer, not a participant.

Their cots were too narrow to cuddle in. Once or twice a week, when Jordan would crawl in her cot and they'd make love, it was an inhibiting act, for any murmurs could be heard by everyone in the camp. It was just sex, not making love. It had none of the passion and wildness she and Jordan usually experienced. Her body never sang. She could never let herself go. .

Sydney realized she was not the woman with whom Jordan had fallen in love. He had been attracted to a woman in red who danced on top of a piano, sure of herself, in love with the world, ready for any challenge. And now she never wore red and never felt that confident.

Drinking was not a solution. It only depressed her more.

Lili did what she could. One day one of the crew stumbled over a dead monkey, clutching a baby in its hands. He brought it to the set.

"Ah, a project for Sydney," cried Lili, taking the little animal and bringing it over to Sydney, who was seated under a tree by the river. "Look, a baby for you!"

Sydney reached out for the barely alive creature. Actually, she did not think her maternal instinct included any more than her own two daughters but a baby anything, even an elephant, was irresistible. "I don't know what to do with a monkey," she said. It almost looked human.

"Neither do I." said Lili, "but I'd think if you could find a bottle, and get the chefs to find some evaporated milk or something like that..."

The monkey thrived. The Mexican cameraman called it "Mono," and so it was named. Sydney couldn't believe how far advanced it was beyond a human baby of the same age. Within days it was following her around, reaching up for the improvised bottle-a ketchup bottle with a nipple-that the chef had come up with. Where he'd found a nipple Sydney didn't ask.

Mono slept with her, curled in the small of her back when she awoke. As she walked along, Mono reached up to take her hand.

"You're quite a couple," Jordan said with a smile.

But Mono was not enough to occupy her days. She wished there were places she could take walks, but walking on the narrow jungle trails could be dangerous. And when the camera crew and Lili and Jordan went upriver to shoot, Sydney was left for a week with nothing to do and very few people with whom to talk.

It gave her time to reflect. She sat in a camp chair under the big trees and watched the river glide by. She asked herself what was wrong, not only with her marriage but with herself

Jordan still had that marvelous energy, that joy in every day that had so attracted her to him. He was often the center of attention, and he thrived on that, but he was happy and busy even when he was not. Even, she suspected, when he was alone. And he needed alone time, big chunks of it. He told her it was necessary so he could find those aspects of himself, which his character needed.

They seldom talked anymore, because Jordan's conversation was wholly about movies and the people involved in them. His focus was on the make-believe lives he lived. He had little time for anything else. She hadn't had all of him since they'd left New York.

She wondered if this life that seemed so empty resembled Big Mommy's and her mother's. Her mother had busied herself with charitable organizations, but was that enough? She couldn't think of any man who would find fulfillment living as she did. Well, perhaps Evan, for he hated any kind of work, but somehow he was always busy. What did he do? He was beginning to breed horses and spent hours studying pedigrees. He followed the sun around the world and spent winters in Florida or on Mediterranean beaches. He'd recently spent three months in Bali. He was thinking of buying a Hawaiian beach house. He might not be earning money or going to a regular job, but he was always finding ways to have fun.

How come she wasn't having fun? Why wasn't she enjoying life? Here she was married to the only man she'd ever loved, she had two beautiful daughters whom she adored, she was sitting in the middle of Africa watching a movie being filmed, and she was so bored she wanted to scream. She had been bored in California, too; now, she could admit that.

There was so much of her that wasn't being used, that was going to waste. There was nothing to occupy her mind. Somehow, along the way, she had lost herself.

When Jordan returned from five days upriver, filled with the sights they had seen, the waterfalls, the animals, the native village, Sydney told him she was going home.

Startled, he looked at her. "You miss the girls. So do I."

"Among other things."

"What's that supposed to mean?" he asked, raising an eyebrow as he always did when puzzled.

"I miss me, too."

"Huh?"

She sat on the cot. "This is your life, Jordan. It's not mine. I just sit around all day. I don't do anything. There's nothing for me to think about. I'm not a sitter. I need more to do to make me feel fulfilled."

"Fulfilled? My God, don't you have everything a woman can want?"

Sydney sighed. "Not all women are fulfilled being wives and mothers and nothing else."

"Sydney." There was pain in his voice. He came over and sat next to her, taking her hand in his. "I thought I've been able to give you all the things you were used to."

"That's true. I lack for nothing that money can buy."

"Well?"

"Oh, I don't know, Jordan. I just know I feel only half full. I love you. I love Juliet and Ashley. But I'm not *doing* anything. Look at me, I've lost all that gaiety you fell in love with. I don't do anything spontaneously anymore. I don't have any work that challenges me."

"You don't have to work. We have enough money so you can do anything you want."

"And that's supposed to make me happy?" He put an arm around her. "I'm happy. Why can't you be? We're leading the same life." He pulled her close to him.

"No, we're not. We're leading your life. Only, you live it and I observe."

"Will you come back? Spend a month with the kids and then come back? Please, Syd? Maybe it's 'the humidity that's gotten to you."

"You only have two more months of shooting. I can get the girls and spend the summer at Oberon."

"How is Oberon so different from here?"

Sydney shook her head, unable to answer. "The girls will be with me. Two more months away from them is really more than I can take."

"But you can take two months without me?"

She reached over to kiss him. "We'll see."

That night when he made love to her, she didn't even care that a cry escaped into the night. No one could do to her what Jordan could.

Three mornings later, two black men paddled her and her suitcases downriver, back to Stanleyville, where she found a plane heading to Nairobi and then Frankfurt. From there she phoned her parents, and Uncle Billy volunteered to fly to Indiana to get the girls and they'd be waiting for her at LaGuardia.

Dear Uncle Billy. He hated the hinterlands. She couldn't believe he'd volunteered to fly to Indiana, of all places. But he did enjoy the girls and even said if she was going to Oberon, he might come down for a week in the dog days of August when Manhattan could be unbearable.

Away from the tropics she felt life surging back into her. She wondered if it was also that she was away from Jordan and his way of life. She liked the idea of doing something on her own. She looked forward to seeing her daughters. They would spend days and weeks together and the high point would not be waiting all day for Jordan to come home. They would make their own fun, and she would teach Ashley to ride and Juliet to swim, even if she was just two. They would have picnics in Martha's Forest, and she'd take them sailing.

As she began to make plans for the summer, excitement simmered through her veins. And none of it included Jordan.

Sixteen

Uncle Billy's slender figure was the first thing Sydney saw as she walked down the steps from the plane. He stood in the forefront of the crowd, dressed in impeccable dove gray, holding Ashley's hand. When Ashley saw her mother, she let go of Uncle Billy and began racing toward Sydney. In one jump, Uncle Billy caught her up in his arms.

He set her down as Sydney approached them and knelt, arms outstretched, as her daughter pummeled into her. Oh God, she thought, motherhood is like a romance. Butterflies flitted across her chest as she felt her daughter nuzzle into her neck, Ashley's little arms thrown around her.

Sydney stood and leaned over to kiss Billy, who wasn't much taller than she was. "It's good to see you," she said. It had been over three years since she'd last seen him.

"Motherhood becomes you," he said in his cultured voice. Uncle Billy might be unconventional but he always observed the amenities. No one who heard him speak, even briefly, would doubt that he was an aristocrat. Even the way he held his head, his nose up in the air, accentuated his background, his sense of superiority of entitlement. Yet, nearly everyone who knew him forgave him this shortcoming, for his sense of humor, his enjoyment of gossip, his penchant for helping people if it didn't inconvenience him too much, were all attributes that balanced his imperfections. The only thing that Sydney didn't like about him was his sarcasm, when he used his rapier like wit to slash someone to ribbons. He did not apply this to many people or very often, but it did make him famous in the circle in which he moved.

"Juliet is home with Silvie. An airport is no place for a baby."

Sydney agreed. "I can't tell you how grateful I am that you flew out to Indiana to bring the girls here."

Billy reached for the baggage check and handed it to Carlos, Big Mommy's chauffeur, whom Sydney hadn't noticed standing behind Billy. She greeted him before he disappeared into the throng to recover her baggage. "I took Warren with me. I mean, can you envision me carrying a baby on a plane?"

Sydney laughed aloud at the picture she had of the two men trying to take care of Ashley and Juliet. "I really can't." And two such rigid men, though they each had a delightful sense of the ridiculous. "How did you manage that?"

"I'll not tell," Uncle Billy smiled.

In the car, while Ashley sat on Sydney's lap, Billy said, "you've lost weight. Are you all right?"

"It was the humidity. I didn't have to do anything and sweat just poured off me. Africa and I were not meant for each other."

"And you and Jordan?" Billy was too smart. He acted as though he didn't care a whit about people, yet he was always the first to see through their façades.

"I think so." Sydney loved the smell of Ashley's hair.

"Where's Daddy?" the little girl asked.

"He's still making a movie." Sydney hugged her daughter. "We'll go down to Oberon and he'll join us there later in the summer."

"Maybe I will, too." Uncle Billy lit a long cigarette in an even longer cigarette holder. Sydney rolled down a window. "I haven't spent time with you in far too long."

"I thought you hated being out of Manhattan."

Billy was barely a decade older than Sydney but she'd always thought of him as part of her mother's generation. "I do, but I've decided I must expand my horizons. I should have visited you in Hollywood while you were out there."

"It's not too late. We'll be going back there in September when Jordan returns."

Billy blinked and said mildly, "Oh, will you?"

Sydney said to Ashley, "Would you like to learn how to horseback ride?"

Ashley's eyes lit with excitement. She loved any animal, even those that slithered. "Oh, I would, Mommy, I would, I would."

"Am I too old to learn?" Billy asked.

"My heavens, what kind of changes are you making in your middle age?"

Billy turned to look at her, eyes blazing. "I'm thirty-six years old. That doesn't seem middle aged to me."

Sydney laughed and reached out to put a hand on his arm.

"Forgive me. It's just I'm feeling old."

"Well," he huffed and then smiled at her. "One is never too old to learn new tricks. I want you to take me sailing, too."

"I thought you always got seasick."

"Well, they have medicines now. I'm planning on coming to Oberon for a fortnight, the first two weeks of August, and your mother said she'd come down and spend three weeks in July with you. None of us has seen enough of you, you know."

"I know." And yet, she'd looked forward to time spent just with the girls and Big Mommy, time to think, time to look inward, time to contemplate her marriage. To think about what it was that might make her happy. She didn't think the goal of life was just happiness, though that was certainly a nice fringe benefit. *Happy* wasn't the right word. *Fulfilled* was more like it.

She wanted more out of life than she was experiencing now, wanted to feel she was *doing* something.

Sydney didn't know quite what the difference was, but she felt a contentment she hadn't known in years. Her days were so filled she hardly had time to sit down.

It was wonderful to be riding again. She was sure the mare she'd had growing up didn't remember her, but nevertheless it felt so familiar and so wonderful. Silvie did come down for three weeks in July.

"I haven't seen you, really seen you, in so long I'll take advantage of it while you're here," Sydney said happily.

But it wasn't her mother she unburdened herself to. She swam afternoons with Silvie, and Silvie played with Juliet while Sydney and Ashley rode. Ashley took to horseback riding as Sydney had, as though born to the saddle. She also delighted in sailing. They took Juliet along, but Juliet was restless. Just sitting in a sailboat wasn't her idea of fun. She wanted to know when she could get on horses with her mother and sister. So, Sydney did let her sit in the saddle in front of her as they walked slowly through the paths in the woods, where squirrels and chipmunks captivated both children..

They picnicked all over the island, riding out several times a week with a basket that Nettie prepared, always with surprises that delighted not only the little girls but Sydney as well. Ashley and Sydney swam in the little lakes that dotted the island while Juliet napped. All of them sat in the reeds and looked at the geese, leftovers from winter that never flew north. Oberon's birds were its jewels.

One day they discovered a seagull unable to fly more than a short distance above the ground. A yellow string was caught around its left leg and on the end of it dangled a fishing sinker, which weighed more than the gull could lift.

Each time they tried to get close to it, it flew only a foot above the ground, but beyond their reach. Sydney said, "We'll come back tomorrow and wait all day if we have to, and we'll bring it some food."

She knew better than to bring Juliet and even wondered if Ashley, at only a bit over four, had the patience to sit ·for the length of time it would require to gain the bird's confidence.

Mother and daughter returned early the next morning to find the bird still trying to lift itself.

"Mommy, are we going to save it?"

"We're going to try, darling. But we'll have to be very patient."

They sat cross-legged, popcorn and crumbs of bread in front of each of them. Other gulls swooped down fearlessly, gobbling up the tidbits. But the one with the weight on its foot only squawked fearfully.

Two hours after they'd sat down by the edge of the river that practically divided the island in half and rose from underground springs that bubbled from emerald green grass, the gull began to edge toward them.

Sydney was impressed with her daughter. Ashley had barely moved a muscle the entire time.

"Now," Sydney whispered, "don't reach out for it if it comes close enough to eat. We'll have to let it come back again and again. It must be hungry. It hasn't been able to find much to eat without being able to fly. Don't say anything and don't move."

Her daughter had done neither for two hours, her gaze fastened on the bird.

It would take several steps toward them, looking at the food, and then its beady eyes would shift to the two humans, and it would back off. But it always took one step closer than it took back. Eventually it stretched its neck and gobbled a breadcrumb into its beak. Sydney wondered if Ashley were even breathing, she was so still.

After another half-hour, when the bird had settled down comfortably to eating, Sydney reached out, so quickly that Ashley hardly saw it, and grabbed the bird, which squawked and tried to peck her. But Sydney had foreseen this and had worn a long-sleeved sweatshirt, even though the day was hot and sweat poured down her face. She grabbed its other leg and said to Ashley, "Quick, the scissors. Make sure you don't cut its leg, but do it as fast as you can."

Ashley, her eyes wide, cut the string, her heart beating wildly, hoping she wouldn't hurt the bird. The weight fell to the ground and Sydney let go of the bird, which soared into the sky before dropping back down. It circled above them, making loud cries before it glided out over the water, swooped down and brought up a small silver fish in its beak.

The expression on Ashley's face was rapturous.

"We saved it, didn't we, Mommy?"

"Yes, darling." Sydney felt exorbitant pride, both in what they had accomplished and in her daughter. "I think this is the happiest day of my whole life," Ashley said as they walked back to the great house, hand in hand.

Sydney did not confide her deepest thoughts to her mother, who played with the girls, trying to teach two-year-old Juliet to swim. Juliet was willing to try anything-she was more of a handful than three Ashleys.

While Ashley traced her fingers across words in books as Sydney read to her, Juliet tried to do the same. She stamped her foot and cried when she could not print letters as easily as Ashley did. She never wanted to sleep, and cried when put down for her naps. She would finally drift off to sleep, but she was not an easy child to raise. Delightful when she got her way, charming and full of life when she was happy, she nevertheless did not radiate happiness as Ashley did.

"Those girls each have parts of you in them," Silvie said, observing them fondly.

"I don't think Juliet's at all like me," Sydney answered.

Silvie laughed. "You just don't want to think that. You were pretty much a handful, you and Evan both. You were a happier child than Juliet is, but like her you were always trying to do things you weren't ready for, always trying to meet challenges."

"I was?" Sydney hadn't thought of herself that way.

"Yes," added Big Mommy, "and Evan was always trying to avoid challenges. He was like Juliet in his brooding. You couldn't read his mind. Now, don't get me wrong, I love him, but he was the difficult child."

Silvie nodded. "That's true, though he could always wind me around his finger."

"And I always resented that," Sydney said, surprised to hear her admitting this to her mother. "When I got a B you and Daddy had a fit, but when Evan got a B you rewarded him."

Silvie didn't seem upset by this confession. "As I recall, you only got a B once in your entire life. Evan struggled for marks. It all came easily to you."

"That's not true." Sydney bristled at this. "I studied hard every night. I spent weeks writing papers."

"It seemed to come easily. You *enjoyea* the studying."

That was true.

"Well," Big Mommy chimed in, "you say Evan struggled for marks. Evan never struggled for anything in his life. Before he struggles, he gives in."

"Juliet isn't like him, then," Sydney said. "She seems to struggle for everything."

"No," corrected-her mother, "Juliet doesn't struggle. She fights."

Sydney liked these afternoons when the three women sat around discussing family issues. The conversation took different twists than it would have had any of the men been around, the way it did weekends, when Oliver flew down. Well, he flew down two of the weekends that Silvie was here. Not really weekends, for he arrived about noon on Saturday and left late Sunday afternoon. He flew into the Baltimore airport and took the ferry across from there. Sydney drove up the peninsula to meet his ferry, hoping she could feel closeness to him that she hadn't felt for many years. But it didn't happen.

He certainly didn't want to hear if she was unhappy with Jordan. He thought she'd made her bed, and if anything was wrong he could say "I told you so." He couldn't understand a family so many thousands of miles away, but it was really Jordan whom he blamed for the distance. He had no business being so many thousands of miles from his family. Families should be together. When Silvie said, "He's the bread winner. Most wives go where their husbands find employment," Sydney gave her a quick look. Was her mother censuring her?

Sydney thought that though their family had been together, they hadn't been close. Oliver never quite allowed that. He might have desired closeness with Evan, but Evan exasperated him all the time. Evan wasn't what he wanted a son to be, so he criticized him constantly, which made for unpleasant mealtimes. Sydney thought Evan must have been relieved to have been sent away to school when he was fourteen. She'd have hated it, but at least at mealtimes he didn't have to hear how lazy he was, how his marks couldn't compare to Sydney's. Sydney suspected that at one time her father may have either paid for an abortion or bought the girl off. She had heard conversations late in the might when Evan was sixteen, but she couldn't be sure. She'd heard her father saying, "I don't mind your sowing your wild oats. That's to be expected, but use a little intelligence, son! Always carry a condom with you, for God's sake."

Sydney suspected her mother was not in the room at the time.

Seventeen

Jordan was not home in July, or in August, or in September. Sydney received only one letter in that time, telling her the filming was taking longer than they'd expected, he missed her, and wouldn't she come back at least for a few weeks? He told her that Lili and Kirk argued but he couldn't quite call it fighting; he personally thought they'd fallen in love. He imagined Kirk had to bend over backward not to focus the film on long, slow shots of Lili's face. He was going to be sorry when the filming ended, except that it meant the family would be together.

He thought when it was over he'd like to take a couple of extra weeks and go over to Kenya and climb Mt. Kilimanjaro. He'd heard that lots of people did it; it shouldn't be too hard a climb, just hard enough to be challenging and make him feel good when he got to the top. A shame to be this close and not do something like that.

He certainly wouldn't want to live in the Congo. God, it was sweltering, but the things he was hearing about Kenya. "Live in Kenya!" Sydney exclaimed after reading his letter to Big Mommy. "Heavens, where does he get his ideas?"

Big Mommy didn't say anything. .

"Well, if he's not back and it's the end of September I ought to see about putting Ashley in a kindergarten. She'll be five at Christmas. "

Big Mommy looked at her. "Are you thinking of going back to California?"

"The only thing that makes living there bearable is Jordan, and even then..." Sydney shook her head. "No. I guess I'll go stay with Mother and Daddy. They have plenty of room."

"Well, I could pack up early and go back now instead of next month. We could all drive up together. I'll phone for Carlos to drive down."

By the time they reached 'New York, Silvie had already made arrangements for Ashley at Chapin, the same school Sydney had attended. The women decided they wouldn't need a nanny, not with the three of them to take care of Juliet.

The first thing Sydney read in the *Daily News*, which Oliver left lying on the coffee table in his study, was that Jordan and Lili were having an affair in the remote reaches of Africa. She knew that wasn't true, but the gossip columnist claimed Sydney had left and Jordan was lonely and she'd heard that Jordan and, Lili were lighting up more than celluloid in the dark continent.

Sydney knew it had to be Lili and Kirk. Maybe no one would believe someone like Lili would become involved with ... well, it *was* rather like beauty and the beast. Funny, a beautiful woman could be in love with an ugly older man but no man could be in love with an ugly woman. Or an older one. Didn't seem fair. .

Or had Jordan been lying to her to cover his own affair with Lili? He wouldn't do that, would he? No, of course not.

She wrote to him weekly, telling him of the girls and how she and Ashley rescued the seagull, and new words of Juliet's, and of the little things that made up the fabric of her life that she found so enjoyable. So much more than whatever it was she felt in California. She was more her own person here.

She called Monday, who had rented an apartment in the Village again. They met for dinner at Mama Leone's and he told her that, much as he loved California, there was no place like New York, even in summer. He was invigorated with all there was to do and see, and he thought if this play really was successful he'd buy himself an apartment in the Village and maybe a house on the Coast and divide his time. He certainly wasn't going back to work for the studio on the same terms he'd had before. It was working on his own scripts from now on or nothing. No contracts.

"Don't believe those things in the papers about Jordy," he told her.

"I don't. Lili's involved with the director."

"Sure," Monday said. "When's he coming home?"

Sydney shrugged. "He's going to stay on and climb Mt. Kilimanjaro."

Monday's eyes lit up. "Wow!"

"Sometimes I wonder how you became a playwright. Your vocabulary is so limited."

"My, my. Sounding miffed. Upset because he's not coming right home to you?"

"I guess so."

"Well, look at it this way. Gives you more time in New York. You hate California."

She looked at him. "Is that what I do?"

"You do. And not even California is lovelier than New York in September."

"It *is* divine here right now."

"We'll take in a couple of movies together. Jordie's new one, the one he finished last winter, opens in ten days. Want to see it with me?"

"Of course."

"Bring Big Mommy, if you want."

Monday and Big Mommy liked each other.

"Billy, too?"

"Sure, we'll make a party of it. Got to entertain you while you're here."

"I've been thinking of going down to the paper and seeing what Daddy does all day long. The last time I was down there I must have been a teenager. He's never encouraged us to visit him at work."

Monday gave her a funny look.

* * * *

Jordan's movie broke box office records. And Oliver frowned when Sydney cornered him in his study one evening and asked, "Daddy, if I come down to the paper tomorrow, will you take me to lunch?"

Oliver looked up, surprised. He'd been reading *The Los Angeles Tunes* in his study. "Call my secretary in the morning and find out if I have any appointments."

"Well, I want to come down to the paper whether you have appointments or not."

Oliver's glasses slid down to the end of his nose as he dropped his head forward and looked at Sydney. "Any particular reason?"

Sydney shrugged. "I just want to see what it's like. I haven't been to your office in a decade, I bet."

"Hm."

"Don't you want the family to take an interest in what you do?" Sydney asked, curling up in the big chair across from him.

There was a fire burning in the fireplace, and it was cozy.

Oliver put down his paper. "I'd like Evan to take an interest instead of doing nothing with his life."

"I'm doing nothing with my life."

"That's different. You're not supposed to work."

Sydney studied her fingernails. "Why not?"

"Don't act silly, Sydney. Women are meant to take care of their children and their homes and their men."

"Oh, Daddy, somewhere inside you, you must know what a ridiculous statement that is. Not all Women have to do the same thing."

Oliver nodded as though he were thinking. "Women who *have* to work would give their eye teeth to be in your position. Sydney, be content to live the life your mother and your grandmother have lived. Have another baby."

Sydney tried to push down her anger. "You're not answering my question. Will you show me around if I come down to the office tomorrow?"

"I'll at least have someone show you around if I don't have time. No one in this family's ever evidenced much interest before."

"I don't have anything else to do, and at least you meet interesting people all the time."

"Well, now that Ike's President, it's some improvement. The country's not going to the dogs as fast."

"You meet the movers and shakers of the world."

He raised his eyebrows and looked at her over his glasses again. "My dear, I *am* a mover and shaker."

Sydney studied him. Having always taken him for granted, not knowing at all what other fathers were like, she suddenly saw him in a new light. She'd never thought of him that way. He was so stolid she often thought him dull. How could he be one of those who shaped the world? He seldom talked about work at home, hardly ever mentioned the people he associated with daily. He did talk politics, and only since she'd married Jordan had Sydney decided her father wasn't always right. Or at least, not according to her lights. His philosophies were too reactionary for Jordan, who called him Neanderthal in his thinking. "A bit to the right of John Birch," was how Silvie referred to him.

He seemed unaware that anyone with less money or less education, or anyone of a different color or not a Protestant, mattered. Perhaps they didn't in his orbit. Maybe that's why his newspaper was always in dire financial straits.

He had backed Senator Vandenberg before the war, extolling the isolationist policies that Vandenberg eventually rejected. And now that the war was a decade behind them, he wanted to revive that policy. He thought anyone who wanted a job could get one. He was sure God had been on the side of the Allies during the war, and that God was a Republican. And white.

He liked women. But he liked women in their place, and he knew exactly where their place was. The funny thing was that Oliver particularly liked intelligent women. His wife had been an honors student. He assumed his daughter would attend college, and approved of her going to graduate school. In fact, he had sternly disapproved when she'd quit the University of Pennsylvania in mid-year. But was that because she'd reneged on getting her master's or because she'd married Jordan? Yet, he wanted these intelligent, well-educated women in his life to keep to women's traditional role. And, Sydney guessed, the women in his life had never questioned that.

Until now.

And she *was* questioning. Not necessarily women's roles, but her own. She was not satisfied with the life she'd been leading and realized she hadn't been in years. *She* was what was wrong with her marriage. She was not satisfied-in fact, she was discontented to be only a wife and mother. Not that she didn't want to be those. She loved Jordan and the girls, but more and more she realized she needed something else, Just what that was, she had no idea, but she certainly wanted to see what men did every day, men in business. Behind the doors that were closed to women.

She wanted to be a mover and shaker, too.

"Talk Evan into leaning, too," Oliver said, "and I'll break any lunch engagements for you."

Evan, who had returned to New York and had his own apartment on Seventy-second Street, refused to go. "You know what Dad'll do. He'll try to push it down my throat. He tries to make me feel inferior..."

"Inferior? I don't think so."

Evan nodded. He was dressed impeccably, as always. "You and Uncle Billy can traipse through life doing nothing, but he always thinks I should be doing something. I think *shoula* is the most disgusting word in the language. I *shoula* follow in his footsteps. I *shoula* be interested in what interests him. Sydney. I don't give a shit if the world goes to hell in a handbag. I can't do anything about it. Even voting doesn't do much about it. I really don't care what the mass of humanity does, or what it *shoula* do. I don't have a social conscience, Sydney. I care about numero uno. Period."

Evan's apartment fascinated Sydney even though she didn't like it. All its rooms were in black and white, and the furniture was ultra-modern, with steel-based lamps and table legs. The floor-to-ceiling windows in the living room overlooked Central Park. Sydney knew that her father financially supported Evan's way of living, even though he disapproved of it. Yet Oliver told her he had cut her off without a cent when she'd married Jordan, wasn't even going to leave her anything in his will. Well, she knew he'd at least leave Oberon to his grandchildren. But he continued to support Evan, of whom he so disapproved.

"Do you go out every evening, Evan?"

Her brother looked across the coffee table at her and smiled. "Do you mean, do I go from one woman to another?"

She shook her head. "No, I mean do you always go out? Don't you ever stay home and just think?"

"What's there to think about?" he asked, lighting a Pall Mall.

"Oh, I don't know. Don't you just need time alone to replenish your soul?"

"Christ, Sydney, where do you get your ideas? No, I don't need that kind of time. My soul's okay. I don't go out every evening. Sometimes I have someone here."

"A woman?"

He laughed. "I make it a practice not to go to bed with a woman in my own place, if that's what you want to know. I want to be able to get up and get out when I want, not have someone around when I'm through with her."

"You sound so crass."

"If that's meant to chastise me, it won't work. I figure we're put on this earth to get as much happiness as we can. And that's what I do. Pursue happiness."

"Does it work? Are you happy?"

"Give me a definition of happiness. Sure, I'm happy. I go where I want, do what I want."

"What do you want?"

He smashed his cigarette out in a shiny black pottery ashtray that was larger than a dinner plate. "It varies from moment to moment. What I want now is to go to '21' for a late supper. Want to come?"

Sydney shook her head. "No. I just came over to' ask if you'd go to the paper with me tomorrow."

"You could have phoned for that."

"Well, thanks!" She stood up and walked over to lean down and kissed his forehead. "I like to see you. We haven't known each other for years. Since before we got married, really."

He took her hand. Looking up at her he said, "If the women in my life had been you, my dear, I wouldn't be going around the world searching for something that I imagine will forever elude me."

"I couldn't stand someone as lazy as you." Sydney walked over to the chair, over which she'd draped her coat. "I want a man with drive."

"I have drive," Evan objected. "Just not for good deeds or work."

Sydney raised her arms to stretch them into the coat sleeves. Evan remarked, "Motherhood's really filled you out, dear sister. You look fantastic."

"From you, that's a real compliment. Your picture never appears in the papers without some beauty on your arm."

"What do you do for sex with Jordan so far away?"

"It's only been four months," Sydney said. She'd never talked about sex with anyone but her husband. She felt uncomfortable that Evan had brought it up.

"Only four? What do you think he's doing to get it?"

Sydney was startled. "The same as I am, I imagine."

Evan's laugh had no mirth to it. "Don't be so sure. I'd never be able to go four months without it. Is he a man or isn't he?"

"Thanks a lot," Sydney said as she left.

The building that housed *The New York Chronicle* was imposing, even though Sydney thought it needed a good scrubbing. It was well over a hundred years old and had been built by her great-grandfather, the real estate baron.

As she walked through the massive oak doors, opened by a uniformed black man, she saw the place as a relic from days gone by. The lobby, empty except for a desk and a gray-haired woman with horn-rimmed glasses who sat behind it, was sterile. Marble floors, marble walls, a panel of elevators along the back wall. She guessed it must have been so long since she'd been here that she had forgotten what it looked like.

The woman nodded tersely at Sydney.

"I'm here to see Mr. Hamilton."

The woman scanned a list of names on a yellow legal pad on her desk. "Your name?"

"Mrs. Jordan Eliot."

The woman's face jerked up, wreathed in smiles. Jordan's name was an open sesame anyplace.

"Oh, you're Mr. Hamilton's daughter. Go right up. Thirtieth floor."

Well, maybe it wasn't Jordan's name, but her father's.

As the elevator slowly wound its way to the top floor, Sydney studied herself in-the mirror along one wall of the smoothly gliding cage. She'd worn a charcoal gray worsted suit, thinking she should look business-like, though a ruffled pearl-gray blouse peeked out of her jacket She'd debated about earrings and settled for the small pearls that had once been her maternal grandmother's. Her high-heeled suede shoes matched her suit. She liked having gray eyes-so few people did. Not even a hint of blue in them, paler than the ocean on a stormy day. Yet she knew they were luminous, that people tended to look at her directly ... people, that is, who weren't connected with the movie industry. Then she'd seemed to disappear. She felt more attractive, more alive in New York.

The elevator doors slid back and Sydney was thrust into a room that housed two desks, with a matronly-looking woman behind each. Hallways ran out of the room, one on either side. One of the women was on a phone, the other looked at her expectantly.

"Mrs. Eliot?" she asked, standing up, smiling.

Sydney nodded.

"This way," said the woman, walking ahead of Sydney down the left hallway. All the offices had open doors except the one at the end, which was her father's.

The woman knocked lightly on the door and then said to Sydney, "You can go right in. He's expecting you."

Oliver was leaning forward, over his desk, talking to a man sitting opposite him. He glanced at Sydney but continued talking for another five minutes, while Sydney waited. Then he stood up and gestured toward her, saying to the man, "Adam, you remember my daughter, Sydney?"

Adam Yarborough, the managing editor, stood immediately, reaching out to shake Sydney's hand firmly, his eyes taking her in. His dark brown wavy hair was flecked with gray at the temples, and he wore rimless glasses. Sydney liked his smile as well as his handshake.

"I haven't seen you since I was a kid."

"The years have been good to you," Adam murmured. Then he turned to Oliver and said, "I'll take care of that and have the information for you by four."

"No, you won't," Oliver said. "You're going to show my daughter around the place. I can wait for that information."

Adam's eyebrows shot up. "I'll assign Chad to that story."

"Good choice. But send whoever you want. That's your department, not mine."

Adam glanced at his watch and then asked Sydney, "What do you want to see?" Sydney looked at Oliver. So, he was going to ignore her here, too, was he?

"What is there to see?"

"Come on. Follow me. Maybe that's the best way to do it."

As they rode down to his office on the sixth floor Sydney explained, "I just thought it was about time to see what my father does and where he does it. All these years and I don't have an inkling about what goes on in the newspaper world."

"My wife doesn't care what goes on here," Adam said.

"I don't think my mother does, either. Daddy thinks a woman's place..."

"...is in the home? Well, your father isn't the most modem of men, is he? I'd give my eye teeth, not that anyone would want them, to have my wife more interested in what I do."

"So would my husband," Sydney said.

Adam Yarborough turned to stare at her.

After they had finished the tour, Adam accompanied Sydney back to Oliver's office. Her father was on the phone and told her he'd be unable to lunch. He couldn't get away for another hour at least.

"I can wait," she said, sitting in a chair.

"No," Oliver said as he nodded to Adam. "You go with her. I'll be there as soon as I can."

Sydney hated being palmed off on a man who had other important things to do and no doubt resented being asked to take care of the boss's daughter.

"Never mind," she said. "We don't have to have lunch, Daddy." But her resentment showed in her voice.

Adam glanced at his watch. "I'm starving."

He'd just taken two hours out of a busy schedule to show the boss's daughter around.

Oliver glanced at her apologetically. "Sorry, dear. The mayor's on his way over right now. Just got off the phone with him."

Sydney stood up. "That's all right. I'll do what I'm supposed to do, walk up to Bergdorf's or stop in at Bendel's and pick up a cute dress or a fox fur piece."

Oliver smiled. "That's a good girl."

Sydney controlled her impulse to scream.

His back to Oliver, Adam looked at her and grinned. "Come on," he said. "The London Grill has the best steaks in this part of the city. And I always carry an extra handkerchief for maidens in distress."

Oliver raised his eyebrows and glanced at Adam. He hadn't a clue what his managing editor was talking about.

Eighteen

Sydney got into the habit of dropping in at her father's office several times a week. She suspected the men thought she was a nuisance, but she was the boss's daughter, so they were invariably polite. No one really had time to spend with her; so she stood in the background watching what they did, thinking it might be smart if she learned to type. What else did she have to do with her life as she waited for Jordan?

Though Sydney knew he didn't approve, Oliver made no objections to her hanging around. Often, at noon, he'd search her out and invite her to lunch.

She'd never seen so much of her father.

She watched him at work and saw a different man than she'd ever known, even though he was his usual confident self. In a business where men shouted most of the time, answered phones at the top of their voices and then rushed out of the building, cigarettes generally dangling from their mouths, her father was an island of calm.

Adam Yarborough was his intermediary. Oliver did not have much to do with the daily running of the paper. That was Adam's job and he moved, shirtsleeves rolled up, collar open, tie askew, through the bastions of reporters, once in a while barking at someone who displeased him. He was always in motion, seldom at his desk, where his phone was always ringing.

Those days that Sydney appeared at the office, Oliver often invited Adam to lunch with them, and Sydney felt a part of something, though she knew she really wasn't. Her father and Adam talked policy, not inviting her into the conversation but not quite ignoring her either. Over the weeks, she was drawn into their world, appearing at the office more and more regularly. Oliver made no comment, but Sydney would have sworn he was enjoying her interest and even her company.

When he was meeting someone of importance, Oliver began to include her, telling her the night before, "The governor and I are lunching tomorrow." Sydney began to sense that she was welcome, if she wanted to be. And she did.

The only one to comment about all this was Silvie, who merely said, "I envy you. I was born too early. You're lucky. If they work at it, women can do anything now."

Sydney wasn't sure of that, but she yearned for a life with more purpose. Just what that could be, she wasn't certain. She felt like a sponge, absorbing everything she heard, all that surrounded her.

She and Big Mommy began to attend the theater once a week. Oliver and Silvie generally went to opening nights and to the parties afterward. The theater had been a part of Sydney's early life. From the age of thirteen, she'd spent most of her Saturday afternoons seeing Katherine Cornell, Lunt and Fontanne, Helen Hayes, and Gertrude Lawrence. Her mother had tried to engender a love of opera in her, but Sydney had twisted and turned in the seat; the soprano's voice sounded to her like chalk on a blackboard.

But now, back at the Broadway theater, she found it much more exciting than movies. She remembered the first years she and Jordan were married, when his life was part of the Broadway scene. What fun they'd had! She had been included in parties and after-theater suppers, belonging in New York in a way she had never fit into Hollywood. ,

She even loved the sharp November winds and the hard, sleeting rain. It brought verve to the city that the constant sun and warmth of southern California never did. It made one strive just to do ordinary, daily things.

The day after she received a postcard from Jordan-a picture of Mt. Kilimanjaro, saying he'd climbed to the top-he appeared. She came home late one Saturday afternoon from playing in the park with the girls, running through the crisp fallen leaves, and there he was, standing in front of the fire in the library. He seemed bigger than Sydney had remembered, handsomer, looking for all the world like the movie star he was.

She felt her heart leap in her chest, the way it always did when she saw him after an absence.

Ashley ran to him with outstretched arms, and he reached down to pick her up, holding her close, his eyes dancing with happiness. "How's my girl?" he whispered, kissing her, hugging her to him.

Juliet reached up and clasped Sydney's hand. She was two and a half and hadn't seen her father in-nearly nine months. She stuck her thumb in her mouth and stared across the room at him, overcome by shyness.

Jordan smiled, still hugging Ashley, and asked, "Has my princess forgotten me?" He set Ashley down gently and started across the room to his younger daughter. He knelt in front of her and said, "I missed you."

Then Juliet began to cry and moved into his arms. He laughed and stood up, holding her close. He reached out for Ashley's hand and stared into Sydney's eyes, leaning over to kiss her.

"I was afraid maybe you had all forgotten me."

That night, after the girls were tucked into bed, Sydney and Jordan headed to Giorgio's, both for old times' sake and because Jordan had said, "I don't want to share you with your parents tonight."

It was like falling in love all over again. Gooseflesh trembled down her arm when Jordan reached over to hold her hand and look deep into her eyes. She felt giddy watching his mouth as he sipped the Chianti. The yearning, pent up all these months, burst forth and she said, "Oh, God, Jordan I've missed you."

"Call your parents and tell them we won't be back there tonight. Let's go to the Plaza or the Waldorf and make love all night. I want to kiss every single part of you. I want to inhale you, drink you, screw you to kingdom come."

He made her feel weak with desire. Before the salad had even arrived she'd gone to the phone to tell her mother they were going to a hotel.

Silvie just laughed and said, "Oh, to be young again."

Sydney couldn't imagine her mother and father ever doing what she and Jordan were going to do. She couldn't imagine anyone else feeling the way she did about her husband. She closed her eyes to steady herself and walked back to the table.

Giorgio waited on them, so proud of his ex-employee, insisting on ordering their wine and food himself. He beamed at them.

"Monday comes in at least once a week," he told Jordan. "I told him the party after his opening is on me."

"You'd think you're his sons," Sydney said.

"Well," Jordan said, still holding onto Sydney's hand as he gazed across the candles at her, "I'll catch you up on the latest African gossip."

Sydney smiled at him. She didn't care what he talked about as long as he looked at her like that.

"Kirk and Lili are getting married."

That made Sydney sit up straight. "She told me she'd never marry. That next month or next year..."

Jordan nodded, laughing. "Well, love does strange things: And being so remote, who knows if it'll last? But I swear she seemed as much in love, maybe more so, than he. And here he is, such an ugly-looking little man and she's so..."

"Glamorous."

"Just so. Proves looks aren't everything. Maybe that's why this picture's dynamite. She took every bit of direction he tossed at her. Sometimes she did it her way and then Kirk would shake his head up and down as if to say, if you think that's right, it's okay with me."

"Can you imagine?" Sydney said, though her heart wasn't in it. She didn't care what happened to any of the cast and crew. All she wanted was to look at Jordan, kiss him, feel him naked against her. She wanted to move her hips against him, feel him enter her, plunge deeply. He was telling her of the exhilaration he felt at the top of Mt. Kilimanjaro. Nothing had prepared him for the sensation, he said, for the feeling of accomplishment. He'd felt like a king.

But he'd wished she'd been there to share the wonder. Nothing seemed perfect without her.

Jordan sat up straight, letting go of her hand as the waiter brought the *melanzane ai forno*. His eyes sparkled with pleasure at the sight of food he remembered so fondly.

"Sydney," he continued, raising his fork, "you should see the wildlife. My God, it's unbelievable. Gazelles, elephants, lions. There are no words to describe it."

Sydney watched his face as he described the scenery and the animals that had so fascinated him. His boyish enthusiasm charmed her. Everyone in the restaurant was looking at him, but he seemed oblivious. He was concentrating on telling her what had mesmerized him. She could tell he wanted so badly to share it all with her. Since he painted such vivid verbal pictures, it was easy to visualize what he described.

Later, when they checked into the Plaza, they barely waited to close the door behind them before they began to tear at their clothes, coming together with fire and wildness. The tenderness came later, after they'd slept, twined around each other. About three in the morning they awoke simultaneously and then they made love slowly and tenderly, the fire and the passion having been spent.

At eight they made love again, laughing as they did so this time, happy and fulfilled. With the Room Service omelet, Jordan announced, "And now the big surprise."

Sydney looked at him expectantly.

"Are you ready for this?"

"I'm ready for anything," she said, believing herself for the moment.

"You've read Pilgrim's Creek?"

"Of course." From the sales figures, one was led to think almost every American had read it. It was last year's runaway best-seller, and still on the lists.

"Julian," he said, grinning. "I'm going to be Julian." Probably the most romantic figure imaginable, Sydney thought glumly. All she said was, "You're not old enough."

"Why do you think there are makeup experts?"

"When did this happen?"

For a second Jordan sensed her mood, though he didn't understand it. Neither, in reality, did Sydney.

"When I was in Nairobi, after the mountain climb. I don't know how he traced me down, but Seth Burgess, who's going to direct it, called me. Impossible connection, and I promised I'd call as soon as I returned to civilization, which is now, but he said he'd be in touch with Mike about contractual details and salary. I want to talk to Mike first, tell him this time I want a piece of the action. Whether it's a good movie or not, everyone'll come see it, just because of the book. And I told him I want to see a script first."

Sydney nibbled on dry bread. "But you know you're going to do it anyway."

"Of course." Jordan's eyes could shine like no one else's.

"How does one turn down something like that? But I thought if I sounded like I might make a few demands, it could up my price. Jesus, Syd, before long we're going to be millionaires a couple of times over."

Maybe now Oliver would be a little more gracious, Sydney thought, but she wondered why she wasn't happier.

"Where's it going to be shot?"

Jordan laughed and reached for her hand. "On the lot, honey. Back home."

Home? LA was home?

Jordan stood up, reached down to kiss her neck lightly, and walked over to the phone to call his agent, Mike.

When he hung up after half an hour, he shook his head, a dazed look in his eyes. "Script approval, leading lady approval, ten percent of the gross proceeds and half a million salary or no percent and a million bucks up front."

Sydney had curled up in bed again, listening to Jordan's half of the conversation.

"Of course," Jordan went on, "Seth wants Sally Miramar but if that doesn't meet with my approval, he'll consider any suggestion I have."

"Sally Miramar?"

"Who the hell wouldn't want to play opposite her?" A smile was spreading across his face." Jesus, Syd, I'm thirty-three years old next month and look where I am."

"You look about twenty-five."

"Then you're too old for me, my old lady."

In some ways, maybe she was. She had just turned twenty-eight and Jordan had forgotten her birthday.

"Come on," he said, "it's Saturday. Let's get the girls and drive out to Jones Beach and walk in the wind."

Ashley and Juliet wouldn't walk more than a few feet from Jordan, preferring to hold his hands as they skipped along. He pushed them on the swings. Then they all took off their shoes, and even though it was gray and chilly, they waded in the water, jumping over the waves.

"Let's get a place on the ocean," Jordan suggested as he knelt beside his daughters, showing them how to build a sandcastle. Their cries of delight filled the air.

"Where? On the Cape?"

Jordan looked mystified. "What Cape? Oh, no, I mean near home. Maybe Malibu or Pacific Palisades or Newport Beach. We can look around. That'll be fun, exploring. I don't have to report to work for a month, though I have to be out there in two weeks to meet with Seth. We can have a couple of lazy weeks just searching out the right cottage. Or a larger place, if you'd like."

Sydney felt a spatter of rain.

Nineteen

They dined several times with Monday. Jordan promised that no matter what, they'd fly back for the November opening of his play. Monday's eyes were bloodshot, his hair needed cutting, he looked' as though he were sleeping in his clothes, and he hardly ate any of the meals they shared. He said he'd never been happier, despite living on adrenaline.

They dined once with Evan but that was abortive, for he hardly said a word. He answered Jordan's questions with monosyllables or was quietly sarcastic. His sarcasm had none of the humor of Billy's.

Oliver managed to be cordial. He could not ignore his son-in-law's success, though it was a high-profile business and he wasn't keen on his daughter's husband's name being known across the land. Hamiltons were low-profile, even if he himself was high key. But he made breakfast table conversation with Jordan one morning when only the two of them were up early, and even promised to come out to California to visit in the spring.

Jordan thought Sydney would be thrilled, but instead she said, "He won't come."

"Perhaps 'you underestimate him."

"No," she said, sitting down on the bed and taking his hand. "Because I'm not going to be there."

A puzzled frown covered Jordan's face. "Not going to be where? In California?"

She nodded, a tear glistening at the comer of her eye. "Not now," she said. "I'm not going back with you."

Jordan stared at her, and she thought at that moment her heart might break. "Jordan, I can't."

"Is there someone else?"

"Oh, Jesus, why do people always have to think that? No, you know there isn't."

"Then what?"

Sydney's sigh was ragged. "The same old thing. Oh, Jordan, I'm torn. I love you. God, how I love you. I love you more than anything in the world. I shall never love anyone as I love you, but I lose myself in your life. I drown. I disappear. There's no me left. I have to find my own direction, do something of my own, not just be your wife. Not just make a home for you and your friends." She burst into tears. Oh, God, she thought. She'd known since she'd awakened that the confrontation would come today. Jordan was leaving in two days for California, and he thought she and the girls were accompanying him, that she'd be happy spending her time looking for an oceanfront cottage.

"Sydney, what you're saying is crazy. You can do anything you want out in California. Find your direction out there, with me and the girls. Shit, you're saying you want to stay here with Ashley and Juliet?" An incredulous look crossed his face. "No," he said, his voice firm. "No, Sydney, just no. I won't even consider it."

"Jordan, my life is not yours to consider."

He reached out, putting his arms around her, pulling her closer. "You know we have a love like few have. Sydney, you can't cast that aside."

She was crying now. "Will you give up what you want to do with your life for me? Will you come back and work in the Broadway Theater? That's what you wanted to do all along."

"Hon, of course not. Give up that money? Are you crazy?"

"And the fame!"

"That, too," he nodded. "I like it, darling. The world's my oyster."

"I know. And I'm one of the grains of sand. I want the world to be my oyster, too."

He pulled away and sat on the edge of the bed, staring at her. "I won't listen to this, Syd. I'm not about to be denied the wife I love and the daughters I adore because you want to be yourself, whatever the hell that means. Sydney, I'll do anything to help, anything you want, just come back and let's try to do it in California. You can do anything in California."

So she went back with him. Within two days he was immersed in plans for the new picture, spending more time with Seth Burgess than with his family. But he assured her, "Weekends, darling. I told him weekends are sacred, no matter what. Meantime, you go on, figure out what it is you want, and I'll back you to the hilt."

The hilt was entertaining at Sunday brunches again, talking nothing but this current picture, and studying his lines late in the evenings. Sydney did cast around for things to do, but lethargy seemed to overtake her. Ashley seemed more introverted than in New York, where she'd been ripped out of the school she was just beginning to like. The only one who seemed truly happy was Juliet. She never fussed, she paid attention to whatever Jordan told her, and was affectionate with her mother. But she wanted all of her mother's attention and since Sydney couldn't find anything else she'd rather do, she spent an inordinate amount of time with Juliet. She was ashamed that, though she loved her daughter, she couldn't find fulfillment spending the entire day with a two-and-a-half-year-old.

If I were a real woman, she thought, I'd find contentment in these things that have occupied women for so long. If I were a real woman...

If she were a man, no one would expect her to stay home and do the drudgery. No one. They'd laugh at a man who did that.

So, if I were a man, what was it Daddy had said about Evan? If he were a man he wouldn't be gadding around Europe, he'd be here learning how to take over this paper. He'd put in a full day of work, and make his life worthwhile.

Well, maybe that's what she should do. Put in a full day of work and make her life worthwhile. Instead, she was babysitting, playing tennis, swimming, showering, and deciding what pretty thing she could put on to look good for Jordan when he came home so tired that all he wanted to do after dinner was collapse and study his lines.

She had to admit, she'd never tried to find work in California. She thought the cause was lost before she even began. Go get a job? Any job? That wasn't what it was all about.

She knew, suddenly, what she wanted to do. She wanted to work at the Chronicle. She wanted to learn all she could there. She wanted to be able to do things on her own, make decisions, be part of the big picture. She knew she'd have to do small things at first, make small decisions. But deep in her heart she knew she wanted to try.

She wanted to work for her father, who didn't even want her to work for him, and she wanted to do it in New York, three thousand miles from the man she loved.

They flew back for Monday's opening, Jordan taking three days off from working on the picture, which hadn't even started filming yet. The critics praised the play, but thought the direction ponderous. They said Clem Howard was miscast in the leading role, whereas Sydney thought he was quite lovely. Anyway, mixed reviews.

"You'd think the play had gotten all bad reviews and was closing tomorrow, from the look on Monday's face," Sydney said the day after it had opened.

"You don't know what it's like to get a bad review."

Sydney laughed. "Neither do you."

Jordan thought aloud. "I've a feeling the play will have a very respectable run. Whether Clem Howard's ponderous or not, he's popular enough that people will come see it. Maybe the producers will even replace him."

"You'd be perfect in the role," Sydney ventured.

Jordan laughed. "Monday says he writes every leading role as though I were going to be it. Sydney, do you know what Broadway pays? Do you know how few people see a play compared to a movie? Darling, forget it."

"No," she said, summoning all her courage. "I won't forget it, because I'm going to stay. If you love me, you'll suggest to Monday that you replace that Howard man."

Jordan gasped. "Shit, I should have known. We should never have come back here."

Sydney shook her head. "I would have come back anyway. I want to be at Oberon for Christmas. I'm sick of Christmases without snow. I'm sick of sunshine all the time. I'm sick of tennis and cocktail parties and loneliness."

Jordan put his hands on her shoulders. "Are we going through this again? Sydney, I can't leave. I'm in the midst of a big, a really big, picture."

"All your pictures are big, really big, pictures."

"Be grateful. I am."

"Well, I want to be in a really big picture."

He hit his forehead with his hand. "So that's it? You want to act, too?"

"Oh, Jordan, no, that's not it at all. I was speaking metaphorically. I don't want to act in pictures. I want to act in life." '

He stared at her. "I wish I knew what to do to make you happy. I'd do it, I really would."

Sydney walked over to him, putting her arms around him. "I know you would, darling. But you can't. No one can, except me. I want to do something, not have things done for me."

Jordan flew back to California alone the next day. Sydney waited until after Christmas at Oberon, which he flew east for, begging her to reconsider. Then she managed to get Ashley back into Chapin and hired a nanny for Juliet. Jordan only stayed three days.

For three years Sydney read in the tabloids about Jordan's affairs. Hedda Hopper doted on him, and reported his most recent romances in her Hollywood gossip column. None of those romances seemed to last. They were usually his leading ladies, the silver screen's most glamorous stars.

He flew east to visit the girls, several times a year, always staying at the Plaza, and asking that the girls be permitted to stay with him. They loved his visits. He took them to the zoo, to the circus, or Radio City Music Hall. He spent all his time in New York with them. Every year he took them to Indiana for a week, to visit his parents. Every year, at least once, he tried to talk Sydney into returning to California with him.

Much as her heart skipped a beat when she heard his voice on the phone or saw him standing in the doorway, she refused. But she did dine at '21' with him, and the tabloids always caught them there, wondering if the Jordan Eliots were reconciling. She couldn't resist going to bed with him. After all, they were still married. Besides, where else could she find the passion and the fire she felt with Jordan? Once he kissed her she was lost. Not lost enough to say yes to Hollywood, but more than enough to say yes to love.

"I do still love you, you know," she said, after they'd made love in the Plaza, with Juliet and Ashley asleep in the next room.

"I can't figure it out." He lit a cigarette, despite her hatred of the smell of smoke. "If you do, why aren't we together?"

She slid out of bed and walked over to the window, glancing out at Central Park. He plumped up his pillow and leaned against it as he stared at her in the dark, her naked body silhouetted against the city lights. Shit, no one, but no one, excited him as Sydney did. What was there about her? She certainly wasn't beautiful like most of his other women.

They no longer had much in common. The fire he'd sensed in her that first night over eight years ago now manifested only in bed when their bodies came together.

She'd acquired an aloofness. She was so caught up in the damn newspaper that little else existed. She could talk more easily about the world, about politics and economics, about other nations and their leaders, than she could about the small, really important things of daily life.

Even Monday noticed it. He was spending half the year in New York now, and he and Sydney dined together frequently. Their friendship had lost none of its warmth. Sydney was always interested in Monday's plays, attending his opening nights, inviting him to escort her to parties. But Monday had confided to Jordan that he agreed: Sydney had changed.

Jordan was changing, too, and he gloried in it. In some sense he knew that if he had been living the life he had before going to Africa he wouldn't be this way. He'd be the father and husband and actor, maybe even in that order. He had not sold the big Beverly Hills house but lived there alone, still throwing elaborate Sunday brunches by the pool when he was home. More and more, his pictures were shot on location.

The tabloids were correct: he had had a series of affairs with Hollywood's most glamorous women. Not one of them touched his heart, but, caught up in making love to them on the screen, it easily moved into the nightclubs and the country clubs of Hollywood, then into the bedroom. When making a movie, he carried the character away from the studio each night, and now—often—he carried the heroine home, too.

They learned their lines together, went to the beach on weekends, or drove down the canyons and out into the desert.

He bought a cottage at Malibu and began to spend weekends there, usually alone unless Monday was on the West Coast. He prowled the beach at sunrise; his sense of loss without Sydney and his daughters overwhelmed him at those times.

Sometimes he raged at Sydney in his mind. She denied him fatherhood. He loved Ashley and Juliet. He didn't want to see them only three or four times a year, to just take them out for fun. He wanted to be a father, be part of their growing up, see them begin to think and write and lose their baby teeth. He wanted to hear them giggle about nothing in particular, he wanted to teach them to swim. He imagined Sydney teaching them to ride and to sail, and he resented Oberon.

He did bring them to the Coast, planning to have them stay all one summer, but he was hardly ever at home and they saw more of the woman he hired to look after them than they did of him. He could tell they were bored, so he sent them back to Oberon after a month and didn't ask for that again.

He decided he must be shallow, for whenever he saw Sydney, whenever they'd been together even five minutes, he wanted to make love to her. Was their relationship only sexual? That seemed to be all she wanted from him.

Once in a while, he would reminisce about the' good old days, the days after they'd first married, when they'd lived on a shoestring and he'd had minor parts in plays. Except for Wednesday and Saturday matinees, they'd traipse through the streets of the city, discovering it, discovering each other, laughing all the time. He remembered fondly that after the show was over, they and other cast members would get together and talk early into the morning. Sydney had told him she was a part of that life in a way she'd never been part of his life in California.

He thought she hadn't tried. He also knew that being married to an actor, a Hollywood actor, couldn't be easy. But he didn't like what was happening to Sydney, because it pulled her farther from him each year. And, as it pulled her farther away, somehow it estranged him from his daughters, too, though they loved him. They were never happier than when he came to New York. The one summer he had surprised them by driving cross-country alone and appearing at Oberon unexpectedly, Juliet would not leave his side. .

"She resents me," Sydney told him,' "for ripping her away from you."

"I do, too."

"I know," she said.

Now, Jordan watched her silhouetted against the city lights, and lit a cigarette. He sighed. "Syd, it's been three years since you refused to come to California. I think it's time we talk divorce."

Did he want to jar her? Did he think asking for an end to their relationship would bring her to her senses? He wanted an answer.

She didn't even turn to face him, but stood gazing over the city she loved. After a minute, she responded. "I know. I knew it had to come sometime."

"Only if I can't talk you into our being together."

"Not as long as you're in Hollywood."

He sat up straight and smashed out his cigarette. "Christ, why not? I love you. You love me. What is it?"

She tossed her head and turned to walk back and sit on the bed, facing him. "I've told you. I lose myself when I live your life."

"How the hell can you lose yourself?"

She thought for a minute. "If you hadn't made it big like you have, and you had to settle for something that didn't fulfill you, didn't feed whatever it is inside you that makes the world wonderful, wouldn't you have lived a life of frustration, of incompleteness?"

"Most of the world settles for that."

"I'm not most of the world." She reached to take his hand in hers, pleading for understanding. "Nor are you. You've found your niche. I need to find mine."

"Being a wife and mother isn't enough?"

Sydney hesitated. "Is being a husband and father enough for you?"

"Christ, you don't give me a chance to know."

"Well, would it be? Will you give up your career, your acting, and come live in New York? Take care of the girls and associate with my friends? Could you do that, Jordan?"

"Of course not."

"Well..."

"I'm not a woman."

Sydney sighed. "But I am, so I'm supposed to be satisfied with a limited role? I can't, Jordan. I just can't. I want to stretch to my utmost, just like you have."

"You sound like a suffragette on a soap box."

"I don't mean to. I can't speak for anyone else. I'm sorry. I'd like to be satisfied with being a wife and mother, but I tried, and it nearly drove me insane. I can't take being a nobody."

Jordan reached out to touch her breast, running his hand over it, leaning over to kiss it. Even though they'd just spent hours making love, he rekindled her desire. She moved over on top of him.

"This is ridiculous," he whispered.

She agreed, but, nevertheless she moved eagerly into his embrace.

Twenty

"Shit," Sydney said aloud to herself. "It can't be. It just can't."

'She knew it, without having to wait for a test. She was pregnant. She didn't know how it had happened, because she used a diaphragm whenever she and Jordan made love. And the last time was when they'd decided on a divorce. Last month.

She didn't even have to wait six weeks to be sure. All she had to do was be five days late with her period and she knew.

She sat down on her bed. What to do? Certainly she couldn't ask Dr. Beckwith for help. He'd be shocked. And she didn't want to fly to Sweden or wherever it was people went to get safe abortions.

And there wasn't a doubt in her mind that that's what she wanted. She wouldn't tell Jordan, or anyone. She wasn't about to louse up her life for a few short hours of fun-well, ecstasy, maybe. Oh, God, are we responsible for our actions, she asked herself gloomily. And how!

It was time for them to get divorced, and this would not only delay that, but add another child for her to feel guilty about bringing up without a father. Juliet made her feel guilty enough. She wondered if she and Jordan had stayed together whether Juliet would be a different child. She acted, even at such a young age, as though she resented her mother for leaving her father. Could that really be such a profound influence? God knows, Juliet was surrounded with love. Everyone in the apartment went out of their way to cater to her. Ashley loved her. Her grandparents loved her. Her great-grandmother loved her. Warren and Carlos acted as though they did, too. So, why was she such a problem?

Sydney shook her head as though trying to clear her brain. Let's worry about this unwanted pregnancy right now, okay? She had no idea where to turn. Would she have to contact Dr. Beckwith?

Shit. Double shit. Shit a brick. Certainly she'd fly to a foreign country before going down some back alley to a quack with dirty fingernails. She wasn't risking her life to get rid of this baby. There had to be some safe way. She'd heard a D and C was an easy operation, but illegal.

Weren't there places where perfectly moral doctors had sympathy for women and unwanted pregnancies? She bet if this could happen to men there'd be ways to take care of it.

Sydney sighed. What was the difference between immoral and illegal? Had it been immoral to sleep with Jordan? Well, not strictly speaking. They were still married, if only legally.

Who could she talk with? Certainly she couldn't tell her mother. My God, she could just see Silvie's reaction! Silvie thought divorce was immoral, though Oliver seemed relieved to think Sydney was leaving Jordan. Nothing could convince him Jordan wasn't after the Hamilton money, even though Jordan already had a couple of million of his own.

Nevertheless, Sydney wasn't going to ask for a cent of alimony. After all, she was leaving him. She had work that was paying her, even if it wasn't enough to support them in style. She supposed Jordan would insist on paying child support. He wanted to be part of his daughters' lives.

"Damn," she said aloud. She should be thinking of how to go about getting an abortion, not letting her mind wander around like this.

Uncle Billy? Could she possibly talk with him? He must know about such things, even if only through gossip.

She asked Warren to have Billy call her at the office when he woke up, and to tell him she hoped he'd lunch with her.

"Sydney," Billy said, rising from his seat when he met her at the restaurant. "This is an unexpected pleasure." He was having his usual vodka martini. Billy had one for lunch and two before dinner. Except for wine with his meals, those were his self-imposed limits. He claimed he'd seen too many people make fools of themselves and he was not about to do that in front of friends.

"Well, I don't know that you'll think it's a pleasure when I tell you why I want to see you," Sydney said, sitting down.

"Oh?" Billy wore light gray slacks, a navy blue blazer, and a navy and burgundy striped tie. He almost looked as though he should carry a cane, not for balance, but just to swing in the air, like Maurice Chevalier.

"Billy, no one in New York looks classier than you do."

Billy smiled. "I work at it."

"No, you don't. It's part of your nature."

"I'm only having salad." It's what he had for lunch every day. That and a hard roll, whenever he ate in restaurants, which was at least sixty percent of the time.

"No wonder you're so trim."

He rested his elbows on the table and leaned toward her.

"You're looking a bit green around the gills. Is something wrong?"

A waiter appeared, and they ordered. Sydney thought the spinach soufflé might go down easily.

"You know, of course, Jordan and I are in the midst of divorcing?"

He nodded. "About time, too. You've been living lives of chastity too long. Time to get on with it."

Chastity? "Well, that's, not exactly accurate, Billy."

"Oh?" He raised an eyebrow.

Was he the one to tell? Well, she had to give it a go. "I'm pregnant."

His eyes opened wide and he just stared at her. "My use of the word chastity was ill-advised, I see. Why are you telling me this, Sydney, my dear?"

"Well, I don't want this baby. I'm just about four weeks."

"Are you sure? Have you had a test?"

She shook her head. "No, but I know. When Jordan was here last time, and that was just a month ago, we ... well, you know."

Billy did know.

"You're not going to ask me, I hope, why we're getting divorced if we care enough to go to bed together?"

Billy smiled. "You know me better than that or we wouldn't be having this conversation. That's the sort of question my sister would ask, not me. "

He sat and waited for her to go on. She sipped her white wine.

Sydney was surprised to discover tears welling in her eyes.

"Oh, Billy, I don't want to have this baby."

They sat, sipping their drinks, while Sydney dabbed at her eyes with her napkin.

After awhile, Billy said, "And you want my help or advice?"

"Help." Then, after the waiter had brought their food she added, "I guess I need someone to talk to and I don't know anyone else who wouldn't stand in judgment."

"You feeling immoral?"

She reached across the table with her left hand and touched Billy's arm. "I do." And she began to cry again.

Billy looked around. "If you're going to create a scene, let's get out of here."

"No, no," Sydney said, her voice ragged. "I'm okay. Really. It's just I feel that what I want to do is so sinful."

"Sinful?" Billy grinned at her. "Well, are we going to have a metaphysical discussion of sin? Because it's illegal, does that make it sinful? Or does sin have more to do with morality than legality? And if you don't think it's sinful, is it?"

Sydney had to laugh. "Okay, we won't use that word. But I don't feel good about whatever it is. And I'm scared."

"You're absolutely sure you do not want this baby?"

"Right. Not unless having an abortion would endanger my life. I don't want it badly enough to die. I mean Jordan would be pleased and I'm not having it out of wedlock-at least, not yet. It won't be final for another five months. I just don't want any more ties to Jordan. And I'm starting a career..."

Billy again raised an eyebrow.

"Okay, so it's at Daddy's. But nevertheless, I'm getting a toehold. I've spent three years there every damn day and I don't want that to be wasted."

"You still love Jordan?"

Sydney shrugged and thought a minute. "More than I imagine I'll ever love any other man. But not enough to suffocate,"

"Well, we're all different. I've never thought I had to make my mark on the world. I'm happy to drift with it." He had finished his lunch and Sydney had barely started hers. "You want to know if I know of some way."

"Yes. You know so many people, and everyone seems to tell you their secrets…"

"And," he smiled, "you've no idea if I've ever been involved in such a thing?"

"No, I didn't even think about that. I just want to know if there's someone safe I can go to, rather than having to fly away to some other country or something."

"How about a weekend in Bermuda with me?" Now Sydney was eating, and enjoying it thoroughly. "Is it legal there?"

"That's not the question. There's a clinic there where everyone goes. It's safe. It's expensive. It's quick, particularly at less than six weeks. Hardly anyone's even sure they're pregnant before six weeks."

How did he know so much about this?

"We could fly down Friday morning and back Monday morning and no one would be the wiser. Five thousand dollars."

"Five thousand…? Oh, my." She didn't have that much of her own.

"I have that much socked away," he said, observing the look on her face. "But it's only a loan. Someday you can pay me back."

"You don't think what I'm doing is wrong?"

"'Sydney, my dear, don't make me your conscience. You decide whether it's wrong or right. I'm willing to help you with whatever you decide."

"Well, I just can't have it, Uncle Billy." When he didn't say anything, Sydney went on, "It's not that it would ruin my life. But is that a criterion?" Billy lit a cigarette, and Sydney brushed the smoke away.

"I just don't want it."

"Then, don't have it."

"It doesn't seem fair." Billy couldn't tell whether Sydney was talking to him or herself. "It never louses up a man's life."

Billy's eyes skirted the room. He didn't see anyone he knew. "Don't say never. Sometimes it affects men's lives."

Sydney cocked her head to the side and studied him. She wondered if anyone ever really knew Billy.

"You're not going to tell Jordan?"

"I'm not going to tell anyone but you."

"Well, when you come to terms with your conscience, and if you still want to fly to Bermuda, let me know and I'll arrange for tickets and for the…for the hotel. In other words, I'll take care of it all."

Sydney felt herself relaxing. "Do it," she said. "I don't want to have to think about it anymore. Are we going for a holiday together?"

"Exactly. And I will come back tan. I will dance in the evening, and I may even snorkel. You will come back and you will not feel weak or traumatized unless you want to flagellate yourself. It's very simple, really."

"You've done this before."

"Once or twice," was his answer.

Sydney did not pursue it. "Have I told you lately I love you?"

He smiled and patted her hand. "You did that by confiding in and trusting me. And you know I love you or you'd never have had the courage to talk with me as you have. I'm flattered, Sydney. There isn't anything, you must know, that I wouldn't do for the family."

Three days later, on Friday afternoon, Sydney and Billy left for a weekend in Bermuda.

All the way down on the plane Sydney felt sick. She hoped she wouldn't throw up. It wasn't the queasiness that comes with pregnancy, but her feeling of guilt, her questioning what she was doing.

The only law Sydney had ever broken was the same one every American over the age of sixteen had also broken, the speed limit. Going sixty in a fifty-five-miles-per-hour zone. Or even sixty-five.

Sydney had never cheated on a test, never plagiarized, had told only little white lies. She had never before had to question her own morality.

Law in all of the United States told her that what she was doing was illegal and, therefore, immoral. In the New York in which Sydney came of age, the drinking age was eighteen, and she had not broken that law. She had always honored her mother and father, remaining a virgin until she met the man she married.

Should she stay married to Jordan, even though they'd lived apart for three years, and have this baby? Was she taking a life, even though the fetus wasn't five weeks old? Was she a murderer?

"What's wrong?" Billy asked. "Your knuckles are white. You're holding onto the arms of your seat as though this were your first flight. Are you alright?"

Sydney didn't open her eyes, but she whispered, "I don't know."

She felt her uncle's hand on hers. "Honey, if you're having second thoughts…"

"No," she said, shaking her head vehemently. "No. I don't want this baby. I want my life to go onward, not backward."

"For whatever reasons," Billy murmured, his voice was soft, "they're your reasons. It's your body, your life. It's no one else's business. Personally, I think it's sinful to bring an unwanted, unloved child into the world. Seems funny to me that the very people who are against abortion, who claim that unwanted children should be born, are the very ones who are proponents of the death sentence *ana* against welfare. Makes no sense at all."

Sydney had never thought of it that way. But, he was talking philosophy and she was wondering about her own morality.

"Daddy'd have a fit, wouldn't he, if he knew?"

She opened her eyes when Billy laughed loudly.

"A shit fit," he agreed. She'd never heard him say anything more colorful than *dam* or *gosh* before. "But your father's uh, er, narrow morality need not be yours."

Later, she told Billy she'd been scared to pieces. He'd had to leave her at the hospital, which looked like a luxury hotel. Her room was elegant. Saturday morning, when she was wheeled down the shining hallway to an elevator, she thought at least it wasn't an unsanitary back room someplace with a high risk of infection.

When the anesthetist held a mask over her face and told her to breathe deeply, she felt that she was dying as she fell deeper and deeper into the swirling black vortex.

She never did see the doctor, and she knew she would never again see her children and Billy and...

She lost consciousness.

She threw up for an hour afterward from the after-effects of the anesthesia, but she didn't even hurt. A nurse suggested she might like to lie out in the sun or under an umbrella in the afternoon. To make up for having eaten so little on the trip, she consumed the steak Diane with gusto and stared at all the other women, rich women from around the world.

Sydney wondered what women who couldn't afford five thousand dollars for a weekend did in such circumstances. Had babies whom they resented forever or whom they gave up for adoption? Jumped off roofs? Doomed themselves and their unwanted children to poverty and ostracism?

Asking herself these questions reaffirmed her feeling that-she'd chosen the right path.

When Billy and a driver picked her up at noon on Sunday, he gazed into her eyes, asking, "Are you all right, my dear?"

He asked no more questions, but amused her all the way back to New York with tales of how three older women had tried to pick him up the previous night.

"What I have never understood," he complained. "is how Evan always gets the young gorgeous ones lusting after him and all I get are the desperate ones. I'm far better looking than Evan, aren't I?"

"You are that," Sydney said, and thought, much nicer, too,

For months afterward, Sydney pondered the difference between legality and morality. Maybe, she thought, men decided what was legal, and morality had to come from one's own conscience.

Once in a while she dreamt she was in jail, bars keeping her from life, and she always knew why she was there.

* * * *

Six months later she was no longer Mrs. Jordan Eliot. Resuming the name she was born with, she was Sydney Hamilton again.

And she finally moved from her parents' apartment, despite the comfort there. She only moved five blocks away, to a brownstone with a small garden in the rear. She bought the girls a puppy, which they named Copper.

The girls' nanny, Bernice, had a room on the fourth floor, which also housed Ella, the cook. Under Ella's supervision, the cleaning lady came in daily.

Sydney didn't have time enough to shop, and much as she thought she'd enjoy decorating the house, she turned the job over to a professional, who followed Sydney around for three days. He wanted to study her personality and lifestyle, the kind of clothes she wore, what she liked. She wondered if the results really did reflect her personality. At first, she didn't even know if she liked it. All the walls were white, a warm candlelight ivory kind of white. The decorator had chosen furniture that changed the accent for each room.

The living room, long and narrow, had flowered sofas and chairs in forest green and wine, with spots of navy and pale green. Pastel impressionist paintings dotted the walls, and Sydney was eventually pleased to find the room both dramatic yet restful. After a few weeks, she found it quite cozy.

The dining room carpeting and chair seats were a rich wine red. Once Juliet saw that, she demanded red for her bedroom, so her bedspread and rug were a bright cherry color that delighted her. Next door, and with a connecting door that was almost always left open, was Ashley's bedroom, in pastels, opposite Juliet's. Lilac and shades of blue and rose were what Ashley requested. At eight she had tastes as definite as her six year-old sisters', but they were not similar in any way.

Nor were the two girls themselves. Ashley's coloring was like her mother's-golden hair and porcelain skin that freckled in the Chesapeake Bay summers. Eyes that were not quite her mother's translucent gray, but blue-gray, depending on what she wore. Her moods were most often tranquil, unlike her mother or father or Juliet. She was a studious little girl, enjoying the challenge of school, not needing to be told to attend to her homework but enjoying it: When she had free time, her nose was almost always in a book. That is, unless she and Juliet were doing something together.

Even though they were so different, they were each other's' best friends. Ashley was patient with Juliet and enjoyed teaching her cursive handwriting, when little Juliet only knew how to print. They received watercolor kits one Christmas and taught themselves to paint horses, which they did by the hour. Ashley was in love with horses. She had begun a collection 'of them and for birthdays and Christmases her mother and father and her grandmother searched for additions. On Saturday mornings the girls took riding lessons. Warren accompanied them, as he had their mother.

Sydney had bought Ashley a pony when she was six, but as she neared eight, she had graduated to a horse, on which she was fearless.

Juliet was like Evan in that she didn't enjoy studying. Books weren't her cup of tea. She always had to be active. She was a moody child, sometimes retreating into herself where no one could reach her.

She was a discipline problem even in kindergarten, because she rebelled against any kind of authority. The only one she let boss her gracefully was Ashley, and anything that Ashley wanted of her, Juliet gave. Juliet enjoyed giving, but only if her largesse was recognized. She was affectionate to the point of ridiculousness. She kissed her nanny and the cook and her sister and her mother, if Sydney was around, whenever she went out the front door. She kissed her grandparents, Big Mommy, and her Uncle Evan, Uncle Billy, and Carlos and Warren. She kissed Nettie when she was at Oberon and she kissed Copper. She loved being held and cuddled. She would hum and sing little songs whenever she was rocked in someone's arms.

Juliet spent much of her time being angry at her mother, because her mother often did not give her enough attention. Sydney made it a rule, and generally was able to keep to it, to be home by six o'clock. She always had dinner with her daughters. If she was going out to dine, she made the engagement late enough so that the girls would already be in bed.

Summers, when the girls spent time at Oberon with Silvie, Sydney flew down weekends and always spent two Idyllic weeks in August there. The three of them rode horses daily, splashed in the pool, and went clamming and sailing.

The summer that Sydney's divorce became final, Evan came down to the island to stay for the first time since they'd been teenagers. Sydney looked at him and wondered what made him so cynical. He'd never had to work a day in his life. He followed the sun and the jet set around the world. He was romancing one of John Power's top models, whose face that spring and summer graced *Harper's Bazaar, Vogue,* and several other magazine covers. Her face peered down from ads in the New York subways, suggesting that Camel cigarettes had something to do with sex appeal.

Evan came for two weeks and ended up staying four, after Sydney left at the end of August. He said he'd bring the girls up the following week, in time for school.

But while he was there he didn't join them in clamming or sailing, though he did accompany them when they rode and swam. He sat on a chaise longue either in the front yard overlooking the bay or back by the pool, and drank.

Sydney had noticed it immediately. "You drink too much," she said.

"Don't start on me," he said, his eyes closed, his mouth tight, as he lay back absorbing the sun.

Sydney studied her brother's body, wire-thin and tanned. "You have the best-looking legs I've ever seen on a man," she said with a laugh.

He didn't open his eyes, but lazily said, "We've always had good bodies, you and I. It's exercise." He had installed a gym in his apartment.

Ashley and Juliet were practicing diving at the other end of the pool.

"What do you do for sex, my dear sister?" Evan asked.

"I think you have a one-track mind. Don't you have anything else to think about?"

"Do you and Jordan still get it on when he comes to the city?"

"That's none of your business."

Her replies didn't seem to faze her brother at all. "You're in the prime of life, Syd. You're not thirty yet. Are you letting these years go to waste?"

"I'm doing anything but wasting my life."

"Oh, you mean I am? Not as I see it. But you without a man? What a waste."

"They haven't actually been hammering at my door, but I do have escorts for parties and plays and when I need one."

"Yeah. Monday Pearson: You getting it on with him? Jordan's best friend?"

"Oh, Evan," Sydney moaned, not knowing whether to laugh or be irritated. She didn't want to "get it on," as Evan so colorfully put it, with anyone. She didn't want any more pregnancies, or any more moral debates. She didn't want to be in a position where she had to break the law or suffer the consequences.

"Sex and love aren't the most important things in the world," she said.

"Yeah?" asked her brother. "Then what is?"

Twenty One

"You know, Sydney, you get better looking the older you get," said Adam Yarborough. He held a cigarette and leaned against the doorway, looking at her seated at her desk.

She smiled at him, her mind preoccupied.

"Aren't you coming out to the party?" he asked. The usual sedate office Christmas party was in progress at two in the afternoon of Christmas Eve. "You don't want everyone to think you're stuck up and won't associate with the peasants, do you?"

"I think people know better than that." Sydney knew the name of just about everyone who worked for the paper. She also knew their spouses' names and their children's birthdays, even though she had to look those up at the beginning of every month. She knew if one of the children or spouses was hospitalized, or seriously ill, or if a family had a new baby.

Not that she was informal with the staff or entered into their private lives. But, unlike Oliver, she was able to call people by their first names, and when they did a particularly good job, she literally patted them on the back. She knew that you didn't get good work and loyalty from people just by paying them well. People needed more than money as reward for work.

Although Sydney often intimidated the people who worked at the *Chronicle*, they liked her, even if she didn't often unbend.

Oliver they simply respected; they didn't know him well enough to like or dislike him. Oliver was the big boss who sat upstairs, seldom showing his face down where the daily work got done. He didn't know the names of many on the staff, although those who had regular bylines were called by name.

Adam was the one they knew. Oliver and Adam conferred daily, and it was up to Adam to set into motion those policies Oliver mandated. Adam was not always tactful, but you always knew where you stood. When he was furious he'd let you know. He'd vent his wrath, and then it was over. He never carried grudges, and when you did something well, he'd tell you that, too. So, though his anger was something to be avoided if possible, you knew that if he was irritated with you, it was usually temporary, and if you were smart, you learned from it. Few who stayed on at the paper repeated their errors.

Incompetence was another thing. Neither Adam nor Oliver had patience with inefficiency, laziness, or lack of ability.

Adam usually gave three warnings, and then you emptied your desk and looked for work elsewhere.

Sydney never asked him but often wondered why Oliver had such faith in Adam. He was a good newspaperman, of that she was aware, and he shared Oliver's political views. He came from a scholarly family. His father had just retired as head of the history department at Purdue. He always dressed well, though he probably bought his clothes off the racks at Macy's or Bloomingdale's. His ties were clones of those Oliver preferred, but he wore the necks of his shirts open, his tie loose and lopsided. He did not travel in the same social circles as Oliver and Sydney.

He lived in midtown Manhattan, though Sydney had no idea whether it was a brownstone or an apartment. He had a couple of teenage sons. She'd met his wife once, but couldn't even remember where, she recalled her as a rather attractive but colorless woman. She had probably been pretty when they'd met in college, but she was faded now, though she couldn't be forty. She'd worn a navy blue dress, Sydney remembered, even though she couldn't recall the occasion, which had to have been several years ago. She looked as though, perhaps, she always wore navy blue dresses.

What troubled Sydney the most about Adam, and the reason she had not developed any real friendship with him, was that she was attracted to him, even though he lacked an ingredient she thought vital, the ability to laugh at oneself and the world. He was not a handsome man. About six feet tall, he was slim but muscular, and weighed about one ninety; he worked out at a gym three times a week.

His face was too long to be considered handsome, his lips too thin and stern, his nose too aquiline. His sandy hair was parted on the left, combed straight, and his whiskey-colored eyes peered out from rimless glasses, making him look like the college professor his father was. His spectacles were usually shoved up above his forehead. Sydney wondered why he even wore them. When he had them on and someone handed him something to read, he always pushed them up on top of his head and read without the glasses.

"Well, going to loosen up and come have a drink of Christmas cheer with all the help?" Adam asked again.

He always treated her as though she weren't quite real, merely the boss's daughter and not a person in her own right. She was aware that was an attitude he had learned from her father. He couldn't quite treat her with condescension, because she was the boss's daughter. But in the three and a half years she'd been at the paper, officially or not, she could tell he only half listened to any of her suggestions, and then did what he wanted, what Oliver sanctioned. He had never given any real consideration to her ideas. Once in a while, something she fought for did impress Oliver. Then Adam would incorporate it, always telling her it was a good idea, wondering why he hadn't thought of it. So, she never really knew what he thought of her, or if he thought of her at all.

She had heard Oliver say, more than once, that Adam was the son he wished Evan were. She knew that if she were the daughter Oliver had wished for, she'd be married now, married to someone who played polo Sunday afternoons, or had his own seat on Wall Street, or was at least a Park Avenue physician. The fact that her father tolerated her presence in the office every day, giving her inconsequential assignments and listening to her once in a while, was as much as she could hope for.

She wondered why she didn't go out and get a real job someplace else. Getting up every morning and dressing for work was like girding for battle. Each day was a challenge, but not the kind she thought she was cut out for. Yet she loved the paper despite Oliver's and Adam's attitudes. She loved the possibilities.

"Come on," Adam said, extending his hand. Sydney was so surprised by the gesture that she stood up and he took her by the arm, leading her out of the office.

She glanced at her watch. "I can't stay long. I have to catch a plane to Maryland."

"Everyone would rather be home trimming the tree, mixing eggnog, tying up last-minute presents. But your father's not here, so I think it'd be nice if you put in an appearance."

Oliver never attended office parties. "You know, act like the powers on high appreciate all that we do through the year. Just one drink won't hurt. After all, the plane will wait. It's your plane. I'll make sure you take off so you can get there before dark. How's that?"

Sydney raised her eyebrows.

Actually, she enjoyed herself so much that she made the pilot wait for half an hour. Oliver had bought a company plane the year before and had flown down to Oberon yesterday, sending the plane back for her today. Ashley and Juliet had already gone, when school let out three days ago. They'd accompanied Silvie and Big Mommy and were no doubt impatient for her arrival, and for Santa Claus's. The adults would trim the tree tonight and then Warren, who always went down to Oberon for Christmas, too, would awaken everyone early in the morning by shouting from downstairs, "Merry Christmas to all and to all a good night!"

Then he'd slam the front door and rush up the back stairway before Ashley and Juliet could get downstairs. Warren didn't look much older than he had when Sydney was in college, though now, a dozen years later, he had to be in his fifties. He could still pass for forty, in both appearance and energy.

Warren didn't take the plane. He motored down, because he wouldn't get near a plane and because he liked driving. When he had passengers he drove at an even fifty-five, but when he was alone he let out all the stops and ate up the asphalt, playing the radio loudly, singing along. He didn't think flying could possibly be as much fun.

Sydney had a great time at the party, allowing herself two drinks. She was surprised to hear Adam say, "It's three-thirty. We'd better get you to Teterboro. Your daughters won't forgive you if you're not there before dark."

How did he know that's where the plane was waiting? How did he know how Ashley and Juliet would feel? But he was right.

"Come on," he said, "I'll get a cab."

She was surprised when he followed her into the cab. It would be dark in another hour; these were the shortest days of the year.

"Your kids will be expecting you, too," she said, but was glad of his company. The two drinks had given her a buzz, and she was feeling kindly toward the world.

"I find reasons to delay going home, even on Christmas Eve."

She didn't know what to say to that.

"Dine with me some evening, Sydney. Do you realize we hardly know each other?"

The streets were jammed with people trying to get out of Manhattan and home to Long Island or Connecticut or New Jersey.

Once at Teterboro, Adam helped Sydney with the packages she was taking to Oberon, walking out to the plane with her, shouting at her above the roar of the twin engines.

"Enjoy your holidays," he said with a smile.

"Thanks," she said. "You, too."

He surprised her by leaning down and brushing her cheek with his lips. "Hope Santa Claus is good to you. Tell him I say you've been a good girl this year."

Girl. She was a grown woman with two children and he called her a girl. Nevertheless, she watched him as he stood while the plane waited for clearance, and thought of him for the next hour, wondering what his Christmas would be like, what he was giving his children, if his wife would like what he had chosen for her.

She wondered if his lips had met hers, instead of brushing her cheek, if they would have lingered and if she would have liked the sensation.

She knew, too, that she should stop thinking such things. Business and pleasure didn't mix. And she certainly didn't want to come between her father and Adam, didn't want any unpleasantness to ruin Adam's future at the *Chronicle*. And, most important of all, he was married. Nevertheless, until it was time to land, she wondered why he had suggested dinner. And she wondered, too, what his kisses would be like.

Twenty Two

Oliver's Christmas present to Sydney was more than she ever dared hoped for. It came in a large box, about two feet by three, and weighed a ton. He insisted it be the last present opened. As she untied the ribbon and carefully unfolded the gay red-and-gold paper, he said, rather smugly, "I wrapped that myself."

Silvie cast him a curious glance. He hardly ever chose his own presents. She did all the Christmas shopping, except for herself. Every year he gave her the same thing: dozens of silk underwear and nightgowns, carefully chosen by himself. It never varied. Sydney hoped that meant they still had a sex life. It was so hard to imagine one's parents making love, particularly when they were older. '

There was a smaller box within the larger box, and a smaller one within that. After she'd opened six boxes, Sydney found a large cement block and a Sunday magazine section of the *Chronicle* tied to it with a ribbon. She turned it around, upside down, and looked at her father.

"I put the concrete block in to fool you," her father said with a wide grin.

"I'm fooled." Sydney had no idea what Oliver's idea of fun was, even after all these years.

Oliver kept shaking his head. "Do you like it? Is it what you wanted?"

Sydney shrugged her shoulders. "I don't understand."

"I'm turning the Sunday magazine section over to you."

As she stared, open-mouthed, at her father, tears sprang to her eyes and one trickled down her cheek. "Oh, Daddy."

Then she began to cry, really cry. She rushed over to her father, hugging him and saying over and over, "Oh, Daddy."

"It's a reward," he said, obviously pleased with Sydney's reaction. "And a token of faith."

Evan got a new Jaguar.

Sydney arose with new zest to meet each day. Much as she wanted to be at her desk by eight, she forced herself to stay home until Ashley and Juliet left for school. Big Mommy didn't think it was safe for them to walk, so she insisted on sending Carlos and her Rolls over each morning and afternoon. Carlos didn't seem to mind at all. The two little girls climbed into the front seat with him, and he could be seen waving his hands and talking to them as he pulled away from the curb.

Sydney saw no need to own a car in the city. If she wanted one to go out of town, her grandmother's or her parents' cars were always available. Uncle Billy saw no need to own a car, either. Of course, he didn't even know how to drive. And now that Oliver had a company plane, Sydney always flew to Oberon. She had become quite like her uncle, though, in that she had little desire to leave the city except to visit Oberon and, once in awhile, Washington. She wondered if Washington was going to become more exciting in the next few years. Next year, 1960, would be Ike's last year as President.

The color of D.C. social life was always tinted by whoever was in power. She personally was rooting for that young senator from Massachusetts, though she never said it aloud, certainly not in front of her father. Long ago she began to move away from her father's way of thinking. Hadn't Jordan had something to do with that? Or had she begun to think independently in college?

She'd taken the week after Christmas off to spend with the girls at Oberon, where they'd skated on the ponds. She took them over to Washington one day, now that the Bay Bridge made the trip so easy, and through the Smithsonian, which bored seven-year-old Juliet so that she fussed and became irritable. Sydney should have known better.

The second of January, Sydney officially began her new job. And that day Oliver provided her with yet another present: a new, and large, office—on the thirtieth floor. It was a corner office, with windows overlooking the city to the north and toward the Hudson River.

He said, "Decorating is not my forte, and besides, I thought you' might enjoy doing it yourself. You have carte blanche. And now you officially have a salary."

She was thirty-one years old and for the first time in her life she was earning her own living. For the first time in her life she was in charge of something. She vowed to herself that the Sunday section was going to be the most read Sunday paper in town. Perhaps she couldn't compete with the old gray lady, *The New York Times,* but she could certainly make her part of the paper more readable. She wanted people to sit up and take notice.

She sat at her desk trying to decide whether to concentrate on decorating her office or think about how she wanted to reconstruct the Sunday section when there was a knock on the door. Without waiting for her reply, Adam walked in.

He smiled at her and held out a bunch of violets, the kind they sold in flower marts at subway stations. Sydney had always loved violets. "I understand congratulations are in order."

"Why, Adam, how nice of you." She reached out for the bouquet and held it while they talked. .

"I've come to offer you a secretary. You'll need one, of course. I have a candidate. She's overqualified for the secretarial pool and I think you two would get along."

Sydney cocked her head. She hadn't even gotten around to thinking about that. "Well, I'll at least interview her," she said.

Was this Adam's way of spying on her, trying to control her?

She didn't totally trust him. She didn't even know if she liked him.

"Her name's Kelley. Mary Kelley. I'll send her up."

He continued to stand there.

"Is there something else?" Sydney's voice was brisk.

"Yeah," he smiled. "How about dinner some night? We're in this business together."

"I like to have dinner with my children," Sydney said. She wondered why she was making this difficult for him.

He coughed. "How about lunch then?"

What did he want from her? Now that her father had given her some stature, she figured Adam wanted something. And she was all too aware that her attraction to him could be lethal. He *was* a married man. And the Sunday section had absolutely nothing to do with him. The whole Sunday edition was not his. They could operate here for years and have nothing to do with each other.

However, he was Oliver's right-hand man. "Lunch would be fine," she said. .

"Today?"

"Why not?" she answered. "One o'clock?"

"One. Any place in particular?"

"Surprise me. I like my men to do the choosing." Now, that was a stupid thing to say, she realized. *My* men? How many men were there in her life? She was aware she'd suddenly put this on a male-female, rather than a business, basis. She could have kicked herself.

He took her to Lindy's, a place she'd never been to despite its fame, and he talked only about the paper and politics. He said if there were any way he could be of help, she only had to ask. His resources were at her disposal.

Sydney thought he seemed to forget she'd been coming to the paper, using a desk that had been abandoned, for over five years.

After she'd listened to him for nearly an hour, Sydney crossed her arms and leaned across the table. "You realize that what you're saying is you don't think I can handle this job."

"I'm not saying that at all. I'm saying we both work for your father now, and if you need any help, I'm willing. That's all."

""This paper is your life, isn't it?"

He nodded. "This paper is my life."

"What about your wife and children?"

"What about them?" ·

."Men don't seem to think families are nearly as important as their work. They take them for granted, it seems to me. Don't you have anything left over for them? Do you help them with what they need?"

He leaned back, looking away from her. "I give them what they need. I earn a handsome salary, my wife has charge accounts at good stores, my sons go to private schools, as does anyone who can afford it in this city. We take a two-week vacation every year to wherever my wife wants to go. I take my sons to the opening of the baseball season. We go up to New Haven to see Yale games, since that's where my oldest has his heart set on going. I expect I'm a reasonably good father."

"I think you're sounding defensive. Are you as good a husband?"

Why was she stepping into this part of his life?

Adam reached for his coffee and sipped it, his eyes meeting hers. After a while he answered, "I don't think my relations with my wife are any of your goddamned business."

She was taken aback, yet somehow delighted with his answer. "I don't think they are, either. And I don't think my needs are any of your business. I can handle this job. I have lots of ideas, and I intend to act on them. If I think there's something I can't do that you can help me with, of course I'll call on you. But right now I don't foresee anything. The Sunday magazine section and the daily running of the paper have little to do with each other."

Adam smiled at her, a lopsided grin that showed his top front tooth was crooked, something she'd never noticed before. "I didn't realize you could be such a hard ass, Sydney."

"Your words imply an insult, but your tone of voice, makes it a compliment."

"For now," he said, pushing back his chair, "I don't know which way I meant it. You may be sure this is the last time I'll volunteer to help."

"Thank you," she said. "Thank you for volunteering your help and for understanding I want to do this on my own."

"Oh." He stood up. "Is that what I understood?"

"Well, you can't be very dense and have this job." Sydney, too, rose from her chair and began to lead the way from the restaurant. On the way out, she saw Estelle Parrington and stopped to say hello. She didn't introduce Adam.

Estelle raised her eyebrows and smiled like a well-fed cat as she watched Sydney leave, followed by Adam. Sydney turned and put her hand through Adam's arm and smiled at him dazzlingly. She laughed to herself, knowing that Estelle must be wondering who he was. As soon as they were outside and Adam started to hail a cab, Sydney said, "If you're in a rush, take it. I'd like to walk."

There was a hint of snow in the air; it was damp and cold. Sydney started off at a brisk clip, thinking the twelve-block walk would be quicker than trying to fight the city traffic.

"Whoa," Adam called, running after her. She shoved her gloved hands in the pocket of her gray cashmere coat and began to hum.

"You don't act rich," Adam said, his long strides keeping up with her.

Sydney laughed. "First of all, this is my first paying job. Second, how do the rich act?"

"They don't walk."

"You know what? I think being rich is being able to do whatever you please. And I please to walk."

"Yeah, your first job," muttered Adam. "So how have you been living so far?"

"Not that it's your business, but on a trust fund my grandfather left."

"Not rich, huh? And is anything about you my business?"

"Not really." Sydney reached out again and took his arm as they walked together, their strides brisk. "But suddenly, Adam, I think it might be nice for us to try to be friends. I don't know anyone else interested in the same things I and who I can talk about this business with.",

"That's all I meant, really," he said, reaching to put a hand over her gloved one stuck through his arm, "when I said I'm around if you need me."

Sydney nodded, feeling more kindly toward him than she ever had. "Do I have to wait until I need you? What about if I just want you? Want to discuss something?"

"Jesus, Sydney, are you playing with me? First you tell me to stay out of your life and then you say let's be buddies. You can confuse a guy."

"I should never have had a drink at lunch. I must remember that. It clouds my mind and makes me want to take a nap. Okay, never again."

On January 2, 1960, on a day when the pewter sky spit not more than a dozen snowflakes over New York City, Sydney felt enormously happy, dizzy with either the whiskey sour or with her new responsibilities, or with sharing her joy with someone. Fate made it Adam Yarborough.

At three o'clock a woman, perhaps six or seven years younger than Sydney, knocked on her open office door.

"I'm Mary Kelley," she said, her voice soft. She wore a black suit with a red blouse, and small black pearl earrings. Her inky hair was shoulder length and very straight, bangs covering her forehead. She wore tinted glasses and a bright slash of scarlet lipstick.

"Come in," Sydney said and gestured to the chair across from her desk. "I'm trying to decide how to decorate this room and how to turn the magazine into something how to turn the magazine into something unlike any other Sunday section. Do you think they're equally important?"

Mary sat down, crossing her legs. "Is that a test?"

Sydney shook her head. "No, merely a reflection of my state of mind."

They looked at each other. Sydney leaned back in the swivel chair. "Tell me something about yourself."

"I'm from Philadelphia. I graduated from Bryn Mawr, which I attended on a scholarship. I'm doing graduate work at Columbia nights."

"So, why a secretary? Are you aiming at being over qualified?"

"No." Mary's smile was serene. "I want to be a secretary to someone who will give me high-powered responsibilities, who will wonder what he- or she-could possibly do without me, and find challenges that will make my life exciting."

Sydney was silent a minute, looking at the girl who returned her gaze. "So, what would you want from me and this job should you become my secretary?"

"To learn enough to replace you as Sunday magazine editor when you take over the paper."

Sydney whooped. "You don't pull any punches, do you?"

"You asked. If we work together you'll find me honest to the point of lacking tact."

"I'll bet you anything you're summa cum laude."

Mary grinned, showing teeth so white Sydney thought she ought to pose for a toothpaste ad. "Bingo."

"I'm a sucker for intelligent people." Sydney stood up and walked over to look out over her city. "I've no idea exactly what this job will turn into, or what I'm going to do. I'd want your home phone number and expect you to be on call. If I travel, I might want you to come along and take care of all details. I'm not a detail person. I'd want your opinion if I ask for it, but expect you not to be upset if I don't take it. Someone today, your ex-boss, just called me a hard ass. I guess that's what I expect to be in this job. You'd have to be a self-starter, anticipate my needs and wants." She turned to look at Mary.

"I mean, in the job, of course. Do you have family?"

"You mean, am I married?"

Sydney nodded.

"No. I don't even have a boyfriend. I go to school three nights a week, and besides, I haven't met anyone I'd rather put ahead of a job that excites me."

"I don't know that this will do that. Right now I've no idea what it will become. I thought I needed someone to write my letters."

"I take shorthand faster than you can talk. I type 110 words a minute."

Sydney sat down again. "Doesn't that bore you?"

"If that's all I did all day, it would. And that's all I've been doing every day downstairs, as part of the pool."

"How do you feel about working for a woman?"

Mary burst into laughter. "Like I've -died and gone to heaven."

"Well," Sydney reached across the desk and offered Mary her hand, "I guess we're in business. Let's see about getting a desk and making that anteroom a place you'll find attractive. Maybe the first thing we better do is decide how to decorate this place. It would be nice to coordinate your work area and mine."

Mary's eyes sparkled.

"Where do you live?"

"The Village. Christopher Street.",

Where she and Jordan had lived. She hadn't been down to the Village in years. Monday still had an apartment there, not that he was in New York much nowadays.

"Okay," Sydney said. "Look over that work area outside this office and think about what you'd like in the way of furniture and whatever else you want. I'll call personnel and get you assigned to me. I'd just as soon you call me Sydney, rather than Ms. Hamilton."

Mary stood up, sensing dismissal. "Starting tomorrow?"

"No, starting now. Whatever you left unfinished downstairs can remain unfinished. It's Adam's own fault for recommending you. How come you didn't talk him into letting you become a reporter?"

"That work doesn't interest me. This does."

"A secretary rather than a reporter?"

"A way to an exciting future that has no bounds."

Sydney hoped Mary wouldn't be disappointed.

As Mary disappeared through the door, Sydney reached for a yellow lined legal pad and began to make notes. Ever since her father had thrown this in her lap her mind couldn't stop reeling with new ideas, with people she wanted to contact. Maybe she'd call Denton Walker and see if he was interested in creating a new photographic look for the magazine. A whole new look.

She paid little attention to Juliet and Ashley while they told her about their day during dinner, but she forced herself not to focus on work until she had tucked them in and read them a story. Though they each had separate rooms, they usually begged to sleep together.

Then she went downstairs and turned the TV on to see what was going on in the world. She never got to the news because the CBS movie was one of Jordan's and she sat, mesmerized, as she always did when she saw him on the screen. Or in person, which wasn't often nowadays, just when he was passing through on his way to Europe or Africa. Last she knew, he'd been heading to Ceylon to shoot a film.

Her heart lurched at the sight of him. She melted when she heard his voice. She hugged a pillow when he looked in his inimitable way at the heroine, a look he'd given Sydney so many times. A tear fell down her cheek. Oh, Jordan, she thought, I can never love anyone again the way I loved you. Maybe I can never love anyone again at all.

She sighed, though it sounded more like a moan when the movie ended. She clicked it off and sat staring into space, wondering what kind of a fool she'd been.

She stood up and, as though sleepwalking, turned off the lights and went up to bed. Sliding between the smooth percale sheets, under the down comforter, she stared across the room looking at her reflection in the mirror.

Shape up, she told herself, looking at her tousled hair, at the sad mouth. If you were still with him, you wouldn't be sitting on the thirtieth floor in an office of your own in charge of the Sunday magazine section of one of New York's oldest, most respected, and dullest newspapers. Well, no one was ever going to say the magazine section was dull. They would soon sit up and take notice. And she couldn't be doing that as Jordan's wife.

Twenty Three

Long before the decorating was finished, Sydney and Mary knew their relationship was something special. Mary was a no nonsense kind of person, yet she had a wonderful sense of humor, and Sydney found herself laughing at work, something new to her. She'd always been so uptight, trying to please her father with jobs that went no place. Now, coming to work each day was a delight.

Denton Walker *was* interested in revamping the look of the Sunday section. He became so absorbed in the project that for a two-month period he gave up all his other assignments. He began to all but live in Sydney's office. He and Sydney and Mary arrived simultaneously at nine, spent the mornings together, and ate lunch together. Sydney soon decided that if she was going to get anything else accomplished, she had to find working space for Denton to get him out of her office.

She had known Denton since her days at Wellesley, when he'd been at Boston University. She'd met him through a friend; Amy McLaughlin, who was dating him rather steadily. Amy's sorority sisters threatened to suspend her because Den~ ton was black.

Actually, Denton was coffee-colored. He had more white in his background than black, Sydney surmised, because his features were Caucasian, but society decreed that Denton was not white. Denton never tried to pass for white; he was proud of his heritage.

He lived, however, in a white world. His father was the principal of a Charlotte, North Carolina, black high school and his mother taught English there. His father had a Ph.D. from Columbia and his mother a master's from NYU.

Blacks thought he lived too much in the white world and whites thought he was too dark to accept him. Except for Amy, who was madly in love with him. She thought he was the handsomest, gentlest, kindest, most intelligent man in the world.

Sydney thought he was, too. She could easily understand why Amy had flipped. But Denton was not ready for marriage and Amy was. Denton decided, after he'd received a BA in English, that he really wanted to be a photographer, and took himself off to France, leaving Amy either to wait for him or to find someone else. She did the latter.

By the time Sydney and Denton were thirty he had made a name for himself as one of France's foremost fashion photographers, commanding enormous sums of money, able to pick and choose his jobs. He decided it was time to return to his native land and see if he could succeed there as well. His fame preceded him, and offers from Vogue and Harper's Bazaar poured in. Within three years he had an elegant apartment in the East Eighties and more work than he could handle. Every model who posed for him fell for him, including the males.

Sydney knew nothing about his personal life since he and Amy had stopped seeing each other, but his career was high profile, and they'd always kept in touch, writing cards at Christmas and usually another letter or two throughout each year. "In lieu of a war, I'll work with you on a new format, Sydney."

"What's that supposed to mean?"

"I'm tired of photographing beautiful women."

"Poor boy," murmured Mary.

He glanced up at her from the floor where he sat surrounded by dozens of sketches. "If there were a war, I'd go give that a whirl. Action. Human interest."

"So, until one comes along, you'll give me some time?"

"Naw," he grinned at her. "You don't pay enough. I'm just doing this for a month or so until we get it off the ground, until you get the look you want."

"I don't even know what look I want."

He nodded. "Until you get a look the three of us flip for, whatever it may be."

"I want a new name for it, too. Not the Sunday section of *The New York Chronicle.*"

"That's a mouthful," Denton agreed.

Sydney left Denton and Mary and phoned Miranda Collins, who had never heard of Sydney, but there probably wasn't a person in the United States who had not heard of Miranda Collins. She was the anchor for the "CBC Morning Show." She had begun as a writer, filling in when Giselle Martin, the token woman, was on assignment. Audiences loved Miranda.

Pretty soon Giselle was gone and Miranda worked with Hank Parton. But within a year Hank left, too, and it was Miranda's show, the first time in history a woman was the anchor of a morning TV show. Sydney took for granted that all the rumors she'd heard were true. Miranda ate co-anchors. Miranda cared for nothing but power and position. Well, you had to be a shark to get to the top in New York.

When Sydney explained who she was to Miranda's secretary, Miranda phoned her back.

"You want to do an article about me?"

"No," Sydney said. "I have other things in mind. Is there any chance we could have lunch soon?"

She heard pages riffling before Miranda answered. "My calendar is full for the next two weeks. Is there a hurry?"

"Sort of. How about dinner?"

"I go to bed by nine," Miranda said, and Sydney could tell she was smiling. . "Six-thirty. My place." She gave Miranda her address. She could hear Miranda talking to someone in the background. "Mrs. Hamilton?" she said to Sydney. "Really, I don't think your paper and I..."

Miranda was noted for her liberal leanings, although her morning show was objective about its political reporting. But one could tell from the people she had on her show what her political bent was.

"My daughters are well behaved, and I'll serve you the most perfect soufflé you've ever had."

Sydney had asked Mary to find out what Miranda's favorite foods were, just in case.

Miranda laughed. "You do your homework, anyhow. Okay. How about Wednesday at six-thirty?"

Sydney returned to the outer office and said to Denton and Mary, "I want you to come to dinner Wednesday. Six-thirty."

"Six-thirty?" exclaimed Denton. "No. one eats at that hour."

"My kids do and Miranda Collins goes to bed at nine."

"Miranda Collins? What's this about?"

"Come find out. I want her to meet the two of you."

Mary Kelley's eyes bulged. "I didn't know people really lived like this," she said.

Ashley and Juliet were drinking cider in front of the fireplace. Ashley, her golden hair straight and fine, was dressed in a dark plaid skirt with a navy blue sweater and a Peter Pan collar. She looked like the perfect little girl. Juliet, her curly raven hair uncontrollable, always looked like she'd just done something slightly naughty. She ran around in her stockinged feet, hating to be imprisoned by shoes. Her skirt was gray flannel and her sweater red, but she didn't look like she'd come from the same home as Ashley. She was mussed and wrinkled and full of the devil.

When introduced to visitors, Ashley was the very picture of politeness, holding her hand out, looking directly in the eyes of the guest and shaking hands, saying as though she meant it, "I'm pleased to meet you." Juliet never stuck her hand out and looked as though she were suspicious of the caller.

Guests found Ashley extremely attractive, but the one they remembered was Juliet.

Sometimes the girls made Sydney nervous because they never fought. They never even argued. She thought that abnormal, remembering the times Evan had played tricks on her, or when she screamed at him, calling him a bumble head when he hadn't done something to her satisfaction. Ashley and Juliet were as unlike as two sisters could be, yet it was perhaps that very differentness that made them so close. They thought like twins, understanding each other's thoughts even though they didn't think alike very often.

Denton, who treated the girls as adults, and Mary were already there when Miranda arrived, wearing a long mink coat that reached to her ankles. Flakes of snow still clung to the fur.

She was more stunning in person than she was on TV. She looked younger and had a grace that one didn't see as she sat behind the anchor desk.

Sydney introduced Mary and Denton and her children.

Miranda seemed delighted. "Oh, how lovely! This isn't a formal dinner then!" One could tell by the way she surveyed her surroundings that she was impressed. "What a charming apartment," she exclaimed, walking over to the fireplace and stretching her hands out in front, of it, warming herself. "I walked over," she said, "since it's only half a dozen blocks."

Her hair was dripping with the dampness of the melted flakes. She tossed her head in the air and sat down on the hassock in front of the fireplace, turning the back of her head to the fire. "It'll dry in a couple of minutes."

Denton fixed-her a Scotch and soda, with a twist of lemon.

"These are my assistants," Sydney said. "But I thought we might get to know each other a bit before we get down to business after dinner."

Since Miranda had a nine o'clock bedtime, Sydney had ordered dinner served at seven. From the lively flow of conversation she could tell that Denton and Mary and Miranda were getting along well.

After the soufflé, salad, and French bread, with crepes suzette for dessert, the little girls bade the guests good night and disappeared.

Sydney said, "Coffee and business in the living room?"

She explained to Miranda that she had taken over the Sunday section, that she was going to change it completely and gave her a few examples of ideas she had already set in motion.

She asked Denton to explain what he envisioned for the magazine visually. And then she said to Miranda, "You're the best interviewer in the business. You know that. The whole country knows it. I'd like you to write for us."

Miranda laughed loudly. "Write?"

"If you'd rather, just give us a tape from an interview. I wouldn't commit you to one a week, but how about two a month? It would be our main feature. *Miranda Collins Interviews.* We'll get people hardly anyone ever gets.

Between the influence of the paper and your clout, we'll get people other journalists would kill for."

Miranda leaned back in the overstuffed chair, crossed her long, shapely legs, and sipped her coffee.

After a few moments of silence in which the only sound was the crackling of the fire, she smiled and said, "I don't have enough hours in my day for all I have to do. Why should I take this on?"

Sydney shrugged her shoulders. "Not money, though I can pay you very well. Vanity? Your ego, I'd think, should already be fairly well fed. I don't have a reason. I just hoped it might interest you."

"So, you get this outrageously handsome, talented man, and this sharp young woman and corner me in a cozy family scene and hone in on something I've done all my life. I started out as a behind-the-scenes writer, you know."

"And got next to no credit for it," Mary chimed in.

"It can even be an in-depth interview with someone you've talked to on the air. Show us something about these people that most people don't know. I don't mean delve into anything unpleasant. You never do that in interviews, which is one of the reasons, I think, for your success. I don't have to tell you what to do. You've got it down better than anyone ever has."

"What's the focus of this-what is it? A magazine?"

"Focus," said Mary. "That's a great name for it."

Focus debuted March fifteenth, with a glamorous Denton Walker photograph of Miranda Collins on the cover. By the following week, advertisers were clamoring for space.

Within six months it overshadowed every other aspect of the paper, and earned more in advertising per page than any other New York City paper.

Sydney moved Mary into the office next to hers, making Mary her assistant and hiring a new girl, Andrea, who served as secretary to both of them. Denton had left for Indonesia, and what he thought were the rumblings of political discontent. By that time Mary was head over heels for him, though she told Sydney she knew it was hopeless. "He's photographed the world's most beautiful women. I don't stand a chance."

So she was surprised to receive weekly letters from him.

Sydney had seen little of Adam since their lunch in early January. In late May, when *Focus*'s success was assured, when Oliver had stopped by Sydney's office and complimented her, Adam came up to her office. Sydney and Mary were bent over her desk, studying a layout, when he knocked on the open door and asked, "Is this where the successful girls hang out?"

He glanced at Mary. "You've come up in the world quickly."

Mary smiled at him. "You told me I would."

He nodded. "I'm often right."

Sydney found herself glad to see him.

"I've come to see if I can talk you into dinner," he said to Sydney.

When she hesitated, he turned to Mary, "You've had dinner with me. Tell her I'm not a big bad wolf, that I didn't seduce you and that I gave you great advice, which is one of the reasons why you're where you are today."

Mary nodded. "That's all true."

"Why?" Sydney asked.

Adam cocked his head to the side and studied her. "I would just like the pleasure of your company for a longer time than lunch."

Sydney returned his smile. "If you can make it after eight."

"Ah, ever the good mother. Of course I can make it after eight. Even after nine, if that suits you better."

"I might fall asleep on you then. And I'd be so hungry I wouldn't be pleasant company."

"How about Friday?" he said.

Sydney wondered if his wife would object. The beginning of his weekend and he was taking the boss's daughter to dinner?

When he picked her up Friday evening, he wore a gray suit with a black-and-gold paisley tie and Sydney thought he looked elegant, a word she'd never applied to him before. She was glad she had switched to a more feminine dress, a turquoise sheath. The only jewelry she wore were large silver earrings that spun when she tossed her head.

"Wow," Adam said. "You look terrific."

Hints of summer were in the air, the leaves losing their spring green and turning darker. Park Avenue looked like a mirage in the lamplight. A taxi awaited them and, as they drove across the city, Adam said, "I wonder why anyone ever lives anyplace but here."

Sometimes Sydney wondered that, too, except she remembered how Los Angeles felt in winter, when snow filled the New York skies and sun lit the golden California landscape. But LA never had excited her the way New York did. No place else ever charged her with so much energy. Ideas poured forth from her here, but in California she languished.

They dined at Passpartout's, where a trio played music from the forties and early fifties and the steak Diane was the smoothest Sydney had ever tasted.

It was the first time, it seemed to her, that Adam had not treated her condescendingly. He poured nothing but praise on her, admiring how quickly she had caught the public's attention with *Focus*, and how wonderful it looked.

"The look is Denton Walker's," Sydney said. "I'm thrilled with what he came up with. I hope we can keep it up now that he's gone."

They talked work all through dinner. Sydney found it stimulating to be with Adam, to talk shop, to be with someone else as consumed with the paper as she was, who understood the hassles and the thrills.

While they waited for dessert, Adam asked, "Dance?"

He moved with grace and expertise, holding her lightly until the trio segued into something slower. Then he pulled her closer, murmuring with the music, "they're singing songs of love…"

Sydney was terribly aware of him. His hand in the middle of her back held her lightly but firmly, his hand around hers felt good. His leg, guiding hers, was closer than it needed to be. And she knew he was thinking of her as a woman, at least while they danced.

Scattered applause indicated an intermission, and Sydney was relieved when Adam, still holding her hand, led her back to the table.

"Do they sing them for you, Sydney?"

Her fork poised in midair, she asked, "Sing what?"

"Songs of love."

She felt a shiver across her shoulders and down her spine. Oh, shit, she didn't want anything personal with a man. She didn't have time for that. And certainly not, of all things, a married man-and someone who worked for her father.

"I've had it with love," she answered, savoring the taste of the pears in wine. "I have too much to do as it is. I couldn't fit a man into my life."

He sipped his coffee and continued to stare at her. "That's not what I asked. You're answering cerebrally. I asked if the songs of love are ever for you."

"I'm not lonely," Sydney said, circumventing his question again.

"Lonely! Ha!" He picked up his fork and began to eat his Black Forest cake.

"What does that tone of voice mean?" She knew she should never ask that, should never let the conversation veer this way.

"Living with someone doesn't alleviate loneliness," he said. "I've been lonelier married than I ever was single."

Sydney stared out at the empty dance floor. She was not going to follow that up with a question. She was not going to make any remark at all, nothing personal between her and Adam.

They finished their dessert in silence. Adam ordered more coffee.

"I see your picture in other papers' society columns. You attend opening nights. You go to charitable functions. You're always on the arm of some man."

"Probably Monday," she said. "Monday Pearson's been a friend for years. He dates bimbos, usually, just so he can take them to bed. I can't figure why else he'd date so many brainless creatures. Instead of bringing them along to his opening nights, or any opening nights, I think he wants someone he can expose to the public and not be ashamed of. Well, I suppose that's not fair to Monday. He and I always have a good time, never run out of things to talk about, and laugh a lot."

"So neither he nor anyone else has locked up your heart?"

"God, you make it sound so romantic. No. I really have no interest in that, Adam. I have my daughters and my career. No man would put up with me. I want to do things on my own. Men don't like to be second fiddles." '

"Which women have historically been?"

She looked at him. "Well, well. I didn't expect that from you. I'm impressed."

"I'd like to impress you. I don't think I ever have."

"Well, Daddy thinks the sun rises and sets on you. Isn't one in the family enough?"

Adam didn't answer. Instead, he shoved his chair back and stood up, reaching for her. "Another dance?"

When his arm went around her and his body moved against hers as they danced, it was the first time since Jordan that she'd responded so strongly to a man.

She looked up at him and smiled, wondering if he were aware he was doing this to her. "What's your wife doing while you're out with another woman?"

"I wondered when you'd get around to that," he murmured. -

He didn't give her an answer.

When they left the restaurant he started to hail a cab, but Sydney said, "Are you averse to walking? It's a beautiful night."

Adam reached out and took her hand. "Suits me."

As they walked along, Sydney felt happy. "I've had a lovely time tonight, Adam."

"You say it as though it surprises you."

"True. It has. Do you know, I don't even know where you live."

"We could walk past it," he said.

"Let's not," Sydney said. "So, it's in midtown."

"I'm in the phone book."

"I've never been that curious."

"Maybe now you will be."

She glanced at him, "Maybe I will. That would be too bad, wouldn't it?"

Again, he gave her no answer, but he tucked her hand through his arm. There was little traffic along the avenue, and the air was spring soft. It took them over an hour to reach Sydney's brownstone. "Do you want to come in?" she asked.

"Whatever I want, I don't think I will," Adam answered. "I'll just continue walking home."

The next morning he appeared in her office about half a minute after she'd arrived.

"I think you ought to know I didn't get to sleep until nearly five."

Sydney raised her eyebrows. "Is that why you look like hell?"

"It is indeed," he said, turning on his heel and disappearing.

She wasn't surprised. For the first time since Jordan had left her bed, Sydney had lain awake wondering what it would be like to have Adam next to her, to feel his hands on her body.

And she had had trouble sleeping, too.

Twenty Four

Later that day, Monday called her. He'd just returned from Hollywood, and needed to catch up on what had been happening. He'd picked up the *Chronicle* at the airport and was thrilled with *Focus*.

"It's smashing," he said. "Last I heard you were working hard on it, not even sure where you were going. I hope New York is appreciative. It's the only worthwhile thing in that rag of your father's."

Neither Monday nor Jordan could condone the conservative bent of the paper. Maybe she could mention that to Adam, see what she could do to influence him, if not her father.

"I suppose you already have a date for it, but 'Olive Branches' opens this week, as I'm sure you know."

"I don't have a date for it," she said. "Nothing opens in the summer. I've never even heard of it."

"Off Broadway," Monday said. "Friend of mine's in it. The world's peculiar, Sydney, or at least the men in New York are. I can never understand why all your nights aren't busy."

"Spoken like a true friend," Sydney smiled whenever Monday called her.

"We're on for Friday then? Supper afterwards?"

"Friday's my worst day, the day Focus goes to press."

"Are you saying no?"

"Monday, have I ever said no to you?"

"Well," she could tell he was smiling, "maybe I'd better learn other questions to ask."

"Why don't you come over here sometime during the week, and see my office. Come see what I'm doing."

"Perhaps I will. It'll be good to see you, Sydney. It always is."

The rest of that day and until four the next, Sydney was very conscious of not seeing Adam. Not that she ever saw much of him, but now she was aware he was in the building, twenty-four floors below, making no attempt to see her.

At four the next afternoon Monday did breeze in, wearing wine red slacks and a bright yellow shirt, sleeves rolled up. He greeted her with a bear hug, gathering her in his arms and swinging her around. "My, my, you sure look important in this big office."

"And you, dear friend, are a wonder to behold. I swear you get handsomer as the years go by."

"Sydney, it's my brain I want you to love."

"It's your brain I do love. Actually you're too tall and too skinny and too … too blond. Too Hollywood-looking for me."

He whooped with laughter and set her on her feet, surveying the room, which was cluttered with piles of papers on the soft Aubusson rug.

Mary entered, her hands full of folders, her glasses askew, her lipstick worn off by this time in the afternoon. As soon as she saw Monday, she stopped, "Oh, sorry, Sydney…" and started to back out of the room.

"No, come in and meet one of the treasures of my life."

Sydney introduced them and Mary's eyes widened. "Monday Pearson, the playwright?"

Monday nodded, pleased to have his name recognized.

"I loved "Wind Chimes."

It had opened last year and was still running.

At that moment, Adam appeared, also in shirtsleeves. He glanced first at Sydney, then at the piles of paper scattered around the room, then at Monday.· He never got around to Mary.

Sydney put a hand through Monday's arm and introduced him to Adam, who stretched out a' hand.

"Sydney's told me about you, Adam said.

"I hope not everything," Monday smiled. "Syd and I go way back."

"Adam's the managing editor of the paper," Sydney told Monday.

"Well, you must be very pleased with her success."

"She doesn't even come under my jurisdiction. I have nothing to do with the Sunday section, and certainly not with *Focus*. She's done it on her own, and for that I do admire her."

Sydney felt an inordinate amount of pleasure at Adam's words.

"I couldn't do it without my right hand here," she said, nodding at Mary. "She does everything. I suggest and she implements, not that she doesn't come up with great ideas, too."

"Her I do take credit for," Adam said. "I knew it wouldn't take her long to get a leg up the ladder."

"So you all have one big love fest here every day, huh?" Monday grinned. "Makes for nice working conditions."

Just then the phone rang and Sydney answered it. The other three went on conversing.

The call was from the publisher of *The Clevelana Plain Dealer*. Sydney had met him two years ago at the national newspaper conference, and tried to remember what he looked like.

"We like the looks of your *Focus*. We've been playing around, trying to come up with something interesting for Sundays ourselves. We've tried a couple of the other Sunday supplements but nothing really catches fire. How much you want for us to carry *Focus*, too?"

Sydney sat down. She'd never thought of that, of its stretching across the country. "I don't know," she said. "I'll have to talk to the people in charge of finances around here."

"Well, think about it. We'd like to introduce it Labor Day weekend. I'd appreciate your getting back to me by the end of next week, one way or another. We think it's dandy. You've done a terrific job. No one's ever come up with anything like it. Where do you get your ideas?"

Sydney shook her head. "Privileged information." she said, smiling into the phone. "I'm flattered, Mr. Jorgenson. I will get back to you by next Friday even if I don't have a definite answer."

"Of course, you realize how much you can increase your advertising rates if your customers get national coverage, don't you?"

"My, my," she said, hanging up.

"What are you grinning about? You look like the cat that swallowed the canary," Adam said.

She told them.

"This calls for a celebration. Come on, it's nearly five. You must have closing hours here. Let me buy you all a drink," Monday suggested.

The drinks led to dinner and, after that, Monday said, "Why don't we all go to see 'Olive Branches' Friday night?"

Sydney could have cut out his tongue.

Certainly Adam would decline.

But he didn't, and the next morning Mary said, "Should I get a new dress?"

In one way, Sydney was disappointed. She wanted Monday to herself. She wanted to hear about the West Coast, hear about Jordan, tell Monday all that had happened to her. In another way, she thought it would be fun to see Adam in a social situation again.

"Olive Branches" was awful. Monday's friend was fine, but the play itself was deplorable. Before the end of the second act, the four of them crept out of the theater.

The night was like most New York summer nights, hot and sticky, yet Sydney loved nights like this. They walked along the streets, four abreast, laughing and tearing apart the play.

Monday knew a little bar they'd never heard of and he led them to it, not too far from Chinatown.

Sydney observed Mary, who didn't look tired at all. You'd never know from looking at her that they'd put their baby to bed today. All the loose ends were tied up on Friday and nerves were always taut, but Mary seemed to relax and thoroughly enjoy herself. Except for lunches, Sydney had never shared social time with Mary, whose emerald dress made her hazel eyes a sparkling green. Monday's joie de vivre was always infectious.

Though Adam sat back in his chair and quietly sipped his drink, he obviously was enjoying himself, too, listening to Monday's witticisms and laughing with him. Somehow Sydney had thought they might clash, but Monday included Adam in the conversation, bringing him out. Adam, so sure of himself at work, was quiet socially. Sydney thought it might be because he felt out of his element around the Hamiltons.

Monday, on the other hand, seemed at home everyplace, and made others feel the same way. Such a nice man, Sydney thought, not for the first time. She was glad their friendship had outlasted her marriage.

Monday titillated them with stories of Hollywood, but insisted that New York was where he belonged. He had begun another play, and that's why he'd come back. He couldn't write in the land of the lotus-eaters. He needed the stimulation of New York.

"Come down to Oberon with me for the weekend," Sydney suggested. "The girls would love to see you, and I yearn to talk with you for hours."

"When are you going?"

"Don't faint. Eight o'clock of what is now today. Daddy has a plane now, you know. It's going to be waiting for me, or for us, if you will. It only takes an hour. You haven't been there in ages. Come on, Monday, we'll fly back early Monday morning.'"

He reached across the table, between Adam and Mary, and took her hand. "I would love to." He said to the others, "Oberon is the world's most idyllic place."

Sydney was delighted to think of having Monday to herself for the weekend. They'd go sailing, and the girls would climb all over him and he'd play croquet with them; losing on purpose. They'd all take a twilight sail. Then she and Monday would sit in the dark, looking out over the water, and she'd hear about Jordan. Or at least hear what Monday would have to say about Jordan.

After a midnight dip in the pool they'd have a drink before bed, and Monday would tell her vaguely what his next play was about.

She'd lie awake in bed, thinking of what he'd said about Jordan, seeing Jordan's face reflected in her mind's eye, wondering what he was really doing. Was he sleeping with some woman he'd made love to on the set that day? Was he happy and fulfilled? The only times she heard from him was when he phoned the girls and she'd hear his voice on the phone. He phoned them regularly when he was in the country, and he breezed through New York occasionally, but ever since she'd had the abortion she didn't see him except to take the girls over to the Plaza. She didn't want to get caught up in his life again. And it wasn't fair to either of them. He still sent her Christmas presents and remembered her birthday, but they had agreed that seeing each other did not permit them to really live their own lives. She imagined Jordan had made love to dozens of women since their breakup.

And she hadn't even kissed a man. Not really. She kissed Monday on the cheek. She pecked friends who escorted her on occasion. But, then, no man had really made overtures. No man had even attempted to kiss her. Six years and no men. She was thirty-three years old. Unexpectedly, she felt sorry for herself. She'd thought she had so much-Ashley and Juliet, exhilarating work, the people she worked with. Suddenly she felt deprived. She'd been denied love and sex, and she realized what she hadn't known in her youth: they were not one and the same. But she hadn't met a man who tempted her with either sex or love. She lived in a man's world, surrounded all day, year after year, by men. Yet none of those men dated her, none of them invited her to anything. . The men she had known as boys were either married or intimidated by her, she guessed. Or just not interested. For the first time since she'd left California, she felt unattractive. Maybe she was being unfair to herself. Most women married young and had only one man in their lives. She'd done that.

Did she need more than one man, even though he was no longer in her life? Did she really need sex? Did she need to feel attractive to some man? She had thought she wasn't like those women who didn't feel complete unless they saw themselves reflected in a man's eyes.

But mightn't it be nice to be kissed again? Wouldn't it feel good to have a man's hands run over her body, to feel a man's tongue on her breast? To know that she excited and fulfilled

Under the table, she felt Adam's leg brush hers. She glanced at him, but he was looking across the table at Monday, who was holding forth on something that was making Adam and Mary laugh.

She wondered about him. He'd said, last week, that he was lonelier married than he'd been unmarried. So his marriage wasn't fulfilling. Was anyone's? Did he find her attractive? And how did she feel about him?

She cast her thoughts aside and began to listen to Monday.

Twenty Five

Ashley and Juliet greeted Monday with open arms and wouldn't let go, clinging to him. The first thing Monday wanted, even before brunch, was a swim, and Ashley and Juliet ran to put on their suits, too. There was no such thing as a relaxing swim at Oberon-as long as the girls were around. Sydney and Monday went sailing in the afternoon and anchored in a cove where the girls cast fishing lines into the water. Sydney's shoulders began to burn and she knew she and Monday would be sore by the end of the weekend.

Big Mommy and Silvie enjoyed Monday as much as Sydney and the girls did. Oliver had flown down Friday afternoon, and though he joined the family for dinner, Sydney saw little of him the two days she was there.

Sunday morning they went horseback riding despite the fact that she and Monday had stayed up until well after two-the first time she'd seen him alone since he'd returned to New York. She deliberately hadn't asked him about Jordan, and Monday mentioned him only briefly, saying he'd seen him often, they'd talked over his new idea for a play, and he didn't think he was seriously involved with anyone. He spent weekends at Jordan's Malibu Beach home-there were usually only the two of them-and they'd solved the world's problems there.

"Unfortunately, the world wasn't listening," Monday grinned. "Of course now he's off to the Seychelles, or is it Africa again? He's been going over to Kenya rather regularly."

He himself had no one particular woman. Writing was a jealous mistress. Sure, he saw women all the time, but only on his terms. He couldn't stand to have one around all the time, not while he was writing and thinking. Not one who would make demands, and any in-depth relationship had its own agenda. Maybe after he won a Pulitzer he wouldn't feel so driven, and could concentrate on other things in life. But he wasn't sure. It would have to be a rare woman who gave him the space he needed, and the excitement he required. As it was now, as soon as the excitement began to dwindle he could pull out. All new relationships were exciting, but excitement soon palled.

"Yet you keep up friendships for years."

"Sure, because you can pull back in friendships. As soon as we begin to get on each other's nerves we can retreat to our other lives. Friendships last much longer than romances. Friendships don't demand the time, the agonizing gut-level emotions, except now and then. Sydney, do you know how wise it's been of you and me never to hop in the sack together?

"Don't think I haven't thought of it. I have. I imagine any man who knows you has thought of that. But once sex enters the picture, friendships change. I plan to value your friendship forever, however long that is. I'm never going to ruin it with a hasty toss in the hay, or even a longer affair. Uh-uh. You and me are going to last a long time. I need your friendship, as I need Jordy's. Friendships have to be nurtured. One doesn't take advantage of a friend. "

"I know some friendships that have turned into love and been great."

"Yeah, sure." They were sitting out by the pool, having taken the midnight swim that Sydney had known they would.

He was right. Much as she loved and treasured Monday she'd never had a desire to go to bed with him. She loved him, but wasn't in love with him. He lit up her life when he suddenly appeared, and she liked it that way.

"But if you don't let yourself become friends with a woman first it's only lust that gets the two of you together."

"So, what's wrong with that?" he grinned. "I still find it one of the more rewarding aspects of life."

She'd forgotten if it was. It had been a long time. Too long.

"What about Adam?" Monday asked.

"Adam? Oh, we just work together. Besides, he's married."

"You wouldn't know it from the way he looks at you."

"Really?"

"Come on, Sydney. You must be aware of it."

"Well, aside from his being married and a father, one doesn't screw around with the boss's daughter any more than you would with a friend."

Monday shook his head and sipped his Bailey's Irish Cream. "You're right, of course. But isn't there any man in particular for you, Sydney?"

"No man in particular. No men in general."

"It must be because you don't want one."

"Jordan's a hard act to follow."

Monday shook his head. It wasn't even chilly sitting out in wet bathing suits at midnight. "Have you had other men, not that it's any of my business?" "Only Jordan." Sydney's voice was soft. Anyone could tell from her tone that she was still in love with him.

"Cut bait," Monday said. "Go to bed with someone. You don't have to be in love. Women complicate sex and life so absurdly. But just go to bed with someone, Sydney. Give yourself that much. Feel a warm body next to you. If you want to be safe, choose someone you know from the start you can't have. Adam, for instance."

Sydney laughed. "I could no more try to seduce a married man than fly without wings."

"I'm not suggesting seduction. It can just happen. You'll know you won't get emotionally involved. So, you'll be safe that way. You'll both know before you even get horizontal that nothing can come of it, and you can even say it aloud. That'll make it easier in the morning when you both go to work at the same place."

"Oh, Monday, don't even talk that way."

"Well, he seems intelligent, and you're always a sucker for intelligence, I know that much. He's nice looking. A bit quiet, but he listens. Most men don't know how to listen."

"Monday, dear, you're a positively immoral influence." Yet, Sydney wasn't offended. She'd already been wondering what it would be like to be kissed by Adam.

In the morning, Nettie packed them a picnic lunch and they rode out beyond Martha's Forest, swimming in the little pond at the edge while the horses nuzzled the long clover. Both girls rode well, sitting erect in the saddle. Juliet had outgrown a pony, now that she was eight. She and Ashley were fearless, galloping ahead of their mother and Monday..

"Great girls, Sydney. I can see why it breaks Jordan's heart to have them so far away."

"That's right. Make me feel guilty."

"He's seldom home, anyhow. Why he makes movies that take him all over the world escapes me. But he thrives on it. If I were the father of those darlings, I couldn't stand to see them only a couple of times a year."

"He could see them every week if he wanted."

Monday nodded. "I suppose so, but he'd have to live three thousand miles closer."

"That's his choice."

"Not exactly. It's your choice, mainly. Most wives are content to live where their husband's work takes them."

"Or, if not content, willing."

"Sorry. I can tell I'm upsetting you, but then, my dear, you're not like most women."

"I'm not unique. More and more, you'll see women taking charge of their own lives."

Monday just looked at the sky and the trees as their horses walked along, side by side. After a while he said, "Oberon's one of the prettiest places in the world, I imagine."

"To me, it is."

When Sydney arrived at work Monday morning, Mary said, "I hear you had a great weekend."

"News travels fast. How in the world did you hear that?"

"Monday called me last night." Mary had a wide grin on her face. "Ah, so," Sydney said as she sat down behind her desk and smiled up at her assistant.

"Ah so, indeed. He woke me up."

"And you didn't object?"

"I objected only to not being able to get back to sleep for three hours."

"Phone calls late at night do that. But a word of warning. I love Monday. He's one of my favorite people in the whole world. But he doesn't believe in long-term relationships. He breezes in and out of women's lives like ... like a breeze. Sometimes even a gale force, I'd imagine, but he does sweep right through."

Mary made a face. "I'm ready for a little diversion, temporary or not. I don't want to get married yet. Not when I'm in the midst of the most exciting career I can imagine. But, thanks for warning me. Personally, I can't imagine I'm in the same ball park as all those Hollywood starlets he dates."

"I don't know who he dates now, but he used to date the stupidest, most vacuous girls I ever met."

"Maybe he's ready for an attractive, brainy, with-it woman."

Sydney reached for papers on her desk.

"Don't I wish I believed what I just said," Mary said as she handed her another sheaf of papers. "Well, anyhow, I'm glad you had a good weekend."

"Is that what I just heard?" Adam's voice came from the doorway.

Sydney looked up to see him, his shirtsleeves rolled up despite the air-conditioning. "You had a good weekend?"

"Indeed I did. Wonderful." -

Mary said, "I have calls to make. Lunch?"

Sydney nodded; and Mary disappeared.

"She beat me to the gun. That's just what I'd come about."

"Sorry, Adam. You heard the lady."

He walked across the room, his glasses glinting in the morning sunlight. The tips of his fingers, Sydney noted, were stained from cigarettes. He had a nice build. Traces of gray at his temples. His eyes, while not cerulean like Jordan's, were a clear blue.

"What else can I do for you, Adam?"

He shook his head quickly back and forth. "Nothing, now that you're already lunching." He turned and left.

As Sydney settled down to work, she wondered what his wife was like.

She and Mary would talk over long-range ideas at lunch, but today she had to begin work on layout and see what articles they had lined up. Miranda Collins had certainly been a great idea. Her features were always on time, always exactly the right length, always amusing or insightful.

Sydney glanced at her watch. Miranda would be off the air by now. She called her at the TV station, before she got involved with the day, and made a date for lunch Wednesday. Maybe some weekend she'd invite Miranda to Oberon. She'd become quite fond of her. She and Mary both had. Miranda's high falutin' reputation, as far as Sydney could see, was unfounded. Sydney had twice visited her at CBC, watching the show live. It had been great fun. Miranda and the people she worked with laughed a lot, and they helped each other. There were last minute jitters, coffee breaks during commercials, an easy camaraderie on the set. Sydney had not once seen Miranda lose her temper or shout at anyone. From six-thirty to nine she was unapproachable, in that she concentrated on who she was talking to and what was coming next. She was well informed about her guests, asked intelligent, probing questions as much as anyone could in the ten-minute interview period allotted, and seemed calmer than she was off-camera, where she was often frenetic.

Some weekend, Sydney thought, she'd invite Miranda and Mary to Oberon. It dawned on her lately that her life was too narrow. There was nothing in it but her daughters and *Focus*.

She went downstairs to talk to the financial department and then came back up to the thirtieth floor and walked down the hall to her father's office.

They'd flown back on the plane yesterday evening, but they seldom talked. Sydney wondered if he'd handed *Focus* over to her to get her off his back and out of his sight.

"Daddy," she said, sitting in the chair across from him. He looked imposing behind his enormous desk, New York skyscrapers outlined behind him. "Last week *The Cleveland Plain Dealer* called and asked if they could carry *Focus*."

Oliver glanced up at her. "Hm." "

"Finance gave me a figure they thought might be fair," she added, and named it. "I don't think that's enough."

Her father's eyes sparkled. "So, they like it, huh?"

"If we could interest more papers we could, of course, increase the rate of our ads. It might spread across the country."

Oliver coughed. "I appreciate your initiative, Sydney, but really, just because Cleveland ... I mean, Cleveland is not the country."

"It's one of the more respected papers."

Oliver nodded. "But Cleveland?"

Sydney shrugged and her voice had a defensive tone. "Well, it's a beginning."

Oliver nodded. "It is that, Sydney. So, I'll tell you what. It's your baby. You charge what you want. Whether it sinks or swims is really immaterial to me. Do what you want."

So, that was it. He thought the Sunday magazine section was nothing. Or at least had been.

She stood up. "We're out of the red, you know."

"I do know. So, you decide everything, Sydney."

How come that didn't make her feel good? She'd felt great when she'd come in to his office with the news.

She took the elevator down to the sixth floor and headed for Adam's office, waiting until he finished 'conferring with two men. Then she went in, closed the door, and sat down, telling him what had happened and asking his advice.

"The big city papers all have their own Sunday sections," Adam said, "but you watch *Focus*. It'll be in papers like *The Portland Oregonian, The Detroit Free Press, The Sacramento Bee, The Omaha Nebraskan*. You'll see, Sydney. Cleveland is just the beginning. *Focus* is going to fan out across the country."

Sydney found herself sitting straighter, her eyes sparkling. "Oh, Adam, do you really think so?"

He lit a cigarette. "I knew with the first edition that you had something special. Yes, I think so. National advertising is going to pour in. You may end up being the big money-maker around here."

"Is all this a promise?"

Adam's eyes softened. "It's what I would promise if I could, Sydney."

"My kids aren't home during the summer, you know. I could go out to dinner one night."

He leaned over and looked at his calendar.

"Wait," she said, leaning toward him. "I'll say it aloud, but you must already sense it. Before you say yes to dinner, you know and I know that we may be playing with fire."

His gaze met hers but she couldn't tell what he might be thinking. His eyes flickered to his calendar again. "You put *Focus* to bed on Friday. Want to celebrate then?"

"I leave Saturday morning fur Oberon, you know. Last Friday night was too late. I was tired all weekend."

"Let's make it tomorrow, then."

Sydney smiled and stood up. When she reached the door and put her hand on the knob, Adam said, "Sydney, as for this fire you refer to, I really don't mind if I get singed."

Gooseflesh sped down her left arm and across both shoulders, inching down her spine.

Twenty Six

"We go our separate ways," Adam said.

"How does this affect your sons?"

"I don't know that it does. We all dine together at least three times a week. We go to church together Sundays. But Shirley and I wouldn't have anything to talk about if we didn't have the boys. She's talking lately about wanting to get a job."

"What kind?"

"Who knows? Something to occupy her mind. I think it sounds like a great idea. Sometimes, even though we hardly ever talk, she just seems to sit around watching TV, waiting for me to get home, as though I'll light up her life."

Sydney finished her Camembert and sipped her espresso. "And do you?"

He laughed. "You've known me for how many years? Could I light up anyone's life? All I want to do when I get home is take off my shoes, put my feet up, and fall asleep in front of the television. I use all my energy at work." '

Sydney doubted that. But energy had to be refueled, and his marriage didn't sound as though it kindled much for either of them.

"Where did you go on your vacation last year?"

He'd told her his wife chose their vacation places.

"A cabin on Lake Umbagog in Maine, on the New Hampshire border."

"What did you do?"

"The boys and I fished. We all went canoeing, some motor boating. I took a gun and the boys and I shot at targets."

"What did your wife do?"

His eyes widened. "I don't know. She took walks and read a lot. Why in the world do you want to know what I do on vacations, Sydney?"

She shrugged. "I really know so little about you outside of work. I thought maybe it's about time."

"There is no me outside of work."

"I can't quite believe that. There's you tonight. There was you last week at 'Olive Branches', and everyone thought you were very good company. I haven't talked with you more over the years because I thought we'd fight about everything, but certainly not because you lacked personality."

He looked surprised "What's there for you and me to fight about?"

Sydney gave a little laugh. "Politics, guns and gun laws, war, the kinds of books we read, religion."

"What about sex? Do you think we'd fight about that?"

She looked at him. "So you've thought about that, too."

They were both quiet, staring into each other's eyes. "I first met you when you were about seventeen years old," he said. "That's what, fifteen years ago? "More or less."

"Sydney, I've thought about you that way ever since."

"Why, Adam Yarborough!" She reached her leg out and brushed it along his, but just barely. "Until this last couple of weeks, I thought there was no chance at all." Again, silence. Sydney sipped her coffee, her level gaze meeting his.

"And now?"

He reached out and put a hand over hers. "Now, I think about it all the time."

"Don't you realize this would be destined to go nowhere? What if I became demanding? Women in sexual relationships almost always do, Monday tells me. I'm your boss's daughter. What if you got fired over a thing like this? Would it be worth it? A roll in the hay couldn't be worth wrecking your professional life. "

"I'd be willing to risk far more than that," he said, his voice husky.

"I thought there wasn't much in your life beyond your job."

"There wasn't."

"What if we do… and it's not so good. How do we face each other tomorrow?"

"God, Sydney, do you have to bring up all these possibilities ahead of time?"

"I've never gone to bed with anyone other than Jordan."

Adam sat back. "Well, I'll be damned."

Sydney pushed back her chair. "Take me home, Adam."

At her door, he asked, "Am I coming in?"

"You decide that," she said, twisting the key.

"I've wondered what your place looks like. How you live." He followed her in.

"You've never been to my parents' apartment?"

"Sure, but that's not you."

Before she could turn the lights on, he reached for her, turning her around, pulling her to him. She moved into his arms, felt his lips on hers, felt the warmth and the taste of their after dinner coffee, his lips opening hers, his tongue searching, and she sighed.

"That feels so good," she said, her voice a whisper.

He held her tighter as his mouth met hers again. She could feel his heart beating, felt his leg moving against hers, his arms holding her close.

Her arms wound around his neck. He kissed her eyelids and her neck and then he took her head in his hands, kissing her so she felt the kiss deep inside her belly.

"I've wanted to do that for years," Adam said, his voice soft.

Sydney heard her breath coming hard. "Wow," she said, taking his hand and leading him into the living room. She turned a light on.

Not letting go of her hand, Adam looked around. "This isn't what I thought it would be."

"How different?"

"It's more feminine than I expected."

"I think I've just been insulted. I'm not supposed to be womanly?"

"I don't think I meant that."

"Would you like a brandy?"

"I don't need one."

They stood gazing at each other, smiling, and he pulled her to him again, holding her close, their breath intermingling. He gave her a little kiss and looked at her again, his eyes searching for answer.

"Where's your bedroom?" he asked.

"Second door on the right, upstairs."

He picked her up, his head thrown back, laughing, and took the stairs two at a time. He put her down so she could turn on the light. "Let me undress you," he murmured.

He began to unbutton her blouse, slowly, kissing her as he did so. She slid out of it, tossing it to the floor. His hands moved around her and expertly undid her bra. Then he stopped kissing her and stood back. "I want to look at you."

She stood there, feeling beautiful for the first time in years.

"Oh, God," he said, bending over to run his tongue over her left breast. A little moan escaped her, and she reached out to undo the buttons on his shirt. For just a second before their naked bodies touched, they looked again into each other's eyes. "It's been so long." Sydney murmured as her breasts met his chest.

"I had no idea. I thought you were probably in bed with every man I saw you with."

Sydney didn't respond but began to unbuckle his belt as he slid her skirt down her legs, onto the floor. She stepped out of it and unzipped his fly, her fingers touching his rigidity. He sighed deeply.

They stood there, until he pulled her close, his hands caressing her breasts. She pushed herself against him, loving the feel of him, of his maleness.

He leaned down and picked her up again, carrying her to the bed, kissing her all the time. When he lay next to her, his hands were all over her, gentle but urgent, his mouth kissing her ear and her neck, running kisses down her arm, across her belly, finally taking her breast in his mouth, nibbling her, his tongue stroking her as she began to move rhythmically against him, her hands exploring him.

"Shit Sydney, how can I be a good lover when you do that to me?"

"Come into me," she whispered. "Be a good lover later."

He straddled her, moving against her, until she was afire, pulling him down to her, rising to meet him. There was no feeling in the world to equal this. He knew just how to excite her, his hands reaching for her buttocks as his tongue met hers, undulating together in a rhythm that pulsed through her blood. She could feel the warm tide rising within her, felt him frenzy her with desire, closed her eyes as stars burst across her horizon, and she cried, "Don't stop!"

Afterward, they lay there, breathing heavily. He rolled from her, onto his side, and they were quiet.

Finally he said, "Jesus, Sydney, I never dreamed it could be this good. Not the first time, that's for sure."

"Ah, are you implying there'll be a second?"

His fingers feathered across her belly. "I could become addicted."

"I guess there are worse addictions." She took his fingers and kissed them, each one. "You have a beautiful body," he said.

"I like yours, too, or could you tell?"

He laughed. "No one's ever told me that."

Sydney sat up and threw her legs over the side of the bed.

"Are you leaving me?"

"I'm going downstairs to get wine, only promise me you won't leave yet."

"Yet?" His eyes smiled at her. "I promise."

When she returned, Adam was in the shower. She sat on the bed and plumped a pillow behind her. When he appeared in the doorway, he said, "Jesus, are you ever the picture of wanton delight."

He walked over and took the glass of wine from her, leaning over to kiss her forehead. "Come back to bed, Sydney. I want to kiss you every place that's kissable, and then some."

Sydney jumped onto the bed. "That's an invitation I have no intention of refusing." She cuddled close to him. "I imagine you've never been six years without sex, have you? You can't possibly know how good it feels after all this chastity and deprivation."

"I intend to make up for all this celibacy," he said. "Maybe even in one night."

She started to ask him if he shouldn't be going home. It was nearly midnight, but she figured that wasn't her business. And besides she wanted what he'd promised. She wanted to be kissed all over. She wanted his tongue every place it could go. She wanted to feel him enter her again. And again.

It was after three before they fell asleep. They might have slept the clock around if it hadn't been for the alarm, which buzzed at seven.

The first thing Sydney wanted to ask was what he would tell his wife? But before she even opened her eyes she figured his marriage was something separate.

They had moved, of course, to a new level, she and Adam, but right now it had nothing to do with his wife. At least, she didn't.

What he told Shirley was between the two of them.

"It's changed forever, you know," were his first words as he stretched to kiss her. "That was the most athletic night I've had in years."

"Are you complaining?" She feathered her fingers down his cheek. "I can't remember when I enjoyed anything more. Good sex makes me feel physically marvelous."

"And that was good sex," he said.

"Indeed."

His fingers played with her right breast, and he leaned down to kiss it. His hand slid down her belly, down her thighs and as his tongue curled around her breast she felt the fire rekindle deep inside her.

"It's seven o'clock," she murmured. "Don't start something you can't finish."

"There's a first time for everything," he said as he stopped kissing her long enough to answer. "I haven't been late to work once in all my years at the *Chronicle*."

"Well," she said, moving as his fingers explored her, "it's too late to stop this, that's for sure."

"This time," he murmured, "you get on top."

It was her favorite position.

They showered together afterward. Sydney giggled, "My maid is going to be shocked. I've never awakened with a man here before." She decided to wear the bright red jersey. It clung, not the kind of outfit she usually wore to work. And red shoes to match. Adam laughed at her attire.

Bran muffins, orange juice, and coffee were waiting on the dining-room table. Sydney said, "I never eat more, but I imagine you eat a hearty breakfast."

"Not today," he said. "Maybe we shouldn't show up at the same time."

"Oh, come on," Sydney smiled.. "How many thousands of people work in that building? Maybe we met a block away, or in front of the building. We don't even get off at the same floor."

"That does put me in my place, doesn't it? I'm on the sixth and you're up with the higher echelons."

"Don't start that." Sydney spread strawberry jam on her muffin. They hadn't even sat down, but stood, ready to leap at any moment. Adam drank his coffee black. "You know perfectly well that next to Daddy you're the one who has the most influence."

Adam nodded. "I do know that. It makes life very pleasant, even when I'm not at work. A kid from Peoria influencing the minds of hundreds of thousands of New Yorkers."

"How about the world?"

"You're the one going to make an imprint on the world, you with your *Focus*." Sydney grinned. "It is pretty impressive, isn't it? Do you really think other papers will fall in line behind Cleveland?"

"Just watch," Adam said. "Come on, let's go. I can still keep my record of being on time if we run."

"I should get a car, just so I have someone to drive us to work at times like this."

"This implies there will be more times like last night?"

"Isn't that up to you? I think it's pretty obvious I've enjoyed myself."

As they headed out the door, without having seen the maid at all, Adam said, "Does it bother you that I'm married?"

Sydney thought a moment as they walked along, hoping an empty cab might come by. "I don't like liars, and you'll have to lie to your wife."

Adam said nothing.

"Won't you? Have to lie?" They stood at the corner and waved as cabs rushed past. Finally, one pulled over and Adam opened the door. Sydney stepped in and he followed, taking her hand after giving directions to the cabbie. "Probably. Yes, I'll lie to her."

Sydney could tell by the look in his eyes that he wanted to kiss her again. But he didn't. He settled back in the cab that honked its way through New York traffic, pressing her hand tightly. She hadn't felt this good in a long time.

The next time Sydney saw him was' at four in the afternoon. . She and Mary had worked hard all day, even during lunch. She'd spent over half the day on the phone. Andrea, her secretary, said, "I don't think the phone's been quiet a total of ten minutes."

When Adam appeared in her doorway, Sydney told Andrea, "Hold any calls." Adam closed the door behind him. "Come here," he said. Sydney stood up and walked over to him, slowly, into his arms, surrendering herself to his kisses.

"Christ, one night in bed and you're all I've thought of the entire day. I don't even know what the hell tomorrow's headlines are going to be."

"It affected me just the opposite. Where I got the energy to do so much work I just don't know," she teased.

He reached out and held her face in his hands. "I want you to know that I've never had as great a night. Never has it been so good. Never. Not ever."

He didn't look as though he'd been up three quarters of the night.

Sydney said, "I'm going home from work, have a snack and fall sound asleep, I expect."

"So, I shouldn't even phone you?"

"Adam, don't phone me from your, home, ever. Okay? When I talk with you, I don't want to picture you there. That's a part of your life that I don't even want to think about."

"Don't ever feel you're second fiddle."

"What I'm feeling is we had a great time. I'd like to do it again if you can get away and you want to. I don't feel any strings. I'm not experiencing any guilt about committing adultery, which is just what I did."

"I did, too, you know."

"Your morality is something I don't have to answer for. But, I'm going to be able to sleep at night without feeling guilty. I liked what we did, and I'm not getting hung up about it."

"Liked?"

She smiled. "Loved." Her voice was soft.

He glanced around her office. "Someday, I'm going to come in here and lay you down on this elegant carpet and we'll screw ourselves silly, right here in your office."

"Promises, promises," she laughed as she reached up to kiss him. "Now, get out. I still have work to do."

"Tomorrow night, before you leave for Oberon?"

"Fridays are my busiest days."

"I won't stay overnight."

"Take me out to dinner first?"

"Ah, you can be bought."

She laughed and drew back, turning and heading to her desk. "Leave the door open. Andrea's already wondering why it's been closed so long." ,

"She hasn't a clue."

"You're right. Adios."

But after Adam had left she stared for several minutes at the spot where he had stood. God, it was so pleasant to think of having sex again tomorrow. It had been so long, so empty.

Maybe now she could even watch Jordan's movies and not weep.

She bent over the papers on her desk but what surprised her most was what an ardent, considerate lover Adam was. She would never have suspected it. He had never seemed to have any tenderness.,

Tomorrow night. How lovely. Tomorrow night he would touch her again, and she would feel his kisses, and a man would desire her. What interested her was that she desired him.

Mightily.

Twenty Seven

After the weekend at Oberon, much as it relaxed and rejuvenated her, Sydney could hardly wait to return to the city and Adam. She felt more alive than she had in years and aware of her body and its needs. She'd have suggested that Adam meet the plane if her father hadn't been along, but she was sure Oliver wouldn't approve.

She wished she hadn't told Adam not to phone her.

He didn't even come to her office until nearly closing time on Monday. She waited all day for him. It was a bit after five when he sauntered in, looking tired and haggard.

He slouched into the chair opposite her desk, starting to light a cigarette, thinking better of it and shoving the pack back into his shirt pocket.

"You look like you've had a tough day," she said, observing his bloodshot eyes behind his glasses.

"It wasn't the day, but the weekend."

"Trouble at home?"

"No, here." He pointed to his head. "I can't seem to think of anything but you."

"Oh, is that all," she smiled, feeling happy.

"How about dinner? Three days without you is more than I can handle, it seems."

When Sydney hesitated, Adam added, "I just phoned home and told Shirley I'd be late."

"I'd like that." She was already wondering how they'd handle this when the girls returned for school. Well, that was still another six or seven weeks away. Maybe she and Adam would be finished by then.

She frowned at herself. She'd gone to bed with him twice in a week, and she was already envisioning the end.

The only way she wanted him was physically. She'd been without affection, without touching, without sex for so long. But now that she'd had a taste of it, knew she could go to bed with a man without being married to him, that she could crave to be back in his arms, to feel his naked body against hers, his hands on her body, his kisses. She closed her eyes. "Well, are you ready? If so, I'll get my jacket and meet you in the lobby."

"I'll be there in ten minutes."

As Mary walked in, Sydney said, "Make it fifteen."

Adam nodded to Mary and left.

"He's getting very friendly lately," Mary commented, tossing a folder on Sydney's desk. "Does he want to know the secret of your success?"

"I doubt it." Sydney nodded at the folder. "Can that wait until morning?"

"Longer than that." Mary narrowed her eyes' and looked at Sydney, but only said, "See you in the morning. 'Night."

Sydney reached out to touch her friend. "Wait a second. We've been together all day and I haven't heard a word about your weekend."

"You seemed preoccupied."

"Did you see Monday?"

Mary's face lit up. "I not only saw him, I spent the weekend with him."

"And?"

"And it was divine."

"Oh, my. What did you do?"

Mary laughed. "We walked through Central Park and Monday cooked some Chinese stuff, and generally I studied the ceiling."

Sydney burst into laughter. She was partly delighted with the turn of events. Mary was not at all like the girls Monday usually dated. On the other hand, she hoped Mary's heart wasn't about to be broken.

That her own heart could be touched and perhaps broken was something she hadn't considered, even though she was sleeping with a married man. Not just sleeping with, thinking of all the time. Eager to see, to be with. Anxious to make love again.

Adam left her a bit before midnight, saying as he pulled on his shirt. "I don't want to leave, you know that, don't you?"

Sydney smiled. "Adam, I'm not possessive. I don't need all of you. Whatever it is that's happening between us feeds something in me that's been barren all these years."

"You're not the only one who's had barren years," he said. "I may have had sex with Shirley, but you touch something in me that she never has. Not," he smiled at her, "that sex isn't great. You do something here, too," he added, touching his chest, "that's never happened to me. You're screwing me up. I spend my time thinking about you, remembering what your body looks like, how you feel to my touch, the little moans you make. You don't hold anything back. Your open enjoyment is novel to me."

"Well, it's what you do to me that's so wonderful," Sydney said, reaching out for his hand as he was trying to tie his tie.

He sat down on the bed next to her. "Do you think of me when we're apart?"

"I thought of you all weekend," Sydney said, giving him a little kiss. "And I was aware all day that I didn't see you."

"Do you have to go to Oberon every weekend?"

She nodded. "I want to. Isn't four nights a week in the city enough?"

"I want to spend all night with you again sometime."

"Well, arrange it."

He stood up and reached for his jacket, which had been slung over the back of a chair. "Easier said than done."

"I know. I have it easy."

"I've always thought everything in your life was easy."

"Because I've had money, you mean?"

"Money. Social position. Power."

"And those things appeal to you?"

"Those things always appeal to those who don't have them. You've taken such things for granted all your life. You're one of the chosen few, Sydney." He reached out, putting his arms around her, and drew her close, his lips meeting hers. "Christ, I don't want to leave. I can't get enough of you."

"You do kiss nicely, Adam."

"How about Friday?"

Sydney kissed him, nodding, and then walked over to her closet to pull out a lilac silk kimono which she slid into. "If I'm going to walk you to the door…"

As they walked down the curving staircase, holding hands, Adam said, "Sometime, Sydney my darling, why don't you invite me to Oberon? I've been hearing about it ever since I came to work at the paper."

"And Daddy's never suggested you come down some weekend? Maybe I could wangle an invitation but only if you bring your family. Daddy believes in the sanctity of marriage."

"I do, too," said Adam.

"And I. But I figure if your marriage were in really good shape we wouldn't be involved. Or at least hardly waiting to tear off our clothes when we enter this house."

"I can hardly keep my clothes on when I walk into your office." He stood in front of the door and gathered her in his arms again. "I don't want to bring my wife and children to Oberon. I want to be with you. I've just always been curious. I've seen photographs of the place, but I've always wanted to experience it. Or maybe it's just that I've yearned to be invited. You people don't invite many there, do you?"

Sydney shook her head. "It's our haven. We used to invite Presidents, but Daddy stopped with FDR. And of course, he had no use for Truman. Ike he's liked, but Ike flies to Camp David weekends. If Jack Kennedy gets elected, Daddy'll have another one of his fits. He'd never invite a Democrat or a Catholic."

"I'm a Republican and a Methodist."

"Oh, dear," Sydney said as she kissed the end of his nose.

He laughed and opened the door. "Good night, my love."

Sydney stood in the doorway, watching him grow smaller as he walked down the street. At the corner, perhaps he could hail a cab, even at this hour.

Good night, my love?

On Tuesday Sydney didn't see Adam at all. She and Mary worked nonstop, having Andrea order Reuben sandwiches sent in. He phoned her from his office at four in the afternoon, and said simply, "I miss you."

Miranda phoned to ask if they could possibly dine tonight instead of tomorrow, and Sydney agreed to meet her at seven at Tartuffe's. She asked Mary if she'd like to come along.

"I've spent every evening with Monday, and I'm not about to give that up for anything. He goes back to the Coast in two weeks."

"Ah, just evenings with him?" Mary grinned. "I do go home mornings to change my clothes, but Monday surprised me last night with my own toothbrush in the holder next to his. I felt like a kid at Christmas, I was so pleased."

Sydney had never known Monday to have his girls stay overnight arid interrupt his working routine, but perhaps the fact that Mary had to be at work all day changed that. Maybe she should say something to him about not hurting Mary. On the other hand, no matter what happened afterward, Mary might consider it all worth it even with a bad taste in her mouth. Sydney thought a minute. As far as she knew, Monday's record had been three months. Though long ago, when they were all out in Hollywood, she thought one of the interchangeable Barbie dolls had lasted about six months.

Miranda, stunning in a royal blue and white polka dotted dress that had an enormous ruff around the neck, said, "Remember, I want to be home and in bed by nine."

"How do you live a full life getting up at four-thirty every morning?" Sydney asked as they ordered daiquiris.

"A full life? You've got to be kidding. But, then I suppose it's what you mean by a full life. I love my life. I wouldn't change it for anything or anyone, no matter how delicious he was. Well, I might give up this morning shift if I were offered an anchor on the evening news, but I don't see that in the near future. So, I'm not much in the social scene. That can wait, Sydney, my dear. I have no desires that aren't being met right now."

Sydney studied the menu. "Aren't you lucky."

Miranda reached out and put her hand on Sydney's arm. "What does that imply? That your life's desires aren't being met?" "

Sydney looked across the table at her. "Don't you get lonely, sometimes, even when you're surrounded by people?"

"Oh, darling, I was far lonelier the decade I was married than I've ever been since."

Adam had said something like that.

"I have a dog," Miranda went on. "Every time I walk in that apartment, she wags her tail and follows me, even when I go to the john. She's attuned to me. She can tell when I'm upset, even if I don't verbalize it, and she comes and sits beside me, staring up at me with love in those big, brown eyes. She watches for me to pull out the leash and she nearly jumps out of her skin. She sleeps in the bed with me, as close as she can get. She gives unconditional love, and I'm the center of her life. No, I'm not lonely. I'm never lonely. Haven't been in years and years."

The waiter appeared. Sydney ordered the veal scaloppini, Miranda the quiche.

"I brought my next month's articles." She smiled. "Aren't you proud of me? I bet no one else is ahead of schedule like I am."

"I appreciate it," Sydney said as she sipped her drink. She really liked Miranda. Each time they got together a deeper degree of intimacy developed.

"I want that ex-husband of yours on my show," Miranda said, "and I can't even find him. I heard he was coming through New York on his way from Kenya or some other far off place."

"Oh, really?" Jordan hadn't let her know he'd be in the city.

"So you don't know anything, huh? If you find him, will you 'give him my phone number? The only time he willingly gives interviews is to plug a new picture."

When Sydney arrived home, shortly after nine, she poured herself a Bailey's and turned on the TV. For the first time all summer she felt alone. No Ashley and Juliet. No Adam. No dog.

She sat watching, half falling asleep when the phone rang.

"Hi, princess." No one but Jordan called her that.

Dammit! Why did her heart skip a beat? She thought she was long past that. She'd hoped going to bed with Adam would get Jordan out of her system.

"Someone told me you were coming through town."

"I'm at Oberon." His voice, as always, was joyful. "I knew the girls were here and since I was flying into Dulles I thought I'd come over before I come up there. You coming down this weekend?"

"I was planning to." like the beat, beat, beat of the tom-tom.

"Good. Then we can fly up to New York together Sunday and spend the weekend together as a family. That okay with you?"

"Of course."

"Not very loquacious tonight, are you?"

"Jordan, you haven't let me get a word in. I'd love to see you and be with the girls at the same time."

"Your grandmother treats me like I'm still a family member."

"No one's forgiven me for divorcing you."

"Except Daddy, huh? He was thrilled, I'm sure."

Yes, Oliver never had accepted Jordan.

"That's water over the dam. Daddy flies down every Friday and I usually come Saturday mornings."

"Can't you come Friday, too?"

"Jordan, that's the day I put *Focus* to bed."

"Do you have to be there?" Sydney' hesitated. Maybe, if they worked really hard the next two days.

"I'll see what I can do. I can't promise anything."

"Try. I'd love to see you, Sydney. It's been far too long. I hear you're having great success."

"Thanks, Jordan. I'll try."

"I'll be disappointed, so will the girls, if you can't make it Friday. We could take a picnic lunch and go sailing Saturday."

Mary would probably jump at the chance to take charge. She, herself, could work late tomorrow and Thursday nights.

"I'd love the chance to *try*," Mary said.

They did it together every week. Mary knew as much about *Focus* as Sydney did. But, Sydney told herself, it was her baby.

"We'll work late tonight."

"No." Mary shook her head. "Monday's mother's in town, and I'm not backing out of that for anything."

Sydney looked up at her. "You've only known each other three weeks."

Mary shrugged.

"Okay, we'll both work tonight and tomorrow. I don't have to leave until Friday afternoon anyhow."

Mary nodded just as the phone rang.

"*The Omaha Nebraskan* calling," Andrea announced.

The managing editor said that he'd seen several copies of *Focus* and he'd been talking with Cleveland and with Adam Yarborough and he'd be interested in carrying *Focus*. Could they talk business?

So, Adam was trying to help her, was he?

"Yes, of course." A smile played across Sydney's face.

After she hung up and told Mary the good news, she rang Adam. "I guess thanks are due you."

She told him about the phone call.

She could almost hear Adam grinning. "That's not the last of it, Ms. Hamilton. You free at least for a drink after work?"

"No. I've got to work tonight."

"Oh?"

"I'm going to leave early Friday with Daddy when he flies down to Maryland."

A moment of silence and then Adam asked, "Any particular reason?"

"Jordan's there. He phoned and asked if I wouldn't come down early and he and the girls and I'll go sailing Saturday."

There was no response.

"Okay." Adam hung up.

At six-thirty, when Sydney was the only person left on the thirtieth floor, Adam strode through her open door. He slammed it shut behind him and stood there, his eyes blazing.

"I've never been consumed by a woman. I've never experienced jealousy in my entire life. But ever since you told me you were going to see Jordan this weekend I've been ready to explode."

Sydney stared at him.

"Don't tell me, you don't have to, that it's not fair or that I'm unjust. I know that. I have another woman I go home to every night. You're the one who should be jealous, and the fact that you're not drives me nuts. My work is suffering, my mind's going, you're all I think of."

He strode over to her desk, leaned across it, and said, "Stand up."

Sydney cocked her head for a moment and then did as he asked. As he'd ordered.

"I told you sometime I was going to come up here and throw you on the floor and screw you silly. Well, the time has come."

He walked around the desk and took her in his arms, his mouth meeting hers with roughness and urgency. "Goddammit, Sydney, the whole time you're with Jordan Eliot this weekend you're going to be remembering what we're about to do here tonight."

Twenty Eight

It almost, but not quite, succeeded. For the three days arid nights afterward, Sydney walked around in a glow.

As he'd pulled his shirt off, Adam had said, "I'm going to fuck your brains out."

Well, it hadn't been her brains, but ever since then her brain hadn't functioned logically.

This was all happening between her and Adam, she told herself, because after all these years sex had reared its head and they'd made love. Love? She really didn't think love had anything to do with it. She'd been celibate so long that now she was making up for it, with abandon.

After two hours with Adam on the Aubusson carpet there was no way she could return to work. He knew that. So, they had gone out to a late supper and a couple of drinks, his leg resting against hers as they dined.

"How will I get *Focus* out when you do these things to me?"

"Maybe it's because of *Focus* that we do these things," he said. "You're the only woman I know who's interested in the same thing I am."

"Sex, you mean?" Sydney asked with the smile that hadn't left her face for the last hour.

"That, too." He laughed. "Sydney, my dear, you do things to me that no other woman has even thought of."

"Poor deprived darling," she said, picking up his hand, turning it palm up and kissing it. "I like your style, too. You make me forget the real world."

"Is that all I do?"

"I'm not going to feed your ego. If it's not perfectly clear how I react to you, then you're blind. If this week's *Focus* is inferior, I'll blame you."

"No. Blame Jordan for being able to talk you into leaving town the day you put Focus out. You wouldn't do that for me."

Sydney sipped her coffee.

"Would you?"

"Adam, don't start that. But let me tell you, if you ever offer me something like we did tonight again, I might even fly to Timbuktu."

He settled back in his chair and grinned.

She lunched with him Friday before taking off for Oberon. She and Mary had *Focus* under control. Mary knew just what to do and Sydney decided she'd rather have lunch with Adam than exhibit a lack of faith in Mary.

"Add *The Sacramento Bee* to the list," Sydney said. "Thank you, sir."

"What makes you think I had anything to do with that?"

"I just do."

"I merely sent copies of *Focus* to some of the managing editors I know pretty well. Our annual conferences give us all sorts of great contacts."

Sydney leaned forward. "I appreciate it, Adam. I really do. It's all so exhilarating. I don't think life could possibly get more exciting. "

"Am I part of that?"

"You are, indeed. Hey, why do you always need reassurance? Doesn't action speak for itself?"

Adam shook his head quickly. "I guess I've thought about you for so long that I don't believe all this. You electrify me, Sydney. Weekends drag. I think of you and you only. I hardly hear what Shirley says to me. I go through actions with the boys, but I'm not there really. I want to meet your plane."

"Daddy wouldn't approve, you know."

"I suspect he wouldn't."

"How can you get away Sunday night? No, don't answer. That's none of my business. But, if you can get away, we'll be back before dark."

"Dark isn't until after nine at this time of year."

"So, how about ten?"

"I'll try, Sydney. I'll try. If I'm not there by ten-thirty, you'll know I couldn't think up a good enough lie."

"Why don't you wait until Monday, then?"

"That would be easier, but God, twenty-four hours stretches into an eternity."

She wasn't sure she'd be ready for him after a weekend with Jordan.

"No, better wait until Monday. Jordan will be returning with us. I imagine he'll stay at my place since it's such a brief time. So, Sunday night's no good."

Adam gave her a sharp look, but said nothing. Sydney glanced at her watch. "I have to run. I told Daddy I'd meet him at Teterboro at three-thirty."

She glanced around the restaurant. There was no one there whom either of them knew. She leaned over to brush her lips across his.

"Don't lie. At least not on Sunday."

"I don't like lying at all."

"I know," Sydney said, standing. "You have it much tougher. I'm just having fun." He grabbed her hand and held on to it as they left the restaurant "Shall I hail you a cab?"

"Fine," she said, squeezing his hand.

Once the plane flew over the rich, brown earth of northern Maryland, Sydney was hypnotized.

Surprisingly, Oliver talked nearly the whole way down. He knew about the *Bee* and the *Nebraskan*. He thrilled her by saying, "I'm proud of you, Sydney. I never even imagined the Sunday supplement as a money-maker."

That was even better than Tuesday night, and she'd thought nothing could surpass that.

Walt stopped what he was doing and said, "I'll motor you over."

Ever since the Bay Bridge had opened, he had more work than he could handle alone and now employed two men. He and Oliver hunted together in the fall, and he dropped everything on summer Fridays when Oliver arrived in order to take him over to the island. He usually stayed for dinner.

Oliver's only venture into egalitarianism.

Walt's marina, greatly expanded, was filled with boats that were invariably missing from the moorings on weekends.

As happened whenever Sydney knew she was about to see Jordan, butterflies fluttered across her chest and inside her belly. Why, after all this time, did she feel like she had years ago? Could she never shake him out of her system? He had never done to her what Adam had Tuesday night. Maybe she should keep that in mind all weekend.

She hadn't slept with him since that time that led to her abortion. Once they were no longer married he had made no sexual overtures, but their relationship still contained a level of intimacy. She never felt completely platonic about him.

Even though she came to Oberon every weekend of the summer, and had all her life, motoring out to Oberon never failed to touch something deep inside her. Oberon had to be the most beautiful place in the world, even if there were no mountains, no red-rocked canyons, no towering fir trees. There was tranquility about the Chesapeake, a sense of belonging. .

Only minutes after they rounded the point and the house came into view, she saw figures racing across the lawn, their waving arms looking like sticks in the distance. Jordan must have had the girls searching for any sign of their arrival.

By the time they pulled up to the dock, Sydney's heart was beating like a moth's wings. "Hmpf," said Oliver. "That man is never going to be out of your life?"

"He is the father of my children."

"Should have found a man like Adam, if you couldn't marry someone like us."

"Adam?"

Oliver shaded his eyes with his hand. Before he could leave the boat, Jordan jumped onto it, barely nodding at Oliver. He took Sydney in a bear hug and smiled at her, saying, "Well, well. You do look the picture of success." He planted a kiss on her cheek.

Oliver stepped onto the dock and leaned down to say something to his granddaughters, whose attention was focused on their parents.

That, Sydney reminded herself, is what she couldn't have had as Mrs. Jordan Eliot. Her own success. Keep that in mind, she told herself.

Walt followed with a basket of fish; his weekly contribution to Friday nights.

Jordan devoted himself to his daughters all weekend. Rules and bedtimes were suspended in summer, so at eleven the four of them were in the pool, splashing each other. Then Jordan told them stories, and the three women in his life sat absorbed, fascinated as he spun his tales.

Sydney always took Ashley and Juliet to his movies, even if they were too adult for the girls to understand. She took them to see his name in lights, as high as a house, in front of theater marquees. She cut out reviews from all the New York newspapers and kept a scrapbook for them. She herself saw the movies two and three times. She watched him interviewed on late night TV or on the *Today* show.

After the girls went to bed, around midnight, and she and Jordan sat on the patio sipping wine, Sydney told him, "I've only seen Monday one weekend. He's taken up with my assistant and I haven't even heard from him."

"Poor girl. Did you warn her?"

"I tried to. But what good does that do? You know him. He sweeps them off their feet. But she's not like the others. She's brainy."

"Maybe he's met his match."

They were silent as fireflies glowed in the darkness.

"What about you, Syd? No men in your life at all?"

Sure. A married man, she thought to herself. She shook her head. "Not really."

"All of the wonderful you, going to waste."

"I wouldn't say I'm doing that. I'm getting quite a name in the newspaper world."

Jordan nodded. She had to control the urge to reach out and touch his wavy hair, long enough to show the curls he'd always had cut off.

"But I know you well enough to know you need some human warmth. You need love."

"Doesn't everyone?"

He nodded. "Perhaps. But I don't know others as well as I know you."

"Obviously lack of love is not something you suffer from if I'm to believe the tabloids."

"Love or sex? They're not the same, you know."

She was learning. "Once sex enters the picture, women - so Monday tells me - get it confused with love."

Jordan smiled. "There's truth to that. But, no, Syd, I haven't fallen in love with anyone. You still own my heart."

"Oh, Jordan, for heaven's sake, that sounds like dialogue in a grade-B movie."

"I'm only telling you how I feel, how I've always felt."

"But that doesn't rule out other women in your life."

"True. I am a rather normal, red-blooded male. Not just sex. I need companionship. Someone to share things I'm interested in."

"That's what we could never do after we moved west. Your movie colony never included me."

"You were never interested in becoming a part of it."

"Are we going to spend the little time we're together quibbling?"

"Sorry. I just spend a lot of time wondering how we could have stayed together, and what went wrong and how."

When Sydney didn't respond, Jordan said, "They're wonderful girls. I do miss having them in my daily life, but you're doing a fine job. They're affectionate and delightful."

"Juliet's a handful."

"She's mischievous."

"She's moody. The only one who seems to understand her is Ashley." Sydney stood up. "I'm heading for bed if we're going sailing early. Nettie's packing us a picnic lunch. You want to leave about nine?"

Jordan stayed seated. "I'm going to stay out here a bit and absorb a little more of Oberon's magic."

Sydney's back was to Jordan when he said, "You've grown beautiful, Sydney. It's great to be with you. I promise, no arguing tomorrow."

"Where are you on your way to this time?"

"Back home, but in two months we're shooting in Thailand. We'll be there four or five months. Then, I'm thinking of buying some land in Kenya."

"Buying land in Africa?" She turned to face him, partway to the house. "Jordan, you're nuts."

He grinned. "Isn't that part of my charm? Do you know what droughts and hunters are doing there? Pretty soon all that wonderful wildlife, even elephants and lions, are going to be extinct if we don't protect them. I'm going to do what I can."

"Have your own wildlife preserve?"

"Your tone of voice indicates you think that's funny, but that's exactly what I'm planning."

Sydney shook her head. Jordan didn't have a practical bone in his body.

As she lay in her four-poster that was so high she had to use steps to climb onto it, she couldn't sleep. She tried to concentrate on Adam's love-making, the things they had done together. Tuesday night she had been exhilarated, so energetic and fulfilled that she could think of nothing else. So, why couldn't she concentrate on Adam now instead of being so aware of Jordan? The tension had disappeared in the morning when Jordan and the girls took the picnic basket, and Ashley and Juliet, in their brief bathing suits, danced around him. He had never become an expert sailor, so Sydney took the tiller, and they headed south where the sapphire sky had not even a hint of a cloud. Instead of staying out in the bay, Sydney took them up a river so the girls could swim. They anchored in a cove and swam before lunch. While Jordan and the girls splashed and shouted, Sydney climbed back on the boat and stretched out on the, deck, lying on her stomach. Pillowing her head on her arms, she closed her eyes and tried to think of Adam, of his lips on hers, of his kisses, but the sound of Jordan's laughter blocked out the married man in her life.

Twenty Nine

Saturday evening Oliver announced he was taking a week's vacation, something he had never done in the middle of the summer. He was going to sit in the sun and maybe ride a bit, sail a little. None of which he had done any of the weekends Sydney had flown down. No one was more surprised than Silvie. You'd think she'd been given a present.

So, alone, Sydney and Jordan motored over to Walt's, and from there the local boy who drove the Hamiltons on errands met them. It took less than twenty minutes to get to the little airport, always filled with commuters' planes.

"Not like the old days, is it?" said Jordan, not expecting an answer. "Remember how long it took us to drive down here all those years ago."

"I'd never get down here to weekend with the girls if Daddy hadn't bought this plane."

"I've thought of taking flying lessons," he said, looking out the window, studying the terrain.

"I'm surprised you haven't."

"Am I staying at the Plaza?" he asked.

"You can stay in my guest room."

"You've been terse all weekend, my dear. Is it something I said or did?"

"No," she said sharply.

"'You don't want me cluttering up your life, do you?"

"Oh, Jordan, I don't. I'm happier than I've ever been."

"Happier than when we were first together?"

"I'm doing more. I'm proud of what I'm doing. We were young and in love and nothing else mattered."

"Tell you what," he settled back in his seat and closed his eyes. "I'll stay at the Plaza."

Sydney breathed a sigh of relief. Whenever he was in her life she couldn't think straight.

In the morning, Adam was waiting for her when she arrived at her office. For just a second, Sydney felt irritation. Was he checking up on her? His legs were crossed, he was in his usual shirtsleeves, and he looked completely at home in her office. He and Mary were having coffee, laughing about something. Sydney glanced at her watch. It was five of nine.

Mary handed her yesterday's edition of *Focus*. Before Sydney even said hello to either of them, she sat down behind her desk and opened it. She read it through before looking up to say good morning, but before she could do that the phone rang.

"*The Daytona Sands*," Andrea told her.

Sydney already knew what they wanted.

Adam waited for her to finish, waited for her to compliment Mary on yesterday's paper, and then when Mary left for a few moments, he said, "Are we on for tonight?"

"I don't know, Adam. I feel pressured. Give me a rain check?"

"Goddammit. I knew it. I've known it all weekend. I knew it last week before you even went down there. No one can hold a candle to that big Hollywood star, can they?"

Sydney stared at him. "Adam, I have work to do."

He stood there for a minute before Sydney said, "I know you want to ask it. No, I did not sleep with Jordan. He did not even stay at my place last night. Tell me, though. Since you and I have been fucking, have you also fucked your wife?"

Adam's mouth tightened. Sydney thought it must be the first time in her life she had used that word and she'd used it twice in one sentence.

"You have no right to act jealous," she went on. "We have no strings attached. What we do when we're not together isn't the other's business. Whether you've made love to your wife or not is quite immaterial.

"How we are when we're together is what matters, Adam. Stay out of my life beyond that, and I'll not interfere with yours.'"

Sydney picked up the coffee cup that Mary had left on her desk and sipped from it, her elbows resting on the desk. She stared back at Adam. '

"Well, we certainly started this week off well."

A week ago she couldn't wait to see him, feel his kisses. Now, her nerve ends, which had been raw all weekend, were on fire. She lowered her head as Adam walked out.

Mary popped in with her usual sheaf of papers. "Exhausting weekend?"

Sydney shook her head. "No. I'm just in a bad mood. If I snap your head off, don't take it personally, and if I'm still this way tomorrow, shake me."

At five she phoned Adam. "Hey, I'm sorry about the way I acted this morning. You did nothing. I had no right to shout at you and say the things I did."

"You were too close to the mark for me to get angry," he said. "But I appreciate your calling."

"I don't want to spend the night, but I am available for a quick drink if you're so inclined."

"Sixish."

"Okay. Give me a ring when you're ready to leave."

They walked three blocks through the summer evening to a bar where no one from the paper hung out. It was a sweltering July night, with no respite in sight.

When they'd ordered their drinks, and made themselves comfortable in the, air-conditioned darkness, Adam said, "I have to ask, Sydney. Are you still in love with him even after all these years?"

Sydney hesitated. "Adam, I'm the one who wanted out. I felt I was drowning. My whole being was lost. I didn't know who I was anymore. I wasn't anything but a shadow, Mrs. Jordan Eliot. I couldn't stand it. Yet I loved him—oh, how I loved him, but I guess not enough to live my life vicariously."

The waitress brought their drinks and Adam gulped his down. "You haven't answered my question."

Sydney picked up her whiskey sour and twirled it around, peering into it. "I don't know, Adam. I guess not, but somehow when he's around I'm ruffled. There's a tension. It used to be exciting, but now it's stressful. I was sarcastic all weekend, like I was this morning."

He reached out and took her hands in his. "Self-protective, my dear. With him and with me. Keep us at arm's length and you won't get hurt."

Sydney looked into his eyes. She sipped her drink, one hand still ill his, their eyes locked. "Adam, I didn't know you were this sensitive."

He laughed. "I don't know if I am, Syd."

"Don't call me that, please."

"Okay." He took his hand away and ordered another drink.

They didn't say anything for a few minutes, and then he asked, "How about tomorrow night?"

"I'm going to the Harrimans for dinner."

Silence.

And then he said, "A world completely alien to me."

"Maybe it's no more interesting than your world."

"What will you talk about?"

"Politics, particularly with the Presidential nominations coming up. Everyone will talk about that. Of course, you're for Tricky Dick, aren't you?"

"You know perfectly well what my politics are."

"Well, the Harrimans aren't Republican, though I have no doubt that many of the people there tomorrow night will side with you. The people I socialize with love the *Chronicle*. It espouses all their causes."

"And whom do you entertain for dinner?"

She smiled and reached out to run her fingers over the back of his hand. "You. You're the only one I've entertained in a long, long time."

"Wednesday night?" he asked.

She thought a minute. "Call your wife. Let's get a bite to eat and go back to my place and make mad love. Or better yet, let's go tear our clothes off and then see if there's anything at all to eat in my house. "

"Shit, you sure are confusing." But he stood and headed toward the phone booth. They ended up not eating at all.

Thirty

In the next two years, forty-six newspapers across the country carried *Focus*. Eventually it would be twice that many.

During that time, Silvie was found to have inoperable cancer. Within three months she weighed only ninety-eight pounds and within four months she was dead. Oliver was bereft and didn't go to the office for three weeks, and then he decided to withdraw from his world.

He called Sydney into his lair and said, "I have a proposition for you."

"Daddy, don't make any sudden decisions now."

She'd wondered, all her life, why she and her father weren't closer. She'd wanted to love him. Or rather, she'd loved him and wondered why he didn't quite love her. They had no camaraderie at work. In fact, she might have been working for a different company, in a different building.

"I want to stop working so hard. I'm sixty-four years old. I'm going to kick myself upstairs. Create a job for myself as Chairman of the Board."

Sydney listened, sensing something important. Certainly he wasn't going to replace himself with her. He'd never had that much faith in her. Besides, he'd never let a woman run his newspaper, his baby.

"Sit down," he said. "This is likely to be a prolonged conversation."

Sydney sat, crossing her legs, looking at her father rather than the spectacular view out his window.

"Let's talk about Adam."

"Adam?" So, that was it. He was going to make Adam the publisher.

"Yes. Do you think I don't know what's been going on with you two for the past couple of years?"

Sydney found herself blushing. Was he going to censure his thirty-five-year-old daughter?

"If I hadn't approved, do you think I'd have let it go on?"

She didn't know what to say.

"Adam's the sharpest newspaperman around."

"He's good, I know, Daddy."

"At least your taste in men has improved." Oliver hunched his shoulders and leaned forward. "You in love with him?"

Sydney took a deep breath. "I don't know, Daddy. Sometimes I think so."

"He in love with you?"

She stood up and crossed to the windows, gazing over the city. "I've tried to keep that word out of my vocabulary the last couple of years."

"Shall I ask him?"

"I'd rather you didn't."

"Why?"

She turned and looked at him. "I might not like the answer. Besides, how honest would he be?"

"I'd like to find out."

"Daddy, it's really none of your business."

"Yes, it is. What I do about this paper concerns you and Adam."

"So I surmised or else we wouldn't be having this conversation."

"I'll give you what you've been heading toward for the last decade. You marry Adam and I'll make you co-publishers."

Sydney walked back to the chair across from Oliver's desk and sat down. A double whammy.

"You seem to forget he's married."

"If he weren't, I'd have spoken up sooner. Have you ever met her?"

Sydney shook her head. "Once or twice, sort of across crowded rooms."

Across a crowded room

Why did Jordan always crop up unexpectedly in her life?

"Then you don't know her?"

"Not really."

"Adam doesn't love her. Not like I loved Silvie. You and he are a perfect match."

"He has sons, you know."

"They're big enough. One's at Yale and the other's ready to go away next fall."

"Maybe he doesn't want to leave her."

Oliver lit a cigar. Sydney hated the smell.

"Maybe he thinks he can't have you."

"He has me whenever he wants."

"I doubt it. Okay, Sydney, that's my proposition. Why don't you talk it over with him? Or would you rather I did?"

"Oh, God, Daddy, no. You're putting me in an awful position." She hesitated and asked, "What will you do if he doesn't want to marry me?"

"I'm willing to bet he does want you, that he loves you and not his wife." He squinted at her. She didn't think he looked sixty-four. Maybe fifty-five. "Would you like to be married to him?"

Sydney had to think. "I've been pretty satisfied with my life as it is."

"If I'm going to make him co-publisher I want him in the family."

Sydney wanted the job so much she tasted it.

"How much time will you give me, Daddy?"

"How much do you need?"

"I don't know."

"How about two weeks? A month at the most. I personally think you two go well together. You can give each other what you need, and together you can give me what I want."

As Sydney fumed the doorknob, her father said, "Are you going to propose to him?"

"I have no idea what I'm going to do. This is pretty sudden."

"Turn around, Sydney."

When she did he looked across the room, meeting her gaze squarely. "A suggestion? Talk about your relationship and its future before telling him I want you two on the masthead. Otherwise, you'll never know inside you, no matter what I tell you or he tells you, whether he's marrying you for power or for you, will you?"

Sydney would have to think about that.

"I'll make it worth it for Mrs. Yarborough. She'll never want for money."

"Buying me a husband, Daddy?"

"If that's what it takes."

Damn. He had put her between a rock and a hard place.

"You don't think I could do it alone?"

A moment's silence. He looked down at his cluttered desk. Then he raised his head again,

"Do you?" he countered.

"Sometimes I think so."

"I don't think you're ready." Maybe he was right. All she really knew about was the Sunday supplement, wildly successful as it was.

As she opened the door Oliver said in a quiet voice, "Sydney, you've already proved you can operate in a man's world and do it better than most men I know. You're just not ready to go solo on this."

"And Adam would be?"

"Adam knows what it takes to put out a paper. He has much to learn about the difference between being managing editor and publisher, but both of you enjoy challenges. No, I wouldn't make him publisher alone. It's a family-owned paper, and I want Adam to be family."

Adam had been Oliver's replacement for Evan. She'd always known that.

"Okay, Daddy. But don't say anything to him, will you, until I've had time to think."

"Of course not."

It was April. Spring was coming slowly to New York, but Sydney imagined it was in full bloom in Maryland. The dogwoods would be dotting the forests with their pink and white blossoms, the azaleas would be ablaze with color. The air would be soft in a way New York air never was.

Taking the elevator down to Adam's office, she wondered how she looked. Her coral red Givenchy suit was one of her favorites. The lapels of a white silk blouse edged the jacket. Pearls hugged her throat and small matching earrings lent femininity to the tailored suit.

Adam was on the phone, but she walked in and shut the door behind her. He winked and signaled he'd be off the phone in a minute. She seated herself.

When he hung up he said, "This is an unexpected pleasure. You hardly ever drop in on me."

"In our two years together I've not asked you for much, have I?"

"You've hardly ever asked anything. In fact, I never even recall your making any kind of request. What have I to give you? You don't even demand much of my time."

"Can you get away for the weekend?"

His eyes danced. "Sydney, whenever I've suggested such a thing..."

"I know. But, can you? This weekend?" "Tell me why." "I want you to come to Oberon." "My God," he said. "At last. This must be serious." She smiled at him. "I'm in the mood to have you all alone for a weekend. And I want to show you Oberon."

"I've always wanted to..."

"I know."

"Who else is coming?"

"Just the two of us and the housekeeper."

"You're taking a weekend away from your children to spend with me?"

"I spend summers with you," Sydney said.

"Nothing could keep me from this weekend."

"Friday about three?"

"I'll arrange it."

"Tell your wife where you're going."

He looked at her.

"What's up, Sydney?"

"You don't have to tell her it'll just be the two of us. But, certainly, she's heard of Oberon. Tell her you're going there."

"Why?"

"I really don't know. But, will you, please?"

He nodded a mystified look in his eyes.

As Sydney started to leave, Adam asked, "I'm not seeing you until then?"

"It's only two days. No, I don't think so. Let's grab a bite to eat at one and fly down right after. See you then."

She needed time to think.

If she did this, she'd turn *Focus* over to Mary.

Monday wasn't in town. When Monday was, which less than half the year was, Mary practically lived with him. When he was in Hollywood she seldom heard from him. The situation drove her crazy.

Sydney didn't even question why Oliver was doing this. She'd never understood him. He must have his reasons. Her only concerns were with how she felt.

She wanted this paper. She wanted to be publisher. She wanted the power, the control, the influence. Perhaps her father was right. She wasn't ready for the job as a solo. She still had much to learn, and the ones to learn from were her father and Adam.

But, marry Adam? How would he feel about it? They'd never talked marriage, they'd seldom used the word love.

Spend more than twice a week with him? Spend every night together? She smiled at that. Their sexual passion had diminished not at all. Adam continued to be a tender, inventive lover, and they were totally uninhibited together.

Even during the school year, they managed to make love twice a week, and once a week he stayed overnight, always setting the alarm to leave before Ashley or Juliet would awaken. The girls had become fond of "Uncle Adam," and once in a while he even dined with them. Sometimes on Sunday afternoons the three of them met him in Central Park or at the Bronx Zoo or at the Museum of Natural History. He refused to go to the Metropolitan, saying that kind of art totally escaped him. He bought them ice cream cones and talked with them as though they were adults.

He gave them Christmas presents and told them he'd miss them when they went to Oberon for the holidays.

He talked only rarely about his sons. Jim was a sophomore at Yale now and on fall Saturdays Adam and Shirley and Steve drove up to New Haven for football games.

What Adam told Shirley when he didn't come home, Sydney never asked. Adam seldom mentioned her, except to say she had gotten a job with the Red Cross, and now she talked of nothing else. Sydney envisioned him in bed with his wife and wondered if it was as exciting as when she and he made love? Was the most interesting thing about their relationship the illicitness for him? Is that why he saw her? To have something to hide from his wife? To feel he had control of something in their marriage, something about which his wife knew nothing?

Did Sydney want to marry him? Spend eternity with him? Give up the freedom that she enjoyed? Would her life have to change greatly? Couldn't Adam just fit into her life, along with the girls? He'd be there for dinner and for breakfast, and he'd be a warm body next to her every night, but they'd stop meeting Sunday afternoons in the park or anyplace else. Would sex, if it were available every night, lose its zest?

Was any of that important? Weren't there intimations that it could be a great marriage, with so much they'd share? The power they'd have? The decisions they'd make together?

Yet, what about love? If Adam really cared about her, wouldn't he have already left his wife? Wouldn't he have said something about love before this? Sure, he'd told her she made him wild with desire. It had gotten so after they'd made love they'd lie in bed sharing frustrations about work, tossing ideas back and forth.

Did she love him? Certainly not the way she had loved Jordan, but Adam and she moved in the same world, and she and Jordan had not though Adam did not move in the same social strata she did.

In all the years she'd been on her own, she'd never even given a dinner party. If she did, would Adam be someone she'd invite? Well, perhaps, to see how others would react to him. Managing editors weren't New York's movers and shakers.

The publishers were, however. Would he be more acceptable if he were her husband and the publisher of the *Chronicle*?

Husband and wife publishers. She smiled to herself. That would create quite a stir, wouldn't it? The daily paper had always been his arena, one she'd had nothing to do with since *Focus* had taken over her life. How would this change, their relationship? She was sure it would. They would be working in the same arena.

What would Oliver do if Adam said no? Or would he marry her just to get the job, the title? Could he be bought? Would she be willing to marry him if the title didn't go with the marriage?

She'd have to give this more thought. How much would she talk over with Adam this weekend? And why did she want the talking to be done at Oberon? Because he'd always wanted to see it? Had forever wanted an invitation there? Because it would be her world and he'd be somewhat intimidated? Is that why she'd chosen it?

She wished her mother were still alive, not that she'd talked to her much about her feelings. But Silvie had been a comfort.

So Oliver had known about her affair with Adam. Had he known from the beginning? Had her mother known and, if so, approved? Or would she have been shocked to think Sydney had been committing adultery for over two years?

At least she didn't cry when she looked at Jordan's movies anymore.

Adam was only the third man she'd ever taken to Oberon. First Jordan, then Monday, and now this man who might become her husband and partner.

Walt looked him over carefully. She'd phoned to tell him to get the boat ready, as she'd be needing it this weekend. The weekend crowds hadn't started yet, though those who came down to open their summer cottages were thronging the Bay Bridge. Thank goodness she and Adam could land at the small Easton airport. They took a cab to Walt's.

"I let Nettie know we're coming. She should have a wonderful dinner. I told her it was special."

"You did, huh?" Adam's eyes took in his surroundings.

Jaded New Yorker that he was, he knew little of geography outside of Manhattan. Queens and Yonkers were the country to him.

"I didn't know it would be this pretty."

"I've been telling you for years how beautiful it is."

As she took the wheel and chugged the motor to life, he came to stand beside her. "I've never visualized you running a boat."

"I'm good," she said.

"Is there anything you're not good at?"

"There's lots. What I'm good at, I'm very good at. And then there's everything else."

He stood close to her, putting an arm around her shoulder, looking on either side of the river as they motored west.

The wind riffled her hair, and she felt good. Maybe this could work out. Maybe Adam would be willing to, leave his wife. Maybe he would want to marry her. .

But guilt coursed through her. When she told her father she didn't feel comfortable about breaking up Adam's marriage, her father had said, "If it were on solid ground you and he wouldn't have been having an affair for these last two years.

"You two have tried to hide this from me, so he certainly hasn't been after you as a way to me. He probably was afraid of being fired if I found out and was willing to risk that. Sydney, my dear, you know how I feel about the sanctity of the family. If I thought for a moment Adam loved his wife, I'd not suggest this-er, alliance."

It had made her feel better. She remembered how Adam had said he'd been lonelier married than he'd ever been alone. They'd really never discussed Shirley and the state of his marriage. It hadn't seemed important. Now, it did. If this weekend didn't work out, they'd be through. Kaput.

Oh, she didn't want that. She'd enjoyed their relationship. It had given her stability and, at the same time, excitement. But there'd been no responsibility. If she had a social engagement, or he couldn't make a Friday night or a Sunday afternoon, neither of them had complained. They'd both known they weren't the center of each other's lives.

The sun felt good, beating on her shoulders. She threw her head back and said, "Kiss me, Adam. I need a kiss from you." He leaned down and his mouth met hers. She laughed. "I feel extraordinarily happy."

His arms went around her shoulders and he stood behind her, hugging her as the boat skimmed the water, leaving the river and heading into the bay.

"See that land over there?" She pointed toward Oberon. "There it is. The most perfect place in the universe."

"So, this is your getaway."

"I want you to see it all. We'll take the jeep out in the morning and I can show you the lakes and the deer and Martha's Forest and the lighthouse and…"

"You're a different person. I can feel you relaxing in my arms. This place does something to you, doesn't it?"

She nodded, her heart, as always, thumping as they rounded the point and the house came into view.

"Wow!"

He grabbed their bags after Sydney slipped into the mooring, jumping out to tie the rope to the pier. She was glad she'd worn slacks, gray flannel with a bright red blouse to give her courage. She'd told Adam they wouldn't dress up. Just a casual weekend, she'd said when he asked what clothes to bring. Comfortable ones.

He handed the bags over to her and she reached out a hand to help him. "Think I'll fall into the water?" he asked. He seemed in a light mood, too.

"I'll rescue you. I'm a very good swimmer."

"Believe it or not, so am I."

"Come on," she said as she grabbed his hand. She never brought a bag. Everything she needed would be here. Except a diaphragm, she thought with sudden panic. Oh, God, she was so used to never carrying suitcases between here and New York that that had slipped her mind. She had never needed a diaphragm here.

Nettie met them at the door, calling Robert to take Adam's bag upstairs. "I've put him in the green room."

"No," Sydney said, "move him to the big one next to mine."

When Nettie disappeared, Adam said, "I think you shocked her."

"Come on, let me show you the house, or do you want to wash up?"

"That can wait. My God, Sydney, this is how the other half lives, isn't it?" Then, peering into the immense living room, he laughed, "Other half? One percent." He amended that. "How about a quarter of one percent?"

Sydney took his hand and pulled him through the living room, whisking him past the Impressionist paintings and family photographs that dotted the walls.

The pool hadn't been filled yet, but the vacuum was out and Sydney could tell Robert was getting ready to set it up for the summer. "Well, we can use the Jacuzzi," she said.

"I've never been in a Jacuzzi."

"You're in for a sensual delight. We'll do it before we go to bed. It gets you warm arid cozy."

"Just being with you is a sensual delight." They walked through the house and out beyond the pool area, out to the edge of the woods. Sydney tossed off her sandals and walked barefoot through the freshly mown lawn. She threw her arms high in the air and skipped. Adam looked at her rather than at his surroundings.

"I don't suppose you want to hear this," he said. "I don't think you've ever wanted to hear it, but do you know how impossibly much I love you?"

Sydney stood stock-still and closed her eyes. She didn't realize her hands were balled into fists until Adam said, "I knew it. I've ruined the weekend before it even started, haven't I?"

She opened her eyes, and he was standing in front of her.

"Sorry. I know you want no ties. I know we move in different worlds, but watching you so filled with joy, so like a little girl, I couldn't help myself. I've fought saying those words since even before we became lovers. But that must be what this place does to you." He put his arms around her. "If I've ruined your day, I'm sorry. I was unable to keep my mouth shut a minute longer."

She gazed into the eyes that were searching hers so profoundly. "Adam, it's not I who have been afraid of ties. It's you. You have ties. You're married. I didn't want you to feel pressure from me. I love you, too." Did she? As she said it she decided it must be true. With whom else could she live a life so full of possibilities?

He kissed her with a tenderness that touched her core. No one in the city office would ever believe there was this part of Adam. Her arms encircled him.

"Oh, Adam, it's so beautiful." He didn't ask whether their confessions of love or the island was what she was describing.

Thirty One

They dined late. It was dark by the time they finished. They had not stopped talking the entire afternoon, and Sydney was surprised that they never mentioned the paper or business at all.

"It might be nice," Sydney said, "to take a walk down by the water and then we can come back and have our brandy in the Jacuzzi."

"I feel I've left reality," Adam said, standing and reaching for her hand.

They roamed across the wide expanse of front lawn, down to the dock, walking out on the wooden planking. Sydney sat down, taking her shoes off and splashing her toes in the cold water.

Adam sat next to her, looking out over the bay at the twinkling lights on the mainland. The evening was warm. There was no breeze at all, and far-off echoes of people talking drifted across the water. Rocking lights indicated boats at anchor.

"I feel I've gone back forty years, to my childhood. Not that where I grew up was this lovely, but there's a quaintness, a sense of the idyllic here."

"Adam, I think you're schizophrenic."

He jerked his head and looked at her, not able to see her face in the darkness. "Because I like it here?"

"No. In the office you're abrupt, you shout, you're hyperactive, you're impatient. Out of it you're gentle, sensitive, tender."

He leaned over and kissed her. "But you're like that, too. No one who works with you would believe the you I've come to know."

Sydney didn't agree with him. She thought the people she worked with sensed what kind of woman she truly was.

"You light up my life," he said.

"Do I make your life complex?"

"You have no idea."

They sat on the dock, holding hands, not talking, but listening to the distant muted sounds. Then Sydney said, "Let's go. It is getting a bit chilly. The Jacuzzi will warm us up."

"I didn't bring a bathing suit."

She turned to him, reaching up to kiss his neck, and laughed. "Don't be silly. No one else is around. You don't need to wear anything."

The pool area was lit. Sydney turned off the lights and left on only those lighting the Jacuzzi. She began to unbutton her blouse, dropping it on the patio table.

Adam looked around. "You sure we're alone?"

"And if we aren't?"

"I had a very middle class upbringing. I'm not nearly as sophisticated about these matters as you are."

"Well, let's start making you more cosmopolitan then. You've lived in New York over twenty years. I think it's about time."

Sydney's clothes were off and she dipped her toe in the warm water. "Ah, wonderful." She slid into the hot tub. "This is great. Come make love to me." The swirling water, its heat sending mist shimmering above the water, felt primal.

Adam joined her, agreeing that this was as close to heaven as one could get. The water lapped at Sydney's breasts, and Adam sat opposite her, saying, "I enjoy looking at you."

"You make me feel beautiful when you look at me like that."

"You are. I could look at you forever."

She paddled over to him, curling up to sit on him, facing him, her breasts against his chest. She wound her arms around his neck and brought her mouth to his, her tongue tasting him. "Let's go slow," she said. "Let's do everything great and good, and wonderful that's possible."

* * * *

Later, she laughed. "I forgot towels." So they walked through the house, trailing drops of water, up the stairs to Sydney's bedroom, and lay on the high, soft bed drinking brandy. Their hands were entwined as Adam said, "You spoil me for anyone else."

She turned toward him, resting on her elbow. "Adam, I don't want to be second fiddle anymore."

Dead silence.

She felt his body go rigid. He put his brandy glass, emptied, on the night table next to him and said, "That means one of two things. Either you've invited me here for a goodbye or you're proposing."

"Which would you prefer?" She was surprised to find her stomach in a knot. He was staring at the ceiling, and he didn't answer her for a moment. "It's not just what I'd prefer. We have other people, other things to consider."

"But that wasn't my question." Now he turned toward her, his gaze so intense Sydney was surprised.

"Sydney, if I had my druthers, I'd spend the rest of my life with you. You must know that."

"That's the answer I wanted to hear. I want to share my life with you, Adam, not have you leave my house at midnight, not know you're lying to

Shirley, not knowing you may possibly be screwing her after you leave me, or the night before you come to me. I find I'm becoming jealous and possessive."

He put an arm around her. "That's something I've been hoping for years, but took for granted I'd never hear."

"I did bring you down here to propose. I know it's not as simple for you. I know you have' sons and a wife to consider, but people do get divorced."

"First of all, I never go screw, as you so put it so genteelly, Shirley after leaving you. I can't touch her after being with you. I don't want her in my bed. I have, however, made love to her, but only when she made the overtures, only so that she will not suspect that twice a week I'm getting laid by the sexiest woman alive.

"I lie awake nights, torn apart by thinking you don't want me in your life more than twice a week. I punch my pillow and Shirley thinks I'm frustrated by work and should take more vacations. I can't tell her I'm in love with my boss's daughter, who has more money than I'll ever earn, who moves in social circles I don't even know about, with people my paper names in headlines. I can't tell her I'm tortured because I have thought I was a toy to you, someone to give you the sex you were denied for years, and someone whom you can talk business over with, but not someone you'd be proud to share your life with.

"Sydney, being in love with you, while it has made me feel alive, has not been great for my ego."

She was amazed. "Have I ever given you cause to think those things? They're absolutely ridiculous."

"You've never told me you cared, that you loved me. I thought..."

She sat up straight, looking down at him. "Adam Yar borough, I want to be your wife. I will be proud to be Mrs. Adam Yarborough. Now, how do we get rid of the present Mrs. Y?"

He had a ready answer. "I've been putting money aside for a couple of years, just in case we ever came to this point, money I can offer her for a divorce settlement. She can have the apartment, she can have anything I own. The boys are old enough so we won't fight over them."

Sydney did not say anything about her father's offer. That could come later. "Labor Day," she did say. "Let's have a September wedding here, at Oberon. That gives you five months to clear it all up."

"I'll try. God, darling, I hardly believe this. Will your father have a fit?"

She shook her head. "I've a feeling Daddy will approve. You're like a son to him. More so than Evan."

"Come here," he said, grinning. He buried his head in her breasts and his hand between her legs. "Oberon *is* magical." His voice was muffled.

He moved out of his apartment and into a studio, but he spent his free time at Sydney's. His and Ashley's friendship deepened, for Adam discussed books with her and history, both of which fascinated the quiet, introverted girl. She had to wear glasses and, instead of letting it bother her, she was proud of them. She thought they lent her an air of intelligence, and she prized intelligence above most things.

Juliet kicked him once. She did not want him standing in the doorway when Sydney read to her at night, or when Sydney tucked her in. She refused to sleep in her own room, but wanted to be with Ashley, which was fine with her sister.

When Sydney tried to converse with Adam, Juliet came and sat on Sydney's lap, demanding her attention. She began to fuss more than usual, losing her temper often.

"She's jealous," Sydney said. "I'm not going to punish her. We'll ignore her tantrums." But she did make sure she gave Juliet more attention and affection. Gradually Juliet softened, but her expression was sullen.

"You're not my daddy," she said to Adam, her voice angry, several times.

"I'm not trying to be," he said. He'd read that in second marriages children were usually the trouble spots, and it concerned him.

Sydney told her father, "I think it would be a nice wedding present to tell Adam about your plans."

Oliver nodded. Adam had already approached Oliver, asking for Sydney's hand. Sydney thought it charming of him, quaint. He told her that Oliver had said, "My fondest dream come true, Adam. Welcome to the family."

Neither of them ever mentioned to Sydney that Oliver offered Adam a million dollars to give to his wife. Adam, wanting to make as few waves as possible, finally accepted, after Shirley said she'd fight him in court. For a million dollars she was willing to fly to Juarez and they'd be divorced over the weekend.

"In that case," Sydney thought aloud, "how about' getting married July Fourth, at Oberon?"

So, on July Fourth, 1961, on the one hundred eighty-sixth anniversary of the Declaration of Independence, Sydney became the second Mrs. Adam Yarborough, with her father, Uncle Billy, Mary, Monday, Miranda, Warren, and Walt as guests and Ashley and Juliet as attendants. As usual, neither Sydney nor Oliver knew where Evan was. The last they'd heard he was either in the Greek Isles or on the Nile someplace, but that was months ago. He was still with wife number three, whom he'd never brought to America to meet the family. She'd had their second child last winter.

Sydney tried to remember how long it had been since she'd seen her brother. Five years? More? She supposed she shouldn't resent his not making an effort to attend her wedding, for he didn't even know about it. After all, he'd been to her first one, and she'd never been to any of his.

It had all happened much more quickly than she or Adam had imagined. Oliver, Sydney thought, was a consummate actor.

His wedding present, he told Adam after the ceremony, was that they would be co-publishers of the paper. He asked only that on the masthead, Sydney also use the Hamilton name. Sydney Hamilton Yarborough.

When they went to bed that night, Adam, his face grave and his eyes serious, asked, "You knew about this, didn't you?"

Sydney smiled. "Daddy mentioned it. I think it's a lovely present, don't you?" She'd thought he'd be more outwardly pleased. It was a big step.

She walked over and put her arms around him as he sat on the side of the bed. "Just think, Adam, all the power and influence. Isn't it exciting? We're going to set New York on its ear."

"Why stop with New York? How about the world?" But he wasn't smiling. He didn't even seem elated.

She leaned down to kiss him, but his lips didn't move. "Is this why you married me, Sydney? Oliver wouldn't give you the paper on your own? Am I the only way you could be publisher?"

The blood in Sydney's veins turned to ice. She suddenly felt so cold that she wanted to turn the air-conditioning off.

"Adam, together we're going to have a marvelous time, be important and powerful and have each other to talk everything over with. And we're going to continue having the greatest sex in the world. We'll be a couple to reckon with. But, I'd have married you even if we had none of that." She smiled at him. "Well, maybe not if we didn't have such great sex."

He looked into her eyes. "I wonder," he said, his voice a whisper. "I truly wonder."

Sydney threw the jacket of her white satin Mainbocher suit on a chair. She flipped off her bra and stepped out of her skirt and panties. She took Adam's hand and drew it to her breast.

"Shit, Sydney, what you do to me."

After they proved they could still have spontaneous, world class sex even though married, Adam murmured, as they were both falling asleep, "Publishers of The New York *Chronicle*!"

"You're on your way to being one of the most powerful people in New York."

"And you, too."

"We are going to be a force to reckon with. Adam and Sydney Yarborough." There was silence, and Sydney was nearly asleep when Adam said, "No matter that you've taken my name. I'm a Hamilton now, aren't I?"

Thirty Two

"We're losing a hundred thousand a year?" Sydney couldn't believe it.

Oliver didn't seem dismayed. He'd been pouring money into the paper for years. But Sydney had never been in on the higher echelon talks before.

Adam looked at the figures. "Circulation's down from two hundred and fifty thousand to a hundred and ninety thou."

Oliver seemed put upon to defend himself in front of the new publishers of his baby. "We reach an audience in between the *Times* and the *Daily News*. We're in-between."

Sydney's exhalation indicated her exasperation. She'd had no idea. "So, what kind of audience does that mean?"

"Sydney, I know what you're thinking, what you've always wanted. I could see it the minute you invented *Focus*. You'd like to appeal to a much-larger audience."

"You'd be losing more than you are if it weren't for *Focus*, if we want to increase our advertising, I'll tell you who we should appeal to. Women!"

The look on Oliver's face wasn't quite a sneer; he was too well mannered for that.

Adam asked, "Why do you say that?"

"Because women are the shoppers. You know and I know women buy everything in the family."

"Except cars," Adam interrupted.

"Well, they choose the colors. I've been doing some studying ever since you tossed those figures on my desk, Daddy. Women love ads. Look at the crowds at stores when they advertise a really good sale. A suburban woman will spend more on gas than she saves driving from grocery store to grocery store to buy an item two cents cheaper. We've got to appeal to women."

"Women don't read newspapers."

Sydney looked at her father, her mouth agape.

He went on. "They don't even know what the hell's happening in the world. They vote for Kennedy because he's good looking, not because of what he stands for. At least I hope not for what he stands for."

Sydney, who was the only one in the room not sitting, let a moan escape. "Do you both think that women are empty headed..."

Adam reached out a hand even though he was ten feet away from her, and shook his head. "Sydney, they're just interested in other things. Their families, cooking, gossip..."

"For crying out loud," Sydney cried, "you certainly don't have much respect for my sex, do you?"

The room was silent. Then Adam said, "You're not exactly typical, my dear."

Oliver hunched forward, looking at his daughter. "Sydney, I don't want a newspaper filled with Pablum..."

"Pablum? So, that's all we think of? Baby food? Fashions?"

Again, neither of the men said anything.

"You'd rather lose money and cater strictly to the businessmen who don't buy the *Times,* the political reactionaries, the ones who prefer the past to the future, the ones who buy gold plated securities? Do you know, both of you, you're behind the times?" Then she laughed. "Well, that was a pun, wasn't it?"

"Sydney, if it costs me a hundred thousand a year, that's all right. I bought this paper forty years ago just so I could be sure the public would get my point of view. Too few people in this world bother to think. And, if I can contribute to anyone's thinking along the right lines, then I don't mind losing money."

Sydney shook her head and started for the door. Then she turned around. "Daddy, just why did you make us publishers if nothing we say is of any importance?"

Oliver stared at her, and then glanced at Adam. "What Adam says makes sense to me, a Almost always." Tears gathered in Sydney's eyes as she walked out of the room, slamming the door hard behind her.

* * * *

One evening, Sydney said to Adam, "I can't reconcile your attitude toward women in general and to the girls and me."

"What's that supposed to mean?"

"You treat us as though we're important only to you."

"And why not? You are important to me."

"But not important enough to help run the world?"

He laughed, though self-consciously. "Sydney, my dear, I wouldn't put anything past you."

"That's no way to get out of it,"

"Come here," he said, reaching for her.

"Go to hell," Sydney said, standing up and walking out of the room, leaving a perplexed Adam staring after her.

When Jordan came that year to visit the girls, taking them over to the Plaza to stay with him for ten days, Adam asked, "You going over there and see him?"

Sydney could sense the tension in his voice. "Darling, isn't it clear to you? I left him. I married you. No. No, I'm not going over there. Look, can't we be civilized? You both seemed friendly last night when he came to pick them up."

Adam nodded. "He did seem rather decent. I told him I hoped he didn't mind that I loved his daughters and he said he didn't think anyone could have too much love, and he was glad I felt that way."

But Sydney began to sense that Adam was not just jealous of Jordan. Whenever they went out socially, he would complain when they came home. "Did you have to dance with Nelson Rockefeller quite so often?"

Or, "Isn't Bernard Baruch too old for you?"

Or, "Simon Wystrander couldn't leave you alone all evening, could he?" Sydney tried, always, to placate him although his jealousy drove her crazy.

"Adam," she would say, putting her arms around his rigid figure, "I didn't marry any of them, did I?"

"No, because they wouldn't have gotten you what you wanted."

She'd kiss him, her tongue running along his lips, melding her body into his, "You're what I wanted."

"No, I'm not. I was the way to the paper and you know it."

"We were having an affair long before that. And that had nothing to do with the *Chronicle*."

She'd start unbuckling his belt and his jealousy always ended up with their making love, but Sydney grew to resent it more and more. She resented making love as a way to appease him. She resented his seeing every other man, every rich, socially presentable man, as a threat. She resented having a delightful time chatting with one of her old friends, only to see Adam's eyes blazing with anger across the room.

She told Mary that being married to Adam and being publisher of the *Chronicle* both made her feel impotent. The only time she'd ever felt important, as though what she did mattered, was when she'd been in charge of *Focus*.

"You want it back?" Mary asked.

"Yes," smiled Sydney. "But it's impossible. Besides, you're doing such a bang-up job there's no way I could follow you."

"I may want some time off," Mary said.

Sydney cocked het head to the side. "Seeing as you don't even take more than two weeks off each year and you've been at it how many years now?"

"Four," Mary answered.

"How much time?"

"A month, maybe."

"Well, that'd be fun for me. I could run it for that length of time. Give me something I really like to do." Sydney smiled. "You getting married or something?"

"Or something." Mary's look was a mixture of confusion and pleasure.

"You and Monday going to take a big trip?"

"I'm going to Hong Kong."

Sydney blinked. "Hong Kong? My heavens, what for?"

"Denton."

"Denton? Denton Walker?"

"He called me from Saigon. Says he needs rest and relaxation and how about meeting him in Hong Kong and we'd go somewhere from there."

Sydney leaned across the table and grabbed Mary's arm. "Denton? What about Monday?"

"What about him? We're not married. He won't even mention the word. He doesn't own me. I'm free to go where I please with whom I want."

Sydney nodded. "Well, this is certainly a new twist. I didn't even know Denton was still in your life."

"I saw him when he came through here last summer."

"You didn't tell me." Sydney was hurt.

"I know. It's just I know Monday is one of your best friends and..." She shrugged.

"Are you sleeping with them both?"

"Oh, Sydney," Mary giggled. "No one but you would ask such a question."

"I hope not." When Mary didn't answer, Sydney again asked, "Well, are you?"

"Denton was only here for a week, and Monday was in California. I sometimes go months without having more than a weekly phone call from Monday."

"So you are, then. Well, well."

"I know when Monday's in California he dates gorgeous women. I'm not the only one in his life."

Sydney knew the truth of that. "When are you going?"

"If it's okay with you, in two weeks."

That wasn't much warning, but what fun it would to take over *Focus* again for a month. Adam and Oliver would probably be glad to get her out of their hair.

"I'll come down to your office tomorrow morning and we'll make plans," Sydney said. She patted her friend's hand. "Good luck, darling."

Thirty Three

In 1962, when Lyndon Baines Johnson was Vice President of the United States, he'd lost the immense power he'd wielded as majority leader of the Senate.

He and President Kennedy disliked, perhaps hated, each other. He tried to find things to do, since JFK excluded him from most decision-making.

Sydney's secretary told her the Vice President was on the phone. "Mrs. Yarborough," the thick Texas accent addressed her. "This is your Vice President."

Sydney had voted for him and Kennedy, without telling her father and Adam. She couldn't imagine voting for Nixon. Her ideas and beliefs were changing from the ones with which she had been raised, and Nixon didn't strike her as trustworthy. He was peculiar. She couldn't quite define how.

"Yes, Mr. Vice President?"

"I'm in your fair city, and I wish to tour all the newspapers."

What in the world for? she wondered.

"Yes, sir."

"How about noon today? Would that interrupt anything vital at your place?" His voice was surprisingly warm. Sydney glanced at her calendar. "No. I'd be happy to show you around."

"Be there at noon. Sharp."

Sydney didn't tell either Adam or Oliver. Oliver might even have forbidden Johnson to enter his building. No, she knew he couldn't do that, but certainly the Vice President had a reason for calling her rather than her husband or father.

The only person she told was Mary. "Do you think he wants a tour of the place?"

"That's probably not his real intent, but you may never know his reason. If he's going to be here at noon, you should offer to feed him."

"How about a chicken sandwich?"

Mary laughed.

But Sydney was serious. She ordered chicken sandwiches, beer and Cokes sent in. Better include pickles and potato chips. LBJ was a man of the people. Besides, that was all Sydney ever had when she didn't have a luncheon engagement.

She did warn the doorman who whisked the Vice President of the United States to her thirtieth floor office with no fanfare.

His handshake was hearty, and he was bigger than she'd thought him to be. "Let me introduce you to the Chairman of the Board and my co-publisher."

"I know who they are." He wagged his finger of his big, meaty hand at her. "And you can do it. But it's you I've come to meet."

She was flattered.

Oliver didn't even stand. Adam at least smiled and crossed the room to shake hands with Johnson, casting a questioning glance at Sydney.

"I'm going to give him a tour of the plant," she said. "I'm sure the staff would be thrilled to meet our Vice President." She found herself taking great pleasure in this, knowing she was bewildering her father.

"We hear good things about this little lady down in Washington," LBJ said.

Though Sydney didn't like being referred to as 'little lady," she did feel a tingle. What could they know about her in Washington?

"Here," Adam said, walking hack to his desk and getting his jacket from the back of his chair. "I'll come with you."

"That's not necessary, Adam," Sydney said. "Though, if you'd like, do join us for lunch in my office."

Adam looked confused, but stayed behind his desk.

"I'll call you when we're ready," she said, smiling sweetly at him. The thrill of power shot through her. She didn't know whether or not LBJ really enjoyed himself or what he got from the tour, but he shook hands with everyone within reach, having a ready smile and a hearty word for each. Energy radiated from him.

"Is this an official visit?" Sydney asked.

The Vice President shook his head. "Not at all. Just thought I'd visit the real power brokers, the press."

Sydney smiled. "Why me? We're a conservative paper, always against your administration."

"You?" His grin spread across his face. "Word is you're changing. We have a chance with you. And if we have, I want to know you. No chance at all with your father, bigoted soul that he is." Then he coughed. "Didn't mean to offend you. But you, you march for civil rights. You come out on TV and say you're for abortion…"

"Well, more accurate to say I'm for a woman's right to choose," she said. "I do think there are better ways to handle not having babies, but abortion should be a viable choice."

"See?" said Johnson. "That's what I mean. I caught you on that 'Meet the Press' and was impressed. Only other women in your league are Patterson and Graham," he said, naming the publishers of *Newsweek* and The *Washington Post*. Sydney admired Alicia Patterson, and she thought Kay Graham and she were rather gray in comparison.

"Kay Graham and I aren't in the same league with Alicia," she said.

"Not yet," he nodded. "But you will be. Lights hidden under barrels."

How nice, Sydney thought, taking a liking to this effusive, unpretentious Texan.

He even acted as though the idea of having chicken salad sandwiches in her office was the most interesting thing he could do today. She could tell Adam was ill at ease. LBJ couldn't tell that, but she could.

"'What did he want?" Adam asked after the Vice President left.

"I haven't the foggiest," Sydney acknowledged. "Said he had come to New York to meet all the publishers."

"'How come not Oliver, then?" He didn't say, Sydney noticed, *or me...*

"He saw me on 'Meet the Press' and liked what he saw."

"Oh, that," said Adam. He'd been embarrassed by Sydney's views and her openness. Oliver had never even commented on it though Sydney was pretty sure he'd seen it. He'd known she was going to be on. They'd even invited her back.

The next time Sydney heard from LBJ was in 1964 when he'd been President of the United States for seven weeks. He phoned her at her home on the second Thursday evening of January.

"I've, been sitting here reading those editorials in your paper," he said, "and I thought I better phone the little lady and tell her how much I 'preciate them."

"Don't get too excited. I've had to fight to get them in. They're just saying you're taking over well; they're not approving Democratic policies. "

"It's a beginning," he said. "I'd like you to come down and see me next week. I'd like you to meet Lady Bird; too. Come down for lunch."

"May I bring my husband?"

LBJ laughed. "Of course, if you think that'll protect you."

Sydney hated it when men turned business into sexual flirtation.

Adam couldn't refuse a White House invitation; in fact, he even evidenced excitement at the thought. They flew down in Oliver's plane and Lady Bird took them on a tour of the White House before lunch. Her southern accent wasn't as pronounced as when Sydney had seen her on TV, and Sydney thought her far more sophisticated than she'd expected. Far more attractive, too, in a fashionable, yellow linen dress, her hair coiffed stylishly. But her voice was tremulous, and Sydney imagined the woman had not yet adjusted to the role she had been thrown into. "I'm trying," she said, "I'm doing my best."

"Of course you are," Sydney assured her. She liked her.

At lunch, to Sydney's surprise, there were just the four of them. The President said, "I have little hope of my civil rights bill getting through Congress. There'd have been more chance if I were still majority whip," he laughed.

"Civil rights? You mean black rights; don't you, sir?" Adam's voice was polite, but Sydney was so embarrassed. She wanted to kick him, but the table was too wide.

Johnson turned to him, his voice strong and his gaze level. "There are big pockets of poverty that still exist in this wonderful country of ours, and I want to wipe them out. We should be color blind. Poor, not able to find jobs or keep roofs over their heads, having to apply for food stamps. It's humiliating. This is a big, rich country, and I want to see that the poor aren't neglected. Black rights? Maybe, Mr. Yarborough, but fundamental to all human beings."

Sydney noticed he'd called Adam "Mr. Yarborough," but was calling her "Sydney." Was this a difference in the way the President treated men and women or did he feel more informal with her?

One thing Adam and the President agreed on: this war in the Far East could not be called off and America shown to be a weakling. America had won every war she had ever entered, and therefore considered all wars she entered to be moral. And, of course, morality had to triumph, for God was always on its side. Sydney wanted to ask what was moral about killing young men over tin, which is what Viet Nam had, or over Communism when it did not threaten them.

"It seems," Sydney said, "that anything that has a tinge of Communism has to be snuffed out wherever it shows its head in the world. I think there are worse things than the threat of Communism. It's never going to take over the world."

Both men looked at her.

"What's worse?" Adam asked.

"Well, I don't like Communism," Sydney quickly said. "But there are countries where the bad guys aren't the Communists, like in so many new African nations. We tend to back anyone, no matter how much he enslaves his people, if he's not a Communist. Like Sukarno. Or in Chile."

"Would you have me pull out of this war?" asked the President.

"You said you were going to."

"I did, didn't I?"

Actually, the luncheon ended on a pleasant note, and Adam came away saying there were some points with which he could even agree with the President. "Though I don't like the way he looks at you."

"Oh, for God's sake, Adam. You think every man I talk with is out to bed me. Have you taken a good look at me? I'm not beautiful."

"You are after you start talking."

"Well, I'm not about to shut up." So, she looked good when she was animated? That was nice to know.

"And," laughed Adam, leaning over in the plane to put his hand around hers, "if anyone knew how great you are in bed, every male in the whole goddamned country would want you."

But they were making love less and less often. Was it because they were both so tired nights or because she felt such despair at their diverging viewpoints? She was changing and Adam wasn't. Their arguments during the days affected their actions, or lack of them, at night.

Whenever she'd see an old movie of Jordan's on TV, or she and the girls would go to Radio City or the Paramount to see his newest, she didn't want Adam to touch her afterward. She wanted to lie in bed and remember how Jordan's kisses felt and how her body responded to his hands and his tongue and his sweet words.

Jordan was the one who had gotten her started thinking the way she did now. Made her think for herself. Not just spout those ideas Oliver had inculcated in her but about those with less money than she had, less freedom, less education. He was the one who started her thinking about these things, and once she began examining those ideas she'd been practically born with, once she began studying and reading about them, once she opened her mind, there was no going back. He was also the first one who'd made her realize the resources of the planet were finite and needed protection.

He'd said of Oliver, "your father's a goddamned bigot. No one, but no one, uses the word *nigger* nowadays except your father. I'd think a man of his education and worldliness would have more sensitivity. Even if he feels as he does, Neanderthal as it is, you'd think he'd have better manners."

Sydney had to agree.

A few months later, after Mary returned from another Far Eastern trip, and after Monday had just spent a month in New York, Sydney asked her friend at lunch, "Does Monday know about Denton?"

Mary shook her head. "Not really. I lie. Well, I didn't lie exactly, except by omission. He thinks all my trips are for the paper. Hong Kong, Singapore, Australia. I didn't exactly say that, but..."

"If they both proposed to you the same day, which would you accept?"

Mary shook her head. "God forbid, Sydney. Besides, neither of them is ever going to propose. I'm involved with two men who hate the word *marriage*. I'm not sure how I feel about it. I don't want to give up my work. They're both very macho, you know. They think women are here to make men's lives comfortable."

"Yet Monday's plays always have liberated women as heroines." Sydney broke her French bread in half and buttered it.

"Hey, intellect and what we think has little to do with how we live our lives," Mary said. "I'm flying to Singapore this weekend and I'll be back in a week. *Focus* is ready for the next two weeks."

"I'm impressed."

Two months later Mary told her, "I'm pregnant."

"Oh, God. Do you know who?"

Mary nodded. "It's Denton's, I'm sure of the time."

"How do you feel about that?"

"You mean am I going to tell him?"

"I don't know what I mean."

Mary leaned across the lunch table. "I've thought about it a lot. I'd like to have Denton's baby."

Sydney looked startled. "So, you're going to have it?"

Mary nodded. "I am."

"Are you going to let him know?"

"I wonder. I don't want him to feel he *has* to marry me, but on the other hand, don't I owe it to him to let him know he's going to have a child, too?"

Sydney wondered if Mary was thinking of quitting *Focus*. Mary answered her silent question. "I hope this doesn't mean I have to leave work?"

Relief Swept over Sydney. "You make whatever arrangements you want. I'll back you up. Of course I don't want you to leave. This *is* 1964, after all. Women can work and have a family, too."

But Denton Walker was killed by a bomb before he ever knew Mary was carrying his child. And Monday surprised them by offering to marry Mary and make the child his.

"No one would ever believe a black child was his, and I told him that. Of course I won't marry him, but can you believe it? I thought he'd be angry at me."

"He can't call the kettle..." and then Sydney laughed at what she'd nearly said. "But I didn't know he was that chivalrous."

"He told me it took the thought of losing me to another man to make him realize he's in love with me. I think, though, that Monday just likes drama. I'm not about to marry him."

"So you're going to have an illegitimate child?" Sydney asked.

"That I am," Mary said, "and I'm not even ashamed."

Sydney admired her friend.

"I'm going to do it all. Be a mom, have a high-stress career, and not have to give up my freedom to a man." She sounded as though she should be proud, but instead she was mourning for the loss of Denton Walker, and would be until long after his son was born.

The person who changed the most from this was Monday. He bought an uptown apartment in New York, selling his Greenwich Village flat. He made his headquarters on the East Coast and stopped dating starlets and other pretty young things, and, if he didn't see her every day, called Mary daily. He was the first to see her son, David. He volunteered to be David's godfather.

Mary said she didn't believe in such nonsense.

Thirty Four

Adam enjoyed summer weekends at Oberon as much as Sydney did. But the zest for life seemed to have left Oliver, ever since Silvie died. He sat on the porch with Big Mommy and stared out at the bay, seldom finding the energy or desire to do anything else. He began staying at Oberon for several weeks at a time.

Adam and Sydney sailed either Saturday afternoons or Sunday mornings, taking the girls with them, exploring creeks and rivers that Sydney had not seen since her youth, when she and Evan would take off on a summer's day. They walked through the woods, and, once, to the north marsh. They swam in the little lakes, or sat among the trees and watched fawns and does, seldom seeing a buck.

On all the ponds there were always geese or ducks and now and then a swan and its brood. Why these had not gone north with the rest of the flocks was a moot question. Ashley and Juliet had found a snow goose, wounded from an out-of-season gunshot, the bullet having passed through its wing. It couldn't be more than a year old, Big Mommy had said, and she'd gotten out bandages so that together the three of them could make a homemade splint.

Robert had made a pen for the bird, which by July had become a pet, waddling after the girls when they let her out.

Sydney said to her grandmother, "I hope they know that someday it's going to fly away."

Big Mommy nodded. "We've discussed that, and whether they'd prefer losing her to freedom or keeping her cooped up."

The old woman smiled through her ghostly makeup. Sydney suspected that her daughters gave meaning to her grandmother's life. She seemed no frailer or more infirm than she had twenty years ago. Though she walked slowly, and sometimes with the help of a cane, her eyesight remained sharp; she still won more often than not at cards, and she could walk through the woods to help a wounded bird.

"I didn't know geese were so big," Adam said. He was not the animal lover that the Hamiltons were, but his eyes grew tender as he watched Juliet and Ashley care for the beautiful bird.

That summer they were also surrounded by seven puppies that Copper produced. Sydney insisted Copper and the puppies spend the summer at Oberon and that when they returned to New York, the puppies stay behind. Robert would then have instructions to find homes for them on the mainland.

She suspected he might want to keep one or two. There hadn't been a dog at Oberon for seven or eight years.

Juliet wasn't so rebellious on the island. She and Ashley were always busy. There weren't enough hours in a day. They often asked Nettie to pack picnic lunches and took off after breakfast on their horses, not returning until late in the afternoon.

"Doesn't anyone worry about them all day?" Adam asked.

Sydney just looked at him. She'd done the same thing when she was young.

When they were in the city, and Adam's sons were home for the summer, they dined together weekly. Sometimes they'd dine out and take in the theater afterward, but more often they just dined at home and spent the evening talking. Sydney and Adam were usually in bed by nine.

Even from the first, Adam's boys had not seemed to resent Sydney. As the· older one explained, "Mom and Dad were never happily married. We used to ask each other how come they'd ever gotten together anyhow. Mom's happier, even though she won't admit it She likes her job arid she has more life. She says she'll never marry again."

Over the next few years Sydney read that Jordan had bought land in Kenya, and he corroborated that when he came through New York.

"I spend most of my free time there. We're building a lodge."

"Who's we?"

Jordan laughed. "Not a woman, love, not a woman. I was using the regal we, I guess. I'm building a lodge, which I may offer to organizations I approve of. You know, the Audubon Society or ones who are active in helping, or at least hoping, to preserve wildlife. Elephants are becoming extinct in Africa. Can you believe that? Elephants extinct! Use the place as a teaching haven.

"'Come spend a week or two in the African wilds, and fall in love with what must be preserved.' That should be good propaganda for the cause. You should come see it, Syd. It's so beautiful. I almost bought land in Tanzania so I could be right where Kilimanjaro is, but politically I prefer Kenya. You can see the mountain from where my lodge is going to be. My room has windows framing it. It's near Tsavo Wildlife Refuge."

This meant nothing to Sydney. "Aren't you bored there?" she asked.

"Bored?" Jordan laughed. "I'm busier there than I am in Hollywood. I'm beginning to see why you felt as you did out there. No, Syd, Kenya doesn't bore me."

She wondered if that was because Maile Rowe, his latest leading lady, would be accompanying him.

"Next year," he said, "when the lodge is habitable, even if it's not finished, I hope I can have the girls for the summer and we'll go to Africa. I want them to see it before it's ruined. I want to show them this place I love so much and expose them to some of the things I care most about in the world."

A summer without the girls? But she knew she'd let them go.

* * * *

There wasn't a day of the following year that Juliet didn't think of the coming summer. She was going to be spending it with the person she loved above all others-well, except Ashley, of course—in the universe. And there was hardly a time that year when she had to be disciplined, despite the fact that she was fifteen.

Her mother, she thought, paid more attention to the President, who was not going to run for re-election. Sydney daily bemoaned the fact that she feared Richard Nixon would be elected. Adam had learned to keep his mouth shut at home when Sydney was on her political high horse, but it was his views that predominated in the *Chronicle*. And if there were arguments, he and Oliver overruled Sydney.

Sydney and Adam were invited to one of the last White House dinners the Johnsons would host.

The President and Adam agreed only on the war. Sydney and LBJ disagreed on that point but agreed on virtually all other policies. However, she wasn't as sure how she felt about him personally as she had when he first became President.

They'd met at a dinner party in New York, a thousand-dollar-a-plate dinner to raise money for Senator Javits and, to her surprise, Sydney was seated next to the President on the podium. He grinned at her and leaned over to whisper, "I didn't bring Lady Bird because I knew I was going to see you tonight." As his leg brushed against hers under the table, she abruptly moved. He made no other overtures, but she hadn't liked his implication. Did all men in power try to abuse it she wondered.

When Adam accompanied her to the White House, she'd carefully chosen a pale blue Cassini evening gown that flattered her coloring. Mr. Howard had suggested wearing a hairpiece so it would look as though her hair was piled on top of her head, tendrils tumbling down over her left ear. Big Mommy suggested teardrop diamond earrings from the jewelry collection she'd kept in a vault for over fifty years. When she showed them to Sydney, her granddaughter asked if she'd mind if she had them reset. They were too ornate for the sixties.

"My God, you look stunning!" Adam's voice radiated approval. "If he's the President, you look like a princess." She was glad he hadn't compared her to the Queen.

Sydney studied her reflection in the mirror. She might be thirty-nine, but her waist was still enviable and she guessed Adam had been right a decade ago when he'd told her she improved with age.

The President confirmed this. "You look beautiful, Sydney," he said, kissing her on the cheek and holding her hand.

Then he introduced her to U Thant.

A hand-picked Air Force string band played music from the forties and fifties, spreading out so that there was a musician at each of the twenty dining tables. Sydney was seated at a table that included the British ambassador, Shirley MacLaine, Leonard Bernstein, Senator O'Malley, and the wife of the Secretary of the Treasury. The conversation was stimulating; she couldn't get enough.

After dinner, they were led to the East Room, where chairs had been set up and a trio entertained them. She found Peter, Paul, and Mary quite charming but their music couldn't compare to that with which she had grown up. She didn't much like Frank Sinatra, but he knew how to dress to entertain. He'd never come on stage unshaven and in blue jeans.

After dinner there was dancing, and Sydney knew Adam would stand on the sidelines. He'd never been able to teach her chess nor could she teach him how to dance.

She was dancing with Senator McCallum when the President cut in and twirled her around the room.

"You're a very good dancer, Mr. President."

The years had taken a toll on him, and the lines in his face were pronounced, but there was a twinkle in his eyes as he held her firmly, closer than necessary, and Sydney thought, why, he's really portly. His excellent tailoring hid his stomach from the public. He murmured into her hair, "The better to hold you close, my dear."

As the orchestra segued from one medley to another, she hoped someone would cut in before she realized one simply didn't cut in on the President of the United States. Finally, when the music stopped, Sydney held out her hand and said, "Thank you, Mr. President," and started to walk away. But the President put an arm around her waist and began walking off the floor with her when she ran into Senator Javits. His wife had made one of her infrequent trips from Manhattan for this unofficial farewell. Johnson still had over four months as President, and the election was six weeks away.

"Ah, isn't this next one our dance?" asked the senator. Later, Sydney thanked him. He actually was a better dancer, too, and dancing with him didn't make her feel uncomfortable.

In a cab on the way to the Shoreham that night, Sydney said, "Again, newspapers aren't the only news sources. Let's buy a radio or TV station."

Sydney suspected the idea was anathema to Adam, as an old time newspaperman. They seldom even looked at TV, and she couldn't remember when she'd last turned a radio on.

As Jordan used to think of Hollywood, as a bastard child of the Broadway theater, so Adam viewed TV and its news coverage. "Entertainment, not news." His voice would be filled with derision.

In the morning, as they were rushing through their room service breakfast in order to catch the plane and be in their offices by nine-thirty at the latest, Sydney mentioned her idea again. "You know, a radio station in Binghamton or TV in San Francisco."

"Binghamton?" Adam's voice cracked. In the plane, they each skimmed through the early editions of *The Washington Post* and *The New York Times* during the forty minute flight.

That night at dinner, Adam said, "Binghamton's out. One should concentrate where there's power."

Sydney raised an eyebrow and cocked her head.

That night they made love, laughing as they sat in a bubble bath and ended up on the thick-piled bath mat.

After that, for the first time that Sydney could remember, Adam flicked the switch of the TV in their bedroom. They sat naked, holding hands, commenting on the eleven o'clock news before they turned to each other and again made long, slow, love until the covers were so tangled that they could hardly stop laughing trying to extricate themselves.

Six weeks later, Adam walked into Sydney's office and sat down across from her desk. He crossed his legs and smiled at her.

"Happy Birthday," he said. At breakfast she'd thought he'd forgotten because she was nearly dysfunctional at hearing so early last evening, of Nixon's victory,

It was all she could do to smile, thinly and say, "Thanks."

"Something to cheer you up." He slid a sheaf of papers across her desk.

She glanced at them. "What's this?"

"We're the owners of KP'IV in Chicago," he said.

"Thought you'd like that."

Sydney looked at him, at the expectant look on his face, at his wanting to please her, and forced a smile. She stood up and walked around the desk, leaning down to kiss him. "How nice."

She wondered why she wasn't more pleased. He'd listened to her for once.

But he hadn't even consulted her. Half of the fun would have been exploring what station and where, flying around the country to talk to owners and managers. Studying the demographics. Making the final decision.

He'd taken all that out of her hands.

"Your father and I decided that was a good idea of yours. Now, you can have fun running it."

A new toy.

That's what they always offered her. Toys. *Focus*.

Her name as co-publisher on the masthead. No real responsibilities, just enough to keep her busy and out of their hair.

Now, a TV station in Chicago. If she had to fly out there often, she'd be out of the way. Neither Oliver nor Adam considered TV real. "The little screen," they'd say, denigrating it.

And she was pretty sure, when she began to study its balance sheets, that it would be a losing proposition, a tax write-off. If she failed with it, it wouldn't matter.

Toys. Well, why not? After all, women weren't capable of handling the major things in life. Look at Congress. How many women were there? How many judges were women? How many CEOs? Adam and Oliver probably thought it was because women just couldn't cut it.

Well, she'd show them. But she wouldn't spend most of her time in Chicago. She'd stay right here and not let them ignore her. They might want her out of their hair, but she'd damn well mess it up instead.

Part of her was furious that Adam hadn't consulted her about the negotiations, hadn't let her study the demographics and the balance sheets, and hadn't given her a choice. Another part of her realized he was trying to be sweet. She'd been the one to suggest branching out into TV. He'd probably had to do a lot of talking to convince Oliver to go along with this.

She smiled brightly at her husband. "Oh, what fun it'll be," she said aloud and told her inner self that she'd make sure that's exactly what it would be. "I love new challenges."

Adam beamed at her. "I hoped you'd think that way." He reached a hand out to brush against her cheek.

Thirty Five

"For heaven's sake," Sydney's voice was raised, one of the few times Juliet could remember her that way. "You're driving me crazy, ever since you came back from Africa, or ever since Ashley went to Cornell. Whatever it is, nothing I do is right, nothing I think is correct, and nothing..."

Juliet, her voice so quiet Sydney had to strain to hear, said, "Here I thought it was just the opposite. You don't approve of anything I do."

"No wonder! You want to go out on school nights until all hours..."

"Not just school nights. You want me in by midnight weekends."

"Darling, you're not yet seventeen."

Her mother drove her insane. She was so archaic. "Every boy I date has hair that's too long, or wears jeans that are too tight..."

"They always wear jeans. Doesn't anyone in your age bracket ever get dressed up anymore?"

"Oh, Mom, for heaven's sake."

"That's another thing. I hate Mom. Can't you call me Mother?"

Juliet gazed at Sydney through hooded eyes. "Oh, you're so old-fashioned. No one calls their mothers Mother anymore."

"You could try, especially since I like it."

Juliet wouldn't. She'd be damned if she would. Sydney had read that this was called passive resistance. Civil disobedience was more like it.

"You're flunking out of school."

Juliet studied the wall behind her mother. "You haven't handed in homework since school started. That's six weeks."

Juliet looked at her shoes. "School's boring. There's nothing to learn there."

Sydney sighed. When did you acquire all the wisdom of the universe?"

Juliet could tell Sydney didn't expect an answer.

Sydney walked over and stood in front of her daughter. Juliet did not look at her but studied her fingernails, which Sydney noted were rather nicely shaped. "The only thing you think about is boys," she said. "I hope you're being careful."

"Why don't you get me a diaphragm if you're so worried?"

"Oh, dear God." Sydney pulled a chair over and sat down next to her daughter, putting a hand on Juliet's arm.

Juliet pulled away. "I don't just think about boys," she said. "I think about lots of things."

"Like what?" Sydney was struggling not to show how angry and frustrated she really was.

"Oh, about … values, what's right and wrong, that stuff." Even Juliet's vocabulary had become stunted lately.

"How about an example." Sydney's voice had a pleading quality to it.

"You wouldn't understand."

"I wouldn't understand about values? Try me, Juliet."

Juliet thought a minute, and began to mumble. "Oh, you know, like animals. You spend your money on fur coats, and Daddy spends his money so that animals don't have to die, so they won't become extinct."

Sydney studied her.

After a minute, Juliet came up with another one. "Your idea of success is having power. You never take the time to just live. You never seem to have any fun. You don't know how to talk about anything but business and politics."

Sydney sat back and looked at her daughter.

"You think smoking pot is immoral, you think sleeping with a guy without being married is sinful…"

"Whoa.'" Sydney held out a hand but didn't quite touch Juliet. "Where'd you get that idea? I just don't believe in sex without the willingness to take on the emotional responsibility, including the possibility of pregnancy."

Juliet looked up at her mother, their eyes meeting. "What do you mean, emotional responsibility?"

Sydney sighed and shrugged. "Sex is for grown-ups and not all of us can handle it that gracefully. What if the boy tells you he loves you just to get you in bed with him and then leaves? Are you up to handling that? What if you become pregnant? Are you up to deciding whether you want to have an illegitimate child, whether you want to put it up for adoption, whether you want an abortion, whether you're ready to marry the boy?"

'Jesus, Mom, you don't think of all those things when you're in the midst of passion."

"That's what I mean. You're not ready for that responsibility. Are you ready to insist he practice birth control every time, are you prepared to do that?"

"Doesn't that take the romance out of it?"

"Sex is more than romance. For twenty minutes of fun, women's lives have been ruined."

"Twenty minutes?" Juliet laughed. "God, I feel sorry for you."

It was all Sydney could do not to slap Juliet. She'd never even been tempted before, though Juliet had been a problem child most of her life. And now, all one had to do was look at her and know how many boys were after her, or would be. That cloud of ebony hair haloing her head, that heart-shaped face with those eyes simultaneously innocent and seductive.

That body, no seventeen-year-old should be that developed, so … so ripe. That was the word for Juliet, her mother thought. She wanted to ask if she was still a virgin but dared not. She wanted to know if her daughter was into drugs, but was afraid to hear the answer.

"Do you know how different Africa was?" Juliet asked, her fingers clasped together. She wore her usual tight Levi's and a tank top that looked like she'd been poured into it. Black. Everything had to be black. "It was pure. The air was pure, clean, no factories and cars polluting it. The people innocent…"

"…and starving." Then, Sydney could have bitten her tongue off. She hadn't wanted to interrupt.

Juliet's eyes gave warning signals to her mother. "People care about each other there. They take care of each other. They don't care about acquiring money and power. They just care about each day. Eating and doing their work. Never having work take over their lives. Never caring about moving up the ladder, never thinking…"

"Never thinking," Sydney's voice sounded tired.

"Oh, Mom, it's you who doesn't think. Well, you think only about politics, not about morality."

"Honey," Sydney said and put her hand on Juliet's knee. "Politics *is* morality."

"You think about how many people buy your paper and about advertising rates and winning Pulitzer prizes. You don't think about individuals. You run around with people who just don't care about other people, who…"

Suddenly Sydney stopped hearing her daughter's voice. Her daughter had no idea what she believed in, what she thought she was doing for the world. Apparently her values and moral judgments had not seeped into her daughter; she had had no influence whatsoever.

"You left Daddy just so you could do what you want, just so you could get famous and powerful. You never even cared how much you hurt him, did you? You married Adam just to have total control over the paper, didn't you? You don't even know what the word love means!"

That stopped Sydney's thoughts. Maybe she didn't. Maybe that was where she'd gone wrong. Maybe she didn't know what love meant. Certainly she'd never experienced love where she was willing to sacrifice herself to that other person. Oh, sure, she'd give her life for her daughters in a minute, without even thinking about it. So, she loved them in that way. But a man? Give up all the facets of herself to be a wife and mother and that only? Always to live life vicariously through a husband and children?

Maybe she didn't know how to love unselfishly. And she knew, too, that in order to sustain love, she had to get it in return. She wondered if her love for her younger daughter was being tested right now.

"You think I haven't loved you enough, right?"

Juliet's eyes shot darts at her. "If you did, you'd never have left Daddy. You'd have let us be a family. You wouldn't have needed to have the paper, you could have been…"

"Hey, enough." Sydney wondered how they could view their life together so differently. "Just name one time, when you've wanted me that I haven't been here for you. Name me one class play, one recital, one time you wanted to go shopping or to a movie that I haven't been available. Tell me when you and Ashley have had problems that I haven't been willing to listen."

Juliet's face scrunched up. "You've never been there for me. You don't know that the only important thing in the world is love. Money doesn't matter, not at all."

Sydney's mouth fell open. She'd thought one of the things she'd done best was be a mother. She felt as though a knife had sliced through her heart. "Oh, for heaven's sake. I've raised a hippie. The only thing that matters is love and pleasure of the moment."

Juliet ignored this. For her, the word had no pejorative connotations. "Daddy is a real father. Or he would have been if you'd let him. But you took that away from him. You took away the most precious thing in the world. If Daddy had always been with us, if you'd ever put any of us before yourself…"

Sydney stood up and looked down at Juliet. Then, she walked over to the phone and dialed Jordan in California. Jordan answered on the second ring. Sydney spent no time on preliminaries. "Our younger daughter seems to think she'd prefer living with you. Do you want to try it?"

Jordan, taken aback, said, "Wait a minute, Syd. Give me a, minute. I'm unprepared for this." '

Sydney glanced across the room at Juliet, who was sitting with her mouth agape, her eyes locked on her mother. "Do you want her or not?"

"I've always wanted her, but you know my life here. I'm going to begin filming in a couple of weeks, and I'm not sure whether it'll be here or in Canada."

"She's playing hooky half the time, she's not handed in any homework in six weeks, she's flunking every subject. Yet supposedly she's one of the brightest girls ever to go through Chapin."

"My God, what's happened?"

"Who knows, Jordan. All I know is I can't get anywhere with her. She thinks I've been a lousy mother and you're a great father. You have values and I have none."

"Oh, Christ, Syd, stop this. She must be right in the room and you're trying to punish her. What's happened?"

Sydney's voice dripped icicles, but her heart was pounding: "I've no idea what's happened. Ashley isn't here for Juliet to turn to. She has no respect for me, and apparently never has."

"Or, for God's sake, she's a teenager. When have teenagers ever respected their parents?"

'Just answer me, Jordan. Do you want her or don't you?" She didn't know what she wanted Jordan to answer. Did she want to be able to say to Juliet "your father's too busy." Did she want to punish her for hurting her so? Or did she really want Jordan and Juliet to try to forge a deep relationship, hoping that Juliet would find answers with her father?

"Here, put her on the line, will you? I know she's right there. I can tell by the tone of your voice."

Sydney held the receiver out to Juliet. "Your father wants to speak with you."

* * * *

Juliet wasn't as lonely in California as she'd been in New York. No one told her she was too young to smoke or complained that her dresses were too short, or made her date come to the house to pick her up so her mother could meet him.

Her mother had sighed at the length of the hair of the boys she dated. She'd said sixteen was too young to stay out until two and three in the morning, even if there was no school the next day.

Juliet laughed. Her mother was naive about so much. She thought "Puff, the Magic Dragon" was just a darling kid's song; she was surprised so many adults liked it. She didn't have a whisper of an idea it was about pot.

What Juliet really wanted was to go to Haight-Ashbury. She suspected if she could get up there she would find hundreds of others like herself.

Once her father had left to go on location in Vancouver, she'd had to promise him she'd be home every Friday night to receive his call, see if she was all right, if she needed anything.

He loved her, she could tell. He cared if she was all right. He hugged her, and he kissed her a lot. He talked with her like she was an adult. She appreciated that, but sometimes she just wanted to be a little girl. It seemed, though, that it was too late for that. Too late to sit on his lap and have him rock her to sleep. Too late for him to solve all her problems.

She began to have the same nightmares again, ones she hadn't had in nearly a year. She'd be alone, staring out the window at hundreds, thousands of people passing by, calling out to them and no one hearing her. She heard herself calling, "Mommy." And then, "Daddy," but no one answered. She would cry and cry, unable to stop. When she awoke her pillow would be wet with tears. She put off going to bed as long as she could, until she fell asleep in a chair while looking at TV. She stopped eating peanut butter and jelly crackers after dinner, thinking they might contribute to her dreams. She began to drink a bottle of beer before going to bed. Or wine. If she drank enough she fell asleep in a stupor and didn't dream. But she felt terrible the next morning.

Her anger at her mother didn't subside. If Sydney hadn't left Jordan, she'd be here now, and she'd take care of her while Daddy was gone, doing what daddies should. Working. Mothers didn't work. Mothers gave love and comfort. She wasn't angry at Jordan for leaving her here in his big house, but at Sydney for not being here to comfort her while Jordan was away.

She managed to get to school most mornings, even if not on time. And in that public high school, the first one she'd ever attended, in that town where it cost a million dollars to own a home, where kids had any and everything money could buy, there were others like her, and she gravitated to them, went to the beach with them, and began to feel a part of a group for the first time in her life.

On the beach one day, early in an afternoon when they'd all cut out of school early, a couple of young men-they were too old to be in school—sauntered over and began talking with the girls.

They were punks, said one of the Beverly Hills boys. And they were. Their hair was long and one of them looked like he'd never even combed his. They smoked pot openly. They were tanned and good-looking. Surfers and bikers. They rode out in the desert on Sunday mornings, one of them told Juliet.

Did she want to come? -

The way he looked at her twisted her insides, made her afraid of him yet at the same time challenged her.

"Yeah, why not?" she said.

His name was Cool Wellington, he told her.

"Cool?" she laughed. "Where'd you get a name like that?"

"I play in a band Saturday nights," he said. "You oughta come hear us sometime."

"Sure," she said.

"Once in a while famous bandleaders come over to the place where we play and pick up one of us to replace someone who's left 'em. Why, last week we had Johnny Mars come in."

He was trying to impress her. Johnny Mars. Sure.

"A couple weeks before that the guy who arranges for Joan Baez came in."

She nodded her head, not believing a word. It didn't matter, though.

"You're pretty," the young man said, looking 'down the front of her bathing suit. It made her feel like she had nothing on.

"You're pretty good-looking yourself," she found herself saying.

"Quite a couple, huh?" He laughed, reaching out to take her hand. "And I don't even know your name."

"Julie," Juliet said. No one had ever caned her that before. "Julie Elliot."

"Want me to pick you up Sunday morning?"

"No. I'll meet you someplace."

"I'll find you a helmet. It doesn't matter what else you wear."

Her mother would have had a fit. Cool had hair down below his shoulders, streaked from time spent in the sun, and his bathing suit was so skimpy and tight it left nothing to the imagination. He handed her a cigarette, and she accepted it, inhaling. It was pot. It felt good. She took another puff.

"Good girl," he said, studying her.

"I'm not," she said, "good."

He grinned. "That makes it even better."

Thirty Six

She'd never experienced anything like it before. The wind hit her face like a knife. She understood why Cool had insisted she wear a helmet and visor. The exhilaration shot through her whole body, elevating her mind to a level she'd never known. She realized they weren't going faster than cars went, but it seemed like it, and she felt more a part of things, of the trees that zoomed by like telephone poles, of the yellow daisies and the rolling hills and straight roads of the desert.

She'd never been in a desert before. Long, treeless stretches where the asphalt stretched like a black belt ahead of them. Then the fifteen motorcycles turned off onto a country road, and pebbles flew into the air as sand swirled around them. Juliet couldn't even see the bikes in front of theirs through the haze of dust and sand. The roar of their engines indicated that they were probably within arm's length.

They drove for miles back into the scrub country, back where no one lived, except maybe an Indian or two, or maybe a prospector. Toward noon they stopped on a cliff that overlooked a sandy valley broken by a crystal brook not six feet wide. Cottonwoods shaded the rivulet, and big black birds with spread-out wings circled above, crying out with sharp, piercing calls.

All the bikers, most of whom had girls with them, tore into their saddlebags and brought out six-packs by the dozen. Maybe by the hundred, Juliet thought. She'd never seen so much beer in one place in her life, except maybe a grocery store.

"Who's going to drive?" she asked Cool, looking around.

"Oh, we won't be heading back 'til dark, and by then it'll be all worn off. We'll sleep it off. Well, didja like it?"

"It was wonderful." Juliet accepted the bottle of beer he handed her after loosening the cap with his teeth. "About the nicest thing I've ever felt."

He squinted his eyes and studied her. "Well, hon, you haven't been with me very long." His grin was wicked. Juliet placed her helmet on her seat, and ran a hand through her tangled hair. The sun beat down on the parched earth. It was as hot, though not as humid, as Maryland in summer. Cool jerked his head toward the other bikers. They walked over to those who had formed a circle, sitting cross-legged, drinking their beer, already laughing raucously. He introduced her to a few, who merely nodded at her, their eyes focusing mainly from the neck down.

"You still in school?" Cool asked when they'd seated themselves. Juliet admitted she was.

"How come you're not in the Army?" she asked him. "I thought all guys who aren't in school were in the service?"

Cool gazed off into the horizon. "I'm just not. I'll go off to Canada or Sweden or even jail before I go fight over there."

Juliet studied him. "Even jail?" He didn't answer. They sat that way for nearly an hour, listening to the jokes, to the laughter, to the ribald conversation. Sweat began to pour down Juliet's neck, a trickle running down between her breasts.

Cool looked at her. "Wanna go down there?" he asked, nodding down the canyon. "Go swimming?"

"Okay." He stood up and reached a hand down to help her up, grabbing two more bottles of beer. They slid their way down the cliff, which wasn't as steep as Juliet had thought. How they'd ever get back up she didn't allow herself to think about.

"Are there snakes around here?" she asked.

Cool didn't answer. When they got to the canyon floor he reached out and grabbed her hand, leading her to the cottonwoods and the clear creek. They could see the bottom, not much more than four or five feet. The stones in it were copper colored.

They sat on the bank of the running water and dangled their feet. It was cold and Juliet wanted to dive in, swim along with it as it went who knew where. Cool offered her a beer, but she'd had three already and refused. He twisted the cap off with his teeth again and said, "Wanna go in?"

She figured her bra and panties were no more revealing than the bathing suit she'd been wearing when she met him…"Okay."

He stood up and stripped off his tank top and slid out of his jeans. He wore no underpants. His whole body was tanned. Suddenly he frightened Juliet. She wanted to get up and run away. He grinned at her. "What you see is what you get."

She stood up and unbuttoned her blouse, slowly. The very act of unbuttoning aroused him, she could see. She tossed her blouse to the ground and unzipped her jeans. Part of her found pleasure in being able to excite a man so easily. It gave her a feeling of power, though she knew, she always knew, that she was never in control. The man always was. So, for the brief time when she felt the power, she luxuriated in it.

"Jesus," he said, "you've got great boobs. Take off your bra."

"No," she said, jumping into the water, which came just above her knees. She inched forward into the fast flowing water, stretching out into it, raising her feet, so it could take her on its journey.

Cool grabbed hold of her foot and jerked her. "Where you think you're going?" he grinned. His hand came up her leg, holding her off balance. She wanted to slap his hand, throw it off her leg, yet at the same time she felt the thrill that being touched gave her. He let go of her leg and she stood up, aware that being so wet her underclothing was transparent. She might as well have been wearing nothing.

"I like it that you don't talk much," he said, as his mouth neared hers. She closed her eyes. Kissing was the part she liked most. Yet so few of the boys she'd been with knew anything about kissing, knew how to make their mouths soft, knew how to make you melt into them. Cool kissed her, but like it was something he knew he should do at this point, not as though it really excited him. His arms, winding around her, unfastened her bra, and then his mouth was on her breasts, he was furiously tugging down her panties, dragging her out of the water and onto the bank, and before she knew it, it was all over. He lay panting under the cottonwood, rolling from her, replete. She stayed where she was, on her back, staring up into the trees, their lacy leaves silhouetted against the overhead sun.

The brook made a rippling sound. In the distance she could hear the laughter and the shouting of the bikers.

Finally, he said, "I could teach you something."

She thought he meant about sex. She hadn't done anything, just lay there. But that wasn't it. "Would you like to learn to ride a bike? Do it yourself? Or would you like to learn to play the guitar? I'm good. Real good."

"Do I have to make a choice? Just one or the other?"

He turned from his back and leaned on his elbow, on his side, laughing into her eyes. "You want both? Yeah. I'll teach you both."

She closed her eyes. And, if I had the inclination, Juliet thought, I'd teach you how to kiss. But she didn't think it was worth the trouble. This boy was never going to ignite her. He was never going to touch her, not deep inside. So, why expend the energy? Save her exertions for learning new things.

She spent more time in the next month studying the guitar and learning to ride Cool's cycle than she spent in school.

Jordan phoned one Saturday. "I tried all last night to get you," he said.

"I was down at Ambrosia's."

"What's that?"

"A place where they've got bands. New acts. A sort of hang-out for comedians and musicians."

"Oh, great. Just the sort of people you ought to hang around with!" But he didn't pursue it. Juliet was on her own, and he knew it was his fault if he wasn't there to be a real father. Sydney had had a fit when she learned he'd left Juliet alone. But Mrs. Harkins stayed overnight in the little apartment over the garage, so he knew Juliet was okay.

"Daddy, I want to learn to play the guitar."

"Fine with me."

"But that means I need a guitar."

He laughed. Neither of his daughters had ever asked him for money before. "Here's my credit card number. Get the best one they make."

She didn't go that far, but Cool showed her one that he'd buy if money were no object. She didn't buy it while he was with her, but went home and ordered it on the phone, giving the clerk Jordan's credit card number. She still hadn't invited Cool to the house, always meeting him in front of the school at three o'clock, or at the beach, or at Ambrosia's. She went there every Friday and Saturday.

Sundays they went biking. She was beginning to know different parts of southern California, always the desert. She spent Sunday afternoons swilling beer and having instant sex with Cool Wellington. But, during it, she'd close her eyes and mentally finger her guitar, exploring new keys and movements, humming to herself.

She didn't know which she liked better, the guitar or biking along country roads into deserts, the wind whipping her face. Every Sunday afternoon Cool gave her biking lessons, let her drive his cycle around in circles, slowly down canyon roads.

She used Jordan's credit card and bought herself a leather outfit to wear when biking, like the other girls wore.

One Saturday night, as she sat alone at the table where she always sat waiting for Cool's band to come on, a tall, big-set man in a Stetson and an embroidered western jacket walked into Ambrosia's. He was surrounded by four other men, all towering, with cigarettes in their mouths, wearing big cowboy hats and boots. The waiters buzzed around, him like bees around honey. When he sat down, leaning back in his chair, facing her across the smoke-filled room, Juliet realized it was Johnny Mars. Cool had been telling her the truth. Imagine Johnny Mars in a place like this!

He acted like a king. Everyone was staring at him and he knew it, taking it in stride as his due. He lived his life like this, Juliet guessed, always the center of attention wherever he went.

But he was quiet. He did nothing to call attention to himself. The men with him were well-behaved, drinking beer, nothing stronger. Johnny listened to the comedian but didn't laugh. He was waiting for something else.

When Cool's group came on, the men at Johnny's table looked at him, and there must have been some kind of signal, for they all sat straighter and just by studying them you could tell they were listening. Listening real hard, and looking. After the band's numbers were over, Johnny had the waiter send Cool over to his table. Juliet watched it all, holding her breath. She'd never seen a big-name country-western star before. Not that she listened to much country, but everyone knew who Johnny Mars was.

Cool didn't play country. He was solid into rock. Juliet didn't know an awful lot about his kind of music, for she'd been raised more on Schubert and Mozart and Frank Sinatra, but she knew Cool was good.

Cool sat at the table with Johnny Mars and his friends and nodded his 'head, and that's all she could see. He was facing Johnny, not looking at her. He hunched over the table, leaning to hear Johnny say something, and then sat up straight, very straight. The men around Johnny rose and Johnny got to his feet. He was big.

Juliet couldn't see his hair, except that it curled out from under his cowboy hat. He put on dark glasses, even though it was so dark you could hardly see. He reached out his hand, and Cool jumped up, stretching to grasp it. He kept nodding his head, and when he turned around, Juliet could see he was grinning.

Everyone watched Johnny Mars leave. It seemed, after he left, that the electricity had been turned off. Cool looked around, saw Juliet at her usual table, and came bounding over, unable to wipe the smile from his face.

"Didja see that?" he asked. "Johnny Mars? You know what?" He sat down at the table, hardly able to contain his excitement. "He said he came back just to see me. Just to, my God, hire me! He's beginning a tour next month, and he wants me to go along, to be part of the Mars band. Jesus, God Almighty. Can you believe that?"

Juliet tried to feel something, but her main concern was that she wouldn't get any more guitar lessons and wouldn't feel the wind whipping her face. She wouldn't have anything to do weekends, no one to go to the beach with after school.

"I'm to go over to his place tomorrow and start rehearsing with the band. He said plan to do it all day and night every day until we leave."

Juliet wondered what was to become of her.

Well, at least her father was coming home. Christmas was in two weeks, and Jordan had told her on the phone Friday night that they were wrapping up the picture and she'd better start thinking about what she wanted for Christmas, because, by God, it was going to be the first Christmas they'd been together in Juliet's memory. They'd buy a tree and trim it together and make up for all the lost years. They'd roast a turkey themselves and have enough left over to have cold sandwiches for days. Would she rather spend Christmas at the big house or at the cottage in Malibu? Or they could spend Christmas in town and go to Malibu for New Year's. Would she like that? He thought now that she was seventeen he'd even let her celebrate and have champagne on New Year's Eve.

When she hung up the phone, Juliet thought that her Daddy didn't really know who she was. Well, he'd never been what she wanted him to be either.

It was the first time she had permitted herself to think that.

Thirty Seven

Juliet didn't miss Cool at all. She had Jordan all to herself. She couldn't remember when she'd been so happy.

In the ten days before Christmas her father undertook a spree of shopping, buying extravagances for Ashley and even for Sydney. He bought presents for people Juliet didn't even know, but whom he promised her she soon would. He bought scarves and jewelry and fine leather purses. They scoured the shops on Rodeo Drive, and at all of them Jordan was recognized and given special help.

When he had finished his shopping whirlwind and had sent off his packages, he turned his attention to buying a tree, asking Juliet's opinion until they found one they thought was perfect. He went up to the attic and found boxes of ornaments, some of which he'd had on trees when he was a boy. Juliet couldn't remember when she'd felt such contentment. She and Jordan sat around drinking hot mulled cider after they'd finished trimming the tree. They admired it, circling it, considering it from all angles. Jordan said, "I know it's corny, but then, isn't that what Christmas is?" Then he put a Mitch Miller Christmas record on, singing along with it.

Juliet thought he was like a little boy at Christmas. He asked her to play "Jingle Bells" on her guitar and was impressed when she was able to improvise. They laughed a lot.

He didn't think anyone should have to work on Christmas, so he'd let Mrs. Harkin have the day off to go over to Glendale to her son's, and when Juliet awoke, he was already in the kitchen stuffing the turkey. The aroma wafted through the house all morning.

He served popovers for breakfast, along with melon and papaya with lime and hazelnut coffee and freshly squeezed orange juice. "You didn't know your old man had these talents, did you?"

No, she hadn't. It seemed to her Jordan was always happy, humming and singing and charged with energy.

She had no urge for pot, didn't have a beer, and drank coffee all day, along with her father. He had a glass of wine before dinner and told her when she was eighteen, next year, he'd allow her to join him.

He asked her, when he'd first returned from Canada, how she was doing at school. She answered, "Fine," which was a lie.

"Much different from Chapin?"

"I like it lots better."

He'd given her three hundred dollars, enabling her to buy carefully chosen presents, which she sent off to her mother and Ashley and to Uncle Billy and Adam as well as her grandfather, but the rest she spent on Jordan. She wanted to watch him grab a present from under the tree and open it and see how he reacted to something she'd chosen, even if it was with his own money.

She bought him a tie that she really liked and a pair of round sunglasses, since everyone in California seemed to wear them all the time. But she knew that he could buy anything he wanted so she searched for something she could give him that he could not buy, that no one else could give him. She came up with something that pleased her extraordinarily and, as it turned out, elicited an unexpected reaction from him.

On Christmas morning, there were presents for him from people she'd never met, but of whom she'd heard. They were, for the most part, clever and witty and drew chuckles of appreciation from her father. And there was a mountain of presents from Sydney, two from Ashley, several from Big Mommy, one with Oliver's signature on the card but Juliet knew her mother had bought it, and one from Uncle Billy.

When they were halfway through opening their gifts she could contain herself no longer.

"Daddy, I have something for you that's not under the tree. I want to give it to you now, though. Just sit there a minute."

"May I get a cup of coffee first?"

When she returned with her guitar he was seated on the sofa, looking at her expectantly. She sat down on the floor, cross-legged, and began to sing and play, closing her eyes as she often did when lost in the music.

He came from a place behind,
Like a shadow looming in the sky,
I knew him without having met him,
Knowing why.
Slowly my heart opened a path of light,
Slowly the past found its balance.
Slowly my heart opened a path o flight,
Slowly the past found its balance,
Slowly freedom was for the asking, with no fight.
Through a lifetime of blindness
We finally saw ourselves.
Through the mistrust and misjudgment,
We finally heard ourselves.
Through the child and the man, we finally loved ourselves.
Slowly my heart opened a path of light,
Slowly the past found its balance,
Slowly freedom was for the asking, with no fight.

When Juliet finished and there was silence. She looked up, and there were tears in Jordan's eyes. "You wrote that, didn't you?"

Not even riding a bike had given Juliet such a high. She nodded, feeling a tear near the surface.

He got up and walked over and knelt down next to her, putting his arms around her and pulling her close. "Oh, honey, that's the most wonderful thing anyone's ever given me."

She felt like bursting into tears.

"I didn't know you could write something like that. My little girl."

"It's the first song I ever tried writing."

"You hit the jackpot," he said, smiling at her. "Have you written it down? I want to frame the words."

"Yes," she said. "I wrote it down for you."

"I'll keep it always. Forever. No one ever wrote a song just for me. And such a lovely song. You're a poet, you know.'"

Juliet had suspected she was.

When they'd finished opening their presents, interrupted by a phone call from Oberon and her mother and sister weeping that it was the first Christmas they'd ever been apart, Jordan checked on the turkey.

Barbara Bickmore

"Now," he said, "it's my turn. If you could have anything you wanted, what would it be?"

"Oh, Daddy, just being here with you. Today's the most perfect day of my life."

"One thing. One thing that money can buy."

Juliet shook her head in puzzlement, her hair swinging in front of her eyes so she had to brush it back. "I have everything," she' said. '

"No," her father grinned "you don't. Something I've been hearing about for the last ten days."

She thought a moment. No, it couldn't be. "Oh, Daddy, you didn't!"

"Come on," he said, getting up and walking over to her, reaching down to help her to her feet. "Let's go look in the garage."

A shining metallic wine-red Harley-Davidson Heritage Soft Tail motorcycle sat between Jordan's black Mercedes and his silver Porsche.

Juliet stood there, open-mouthed, before walking over to run her hands along it, to look at its leather seat, to caress it.

Jordan beamed. "You can exchange it for color and even for style," he said. "You can get exactly what you want, but the clerk told me this was the best money can buy. I described your height and what I think your weight is and this is what he recommended. I bought the color I liked, but we can take it over tomorrow and exchange it for…"

"Oh, no," Juliet could hardly talk. "I love it just as it is."

While they were in the midst of their turkey dinner, Cool phoned. "Merry Christmas," he said, an obvious smile in his voice.

"Hi." He had died, as far as she was concerned.

"I just wanted to call and say hello. I miss you."

When Juliet didn't respond, Cool asked, "Have you had a good Christmas?"

"Wonderful."

Why didn't she tell him about her bike?

"We're opening in Minneapolis on the tenth. Then we go over to Madison."

"So far north in the winter?"

It was about all she had to ask him.

"This is the life, man," he said instead of goodbye.

She took her bike out every day, but she didn't spend hours on it. She wanted to be with her father, who was home all the time. He wouldn't start a new picture until February and then it was going to be shot right here, at home, in Hollywood. He didn't know how his public would react to it. He was going to play a con man. A con man, as it turned out, with integrity, or else he wouldn't have accepted the part. But would they believe him as a con man, slightly seedy? One of his favorite directors, Bernie Kellerman, had talked him into it.

Since Juliet had been in California with her father, he'd had none of his famous Sunday morning brunches and so she had met only a few of his friends. One was the photographer Jordan always insisted on having on any picture he made, Alan Hawke. Another was Paul Mellon, who did something with the movies, though Juliet wasn't sure what. In fact, Jordan didn't know anyone who wasn't connected with movies. She hadn't met anyone whose face she recognized, no stars, but that didn't matter. What mattered was that she and her father did every thing together, now that he was home.

"When I'm filming this next one, we'll be able to have dinner together every night, even if I'm gone before you wake up for school."

School, yeah. Now that Cool was gone she had no one to do things with. Well, she could ride every day after school, ride up into the hills, along the canyons, even along the beach road.

She asked if she could take the bike to the beach house when they went up to Malibu on the thirtieth.

"Of course. I've been thinking of having a little party New Year's Eve. Not many. But I'd like some of my friends to meet you."

He made it sound as though he were giving the party in her honor.

Juliet thought she had everything in the world she could ever want. She awoke every day smiling and kept that feeling all day, every day. Her father, her guitar, her bike. She couldn't imagine ever wanting more.

Jordan had only invited twelve people for New Year's Eve. A couple had previous commitments, but ten said yes and brought a few extras.

Juliet loved the beach house. It was unpretentious. A two story wooden structure with a balcony overlooking the ocean from the second floor; where the two bedrooms had seafront views. Jordan had furnished it almost puritanically in glass and black leather. Not the warm, comfortable colors and style of the Beverly Hills house, which Sydney had furnished nearly twenty years before. There was informality to the beach house that appealed to Juliet. You walked into the kitchen and then, stretching toward the ocean view patio, was the combined living-dining room, really just one large room, stretching sixty feet long and twenty-two feet wide. Around the patio flowers ran riot, and the large hedge, which Jordan had planted for privacy, precluded seeing the ocean from the downstairs patio, though one always heard the ceaseless, timeless breaking of waves.

On this New Year's Eve it was balmy enough that the patio glass doors were open and the smell of salt air penetrated the house. A nearby caterer had been able to supply someone at the last minute.

Alan Hawke came with his wife, and Paul Mellon appeared with a most attractive man whom Juliet thought was effeminate, but he was witty and a clever conversationalist. Carole Cooper and her husband arrived and that made Juliet's mouth drop, though she tried not to show it. Carole Cooper had been Jordan's co-star in two movies. She wasn't nearly as beautiful as she appeared on film, but nevertheless she had an excitement about her and immediately became the center of attention. She wore little make-up, and Juliet figured that must make the difference. Her bone structure was wonderful, but it was her eyes and her voice that had catapulted her to fame. That husky voice was recognizable any place, and she fairly reeked of dramatic presence.

She made a fuss over Juliet, saying, "I've heard so much about you and your sister. This is wonderful for your father to have you here, at last. I know how much he's missed you over the years."

Juliet liked her. But the one who knocked Juliet for a loop didn't arrive until eleven.

She didn't ring the bell, but walked right in, obviously at home. She wore a white chiffon dress and her silver earrings spun as she talked. She smiled easily and her voice was so soft one had to lean toward her to hear her. She sounded like a little girl, Juliet thought. Her wide blue eyes were innocent and trusting, questioning. She put her hand through Jordan's arm and smiled up at him as though they had a secret. He leaned down and kissed her cheek, seeming to revel in her possessiveness.

Juliet knew who she was; her photograph had appeared on every magazine cover in the country, and not just movie magazines, but *Time* and *Harper's Bazaar* and *Vanity Fair*. In the last year she had had more coverage than any movie star, than any President. Hildy Vandenberg.

"Come on," Juliet heard her father say. "Come meet the other woman in my life." Hildy stretched out her hands, a smile on her wide, sensual lips.

"I've been looking forward to this. I'm sorry I couldn't spend Christmas with you, but I always go home to my folks, in Austin." She had just a faint Texas drawl.

For the first time since she'd been in California, Juliet felt cold.

"Your father couldn't do a thing Friday nights until he got hold of you on the phone."

So, she'd been in Vancouver, too. Jordan had not once mentioned her name. Was she in the picture, too, or had she just been there with him?

The evening stopped there for Juliet. She didn't remember much of the conversation. She couldn't recall what people laughed about, or who else was there. At midnight, she did remember, her father poured her a glass of champagne and leaned over to kiss her before he kissed Hildy as 1969 was ushered in.

"After I finish this next picture," Jordan said, "if Hildy and I are between roles at the same time, I'd like all three of us to go over to Africa. Show her my place there. Let her see nature as it should be. I think she'd like it, don't you?"

Juliet didn't answer.

"You'd like it, I know. Maybe as soon as school's out. A graduation present, sort of."

"I'd love that,'" Hildy said in her breathy voice.

Juliet drank four glasses of champagne, though Jordan didn't know that. And, while the party was still going on, about three o'clock, Juliet went up to her room and fell asleep without even taking off her clothes.

When she awoke, she had a terrible headache. She could see the ocean from her bed and decided that cold as it might be, she'd dive into the water, briefly. That should wake her up, give her a good start for the New Year.

She stopped, in her bathing suit, in the kitchen and poured herself some orange juice. Glasses were scattered over all the tables. Dried carrots curled up on plates, black olives wrinkled, dips had crusts on them.

Maybe she'd surprise her father and wash the dishes, clean up the place before he woke up. It was only eight. She had no idea what time the party had ended, when people finally left, but he would probably sleep for a good long time.

She ran down the beach in the cool morning air, knowing that if she just dipped her toe in the ocean she'd never go in. So she gave one headlong dash, plunging into the icy water, diving under a wave that was hardly worthy of its name. The ocean was calm-gray and calm and frigid.

One dousing was all she could take. It was just what she needed to wake her up, give her energy. Surfacing, she turned around and ran out of the water to see her father waving at her. He stood on the balcony, his chest bare, wearing only his pajama bottoms. She could tell he was smiling. Happy.

She waved back at him at the same time Hildy appeared next to him, emerging from the sliding glass doors wearing the top of his pajamas, brushing her tousled hair back with her left hand, looking beautiful even with no makeup, sleep filling her eyes. She faced the ocean and put her right arm around Jordan's waist. She barely came to his shoulder. Jordan's arm went around her shoulders and he leaned down to kiss her briefly before waving again to Juliet.

Juliet did not wash the dishes. She took a hot shower, poured herself some leftover coffee, and ate a hard roll without butter. She found three hundred and twenty-four dollars in the jacket that Jordan had left hanging in the hall closet, and rolled the few clothes she had brought to Malibu in a towel. She stuffed that into the motorcycle bag, tied her guitar on with rope she found in the garage, and called out, "I'm going for a ride."

"I'll have crepes for breakfast in half an hour," Jordan shouted down the stairs.

Juliet didn't answer.

She figured she'd pick up maps as she went along, from one state to another. What was the next one? Nevada or Utah? Or maybe Oregon? She'd never been very good at geography. She hoped it hadn't yet begun to snow, as she'd head northeast. Minneapolis was about as far north and as far to the middle of the country as you could get. She was pretty sure of that. She guessed she'd ride through Nevada. She liked the desert, and maybe it wasn't snowing there, though it might be in Montana.

She liked long, straight desert stretches. She told herself she'd love every minute of riding her bike halfway across the country.

Thirty Eight

Juliet realized she'd never known what the word cold really meant before.

One thing, though. The roads were clear. Wet but clear. Snow was piled high by the sides of the roads, but all the way north, from Kansas and through Iowa, there was no snow on the highways. But it covered the fields and the sidewalks and ice hung from trees, crystal sparkles against a Technicolor blue sky.

She existed mainly on peanut butter crackers and orange juice, paying six dollars a night at a cheap motel, keeping her money for gas and for when she got to a big city.

The highways were perfect.

It didn't snow until she hit Minneapolis. She'd assumed it would be easy to find out where Johnny Mars and his band were, but the most she could find was that they opened at the auditorium in five more days.

What to do until then?

It wasn't until the third day, holed up in her usual motel, that she thought to call around to other motels and hotels, and sure enough, Johnny's band was in one of the ritzier places. She left a message for Cool and hoped he'd call back, hoped he'd be glad to see her.

He did and he was.

The night manager woke her up at, three A.M., saying there was a call for her and the phone was down the hall. She pulled her leather jacket around her, for she'd forgotten to bring any night clothes, and stumbled down the dimly lit hallway.

"Hon, what're you doing in Minneapolis?" Cool's pleasure was obvious even though his voice was slurred.

"I came to hear you play." Because she couldn't think of anywhere else she wanted to go. Or anyone else who really wanted to see her.

"I'll come over and get you right away."

"No," Juliet mumbled. "I'm still half asleep. Do it in the morning."

Cool laughed. "We don't even wake up 'til two."

"Well, I'll come over to your hotel about then."

He gave her his room number. She wasn't prepared for what she found. His room contained three other young men and two women. There were two double beds. Cool and one of the other men were sleeping on the floor, on blankets.

But he seemed to think nothing of it and put his arms around her, smiling. She thought he was stoned. So was everyone else. He hadn't shaved in several days and his hair was mussed, as were the clothes he'd been sleeping in.

"Jeez, it's sure good to see you. Wait'll I brush my teeth and we'll go get something to eat. I can't believe it."

The others on the beds rolled over to see who he was talking to. One of the women's breasts were exposed.

"Are they with the band?" she asked as they headed down in the elevator.

"No," he said. "We don't have women in the band. They just sort of travel with us, and then after a couple of towns, drop off."

In the coffee shop, Cool ordered a hamburger for breakfast, and Juliet had a bacon, lettuce, and tomato sandwich, the most substantial food she'd eaten since leaving Malibu.

Cool didn't ask her how she got there, what made her decide to come, what he was going to do with her. He told her how great it was to be with Johnny, that the band was like a family. That touring by bus, and Johnny had two enormous ones, one for the musical instruments and audio equipment and one for the guys, was the real way to live. The real way to see the country. They had a tape player in the bus, and they played cards and just yakked. Along about late in the afternoon, they'd get to playing music, not really rehearsing; but playing around with new sounds. Cool thought he, himself, had improved about two thousand percent since joining the band just twenty-nine days ago. Just shows what inspiration could do, he said. He'd never met better guys than the ones in the band.

Already it felt like they were brothers. No jealousy. Just helping each other standing up for each other. A real family, though without the criticism that went with most families. Johnny had told him he'd been looking for a guitarist to play along with him for over six months and hadn't found one he wanted to make a permanent part of the group 'til he'd discovered Cool. That's why he'd come back three times to hear him, to make sure. He'd had each of the other band members come, too, and they'd all agreed. Johnny told him he knew he hadn't made a mistake.

They were going to rehearse at the auditorium that night, and she could come along and see what he was talking about.

What he was talking about was music that entered Juliet's pores and moved around inside her, making her blood pulse and her heartbeat with the rhythm. The guy who played the harmonica made it talk, made it sing, and made it make love to her.

She'd never heard a harmonica played like that. And when Johnny began to sing, even though Juliet hadn't been much into country music, she could tell what all the fuss was about.

Johnny wasn't dressed up tonight, just had on an aqua cotton shirt and jeans. He wore a wide belt that looked Indian, like it had come from Arizona or New Mexico, with a big silver buckle that had a turquoise stone in the center. His cowboy boots were scuffed and, peeking out from under his open necked shirt was a bolo that matched it, turquoise. His Levi's were so tight it looked like he'd been poured into them.

He didn't have a real singing voice, but what he did with his voice made you listen to every syllable, made you feel a thrill with every phrase. Made you melt.

He was big. As tall as her father, but bigger boned, heavier. Not fat, but solid, yet he moved across the stage with a light-footed grace. When he stopped singing and began strumming away on his guitar stamping his foot to the rhythm of the music, Juliet thought her blood vessels might burst. He made that guitar sing. He made it wail. He made rockets ignite in that dark auditorium, and Juliet had to take off Cool's sweater.

Later, they walked through the snowy night to a bar that was already familiar to the group. When Johnny entered, everyone broke into applause. He just grinned and headed for a dark corner. Along the way three women had materialized, two of whom Juliet thought were the ones she'd seen in bed that morning. She found herself seated directly across from Johnny, and after he'd looked around the room, after he'd ordered, his eyes latched onto her, and he sat quietly observing her. She returned his gaze. He was certainly one fascinating man. She guessed he must be about thirty-five. Close up, he looked tired. His eyes hardly ever smiled.

After about half an hour he leaned over the table, which was so large he had to shout to make himself heard. He nodded to Cool. "She yours?"

Cool laughed. "I don't know. But she drove a couple thousand miles to come see me."

Johnny raised his eyebrows, then reached out his hand to her, and said, "Let's dance."

The dance floor was roughly the size of a postage stamp.

"Got a name?" he asked.

"Julie Elliot."

He pulled her close and moved around the floor. He emanated power, and Juliet noticed people staring at them. Minneapolis probably didn't get a lot of big-time stars.

"You jail bait?" he asked.

Juliet didn't know what he meant.

"Under eighteen," he explained.

"No," she lied. "I'm just eighteen!"

"You got class," he observed. "You're not like the others."

"I'm never like anyone else," she said. That had bothered her all her life.

"How long you known Cool?"

"A couple of months."

Johnny smiled, but not with his eyes. "You're not real talkative." Juliet didn't say anything.

He pulled her so close she could feel the sharpness of his belt buckle. "You spending the night with Cool?"

"I'm sure not spending it in a crowded hotel room. I have my own room, in a motel."

"Will you spend the night with him if he comes to your place?"

Juliet looked up at him. "I have to tell you I don't think how I spend my nights is any of your business."

When they returned to the table a cigarette was being passed around the table. "Mary Jane," Cool murmured when he passed it to her. She inhaled deeply. It had been weeks.

From across the table Johnny Mars stared at her. One thing she liked. He stared right into her eyes, not at her breasts. He didn't act like he'd even noticed her body, except when he held her tight, but he liked what he saw behind her eyes. No man had done that to her.

By the time they broke up well after two, Juliet could hardly keep her eyes open.

"I'm not spending a night in bed with other people," Juliet said to Cool. "You want to be with me, you come to my place. You don't want to be with me, I'll see you tomorrow."

Cool grinned. "Not want to be with you? You nuts or something?"

He told the rest them he'd meet them at three. Their performance was tomorrow night, and the auditorium was already sold out, SRO. The evening TV reported that traffic jams were expected.

Johnny got up and walked out before anyone else did, walked out alone.

Cool really didn't know diddly about kissing, Juliet thought, not for the first time. If I'm going to be with him awhile, I better start showing him. But by the time she got up the energy, he was already inside her and five minutes later was snoring on his back, a smile on his face.

Juliet didn't care. She just did it to have someone near her, to be with someone. Just did it to please the guy enough so he wouldn't leave. She wondered if Hildy Vandenberg felt that way when Jordan made love to her.

She tried to picture her mother and father doing it and couldn't. Tried to imagine her mother in bed with Adam, and wondered if she enjoyed it or did it just to please him. Wondered what all the fuss about sex was. Wondered what an orgasm felt like and what had to be done to reach that point. And if it was as fine as she'd heard, if it made it all worthwhile.

Lying there, listening to cars rush past in the muffled hollowness the snow created, she thought of Johnny Mars and the way he looked at her across the table, the way he held her so close she knew if she could feel his belt buckle he could feel her breasts, and if that's why he held her so close. She thought of the way he made her feel when he sang in that scratchy voice of his that penetrated right into her soul. She wondered if the words that so touched her were ones he wrote, and wondered if he really felt the words, or if they were just part of his stock in trade.

He wasn't like the younger men ill his group. He didn't give parts of himself away. He'd said she wasn't talkative. He didn't waste many words himself.

As she lay there, a tune she couldn't recognize played in her head, and words came tumbling out of nowhere.

In a snowstorm's grayness
I swallowed to forget my fear
the cold was courting

She thought of Johnny on the stage, a spotlight dancing on him, and wondered how he'd sing those words. Could he know fear?

Outside, in the muffled darkness, the snow came down in large, wet flakes.

After Minneapolis, there was Madison, Wisconsin, and Cedar Rapids, Iowa, and one city after another, stretching across the winter landscape.

Juliet spent the afternoons sitting in empty auditoriums or theaters, in the darkness, listening to rehearsals. Or they all rode in the bus, sleeping or playing cards, talking about nothing much, strumming guitars and listening to that fabulous harmonica. She wanted mightily to take her guitar out and play along, see what she could learn, but she didn't dare. Even if they didn't make fun of her, she'd feel like a fool.

There were always a couple of other women in the bus, though not always the same ones. The girls the band picked up were interchangeable. She never remembered any of their names. Sometimes they slept and the bus just kept whooshing along the road through the night. Those nights, when she and Cool didn't have a room of their own, she'd hear giggles in the darkness, hear moans and she knew what was happening, right there on the bus.

Most of the time they were high. She was, too. So that when Larry Martin, the harmonica player came and sat by her one night, she wasn't surprised when his hand touched her knee. She didn't say anything, but he kept mumbling something like, "You're not like the others." She was so tired of hearing that. She wished she knew what to do to make herself like the others. She'd always wondered how to be like other people.

But when his hand moved up her leg, she said, "Cool won't like what you're doing."

"What about you?" he whispered, leaning over to kiss her neck.

"He'll be angry with you."

"No, he won't. We trade like this all the time."

She sat up straight and looked around, but couldn't see in the darkness, not way into the back, anyhow.

"Yeah, he's back there with the blonde. It's okay." His hands moved to her crotch. She didn't know why she didn't stop Larry. She was furious with Cool. What the hell was he doing back there with another girl?

Larry took his hand away and lit a cigarette. He offered it to her. Why not? So what if she'd had three beers since dinner? She inhaled deeply. He twisted in his seat and cupped one of his hands over her breast. He reached over her and hit the reclining seat button, and the seat slid back to a prone position.

He climbed on top of her, kissing her wetly, saying, "You have the greatest boobs."

Did men think of nothing other than breasts? At least he kissed better than Cool did, but she didn't like the feel of his tongue in her mouth. She wondered how he could play such beautiful music on his harmonica. And then she felt him against her, felt him pulling at her jeans, unzipping his, felt his flesh against hers, felt his maleness between her legs, felt him thrust into her without any foreplay at all; without anything. Felt his thrusting, heard him grunt, and then he slumped against her, lying there for a minute, before he moved back in the seat beside her, zipping himself up.

Ever afterward, for all the time she was to know him or hear of him, his music never again sounded the same.

The next night, after a concert in Bloomington, Indiana, where they were going to spend the night in a hotel, it was not Larry who took his turn. In the dark, smoke-filled nightclub they had gone to after the show, it was Johnny Mars who said to Cool, "Find someone else tonight."

No one asked her. And Cool didn't say no. He cast a quick look at Juliet and nodded. Johnny reached out his hand and stood up, pulling her with him.

"Come on," he said, leading the way to the elevator.

Johnny wasn't like the others. He wasn't like any man she'd ever known. Johnny got pleasure from exciting her, from doing things to her that made her moan, that made her move under him, by showing her things she'd never known about. And he knew how to kiss. Oh, did he know how to kiss. He used his tongue every place, even in places she'd hardly known were part of her. She trembled. Once she felt so on the edge of a precipice. She felt herself falling and falling, then she heard herself cry out. She didn't want him ever to stop, she wanted the feeling to continue, upward and into her core.

He did it to her again and again.

She closed her eyes. For a man as big as he was, he was surprisingly gentle and when he was on top of her he never let all his weight rest on her. And he kept doing those things to her until dawn.

Maybe this was what was meant by making love

As a sliver of pale rose streaked the eastern horizon, she fell into a tousled sleep.

The next night, Johnny said to Cool, "Find yourself another woman. For good."

Cool never even objected.

Thirty Nine

From then on Juliet stayed in Johnny's room, sat with Johnny on the bus. Ate with Johnny. And moved in the bed at nights with Johnny, learning things she'd never known before. Not just in bed. Johnny also spent hours teaching her how to finger a guitar.

Once she became known as Johnny's girl none of the other guys in the band came on to her. They left her alone. They were friendly, but they knew better than to try to fool around with her. Even Cool.

On her eighteenth birthday, after they'd made love, Johnny asked, "You wanna get married?" He sat on the edge of the bed and reached into his wallet and took out a small envelope filled with white powder.

Marry? Be Mrs. Johnny Mars?

Instead of answering, she asked, "What're you doing?"

Johnny was sniffing the powder. "C'mon, babe! You've seen me doing this before."

She swore she hadn't.

"When?"

"Off 'n' on."

"No, I mean, when do you want to get married?"

"Well, we could do it tonight. Where are we?" They were in a different city every night. "I don't know what the laws are here. Do we need a blood test? Is there a waitin' period? We have to be in Nashville this weekend."

Nashville? She never knew where they were going next.

"What're we doing in Nashville?"

He reached out for her, laughing. "Now, what do you think we're doing there? Grand Ole Opry, of course. We're going to stay there a couple weeks, but if we get married in Nashville, there won't be no privacy. It'll be a big do." Marry Johnny Mars? Have Johnny Mars's babies?

"Does that mean I'd have to stay home while you go traveling?"

"No. It won't change life none. Just make it legal."

"Why do we have to make it legal?"

"Hey, gal," he pulled her to him, his mouth coming down hard on hers. "I thought all women wanted to get married."

She'd thought when you fell in love and someone kissed you, bells rang. Your body sang and your heart beat fast. No man had ever done that to her. She felt Johnny's hands on her body, felt him pulling down her bra straps, felt his tongue on her breasts, but everything she felt was on the outside. Nothing happened inside her. Nothing made her yearn for him to start making love to her again, nothing happened to her heart or her mind. It didn't matter whether he made love again or whether he didn't. He kissed better than Cool that was for sure. He kissed better than any man who'd ever kissed her. But his kisses didn't go beyond her lips, didn't touch her soul, where it really mattered.

Would it matter whether or not she was Mrs. Johnny Mars? "I don't know, Johnny," she said. "I sort of like things the way they've been."

He pulled away from her and she saw a look of anger in his eyes. "Do you hear those chicks cry out every night? Do you know what any of them would give to be Mrs. Johnny Mars? Come to my bed every night? And you're saying you don't know if you want to marry me?"

"We've only been together a little over a month. Don't you think we should know each other better?"

"What's to know? Shit, you're just eighteen. You haven't even been written on yet. You don't know not a thing."

He stood up and walked into the bathroom. He didn't close the door, but turned the shower on. Juliet lay there, realizing he was angry. Would this be the end if she said no? What would she do then?

She had an urge to talk with Ashley. She hadn't even called any of her family since she'd left LA. She'd sent postcards to let them know she was all right.

She tried to blank her mind. It was nearly two. Yet she knew she couldn't fall asleep. She reached under the bed and pulled out Johnny's guitar. Sitting up in bed, naked, cross-legged, she strummed a tune she hadn't heard before, making up words to match it. She closed her eyes, as she nearly always did when the music poured into her. She saw the visions, the flowers she sang about. She didn't see Johnny standing in the doorway, toweling himself dry, looking at her with an open mouth.

Before she finished, he said, "How come I didn't know you could sing? And what song is that?"

Juliet stopped, opening her eyes. He was nice-looking. And for once his eyes were soft, almost smiling.

"I can't sing," she said. "I was just playing around."

"Well, it's not a strong voice, but it's good." Johnny walked over to the bed and sat down next to her, taking the guitar from her. "Sing with me."

Shyness overcame her. "Are you making fun of me?"

He leaned over and took the guitar. "Come on," he said as he strummed. He began to sing, soft and not loud like he did on stage. He jerked his head as if to say, come on, please. They sang together and after a verse, Juliet began to relax.

This was nice. This was more like making love than sex was. She felt close to Johnny and reached out to put her hand on his leg.

"Damn, that's fine," he said, grinning and enthusiastic. "Got an idea. Let's find another girl and have you two be backup singers. Give us a new sound."

"Oh, Johnny, I can't do that! I can't sing in front of people. I'm not that good. "

"Not strong enough as a single but perfect for backup. C'mon, babe, we'll be working together. You and me, singing together. That's my wedding present to you. You and me singing."

They found the other girl, Grace Eakins, in Nashville, just waiting for a break. She was a much more experienced singer than Juliet, having come to Nashville hoping to break into the big time. While backup for Johnny Mars wasn't exactly what Grace had had in mind, it was her first step up the ladder, and Johnny was as big-time as you could get. Juliet liked her. It was good to have another woman as a permanent member of the group. And by that time she was Mrs. Johnny Mars.

Everybody in Nashville's country music world came to the wedding

No one commented, even privately, that Juliet was young enough to be Johnny Mars's daughter. And she didn't tell her parents until it was all over, until after it was in the papers and only.

When Juliet finally got around to phoning Ashley, her sister broke into tears. "Oh, Julie, how could you do this without me there? I'd have dropped everything to come."

Juliet had no answer.

"We've been worried to death about you." When Juliet still didn't say anything, Ashley continued. "What's he like? Do you love him a lot?"

Juliet shook her head, even though Ashley couldn't see her.

"He's making me a backup singer," she said, as though that explained everything.

"You, a singer?" Ashley didn't exactly laugh, but she sounded mystified.

"You don't have to tell me; I know I'm not a singer, but it keeps Johnny happy. He sees it as something we can do together."

And it kept him on an even ked. He was drinking less. He smoked pot less. He didn't fool around with the white powder very often. The trouble was, Juliet couldn't really tell when he was stoned. And when he was drinking he insisted she drink along with him. Late nights were becoming blurs. She slept later and later, waking up in the middle of the afternoon, when Johnny did. She thought they had sex every night, but most of the time she couldn't remember.

"Are you happy?" Ashley asked.

For a few seconds there was no-response, then Juliet answered with a question. "What's happiness, Lee?"

Ashley changed the topic. "Mom worries about you all the time. She's frantic when she doesn't know where you are. It'd be nice if you'd call her."

"I don't have anything to say."

"Oh, for heaven's sake, Mom's not like you think she is. She loves you. You've just never let her. Just call and tell her what you've told me. Tell her where you are, that you're a singer now, that you're safe."

"I'll think about it," Juliet promised before hanging up. They were going to stay in Nashville until August, making an album, getting together a new act now that they had backup singers.

"I'm sick of always eating out," Juliet said. "Can't we get a place with a kitchen?" And though they did get an apartment instead of staying in hotels, Johnny never ate there. He liked just a bite to eat before working for seven and eight hours in a rehearsal hall, striving for just the right sound before recording.

Then he wanted to be with his boys, be with the band, eat with them, drink with them, smoke with them. And he always wanted Juliet there. Grace came along, too. Juliet thought she was sleeping with Cool. But maybe she was doing it with several of them, like she herself had for a brief while before Johnny took her over.

Johnny. She didn't feel she knew him at all. They'd been sharing beds for nearly four months, and she still had no idea. Was there anything beneath the man everyone saw, beyond the voice and looks that women screamed for, beyond the man who liked to screw her daily and drink and smoke? Was there something else that had escaped her? All he thought about was music, about "the right sound," and once in a while he looked at ball games on TV, but not often. He was more likely to find amusement in a bar, where his band surrounded him.

They treated him with awe. He was always the center of attention. When he talked, no one else did. When he got angry, which wasn't often, his wrath was something fearful. He always apologized afterward, putting his arm around the guy, telling him he really loved him and he didn't know what had gotten into him.

Juliet thought he was an empty shell looking for something that would fill him up. She had no idea why he wanted her.

He wanted the "new sound" ready for the State Fair circuit come August. She thought all they had in common was working on blending their voices, learning how to play the guitar with more finesse, and screwing.

And when he did the latter, she tuned him out now. She lay there, going through the motions, her eyes focused on the ceiling or closed, putting together words, concentrating on them rather than on what Johnny was doing.

"You're the best lay I've ever had," he said one night "I don't even want other women."

"I don't want other men,'" she said, wondering how she could be such a good lay when only her body was present. He rolled over and pulled a bottle out of the bedside table, swallowing from it. He reached it out to her.

"I don't need it," she said.

"Need it? Shit, I don't either. But I like it. C'mon, a little one. I don't like to drink alone."

One little one led to another, and the next thing she knew it was two in the afternoon. And the next thing she would know, it was two years later.

Forty

In the spring of her senior year at Cornell, Ashley stared out the window at the bluebells of spring that dotted the campus lawns. There were usually a few late April or early May days like, this when the thermometer shot to the nineties before returning to normal.

It was hard to concentrate on her studies. Thank goodness, there was only another month until summer vacation. She debated about whether or not to call her mother.

Or should she go through this alone?

Roger wouldn't be there for her, she knew. She was pretty sure of that, even though he had volunteered. She thought about him as the curtain billowed in the soft breeze. She'd admired his integrity and his mind first, and then one thing led to another. Every time he touched her, when his fingers crept under her sweater or he unbuttoned her blouse and encompassed her breast with his hand, caressing her, her body felt alive, electric. It had felt so nice, unlike anything she'd experienced.

She'd met Roger at a party two months ago, when she was the only one not smoking the joints being passed around. She'd tried pot and didn't like the taste, didn't like the idea of something taking over her mind, distorting her view of reality. She didn't want to become addicted to anything, which was why she'd never even tried cigarettes, plain old nicotine cigarettes.

Roger had just returned to the campus from eleven months in a federal penitentiary in Oklahoma. She'd never heard of him, but people at the party sat around cross-legged or in the lotus position, in a circle on the floor, listening to him as though he had all the wisdom in the world. Candles lit the darkened room.

"The hardest part of the whole experience was the lack of privacy," he'd said. "A hundred men in a room of double-decker beds and johns at one end with no doors, no privacy. Lights on all night. Never one goddamned second of privacy."

"Wow!" said a girl.

"Any guys try to fuck you?" someone asked.

"No," Roger answered as Ashley studied him. She couldn't see the color of his eyes in the dark, but she could make out his square face with a lock of straight, dark hair falling over his forehead. Reflections of the dancing candle flames were mirrored in his rimless glasses.

"What did you do all day?"

"Was bored. Monotony and lack of privacy are the two things that can drive you nuts, do you know that? I read a lot. They let us go to the library every day. Probably got more of an education than I get here."

"You free now?"

"Nope." He had not only burned his draft card, but was one of five who had set fire to his local draft board. "I have a trial coming up in four months unless I let myself be drafted. But I'm not going to."

"Why don't you go to Canada?"

"That's not fighting for my beliefs," he said, and that's what got Ashley.

"Civil disobedience," she murmured. "Henry David Thoreau."

"And Gandhi and Martin Luther King. Yup." He peered through the dark at her.

Though she didn't get to speak with him again at the party, when she was searching for her coat about one-thirty in the morning, he found her and said, "I don't even know your name."

She told him.

"How about my walking you home?"

"I live up the hill at Risley."

He nodded. "Suits me," even though big, wet snowflakes were falling.

She liked talking with him. He was intelligent and serious, yet had a sharp sense of humor. She hadn't worn boots because it hadn't been snowing at eight o'clock, so she slipped and slid all the way up the hill to the bridge that passed over the gorge to her dorm. He held her arm to steady her. "I'm proud of my parents," he told her. "They about died when I went to prison, but never once did they even suggest I give in. They brought me up to fight for what I believe in."

Ashley and Roger stood, she shivering with the cold and her wet feet, beneath the street light at the end of the bridge, and watched the fat flakes fall slowly to the ground. In the distance a dog barked, but the snow muted all other sounds.

He asked, "Want to take in a movie tomorrow night? I hear M*A*S*H* is supposed to be pretty good." It was. It was right up his alley.

The day following, that Sunday morning, he appeared at Risley Hall at nine, suggesting they go skating on the pond across the road Afterward they had hot chocolate and talked all afternoon. He certainly was one of the more interesting boys she'd dated.

As she would 'one day recognize, she was first attracted to men's minds. The way to seduce Ashley Eliot was to fascinate her intellectually. Not just with intelligence, but with being a person of honor and principle. It was not until those hooks were in her, not until she was already feeding on the bait, that she began to study Roger's looks. He looked like the boy next door. He was slim and clean cut; he dressed neatly, not in the unwashed jeans or cords that most of her peers wore. His shoes were always polished, and his brown hair was shorter than most of the boys. His eyes were the color of the sea on stormy days-gray-green. Ashley liked his long, slender fingers. She told him they looked like a surgeon's hands.

"I was going to be a doctor. I was pre-med before I got sent to prison. But no med-schools going to take a guy who's been a convict. So, I guess maybe I'll opt for teaching, get my doctorate another way."

"You won't earn nearly as much money."-

He nodded. "So, maybe it's better this way. I think that if money is the goal of life then one has a very narrow morality. Unless I give something back to the world, should I take anything from it?"-

He got closer and closer to Ashley's heart and wasn't even aware of it.

The big drawback was he never asked her about herself. He had no idea who her family was, no idea if she had siblings, if she liked dogs, if she believed in God, or even what she was majoring in.

He did know she lived in New York City, and laughed. "I didn't know anyone actually lived there."

He was from Liberty, Missouri, and thought it was the prettiest town imaginable. "It's straight out of 'Father Knows Best'," he told her.

She visualized it, and thought how pretty it must be. How fine to live there, to be part of Middle America, to share its values.

"Except everyone there thinks I'm a Red," he told her. "Everyone except my parents. Not one other person in town sympathizes with me. They don't even speak to me when I go home now. My parents are going to move into St. Louis. Their lifelong friends hardly associate with them. Friends they've known all their lives feel sorry for them, thinking they must have done something wrong to have a son turn out like me, a son who objects to the war in Viet Nam."

A month later it had stopped snowing and the giant red Emperor tulips poked their heads from the hard ground as lilacs scented the air. They were sitting in Ashley's dark blue Olds, on a butte overlooking Lake Cayuga. Roger reached over and put a hand between Ashley's legs, and she didn't move his hand away. He pulled her close and kissed her, his fingers moving up her leg, caressing the soft flesh there. As his tongue feathered along her lips, she opened her mouth and liked the taste of lemon grass tea and the smell of his aftershave.

She could feel her nipples harden and hoped he would kiss her breasts, hoped his hand would not stop doing what it was doing. She heard him whisper, "Touch me," and she reached out to feel him, his hardness and his desire. Her legs parted, inviting him.

"Oh, Christ," he whispered. He pulled his head back and looked at her, though she could not see his eyes in the night.

"This isn't the goddamnedest best position for this sort of thing."

Ashley reached down and unbuttoned her blouse. "Kiss me," she whispered.

Instead, he started the motor, backing out of the space they were in and driving down the hill. He drove to the Lake Breeze Motel just inside of town. As he drove into the parking lot, he gave her a look. "Is this okay with you?"

She'd been ready to make love fifteen minutes ago, but now the bright lights, the loss of intimacy, his hands not caressing her, she wasn't sure. "I don't know."

He cut the motor and looked at her under the hot pink neon light. "We don't have to, you know. Tell me, have you done this before?"

She shook her head.

"That's what I somehow thought," he grinned at her. "But I don't want you to do something you don't want to. I want to make love to you. I've wanted to do that since the night I first saw you. But only if you want it, too. I don't want to do it cramped up in a car. I'm not mad about doing it in a cheap motel, either, but I don't know any alternatives."

He was nice. He was awfully nice. Ashley had been trying to figure out whether or not she was in love with him. When he touched her, and when he kissed her, he blotted out everything else in the whole world.

As she buttoned her blouse, she opened her car door and got out. "We can at least see what happens."

He swung out of his side and said, over the roof, "If you want to back out, if you don't want to do it, I'm not going to stop seeing you. I won't be angry."

"Are you trying to talk me out of this?"

"Hell, no," he grinned, walking to the motel's office and paying for a room. When he came back, he said, swinging a key, "Room eleven, down at the end."

He wanted the light on, so he could see her. "Seeing is part of making love," he told her. He kissed her and slowly unbuttoned her blouse. Then he stood in the middle of the room and undressed. She had never seen a man totally naked before.

"You've got a great body," she said, trying to push her nervousness away. His body was almost as fine as his mind, she thought. Maybe she was in love.

"That's what I'm supposed to say to you." He smiled at her. But he didn't say it. He never said anything about how he felt toward her.

She was surprised she wasn't more embarrassed, for she'd never been naked before a man other than the family doctor and then she'd had a sheet over her, but the way Roger kissed her and what his hands did to her body did nothing except excite her. He took his time, playing her body as though he were a violin virtuoso, fingering her, exploring her, kissing her, asking her to touch him, showing her what to do, guiding her fingers until she could think of nothing else in the universe except wanting him inside her.

It didn't even hurt much. But no bells went off. It hurt enough to keep her from reaching a peak her body seemed to be climbing toward. He jutted into her, grinding against her in a way that though she hurt a little she still shivered with the ecstasy of their union.

Afterward, when they lay beside each other, holding hands, he turned the light off and said, "Let's not go yet. Let's stay all night. Let's do this again in the morning, when you won't hurt. When I can give to you what you gave to me."

He was very thoughtful. She almost said aloud, "I love you." But she didn't. She fell asleep with him curled around her.

It was still dark when she awoke, feeling his hands caressing her breasts, feeling him move in back of her, felt his erection against her and, with a sigh, she turned on her back.

"Let me show you other earthly delights."

This time he did things to her she'd never even heard of and she climaxed so forcefully that she heard herself cry out, "Oh, God!"

"Yeah," he said. "This is it."

As the sky pearled into dawn, Roger broke away from her and said, "Let's get you back to the campus."

"It doesn't matter. Everyone stays out now and then."

"Okay," he said, "if that's how you feel." So they made love the rest of the morning, until Ashley was so sore, until her breasts hurt and she couldn't let him inside her one more time.

He lay then, his head on her stomach, gazing up at her. "I'd go to jail for you, too," he said. It was the first time he'd ever said anything about his feelings for her.

Despite her discomfort, Ashley felt so happy she thought she might burst.

Just like that, anything about Roger's mind, about character and integrity, any of their political and philosophical discussions, took a backseat. And that's where they made out nearly every night-in the backseat of Ashley's car. As spring warmed up, they sometimes brought a blanket and found an isolated spot in a park beside Lake Cayuga or up in the hills in a farmer's pasture.

There was no awkward fumbling, no hasty clandestine coupling. Their lovemaking was never rushed.

Ashley's cool intellectual attitude fell out the window. She had worked so hard to stay away from anything that could become addictive, yet in a short space of time she had become addicted to being in Roger's arms. He taught her to do things to him that she'd never known women did to men, and she enjoyed them. She had never known a man's body could give her such pleasure.

Her studies suffered. When she tried to read, what she saw in front of her were not the words, but Roger's eyes and the way he looked at her. All she could think of were his kisses.

She wanted to take him to Oberon after school was out. They could make love all over the island. She wanted to lie on the soft earth under the trees in Martha's Forest with him. She wanted to swim in the little lakes with him. She wanted to take him sailing and make love to him surrounded by water. She wanted him to see it, to share the place she loved most. She wanted him to be part of it, part of her.

Yet she never got around to telling him about the place. She never once mentioned Oberon, though she imagined him there all the time.

As she stared out the window through the billowing curtain at the bluebells, graying in the twilight, she thought of their time together that afternoon when she'd told him, "I think I'm pregnant."

After the first night, when making love was so unexpected, he'd always worn a rubber, so they'd felt safe.

Silence.

Then, "How could you be?"

"It must have been that first night. I think I'm just barely pregnant. I just missed my period."

"Have you seen a doctor?" She shook her head. "I thought I'd talk with you first."

"Well, shit," Roger had said, staring in the distance, looking beyond her.

She wasn't ready to have a baby, quit school, and be a mother. She supposed she was in love, but she wasn't ready to give up her life and settle into motherhood. Have a husband who might go back to prison?

Even if he had turned and said, "Well, let's get married. I do love you," she didn't think that's what she wanted. But they'd never even spoken of love.

"Well," he'd said slowly, looking at her, his eyes troubled. "How much would an abortion cost? I could probably pay half of it. I mean, it's my problem, too."

She had no idea what abortions cost.

"You ... you don't want to have this baby, I hope."

She shook her head. "Not really."

"We'll find a way. I'll come with you, if you want."

She guessed that was thoughtful of him.

"Do you have any qualms?" he asked. "I mean, you're not a religious person, are you?"

She shook her head again. He knew next to nothing about her. "I'll make some calls," he said. "And I'll go with you, if you want."

Ashley made a call, too, to Sydney.

"Do you love this young man?" Sydney asked.

"I don't know."

"How does he feel about you?"

"I don't know."

"Honey, I'll be there by noon tomorrow."

"You don't have to do that."

"I'm coming. Right now nothing is more important. I went through an abortion many years ago and I didn't do it alone. I don't want-you to be alone."

Her mother had had an abortion? Her own mother?

"I'll fly up early tomorrow. It's really very simple, darling. Now that it's legal it's a very safe procedure. Not like it used to be."

"Are you disappointed in me?" Sydney's warmth came across the miles. "Darling, you know better. If you thought I would be, you wouldn't have phoned. Of course not. Don't you dare worry. It's not dangerous. Of course you don't want to have a baby unless you're married and want to bring a child into the world right now. I'll be there between eleven and twelve."

Ashley hung up, feeling better. Thank goodness she had the mother she had. Now she thought she had a glimmering of why Sydney was so non-judgmental, why she so seldom stood in censure. Her mother had once had an abortion! Was this before she'd met Jordan? Was this after they were divorced? And, if so, was Adam the father? Or had there been someone else in her mother's life?

Roger did not call her the next day.

Sydney went to the family-planning clinic with Ashley. Earlier, Sydney had asked Ashley if she wouldn't rather come to New York and have their gynecologist do it. Sydney understood and put no pressure on when Ashley said she'd rather have it here and be done with it, be back in classes Monday.

They made an appointment for the next morning; Ashley was out of the clinic by four in the afternoon and stayed overnight in the hotel with Sydney.

Ashley knew she would never forget the fact that her mother had come to share this time with her. What was happening to the *Chronicle* and in the world wasn't as important to Sydney as she was.

Ashley had never loved anyone more than she loved her mother at this moment.

Roger never did call her again. She saw him once, walking across the campus, and she waved. He looked straight ahead.

Forty One

Johnny only treated her nicely when they were in bed or when he had her on his arm when they went someplace. People stared at them, and Juliet was aware of this, not only because he was Johnny Mars, but because she looked the way she did. But the admiring stares seldom gave her any pleasure. They're not looking at me, she always thought, but my covering, the outside skin. Not me. Johnny bought her beautiful clothes, which she cared about but little, and fur coats, which she hated because she kept thinking of the animals that were killed.

It wasn't that he was cruel to her, he just ignored her most of the time. When they dined alone, which was hardly ever, they never had anything to say.

She was soon tired of cold, dark rehearsal halls and singing the same songs over and over.

He always wanted her around. If she wanted to go shopping by herself, or take off and walk around whatever city they were in, he'd suggest she was going out to meet some man. She never responded to these accusations, because she thought he must know no other man would dare get near Johnny Mars's wife.

She felt imprisoned. Sometimes she wondered what on earth she was doing. Why didn't she leave? She never came up with an answer. It was comfortable, and she didn't have to think most of the time. Besides, she got to see a lot of the United States. She'd seen half the university campuses in the country, she guessed, and she liked that. There was something hushed and sort of holy about campuses, and she always wondered what she'd missed by not going on to college. She liked the looks of students she saw walking through the crisp fallen leaves, or the lovers walking hand in hand on balmy days when the budding leaves were green-gold.

What Johnny liked were the screams and thunderous applause. Juliet didn't know why he and all the band members had to take coke to get high. She'd have thought they'd have gotten that just from all the adulation. What she liked about singing with the band and with Johnny and Grace was the rhythm. Her body came alive with music. Music caressed her, and the words just went right through her, words always about lost love. Always. And loneliness because of that lost love.

Maybe she'd never known love, Juliet thought but she'd sure known loneliness. Seemed like she carried it around within her.

She'd refused to try anything more than coke and pot. She thought maybe Johnny was doing a little heroin, but she hoped not. Cool was, of that she was pretty sure. Cool and a couple of the others. Cool hardly ever paid attention to her. He was involved with one pretty face after another, a different one in every city they hit and sometimes a couple at the same time in the college towns. Those girls were getting an education their parents hadn't counted on. She wondered if he'd learned how to kiss.

One of the consistent things about Johnny was he never hurried sex. He always took time, not letting himself climax until he was sure she had. And because he insisted she do so, she fought it. Sometimes she would try not to let herself go, but Johnny never showed any frustration, he just kept doing things to her until she had no control over her body. With Johnny, every single time, even if it was twice a day, she had an orgasm.

Sometimes, though the experience was physically fulfilling, she was furious. She would like not to let him have such control over her. But Johnny knew how to make love. And Johnny liked everything about it so much, even when he was stoned, that he was never in a hurry, and he was always inventing something new. Juliet figured by now there was nothing left for her to learn about sex. In some ways, she knew she was lucky.

Yet, she was not happy.

She spent hours alone in hotel rooms. She could only explore so much of each new town. Sometimes she couldn't tell one from another.

They sat in bars and dance halls and bistros until early in the morning, whether in concert or not. They slept the days away, Johnny more often than not waking after three. Often Juliet, stoned also, would lie next to him and stare at golden bars of sunshine filtering through the hotel curtains, wondering what city they were in.

When she was clean, when she had had only alcohol and was experiencing only the slightest trace of a hangover, without waking him she'd get up and get dressed, stopping in the coffee shop of whatever hotel they were 'in, gulping down orange juice, and she'd go out and prowl the streets in the afternoon, though Johnny was always irritated when she wasn't there when he awoke.

She spent hours fiddling with her guitar, playing around with new tunes and words that went from her head to her hands, words she wasn't conscious of until they came out of her mouth, and then liking the taste of them, the way they rolled over her tongue.

Late one winter afternoon, when Johnny came in from wherever, he stopped in the doorway and said, "What song is that?"

"I don't know," she replied, continuing to strum her guitar.

He raised his eyebrows. "One of yours?"

He always found it amusing that she played around with new words and tunes, but he seldom paid any attention to whatever she was doing .

"Yeah."

He sat down on the bed and listened. "It got any words?"

"Sort of."

"Sing 'em to me."

She knew he'd probably make fun of her, but when Johnny told her to do something, she did it.

She began to sing, in her husky voice that could never fill an auditorium, that needed a mike as a backup singer but that had timbre to it, that could make anyone stop talking and try to listen, to catch every word, every nuance. It was a part of her voice Juliet never understood.

I left yesterday
With blossoms on the apple trees.
The last I saw their faces
smiling, unknowing, innocent.

One step into many
the seasons pave my road
littered with
loose memories, frail faces, and
insecure dreams.

With the depth of goodbye
greater than
the wave of hello,
I steal warm smiles,
gentle kindnesses, and soft words.

One step into many
the seasons pave my road
littered with
loose memories, frail faces, and
insecure dreams.

In my dust the bonds fade,
the intimacy is abandoned,
with each step the doors close
and the fear is nourished.

One step into many
the seasons pave my road
littered with
loose memories, frail faces, and

insecure dreams.

In pale blue neon
another care awaits,
as another round of faces
claim this heart's stake.

One step into many
the seasons pave my road
littered with
loose memories, frail faces, and
insecure dreams.

Johnny didn't move or even seem to breathe as she sang. When she finished, he walked over to her and knelt down next to her.

"Wow, babe, that's humongous. Can you write it down?"

Juliet guessed she could. "Lemme show it to the boys. Maybe we could play it."

Juliet looked up at him with wide eyes. "You mean sing it in front of an audience?"

"Babe," he said, leaning over to kiss her, "I bet I can sing it to the top of the charts."

Which, after making an arrangement, is just what he did. Juliet didn't know because she never wrote home and didn't call for months on end, that the week her first song hit the charts, the song that would eventually give Johnny his eleventh gold record, was the week Big Mommy died at age ninety-four.

She died in her sleep, after a rousing night of poker.

Though infinitely sad to have lost what she considered "her rock," Sydney decided Carlos mourned the loss of her grandmother most. He was so broken up he couldn't drive a car in the funeral cortege. He insisted on flying down to Oberon with Oliver and Sydney and Uncle Billy and sat by the gravestone, in the little cemetery plot surrounded by pine trees, his dark face impassive behind eyes that looked as dead as Big Mommy was.

In her will, Big Mommy left her Rolls and Carlos to Sydney. She wanted him to be sure of a job forever, and she couldn't understand how Sydney had operated all these years without a car. She also left Carlos a hundred thousand dollars. In case he didn't want the job with Sydney, he had enough to last him awhile, anyhow. But Carlos wasn't going anywhere.

"I wouldn't know what to do without being a part of the Hamilton family," he told Sydney.

So, Sydney began to use the Rolls, which Adam loved. They no longer took cabs to work, but Carlos pulled up before their apartment house at exactly eight-thirty every morning. And whenever Sydney or Adam needed to go somewhere, Carlos was at the ready.

Uncle Billy, who had been part of the Friday night poker games for over fifteen years, insisted that Carlos still play with the group. With time, Carlos began to smile again, but the joy he 'used to evidence was never recaptured. A part of his life was buried at Oberon. He told Sydney that he often dreamed of those pine trees, which he'd seen only that once.

When Juliet finally heard about the death of her grandmother two months later, she cried for hours. She'd felt a loss for a long time, and she could pinpoint it beginning at the time Big Mommy must have died. Even though she hadn't seen her great-grandmother for three years, she knew that something had left her life that could never be replaced.

She was also afraid that she was losing her own life, and that it might be too late to regain it. She was twenty-one years old, her first song had just made gold, and she had no life of her own at all.

She did not tell Johnny that Big Mommy had left her half a million dollars. She pretended it wasn't there, sitting in a New York bank, gathering interest.

She didn't know what to do about it.

Sydney wondered how Big Mommy must have viewed her life, and her progeny. Evan was on his third marriage. His third child, the only one by his second wife was responsible for the death of another teenager, speeding so fast in his father's high powered inboard that he'd plowed right into a water skier, smashing him into oblivion. Sydney had a feeling Oliver had come through and paid the family off, as they didn't sue.

Despite repeated efforts to meet with Juliet, even offering to fly to wherever Juliet was, Sydney hadn't seen her younger daughter in nearly four years.

Juliet was into drugs. She was pretty sure of that. She read about her in the *Daily News* or those scandal sheets one found in grocery stores. Those big-time rock stars were all into drugs. And those photos of Juliet, calling herself Julie now, married to a man twice her age.

Sydney had to admit Juliet had turned into the family beauty. Even though she and Adam didn't watch TV, one night Ashley had phoned her from Ithaca and said, "Mom, Julie's on TV. Turn to Channel 11, they're showing a Johnny Mars concert."

Sydney's heart lurched, and her hand flew to her throat as tears stung her eye. Her baby, Juliet, up there in front of millions of people, singing. My heavens, Julie singing on television. A Hamilton showing herself like that. Well, she was Jordan's daughter, too, wasn't she? And she did look lovely, even if her hair managed to look like it had never been combed.

And that Johnny Mars — she guessed he was her son-in-law-well, he did put on a show. Sydney could see that his essence magnetized Juliet.

"He's something," she said to Adam, who was doing a crossword puzzle on his side of the bed. "Isn't he?"

Adam glanced up. "I give up if that's called music," he said. "Though it is better than rock. At least I understand the words."

"He's closer to my age than hers."

"That's what she's wanted, isn't it? A father figure."

Sydney turned to look at him. "Hm."

Adam studied the folded-over paper in front of him.

After the concert, when she'd turned the television off, Sydney said, "Ashley's the only one who's turned out right. Evan's children are hell raisers. And Juliet's doing whatever she's doing. I'm grateful Ashley's turned out so admirably."

"Admirably?" Adam asked. "You call having an abortion admirable?" -

Well, it's nothing to be ashamed of, she thought. But she didn't say that aloud. She knew how Adam felt about it, like breaking one of the Ten Commandments. Well, he'd broken one, too, but she didn't remind him of that.

Big Mommy must have wondered what had gone wrong with her grandchildren and great-grandchildren, Sydney thought. She and Evan both divorced and their children living such unexpected lives.

She turned off the light on her side of the bed and pulled the covers across her shoulder. Adam continued with his crossword puzzle.

Forty Two

"Mom," Ashley's excited voice shot through the phone lines. "Did you hear?" From the sound of her voice, it was something good.

"Hear what, darling?"

Sydney had been on her way out of her office when Dominique said, "Your daughter's on line three."

Dominique had instructions to interrupt Sydney if Ashley or Juliet phoned. Ashley seldom phoned her at work and Juliet, never. Not at home, either.

Sydney stood, the phone in one hand and a yellow-lined pad in the other.

"Daddy's been nominated for an Academy Award. I tried to phone him but the housekeeper said he wasn't home yet from Kenya, though I thought he was supposed to leave there four days ago."

"Well, you know your father," Sydney said. "Always someplace else." But she sat down. "Of course he was nominated five years ago, too."

"I know," Ashley said, her voice filled with pride. "Two nominations. Isn't that wonderful? Well, I just thought you'd want to know."

"Of course, darling. Of course."

"The awards are still two months away, but oh my, I do hope to get hold of him soon."

"When you do, offer him my congratulations."

"I hope Julie knows." Even Ashley was calling her Julie now.

Before Ashley could get hold of her father, Sydney saw him. He breezed through, staying in New York just one night before flying on to the coast. But he called her and asked, "Free for dinner?"

Usually Adam accompanied her when she saw Jordan. He'd listen while they talked of the girls, commiserating with each other about Juliet, wondering why she never contacted either of them. Wondering if she was safe, if she was happy.

Sydney asked herself constantly if Juliet would have been different if she'd stayed in Hollywood, being a wife and mother. When she'd voice those questions aloud, Adam would reassure her, telling her Juliet would probably have been a problem no matter what.

"If you weren't happy, if you'd been filled with resentment at the life you led, that would have communicated itself and Juliet would have picked up on that. I don't know that she'd have turned out like she has, but she'd be screwed up in some other way."

"She should have had another mother." Adam would look at her and laugh. They'd played this scene over several times.

But tonight, Sydney wanted Jordan to herself. She didn't want to have to sit between the two men, feeling she was walking a tightrope. Adam would pick up on every sign of affection and tell her she was still in love with Jordan, and that Jordan obviously had never married again because he was still carrying a torch.

And she'd say, as she must have at least a dozen times in their marriage, "Adam, for heaven's sake, remember I left him."

"Yeah, but not because you didn't love him."

"Because I couldn't live with him," she'd answer, as always.

Tonight, she would be alone with Jordan, in some quiet place. They'd talk about the girls, and she'd find out about his life. She wondered if Ashley had ever told him about her abortion, or if that was a secret between her and her mother. And Adam.

He'd be in a rush, he told her, since his plane left at six-thirty. Could they meet early, maybe five-thirty, unfashionable as it might be? ,

They arranged to meet at L'Auberge, not far from the Plaza. Certainly it wouldn't be crowded at that hour. She could walk home afterward, even though that would disappoint Carlos.

Unless it snowed, as it might.

When she told Adam he wasn't invited, he just nodded, and said, "Okay."

He'd catch a bite to eat with Steve Castor, his managing editor. They had a couple of things to talk over and hadn't had time all day to get to them.

* * * *

But she did not dine alone With Jordan. He brought a woman with him who looked young enough to be his daughter, someone not much older than Ashley, Sydney was sure.

Sydney felt as if she'd been kicked in the stomach. She'd been reading about Jordan and his women for years, but he'd never brought one along when they'd been together.

Jealousy.

She was surprised to realize that's what she felt, after all those years. How long had they been separated now? Eighteen years, and yet she felt wounded that he'd brought another woman along, even when she'd always brought Adam.

When Sydney mentioned the Academy Award nomination, Jordan nodded. "Funny, but it doesn't even seem part of me. I finished that film a year and a half ago. It's a part of my past. It's not even one of the ones I'm proudest of. I just took it so I could work with Kirk O'Malley again. He's nominated, too." So was the picture.

"What's a damn shame is Lili can't get work. She took a cameo role in this picture just to stay active. She's still one of the greatest actresses I've ever worked with."

"Then why can't she get work?"

Jordan shrugged. "She's the same age I am. Forty-eight. Too old for most women in films. But not for men."

"They're still married, aren't they? That's a surprise."

He nodded. "One of Hollywood's more durable marriages, to everyone's surprise."

And then he asked, "What do you hear from Juliet?"

"Nothing," said her mother. "I hear about her. She was on TV a couple of months ago. Johnny was in concert, and lo and behold, there was our darling, singing with another woman, doing what Ashley calls back-up. Strumming her guitar, singing and wearing next to nothing. Well, a pair of jeans, but not much on top."

Jordan laughed. "Show business must run in the family. I met them in Hollywood when they were there last year. He didn't say much. Neither did our beautiful daughter, but I guess I should have been pleased they even looked me up. I got the feeling it was his idea, not hers. Of course, he's younger than I am, but not by much."

You should talk, Sydney didn't say, glancing at the girl seated next to him. Brenda, was that her name? She'd hardly said a word, but then they were talking about their children.

"How do you think Ashley is?" Jordan asked.

Sydney laughed. "When I talked to her last week I asked if there was a man in her life, and she answered, 'you don't hear me crying, do you?' So, she's fine right now."

"I wonder if Juliet's happy."

"I wonder that, too."

When they parted, Jordan kissed her on the cheek, and Brenda took his arm as they walked the few blocks to the Plaza.

Snowflakes were falling gently, and one melted on Sydney's eyelash. Or was that a tear?

Life was certainly complex. If she'd loved him, why hadn't she stayed with him? Why couldn't she have been content to be Mrs. Jordan Eliot, wife and mother? Then her heart wouldn't feel like it was breaking every time she saw him, whether in person or in a movie, and then maybe Juliet would be a college student. And she'd call her mother and father every Sunday evening. She wondered if that would really have happened if she'd stayed in California and not had to make her own mark in the world.

When she arrived back at her brownstone, Adam was waiting for her, and from the look on his face she guessed he was filled with jealousy, wanting to know everything Jordan said. But instead he said, "God, I've been searching for you. Your father's in the hospital."

She grabbed his arm. "What's wrong?" A heart attack?

"A car hit him. I've just been waiting to go over to the hospital until I could find you. Five more minutes and I'd have gone anyhow."

She thought perhaps Adam loved Oliver more than she did. Yet the thought of her father in pain, of his perhaps dying sent chills along her spine.

"Carlos is waiting," Adam said. "I'll call him."

Oliver was bedridden, his legs and pelvis broken. The doctor told Sydney and Adam he doubted that her father would ever walk again.

She begged him to come and live with them, but her father said no, he'd grown up in his apartment, it was home to him. Why didn't Adam and Sydney move in here with him? It would be theirs one day, anyhow. If they wanted to redecorate that was fine with him, he just wasn't about to go live someplace else.

Sydney and Adam talked it over. The apartment was about three times larger than the brownstone Sydney had moved into when she took on *Focus*. She had grown up in that apartment, and Ashley and Juliet had grown up there, and – she had to admit - the apartment, the penthouse that took up the top two floors of the building her grandfather had built, was a part of her. Not quite in the way Oberon was-she couldn't imagine ever living without Oberon as part of her–but she had always loved that apartment. She loved looking down on the city from the twenty-sixth floor, loved the terraced gardens her mother and Big Mommy had made, which Warren still cared for.

Adam liked its ostentatiousness. "For a country boy from the Midwest, the luxury does appeal to me," he admitted.

Jordan was from the Midwest, too, and Sydney wondered why her father had been so adamantly opposed to one and so approving of the other.

Sydney had not bought any furniture to which she was attached, but she also felt that much in her family's apartment was old-fashioned, so she set out to redecorate all but Oliver's bedroom and study. They installed a lift for Oliver's wheelchair so he could be carried on a belt up to his bedroom, providing a change of scenery each day

Sydney hired two people to care for him, arranging for the night nurse to have the room next to Oliver's. Although she told Oliver the day nurse would have to be male because he would have to lift Oliver, her father insisted on a woman, a pretty, young one, for nights, which he spent watching television in his room. He wanted company, preferably female company.

He was a terrible patient, demanding, short-tempered, waiting impatiently for Adam and Sydney to arrive home from work to give him a blow-by-blow of the day.

Between her duties at the paper, her father's demands, and redecorating the apartment, Sydney was exhausted all the time. She even forgot to watch the Academy Awards until

Oliver sent Miss Higgins to interrupt Adam and Sydney's dinner with the announcement that the awards were being televised. Even though the show would be more than three hours long, he thought Sydney might be interested. It was the first time he had ever acknowledged Jordan, or his success.

Sydney ordered their dinner carried into the library, where they ate and listened to acceptance speeches, which seemed interminable and banal. Though he didn't leave the room, Adam busied himself at the desk, reading the daily papers from around the country, until Audrey Hepburn announced, "And the winner is ..."

She tore open the envelope and pleasure filled her luminous eyes as she announced, "Jordan Eliot!"

Thunderous applause indicated. He was a popular winner.

Sydney felt a clutch in her heart, not realizing her hand had gone to her chest.

Jordan's acceptance speech was as trite as the rest, but Sydney thought he had never looked more handsome. As he ended the brief speech, he looked right at her and said, "They may have nothing to do with my winning this award, but I want to thank my daughters, Ashley and Juliet, for just being, and their mother, for having faith in me when no one else did."

Sydney stared through her tears as the music began and a couple in costumes that barely covered them began to dance, gyrating to a rhythm she didn't even hear. She hadn't realized she'd barely whispered, "Oh, Jordan," until Adam swept past her, slamming the door behind him.

Forty Three

In all her years at Cornell, as an undergraduate and at the veterinary school, Ashley never got a mark below an "A." But she should have gotten an "F' in men.

The first year at vet school she had an affair with her organic, chemistry professor, a good-looking doctor in his mid-thirties, with sandy hair and green eyes, who had to be the brightest teacher she'd had. He was passionately in love with his subject, and inculcated that fervor in his students.

At the end of the term, after she'd left his class, he phoned her one evening. "I don't believe in dating my students," he said, "but you're no longer in my classes. I'd really like to see you. How about dinner some evening?"

Some evening turned into many evenings. They went to the movies, and they attended soccer games, which bored her, but anything Whit liked, she wanted to like. He told her she could excel in research, would she think of that?

"No, I want to be a veterinarian."

"You could be that and do research, too."

"No," she said. "I've always known what I've wanted to do."

She kept waiting, each night he brought her home, for him to kiss her. But he didn't. He told her, "You have one of the finest minds of any student I've had." That wasn't exactly what she wanted to hear.

They drove to Corning to visit the glassworks and to Watkins Glen to walk through the ravines. In the spring they sailed on Lake Cayuga in Whit's fifteen-foot *Star*, and he was delighted with her sailing ability. "You really know how to handle a boat."

"I should."

One evening, near the end of the school year, Whit suggested a twilight sail. "I'll bring a supper. There's a full moon tonight."

At last, Ashley thought, at last.

The night was warm. There was next to no breeze and, as they floated in the moonlight after a supper of cold lobster and champagne, Whit said, "I want you."

Ashley turned to him.

"I mean, I want a sexual experience with you," he said.

She smiled. "You could work up to it, you know. It wouldn't hurt to kiss me."

He leaned over and put an arm around her, his mouth upon hers. But that's all it was. Their lips touched.

"Are you a virgin?" he asked.

"No. Are you?"

He laughed. "Come on, let's go back to my apartment."

But once back there, he turned on the lights and said to her, "Well?"

His apartment looked like a monastic cell. It was spartan, neat, and in muted shades of earth tones.

"You could be a little more romantic," Ashley suggested, not knowing whether or not she wanted this now, though she'd been thinking about it for months.

"I'd like to make love." Did he think the words alone would awaken her romantic instincts?

He took her hand and led her down the hall to his bedroom, which contained only a futon and a desk, with a tall lamp in the comer. He certainly didn't spend money on possessions. '

He began to take off his clothes, piling them neatly on the desk. When he was naked he lay down on the futon and looked up at her. She kicked off her shoes and slipped out of her white cotton turtleneck and her jeans. He reached up and turned off the light.

"Touch me," he whispered.

"Kiss me," she said.

He did. But as before, his mouth was closed, his lips rigid. It wasn't a kiss. It was mouths pressed together.

He didn't touch her, breasts, and he didn't fondle her.

She lay there, waiting.

They were side by side, not touching, and he said, "I can't kiss. I mean I don't like to – it turns me off."

Well, Ashley thought, this is strange. "When I was a boy my mother always clutched me to her breasts when she came in to kiss me good night. I got to hate those breasts. I felt I was being smothered. And when I was sixteen, one night she flicked her tongue into my mouth. I jumped and screamed at her. I told her never to do anything like that again, and she fell to her knees, begging me not to tell my father.

"I'm normal, Ashley, really I am. I love sex. I just don't like breasts and any time I kiss a woman it reminds me of my mother and I just can't do anything."

He grabbed her then and moved on top of her, entering her before she even had time to realize that's what he was doing. He moved with frenzy, with abandon, his hands pressed into the bed beside her, so his weight wouldn't be on her. None of it excited her. There were no kisses, no touches.

She did begin to move with him, trying to build up some desire, but it didn't work. When he came, he barely made a sound.

They lay next to each other and, his voice shaken, he asked, "You didn't come, did you?"

No, she hadn't.

He didn't call her again, and when she came back in the fall, they didn't even run into each other.

She bought herself a dog, a black-and-white furry ball-a Heinz 57, she guessed, not knowing what breeds were involved. It took her no time at all to come up with the name Boo Boo, named after Holden Caulfield's sister in *Raise High the Roofbeam, Carpenters,* one of her favorite short stories. But then, anything J.D. Salinger wrote was a favorite.

Boo Boo and Ashley became inseparable. Except when she was in class, Boo Boo accompanied her. Her friends became used to Ashley's coming to supper with Boo Boo, with Ashley's bringing her dog to parties, and to picnics. Boo Boo became one of the more popular beings on campus.

They slept together, Ashley once waking up to find· Boo Boo's paws around her neck. On Saturdays when she'd go to the usually deserted lab alone, Boo Boo came along.

Graduate students had their own desks, and it was nearly noon on a Saturday in January that a voice said, "Do I have to clear it with your dog to ask you to lunch?"

She looked up, her glasses askew as she brushed her long hair out of her face. She'd been so absorbed in her project that she was disoriented for a second. .

Standing in the doorway was one of the older students in her class. Jonathan Seibert had to be close to thirty, a tall string bean of a man with chestnut hair, warm brown eyes, and a rather long face. His glasses were the kind that grayed in sunlight, and he'd obviously just come in from outdoors because they were still dark.

"Hi," she said.

"I've searched all over for you. How about lunch?"

Why not?

"Give me another half hour here," she said.

"Sure." He smiled and she liked the boyish look, a bit like Robert Redford, but not nearly as good-looking. "I'll be back in half an hour."

"We can take Boo Boo home first."

"No, let her come." She liked him already.

They went to a small Italian restaurant on a hill overlooking the lake. The view was spectacular, the hills covered with snow and pine trees. Below them Cayuga Lake stretched like a long finger north into the woods.

"I've never been up here. I didn't even know this place existed."

"It hasn't been open long," Jonathan said. "I have a penchant for little Italian restaurants."

He'd been teaching science for five years, he told her, in a little town called Morris, over toward the Catskills. But teaching didn't pay well, and he decided he liked animals more than he liked junior high kids.

"Actually, I might just have been looking for an excuse to come back to school. I could spend my life studying."

His long, slender fingers were expressive and he used them often, gesturing dramatically. His eyes smiled, and Ashley decided he had a nice sense of humor. "I think a sense of humor is one of the most important things a person can have."

"That surprises me," he said. "You always seem so serious."

He had grown up in Albany and didn't like cities even that large. He wanted to practice in a country town, where cows and horses would be as much a part of his practice as dogs and cats. He would be happy to work in breeding cows, in working with pigs and goats. His particular fondness was for horses. He'd never been able to afford a horse, but he had every intention of doing so once he became a veterinarian.

"You have any area you want to specialize in?"

"I'd really like to work with birds."

"Birds?" His voice cracked. '

"Where I grew up, or at least where I spent my summers, birds are really important. There are more birds in the Canadian Flyway than one can even imagine. My grandmother would nurse birds with broken wings, or those that cats or other predators hurt. I think birds are one of nature's most beautiful creations. I can watch them for hours."

"So why not become an ornithologist?"

Ashley had asked herself that often. "I want to heal. Besides, I really like all animals."

"You could never make a living just treating birds," he laughed.

He introduced her to other restaurants he favored: Anatolia's, a Greek one; Los Papagayos, which was Mexican; a Chinese place; even Japanese sushi, which she hated. There was an Indian restaurant where she loved the tandoori dishes, and a Lebanese place where the food was unlike any she'd ever tried and for which she developed a passion.

In return, she invited him to suppers in her apartment.

"God, I've never seen any student apartment decorated this beautifully," he said the first time he came, gazing around at the second floor of the house Ashley had taken when she was an undergraduate. She had spent a long time decorating it, simply yet elegantly. She felt at home here, and had had no trouble with the landlord about Boo Boo.

"You're a great cook," Jonathan told her. "I could get as addicted to your cooking as to these little restaurants I like so much."

He was seldom around weekends, only about once a month. He went home, he said, to visit his friends. He took the bus on Saturday mornings and came back late Sunday nights. He'd usually call her about ten, after he'd returned.

This was fine with Ashley, for it gave her time to catch up on the work she didn't get done those evenings she spent with Jonathan during the week, which was nearly every evening.

They did research together, and homework together and talked over their individual projects. And they kissed a lot. It wasn't until they'd been seeing each other for nearly three months that Jonathan said, one night after they'd done the dishes and were sitting on the couch with Boo Boo at Ashley's feet. "You must know I want to make love to you."

Ashley smiled at him. "I've been wondering what's taken you so long."

His arms were around her and he leaned down to kiss her neck. She felt his breath in her ear as gooseflesh tickled her neck and her left arm. His hand reached around her to fondle her breast.

"That feels good," she said.

"It sure does."

She turned her face toward him and his mouth met hers, his hand feathering down her stomach.

Ashley had forgotten how wonderful it felt to be touched. A soft moan escaped her. He pulled her plaid skirt up and his fingers touched her inner thighs. She closed her eyes as his other hand tugged at her red cashmere sweater.

"Come on," she said, standing up and reaching out a hand for him. "The bedroom's more comfortable for this." But she stopped in the bathroom to insert her diaphragm. Never again, for her, an unwanted pregnancy.

He was good at this. He took his time, kissing her face and her neck and her ears and her breasts. He kissed her belly and the insides of her thighs. He kissed the back of her knees and the length of her arms. He brought her to the brink over and over again but stopped just before she could climax, so that when she did come it was with a force she had not known before. She cried out, wondering why it sounded like 'a wail of agony rather than pleasure.

"Jesus," he said when they lay exhausted, "you're terrific."

"And vice versa," Ashley said. "My, you sure know how to please a girl."

They began to please each other every night. They stopped going to ethnic restaurants and dined at Ashley's. Once in a while they took in a movie, and they did study, but all day long Ashley looked forward to what she knew the night would bring.

Sheer, unadulterated sex. Long hours spent in bed–slow, erotic time with Jonathan making luxurious love, calling all of Ashley's senses into play. They tried positions that titillated and delighted. He used his tongue in ways for which Ashley was sure tongues had not been invented, but which she began to crave. She'd sit in a class mornings and not hear what the professor said, remembering what Jonathan's tongue had done to her the night before. She shivered in anticipation of the coming evening.

In the spring they expanded their time together, canoeing on the lake in the warm afternoons. They drove into the country to watch the earth being plowed, to see the willows turn green-gold and the fruit trees blossom.

Ashley phoned her mother to tell her she'd fallen in love. She had not said this about any man before, not even Roger.

"When am I going to meet him?" Sydney asked.

"Maybe I can bring him to Oberon this summer."

"Oh, then it *is* serious."

"Well, we haven't talked about it, but I'll invite him. I think he has to work summers to earn enough money but maybe he can take the first week after school's out to come down."

In early May, a month before the summer break, Ashley broached the subject of coming to Oberon. It was as though a veil dropped over his eyes.

"I can't," he said. "

"Got a good reason?" Ashley ran a finger over his naked chest. She leaned over and kissed it. "I'd like my mother to meet you."

"I can't," he repeated.

"Well, how about anytime the whole summer long?"

"I can't," he said again. .

"Can't or don't want to?"

He sat up in bed, drawing away from her. "Oh, shit, Ashley, I knew I'd have to tell you. I hoped it wouldn't be yet."

"Tell me what?" She sat up, looking at him intensely.

"I'm married," he said.

Ashley felt she'd been kicked in the belly. She stared at him.

"My wife's working so I can do this. She teaches art. That and a little trust fund I got from my grandfather make all this possible. That's where I go weekends. Home to her and my son, Caleb."

For just a second, Ashley thought she might be sick. She drew a deep breath. She realized her fists were clenched, and as she looked down at them she drew her arm back and hit Jonathan squarely on the jaw.

He jumped from the bed. "What the hell's that for? We've never talked of the future. You've obviously enjoyed all this. Tell me you haven't had as good a time as I have. Do you think going to bed with a guy puts strings on him? Making love doesn't promise anything permanent. Christ, Ashley, I've had the greatest five months I can ever remember. You're terrific. You're more than that. If I weren't married, Christ, I'd want to marry you. You're..."

"Get out of here," Ashley said, her voice icy and controlled. "Get out of my life."

Ashley told herself all summer, all the long, idyllic summer at Oberon, that she was not nursing a broken heart. Jonathan was right. Sex and love had little to do with promises. She should have learned that before.

Boo Boo licked her hand, played Frisbee with enthusiasm, dashed along beside her as Ashley rode horseback, walked through the meadows with her, loved sailing, and was a warm body next to her in the bed. Dogs gave unconditional love. No man did that. Ashley wondered if men even knew what the word *love* meant.

Forty Four

Juliet felt sick to her stomach. She tried to open her eyes, but when she did so the room spun around and she found herself vomiting again. The smell nearly overpowered her.

She wondered where she was. The last she remembered ... dear God, what *was* the last she remembered?

Her whole body ached. She could hardly move. She turned her right hand palm down, to feel something. Anything. Carpet. She was lying on a floor.

She tried to open her eyes again but they seemed stuck together, glued. Where had she been? Oh, she remembered.

She'd driven out alone—no one else cared about seeing it-to see the Presidents. Impressive? Oh, my. She stood there alone, in the frigid winter day, the sky a bright blue. A pale winter sun shone down on those four faces, where Lincoln's sad eyes stared out over the rocky land.

Even Teddy Roosevelt's pince nez was impressive. To think a man had carved all that and had been able to differentiate among the looks in their eyes, the muscles in their cheeks. Carved into that hard rock, even the minute differences were obvious. Juliet knew she was standing in the presence of something wonderful. Museums bored her, but Mt. Rushmore thrilled her. She'd stood there in her fur-lined boots and down parka, alone on that frigid day when the park was deserted, and spent hours staring up at the great stone faces, enthralled. She was cold. She hadn't realized she'd gotten such a chill, and she shivered all the way back to the motel in the rented car.

Maybe Johnny would be awake by now.

Johnny was not only awake but had been drinking. The moment she entered the room, before she could even take her jacket off, the back of his hand swept across her face, knocking her back against the wall.

She remembered his hitting her over and over, saying awful things. She was a whore, she had made him nothing more than a pimp for her songs. She didn't know what loyalty meant or she'd never have sold songs to Hank Williams and Patsy Cline.

Didn't she know what loyalty was? What the hell did she think? He'd taken care of her all these years; any songs she wrote belonged to him. Ray Price had taken one of them to the very top of the charts. He'd heard it on the radio as he woke up.

Goddamned whore. Fucking disloyal bitch. Who'd she think she was? She belonged to him.

Well, maybe she had, once. But no longer.

Involuntarily, her arm came up from the floor and she threw her hand in front of her face as though to protect herself.

She had to get out of here, away from Johnny. Away before he came back. He'd hit her before, but not like this.

She forced her eyes open; gunk stuck to her eyelids. She looked around. She forced herself to stare at the ceiling, swirling above her. It couldn't be the same motel. That one hadn't smelled of vomit and urine.

She moved her head, and it hurt.

She closed her eyes. She had to get away before Johnny returned. Vaguely she remembered him snarling, "You beg for a shot? Okay, babe, this is the last one you'll ever beg for. For you, there ain't nothing else, babe. It's the end of the line. And I'll be long gone. They'll call it an overdose.

"And, babe, I'm overdosed on you. Goddamn disloyal bitch."

She remembered nothing else. She turned over on her side and every inch of her body hurt. She clawed herself to a kneeling position and looked around the revolving room. A mirror was across the room on the closet door. She crawled, crying, every inch of her body in pain.

In front of the mirror, she raised her head and studied her reflection, hardly recognizing herself. Her eyes were black and blue. No wonder she had had trouble opening them. They were like slits in her battered face. Her bloody lips were so swollen and cracked she couldn't move them. Her blouse was torn and her arms discolored. Her hair was a tangled mass.

The smells of urine and vomit, she realized, were not from the motel room, but from her.

She retched.

She needed water desperately.

Crawling to the bathroom, she could hardly reach to get a glass. She inched herself up, holding onto the porcelain sink, barely able to turn on the faucet and fill the glass. Just a sip, she told herself, knowing she'd throw up again if she took even a healthy swallow.

She lay on the cold tile floor for she didn't know how long. After a while, she pulled herself over to the tub and ran water. She couldn't stand the smell. She had to bathe.

When she got to the bed, the stench still lingered in the room. She climbed between the sheets, but began to shiver so severely her teeth chattered. .

It was hours later, or maybe the next day, that she regained consciousness. And she knew she needed help. She picked up the bedside phone and dialed Ashley. "Lee, I'm sick."

"Where are you?"

"I don't know."

"What do you mean, you don't know?"

"Wait a minute." There were matches in the ashtray by the phone. She reached for them and tried to focus on the lettering. "I think I'm at the Custer Inn in Rapid City, South Dakota."

"What in the world are you doing there?"

"I don't know." It took all her concentration and energy to hold the phone.

"What's the phone number?"

Juliet studied the matchbook and read it to Ashley. "Lee, I think I've been overdosed on purpose. I looked in the closet and Johnny's clothes are gone. I think he tried to kill me, I don't know."

"Oh, Jesus Christ, Juliet. Rapid City, South Dakota. Can one even get there by plane?"

"I don't know."

"Okay, you stay right there. I'm going to phone the motel. What room are you in?"

Juliet tried to think. "I don't know. I don't even know if these are matches that belong here. Maybe I'm not here at all."

"Don't move. I'll call the motel. If you haven't heard from me in fifteen minutes, call me back." Ashley hung up.

Juliet just lay there, no longer shivering, but hungry. In a few minutes there was a rapping at the door.

Juliet weakly called out, "Come in."

A key turned in the lock and a middle-aged man with a beard stuck his head in the door. His nose scrunched up at the smell. He looked around and saw a blotched Juliet lying under the covers. "Good Lord. He told me not to come in for the next five days. He said someone needed privacy to write a book. He paid me for five days and took off in the middle of the night."

The phone rang.

It was Ashley, who said, "The manager's going to take care of you and somehow or other; blizzards or not, I'll be there tomorrow. I don't know how, but I will, even though I'm supposed to have a mid-term. Don't worry, honey. I'll be there."

Juliet began to cry.

"Now what?" Ashley wondered as she hung up the phone. How the hell to get to Rapid City, South Dakota? She tried to think of a map, attempting to envision where it was, relative to Chicago, but she gave up. It was west, that was all she knew. Did planes even fly there?

She called her mother.

"Oh, my God," Sydney said. "Well, let me call a travel agent. Let's see what we can do."

"Mother, don't you want to come?"

There was a moment's silence. "Ashley, I wish I knew what to do. I've never known what to do where Juliet's concerned. She blames me for all her problems. If I hadn't left your father, she could have had a life right out of 'Father Knows Best.' She's always been angry at me for leaving him."

"Mother, you had to do what was best for *you.*"

"Thanks, darling, but who knows what's best? I think she does these insane things because of me. I'd just aggravate the situation, I'm afraid. I've been worried sick about her for years now. But perhaps calling your father would be better. He's what she's always yearned for."

"But, Mother, when she had him..."

"Darling, she ran away because she couldn't have *all* of him. But he's the knight in shining armor to Juliet. She always dreams he'll save her, he'll love her enough that she'll find the answers she's been searching for all her life. So, why don't you call him, and I'll find out how you can get to that godforsaken place."

"Mom, I think Johnny beat her. The manager says she's in terrible condition. She's been lying in that motel for days."

"Oh, dear God. Maybe I should send Dr. Beckwith out there." Concern and irritation were both reflected in Sydney's voice. "You know what I really want to do. I want to rush out there and gather her in my arms and rock her and tell her every thing's going to be all right."

Ashley gripped the phone tightly. "Then why don't you?"

She heard Sydney sigh.

"Because everything won't be all right and Juliet would call me a liar and find something else to hold against me."

"I don't think you're being fair."

"Darling, I'm sure I'm not. I'm just venting my frustrations. Call Daddy and see if he can meet you there."

But Ashley couldn't find Jordan. She remembered he'd phoned weeks ago and said he was going someplace, some country whose name didn't even ring a bell with her, and he said he'd write and he'd phone, but so far he'd done neither. .

When she reported this back to her mother, Sydney said, "Let me phone Monday. He always knows where Jordan is."

Monday told Sydney that Jordan was in the Seychelles. Islands off Africa, he thought. . "Why does he always choose the goddamnedest, most exotic locales to make movies?"

Just then Billy walked in. She explained what was happening.

"Ashley's already driving down from Ithaca. She has to fly to Chicago and change to some rinky-dink plane and if it's snowing, as predicted, who knows whether or not it'll land in Rapid City? My heavens, South Dakota, of all places!"

Billy voiced concern at hearing of Juliet's plight. "Where are the Dakotas? Isn't that Buffalo Bill country? Somewhere between here and California, I surmise? Must be god-awful. What's she doing there?"

"How do I know? One never knows with Juliet."

"Wait a minute," Billy said suddenly. "I'll go with Ashley. Juliet may need some moral support. I've seen more drug addiction than she has, I'm sure. What airline and what time?"

Sydney knew how much Billy hated leaving Manhattan. "She's driving down from Ithaca right this minute. You two can catch the six-thirty American flight which will connect up with whatever the name of the other airline is for Rapid City at seven in the morning."

"We can stay at the Palmer House. If it's snowing, we'll take a bus from there."

Billy didn't even seem dismayed, sounding more resourceful than usual. "Or rent a car."

"Sure, I can just see the two of you driving through a blizzard. Well, dear, I will feel better if you go with her. What would we ever do without you, Billy?"

I hope you never find out."

Even though the manager cleaned up the room and brought Juliet tea and orange juice and toast, the smell lingered. He had, at Ashley's direction, called a doctor, who personally took her to the hospital. Her arm was fractured, her nose broken, and he wanted an ophthalmologist to look at her eyes.

When Ashley did arrive, late the next afternoon, the doctor obviously thought Billy was her father. He recommended that Juliet be institutionalized to cure her addictions.

"Addictions?" asked Ashley.

"Drugs and alcohol," the doctor answered. "She's killing herself, or the guy who did this tried to kill her. She needs to be rescued, and if she won't do it herself, I advise you to do it for her."

He told them the best place he knew for this sort of thing was in St. Louis, but it was expensive. Billy asked him to call and see if they could take Juliet immediately.

Juliet didn't argue. She was so glad to see her sister and Billy that she burst into tears. But to all their questions, she only replied, "I don't know."

Ashley wanted to sue Johnny Mars, but Billy told her that was impossible. "Think of the headlines," he said. "A Hamilton dragged through that? Your mother wouldn't put up with it."

His cooler head prevailed.

"Does Mother know?" Juliet asked weakly.

"Yes,'" Ashley answered.

"She was too busy to come?"

Ashley put a hand on Juliet's. "You must know that's not the reason." She remembered when their mother had left everything and come to be with her when she'd had her abortion. "She thinks," Billy said, "that she's the reason you take drugs and get into these scrapes."

When neither of the girls said anything, Billy continued. "Sydney thinks you've never forgiven her for leaving your father, and that you're trying to get away from her and her coming would only have worsened the situation."

Juliet knew that was only an excuse. Her mother had found the *Chronicle* more important.

Forty Five

Oliver was able to dine with them, albeit in his wheelchair. Sydney was surprised. Illness had made him softer, easier to get along with. She'd have thought he'd become more crotchety, losing his power, not being in control. .

He seemed to enjoy dinner times, asking probing questions concerning the *Chronicle*. Adam reported that it wasn't quite in the black, but they were not losing more than sixty thousand a year.

"Partly," he had to admit, "that's Sydney's handling of the TV station. She turned that around and has talked some of those advertisers into expanding into the New York market."

He smiled across the table at Sydney, an affectionate smile that went on and on until she thought it was downright silly. Then she leaned across the table to ask, "Adam, are you all right?"

From the look of him she wondered if something had stuck in his throat, but he just kept smiling a rather vacant smile, his fork poised in mid-air. His hand didn't move at all.

Her heart beat faster and she got up and ran around the table, putting her arms around him, staring into his eyes.

"Adam, darling, are you all right?" She knew he wasn't.

Panic swept through her. Oliver asked, "What's wrong?"

Sydney shouted, "Warren!"

He must have been only two steps away in the kitchen, for he poked his head through the swinging door, his eyebrows raised.

"Call the doctor!"

"What's wrong, Miss Sydney?"

"I don't know." Her heart was hammering in her chest. Adam's hand was still raised.

"Oh," she said impatiently, "I'll call him."

She rushed up the stairs to the Rolodex she kept on her desk and dialed her doctor.

"I'm sorry. This is the answering service. Is this an emergency?"

Sydney assured her it was and rushed back to the dining room to await the doctor's call, which surprisingly, came within three minutes.

"I don't know what it is," she almost wept into the phone. "He hasn't moved in five minutes. God, Jeff," she cried, "what is it?"

"Sydney, I've never been his doctor. Call his doctor. I suspect it's a stroke."

"For Christ's sake, Jeff, I don't even know who his doctor is. He may have mentioned him over the years, but I've never paid any attention. He's been in such good health he's never seen his doctor except for an annual checkup."

"I'll be right over." She could hear laughter and music in the background and imagined he was dining out.

By the time he arrived within half an hour, Adam's hand, at least, was down, but he still clenched the fork and his vacant stare indicated that wherever his body was, his mind was someplace else.

Dr. Beckwith asked Warren to help and they laid him on the floor. "Let me call the hospital and ask for an ambulance. I'll have to do some tests but, my dear, I do suspect a stroke."

"But he's young!"

Beckwith shook his head and headed to the phone.

"I'm driving with him in the ambulance, just in case he regains consciousness," Sydney said.

The silly grin was gone· now and Adam was unconscious. His skin was ashen, gray, and Sydney was afraid to lean down and see if he was breathing.

"That's supposed to be me, not him," Oliver said over and over. "He's not yet fifty, for God's sake."

Sydney held his cold hand all the way to the hospital. She wondered if he was dead, if the chill of his body had entered hers, for she shivered, her teeth chattering the whole way. She couldn't keep her legs from shaking even though she was sitting.

Dr. Beckwith told her to wait. It seemed like forever. An orderly came along and asked if she'd like coffee. No. She couldn't eat anything. She knew she couldn't. Her stomach was tied into a knot. She sat, or paced back and forth, clutching herself in a tense hug.

When the doctor finally did come, he put an arm around her and began leading her down the hall to the room where they'd taken Adam. "It *is* a stroke, my dear. I don't know how severe or whether he'll talk or walk again."

As they entered the room Sydney saw that Adam was in a bed that resembled a crib. "We gave him paraldehyde," the doctor said, though that meant nothing to Sydney.

"Is he going to die?" Sydney asked.

"It's too early to tell. But he's young. The question really is whether he'll be a vegetable or recover his faculties."

"Oh, God," Sydney moaned as she turned into the doctor's shoulder and began to cry. He patted her back. "I'd better call his sons," Sydney said. She would wait until morning to notify Ashley, but his boys ought to be here.

* * * *

Sydney feared she would split apart, splinter into so many fragments that, like Humpty Dumpty, she could never be put together again.

The two strongest, or at least unbending, men in her life were now dependent on her. Neither wanted to be left alone. They were scared, she realized, and bored. They lay in bed all day waiting for the moment she'd appear to fill them in on the things that had once been the center of their lives.

She'd look at Adam, sleeping. He begged her to sleep in the room with him, but she had to get her rest. She was running the paper now, and she didn't know where she found the energy.

She did sit next to his bed, now that he could talk. He could look at TV, and spent most of his time staring at it, when once he had ridiculed it. Whether or not he understood all that was going on or whether he really paid attention didn't matter.

He could talk, but his left side was paralyzed. Sydney would look at him when he dropped off to sleep and think about how fond she was of him. What had clouded their marriage was their fighting over issues, beliefs, ideas.

They'd fought about Martin Luther King and about Nixon, whom Sydney hated with a passion. Adam, while perhaps not personally liking the man, certainly respected all that he stood for. "And if nothing else, he at least has given us Kissinger." Adam wasn't sure how he felt, however, about Nixon's opening up China. He wanted nothing to do with anyplace that reeked of Communism.

They'd argued over civil rights marches, about Medicare, about Juliet, about whether or not there was a God.

"If you're not sure you believe," Adam had shouted, "what's to keep you from committing murder, or robbing someone, or..."

"Or adultery?" Sydney grinned wickedly. "Doesn't seem your sense of morality kept you from that, darling. I'll tell you what keeps me from committing sinful acts. My conscience. What's deep inside me keeps me moral, not some amorphous God."

"Shit, Sydney, you're no better than a pagan."

That surprised her. She thought of herself as a rather spiritual person, one who had grown compassionate, who reveled in nature, respected the universe, and had more faith in people than Adam and her father did, both of them believing that only the fear of God kept people good. She believed in the basic goodness of people, but she and Adam had argued about that for years.

Now, she found she missed the arguing.

She did not miss her, father's autocratic ways. He had become submissive, almost obsequious, begging her, albeit silently, for some of her time when she was home.

She was so tired she could hardly make it through dinner. She suggested setting up a small table in Adam's room and she and Oliver dined in there while the nurse fed Adam. They wanted, of course, to know what was happening at the paper. Oliver could hardly wait for his copy each morning, and had circled the editorials and numerous articles to discuss with her. To her great surprise, he did not try to run the paper from his bed.

She would be asleep by nine, in the room in which she'd grown up, now that Adam occupied their room. She would sit by the window, brushing her hair, listening to the sounds of the city, knowing that in a few minutes she would drift into sleep with thoughts that nearly always upset her. She was stretched, she felt, as far as she could be stretched. She felt she hadn't had an identity of her own for so long, she'd almost forgotten who she was. Oliver's daughter. Jordan's wife. Briefly, editor of *Focus*; now, Adam Yarborough's wife.

"I'll never marry again," she said aloud. In marriage she had lost herself, twice. She wondered if she had really loved Adam. Their clashes had been so consistent that it tempered any warmth she thought she had felt in the beginning. He had wanted her to love him, she knew that. But God, he was so narrow-minded, so bigoted, so exactly like her father in those respects. Neither he nor her father had been first-class businessmen, but money wasn't their primary concern. Propaganda was.

There was a light tap on her door. "Your brother is here." Warren's voice was soft.

Evan?

"I'll be right down," she said, reaching for her robe.

As she passed Adam's door, she went in for a second. His breathing was regular, but shallow. She sighed before turning to walk down the hallway, down the curving staircase where her brother awaited her in the library.

Evan had already helped himself to his usual bourbon and had lit a cigarette even though he knew it offended her. He sat slouched, his left foot resting across his right knee, in the wingback chair. Flames danced in the fireplace, and Sydney was suddenly aware of how much she liked this room, and how seldom she had used it lately.

"Evan," she said as she walked over and leaned down to kiss his cheek. He smelled of expensive aftershave and looked, as he always did, like an advertisement for Brooks Brothers.

"How's Adam?" he asked.

"I think he's dying," she said. "And Daddy's in terrible shape, too."

Evan shook his head. At forty-two he was as slim as he'd been at eighteen, but his face, from many years spent in the sun, was leathery and lined.

"Did you enjoy Majorca?" she asked, pouring herself a glass of Chivas Regal.

He grimaced and shook his head. "So-so. No one much there."

"That's not what I heard. The gossip columns have you involved with Therese..."

"A temporary thing. Over and done with."

Sydney sat on the loveseat opposite her brother. The warmth from the fire felt good. So did the Scotch. Maybe she should try it more often. "I didn't know you were back in the States."

"I just arrived this afternoon."

"Daddy's asleep by now."

"I came to see you. I'll see him tomorrow."

Ah. He wanted something, she could tell.

"How are the girls?" he asked.

"Ashley's graduated, as you must know. You haven't been gone that long. And Juliet, well maybe you haven't heard about her."

He leaned forward, his eyes intense. "Something happen to her?"

Sydney nodded. "She's been in a treatment center in St. Louis."

"A treatment center?" Evan's voice cracked. "You mean for drugs?"

"I mean for drugs and alcohol. It's a long story."

"Jesus."

Sydney knew Evan played around with pot and, for all she knew, cocaine."

"Tell me," he said.

She told him in as few words as possible, not letting any feeling surface.

"She going to be all right?"

"We certainly hope so. I flew out once a month after she first got there, but between Adam and Dad I can hardly get to the office now."

Evan took a deep breath. "The office, that's what I've come to see you about."

"I should have known it wasn't just to see me."

His eyes blazed and he leaned forward. "Don't give me that crap. When we were kids my sun rose and set on you. You were my life, my whole life. And then..."

"...And then we grew up."

"Yeah, always the little brother. Always the one who's never quite caught up with his always competent, always sure-of-herself sister. The sister who marries a guy who wins the Academy Award..."

"A long time after we divorced."

"And becomes the big-deal publisher."

"I've never been in control, whatever you think. No matter what it says on the masthead, until he was bedridden Daddy was the publisher. He's never relinquished one iota of power except to Adam, never to me."

"Still, you're the first woman..."

"Don't forget Dolly Schiff and Alicia Patterson, and down in Washington, Kay..."

Evan interrupted her with a wave of his hand. "Ball breakers, all of you. Never been satisfied to be normal women. Well, I figure it's time to claim my share, with the old man out of the running."

Sydney stared at him.

"I want to come work at the paper."

She began to laugh.

"I'm not exactly a moron. I figure we might share responsibilities, since obviously now that Adam's dying and Dad's incapacitated, you'll be in charge. I thought I could help."

Sydney leaned her head against the high back of her chair and gazed at her brother. "So, after I've spent fifteen years learning the business, you expect to walk in and do what I do?"

"Well, *with* you."

"Evan, you have to be out of your mind. Do you know what kind of background you'd need?"

"Dad didn't have any when he bought it."

When Sydney didn't say anything, he continued. "People tell me I write great letters."

Sydney didn't know whether to pity him or laugh. "I imagine you don't know the paper loses money annually. It's not the road to riches."

There was a moment's silence and then, his lips thin, Evan said, "I don't believe you. Not for a minute."

"We'd be much wealthier if Daddy had never bought this paper. He's poured millions into it." She let that sink in and then shrugged, adding, "We'd have far more had he not always paid for your peccadilloes and your trips and your alimonies and child support. He's probably poured as many millions into that."

Evan looked up. "I'm his son. What else was he going to do with it? Shit, it's yours and mine."

For the first time it hit her. From the day she'd left school and married Jordan, her father had never given her a cent. She'd worked for everything she'd gotten. And Evan was insinuating that she was the lucky one.

"I'm going to see Dad, have it out with him, then. I'm the son. The heir apparent, so to speak."

Sydney's eyes blazed. "Heir apparent, because you're male?"

She wondered, suddenly, if that's how Oliver saw it. He'd refused to let her take the reins, giving her only one choice: marry Adam if you want to help run the paper or...

According to Oliver, nothing was a woman's business except her home, and perhaps raising money for charity. Of course, it was the men who gave the money for the charities. He couldn't possibly leave the paper to Evan, could he? If Adam died first, would her father leave the paper to her brother? Certainly he'd include her, even though he'd sworn so long ago she'd never get one cent of inheritance from him.

But, surely, now that she'd worked with him so many years, even if he didn't approve of her gradually shifting politics.

When had he last made out a will? Surely he'd include her and Adam ... she hated herself for even thinking this way.

"Don't wake him, Evan. He's an old man and he needs his sleep. Though his mind is still sharp, his body isn't. Please wait until morning. He doesn't get up until nine. Be, here then, if you must."

Evan stood and placed his glass on the table next to him.

"Tell me," Sydney said as he headed toward the hallway, "are you so hard up you have to think of working?"

"I am," he said.

"It's what comes from living the life of a bon vivant. And, of course, having ex-wives who receive a colossal amount of alimony, to say nothing of five children to support. "

"And movie stars to play with on exotic islands."

He grinned at her. "Sydney, I'm glad you're the one who inherited the Puritan ethic. You miss so much in life."

"And you, dear brother, seem to miss nothing."

"If I do, I plan to make up for it."

He was gone.

How, she wondered, could the life he lived possibly give him satisfaction? He did nothing with it. Never had. When they were children, though, in those carefree days before she began to assume responsibility, they had been close, had such fun, laughed so much. Now, there was always tension between them.

In the morning, before dawn, Uncle Billy awakened her.

"I was just coming home," he whispered, "and thought I'd look in on your father. I do every night."

Night? It was almost dawn,

"He's dead, Sydney." There was pain in her uncle's voice.

"Dead? Daddy, dead?"

She jumped up arid went tearing down the hall to her father's room. The nurse confirmed what Billy had just told her.

"I'd been down in the kitchen having tea," she said, her voice guilty, "and when I came back up, he... he..."

Oliver Standish Hamilton.

The end of an era.

Sydney had wept for her mother and for Big Mommy. For Big Daddy when she'd been a girl. She'd wept often for Juliet. She'd grieved for Chessie and for Silver, the horse that died when she' was thirteen. .

But for Oliver, no tears came.

Ashley came down from grad school and Juliet, accompanied by a nurse, arrived from St. Louis. Hundreds of friends from Washington and around the world arrived. A quarter of the Congress and two Supreme Court justices attended Oliver's funeral. Every other New York publisher put in an appearance, as well as the Governor and Mayor.

The burial would be a closed affair at Oberon. Sydney would have to leave Adam just for the day. Billy would accompany her, and she took for granted that Evan would, too. Oliver's personal lawyer, Richard Rubens, told Sydney he'd come to her apartment at eleven the next morning to read the will.

Ashley said she didn't care who'd been left what and she had tests to take, so she drove back to Ithaca that afternoon. She and Juliet had shared their old bedroom, the one they used when visiting their grandparents, and stayed up until after three, talking. They fell asleep with their arms around each other.

Ashley told her mother she thought Juliet was better than she'd been in years. Juliet and the nurse took an evening plane back to Missouri.

Only Evan, Uncle Billy, and Sydney were present for the reading of the will.

Rubens told them Oliver rewrote his will annually, always on September thirtieth. This will was only seven months old, notarized when it was written.

To my daughter, Sydney, from whom I have learned more than I taught, I leave The New York Chronicle. She's the only one who has ever loved it as I do. I realize it's a mixed blessing, and in order for her to be able to afford to continue publishing it, I leave her everything except the other few bequests that I shall make. So long as she stays married to Adam Yarborough, and so long as he wants the job, he is to be the co-publisher.

I leave her the family apartment on the top two floors of the building my grandfather built. The rest of the building is to belong to her and her brother, in joint ownership, with Sydney managing it. The rents are to be divided annually between her and Evan.

Evan, ah, Evan. How you have troubled me, my son. As of this date, September 30, 1971, you have cost me approximately twenty-two-million dollars in alimony payments, child support, and extravagances. I leave you five million dollars.

To Ashley, who, like her mother, has beliefs and integrity and works toward her goals, I leave five million dollars. I am proud she is a Hamilton.

To Juliet, who, like her uncle, has brought nothing but embarrassment to the family, I leave a hundred thousand dollars, which is more than I think she deserves. I imagine her mother and sister will support her and her problems, no matter how little I leave her.

Oberon. Ah, Oberon. It may be Evan's only hallowed ground. I know what happy summers he and Sydney spent there as they grew up, so—trusting that he has some sense of integrity and will revere land that has been in the Hamilton family since the founding of this country-I leave Oberon jointly to Evan and Sydney. If Sydney predeceases Evan, her half will pass on to Ashley and Juliet. If Evan predeceases Sydney, his half will revert to her. Neither of them, I suspect, knows what kind of upkeep it demands financially. I hope they will each consider it worthwhile to spend whatever is needed to keep Oberon in the Hamilton family in perpetuity. I leave Evan's children, Nicholas, Diane, Anthony, Roma, and Rianna, each two hundred thousand dollars, which if they have not inherited their father's careless ways, should last them through their educations, at the very least.

To my brother-in-law, William Seabright Holister, I leave one million dollars. He has brought laughter to my life, been the brother I never had, and has always been there for any family emergency. He has willingly listened yet never given unasked-for advice. Thank you, Billy.

The rest of my estate, all my belongings and assets, I leave to my beloved daughter, Sydney, who is the son I never had, whom I am afraid I have been remiss in expressing my admiration for. I die knowing that what my family before me and what I have created will go on into perpetuity, thanks to her.

Sydney glanced at Uncle Billy, who sat beside her, his eyes glistening. Now, she wept. Why could her father never have told her this when he was alive?

"What the hell?" Evan's voice ripped through the air. "I'll contest this."

"No, you won't, son," said the lawyer. "It's airtight. We saw to that. You have two million dollars. That makes you a very wealthy man. With good investments..."

"And what does that leave her?" Evan snarled, pointing at Sydney.

"Very well off, indeed."

Forty Six

Sydney stared at the phone for a long time. Then she rang her secretary and told her, "Get me Brock Thomas at the *Times*."

She waited three or four minutes before her phone rang. She picked it up. "Brock, this is Sydney Hamilton." There was a moment's silence until she said, "Yarborough.

Sydney Yarborough."

Then, "Oh? Yes, Mrs. Yarborough."

"Any chance we can have lunch?" "Like when?" . "Today?" . . "Are you making an overture or is this strictly business?"

Sydney laughed. "Come find out."

"Yeah, I can make it. It's a slow day. Where and when?"

"How about Caruso's at one?"

"How can I say no? That's not one of my usual hangouts."

"It's near your office."

"Yeah. Well."

"One." She hung up the phone and a smile played over her face. He had no idea what precipitated this call.

She was at her usual table at Caruso's when Brock walked in. He always looked as though he'd slept in his clothes. His tie, a tasteful one in Sydney's opinion, was awry, and his glasses were smudged. She wondered how he saw through them.

The waiter showed him to her table. He smiled at her and said, "Hi," as he slid into a chair.

"What would you like to drink?"

"Scotch," he told the waiter, "on the rocks."

"Mineral water," Sydney said, "with a twist of lemon."

The waiter already knew that.

"The veal blanquette is delicious."

"Veal blanquette, huh?" Brock squinted his eyes and studied her. "You're not as skinny as you used to be. I think the last time I saw you was at LBJ's ranch."

"It can't have been that long ago."

"A memorable weekend, wasn't it?" Brock studied the menu.

She watched him. His finger twisted inside his collar, as though he wanted to loosen it. His blondish hair had streaks of gray at the temples.

"You could have knocked me over with the proverbial feather," he said as the waiter brought their drinks.

"I'll have the pesto," Sydney said. "And a salad, with olive oil and lemon."

Brock ignored her advice about the veal and ordered London broil. "Rare."

"I certainly didn't expect the publisher of the *Chronicle* to call me, especially not so early in the day."

Sydney leaned back in her chair. "What do you think of my paper?"

"Loaded question." He studied her. "First, why are we here together, having lunch?"

"Let's have a little conversation first."

"I didn't realize you were such a typical woman," he grinned. "It seems to me I've heard that line before."

He really was a bit crass.

"Well?"

"Well. Let's see. Well-written paper, but non-controversial, a bit stuffy for me. Too careful, though your politics seem to be improving, even if slowly."

"Would you suggest a tabloid style, then?"

He took a long swallow of his Scotch. "God forbid. I'm not a tabloid man. That's for the average man, and you don't want an average paper. You want a paper that'll continue to win Pulitzers, but will attract more readers. Is that why you're asking me? You want to change it now that you're the chief?"

"That's the general idea."

"Why me? I'm not a conservative."

"That's why. Also, I like you."

He raised his eyebrows. "Do you know you're the first woman to say that to me?"

Sydney nodded. "Perhaps if I were here as a woman I mightn't be saying that, but I'm here as a publisher."

He laughed.

"I want to revamp the whole thing. I've changed over the years, and my father and Adam and the paper didn't. Now, I have a chance to turn my conviction into action. I want to take stands. I don't believe in this war. When it began I took for granted, like most Americans, I imagine, that any war the United States entered was a moral war. Or at least we were on the side of morality. I'm not so sure now. I think we have no business being over there. It's not like World War Two. The students are right. I admire those who burn their draft cards or go to jail or Canada or Sweden before they'll fight in a war they consider immoral."

Brock cocked his head and raised his eyebrows. "Is this the publisher of New York's most conservative paper saying these things?"

"I think we're destroying our air and water and thus the planet."

"Well, well. Now, you begin to interest me."

"I marched in Selma."

"My God, I may fall in love with you before dessert."

The waiter brought their food.

"How much money do you earn?"

He glanced from his plate to her, eyebrows raised in question. "Thirty-five grand."

"Come be my managing editor, in charge of the whole thing. Make it one of the best newspapers in New York, or at least as good as but more readable than the *Times*. How about a hundred thousand for a starter?"

His fork was stuck in mid-air. "How many others have you approached about this?"

"None. You're the only one I've even thought of. When I knew what it was I wanted, Brock Thomas was the only name that came to mind."

His fork continued to his mouth while Sydney waited. "Me work for a woman?"

"I may withdraw that offer."

"I was only trying to be funny. You've overwhelmed me. Last time I was speechless was, I don't know when."

Sydney began to eat with gusto. She could tell he was hooked.

"Me at the *Chronicle?* Do you know how many times over the years I've ridiculed your editorials, your policies, and your politics?"

"Think of the power," Sydney said. "You can change a whole newspaper. You can't fire the people who've been there forever, but you may hire whomever you want. A whole fresh hew start."

"For you, too?"

Sydney smiled. "For us both."

They looked at each other, sipping their drinks.

"No sacred cows," Sydney said. "I'm tired of protecting J. Edgar Hoover. And we were all too silent about JFK and his women, and Bobby and Marilyn. No big names protected.

"And no going over people's heads. I don't want either of us to call reporters directly, but we'll go through editors. I have always asked an editor to be present when I see a reporter. I'd like you to do that, too."

"Christ, I could stand a new start. I'm forty-eight years old and yearning for a challenge. And here it's dropped into my lap."

"Are you saying yes?"

"We may argue."

"I don't hold grudges."

"You'll get mad at me."

"Only dogs get mad. I may get angry with you. Well, I've been angry before and generally kept my mouth shut. With a new start, and being sole owner, I won't keep my mouth shut. You'll get angry with me."

"Sounds like the beginning of a perfect love match, doesn't it?" Brock couldn't keep a grin off his face. "Well, shit a brick. I sure didn't imagine this when I woke up today."

"Do you want another drink?"

"Yeah," he said. "Coke," he told the waiter, and then grinned at her. "With a shot of lime in it."

Sydney felt extraordinarily pleased. "I want a one-hundred eighty-degree change. I refuse to cater any longer to what I consider bigotry, narrow-mindedness, and prejudice. I want to fight all the things it's the business of moral human beings to fight: ignorance, superstition, naiveté. My father and my husband, I must admit, have had an amazing lack of objectivity when it comes to journalists. From now on, subjectivity will only be on the editorial page. In the rest of the paper, I want us to print the facts, wherever the chips may fall. I don't give a damn what a Roosevelt, or a Kennedy, or a Hoover does; if it's newsworthy, it's to be reported.

"On the editorial page, however, I want to take stands for abortion–or, at least, a woman's having the right to a choice. We're going to be for civil rights, for affordable medical care for everyone…"

"Whoa!" Brock put up a hand, palm facing her. "This is almost too much to absorb. You're advocating this for New York's *Chronicle?*"

Sydney laughed. "Indeed. And, in fact, since it's almost a conditioned reflex on my part, you should hit me over the head if I ever seem to be tempted to compromise."

"My, my." He leaned back in his chair, his gaze frankly admiring.

Sydney put her elbows on the table and rested her chin on her hands. "Look, one of my main concerns is financial, how to keep advertising. I don't know anything about rates, and I figure that's not upstairs business. But, getting and keeping advertising is." She paused. "We don't make money."

Brock absorbed this, frowned, and then nodded.

"We pour money into it. However, I intend for us to be in the black within six months."

"Or?"

She reached out and touched the back of his hand. "No, your job won't be on the line. I'd keep on going, but I'd *like* to be in the black within six months."

He nodded again, obviously relieved. "We must, of course, increase circulation to be able to get new ads." She leaned closer to him, her voice lower. "I'm willing to sink half a million into this now, to turn us around. But I can't do it alone."

She watched him. "How long before you can start?"

"I've gotta give notice, of course. Maybe two weeks?"

Sydney took out a small pad from her purse and wrote numbers on a piece of paper. "Here's my home phone number," she said. "Memorize it and give it to no one else. Call me anytime. I'll make an announcement after you've informed your boss."

"Boss. Is that what you'll be? My boss?"

"My husband's name will continue on the masthead but, frankly, he's incapacitated. And, I *do* own the paper. You'll be my buffer between everyone who works at the paper and me. They'll report to you. You report only to me."

"Well, well," he said, leaning back in his chair. "What do I call you? Mrs. Yarborough or Mrs. Hamilton?"

"Sydney's fine. And the cherries jubilee is fantastic."

"Okay, let's go for it. Something other than me ought to be on fire."

His enthusiasm was boyish and she liked that. She hadn't expected to see this aspect of the man. He had a reputation for crassness, for brashness, and aggressiveness, for putting up with no nonsense, for his irreverent humor, and for his free use of four letter words.

"You're noted for being a driving force," she said. "That's what made me call you. Basically, what I want is a liberal paper with a large amount of humor and human interest that will include, but not accentuate, sex as a major phase of the human condition, but not treating it as tabloids do. I still want the concentration to be on news, not scandal or innuendo."

He nodded as though to indicate that that was fine with him.

"I work well under pressure," he said. "I demand good writing and that means intelligent thinkers. I want better editorial writers than you have. How much are you willing to let me spend?"

"I'll let you know when you get near that point," Sydney said. "But do me a favor and hire some talented women."

"Wow." He looked at her. "Just wow."

"You're not at all like I heard you were."

"Wait until you work with me."

"I can hardly. Wait, that is."

It was pouring. When she arrived home, Sydney shook the rain off as she rode upstairs in the elevator. She handed her raincoat to Warren. Uncle Billy was waiting' with a gin and tonic in hand. "I thought you might need this. I'll have one with you."

Sydney accepted the drink and walked into the living room, over to the long windows that overlooked the terrace and the city beyond. The rain slashed against the windows, rattling the panes.

She had felt so great at lunch, so delighted to have latched onto Brock Thomas. Finally the *Chronicle* could become what she'd wanted it to be. She and Brock were going to take this paper places.

Forty-four years old and at last she could take charge of her own life. She could begin to do things she had only dreamed of. She did not have to fight for her ideas any longer. She would not be ignored any longer. Whatever she wanted to happen would happen.

"I feel callous, but I'm going to take over and things are going to be as I want them to be."

Suddenly, with no warning, Sydney began to cry, great, gulping sobs that she couldn't control.

Billy sat down and crossed his legs. "I'm no earthly good with crying women," he said. "So cry to your heart's content, but don't expect anything from me."

"I don't even know why I'm crying," Sydney sniffled. She did accept Uncle Billy's handkerchief. "Oh, Billy, you're always so good in a crisis. What would I, what would we all, do without you?"

"My dear, I hope it's a long long time before you have to find out."

He let Sydney finish her crying and then said, "Something I've been thinking of since the funeral, Sydney. I know I'm not a Hamilton, but I hope you'll bury me, let me be in the family plot at Oberon. I may not have spent much time there, but I can't envision spending eternity without being surrounded by Hamiltons."

Sydney got up and went over and leaned down to kiss him. "You're family. Of course."

"Is' that a promise?"

"It's a promise." Although he made no sound, Sydney sensed his silent sigh of relief. She finished her drink and then sat on the sofa staring into space. "I feel sinful and depraved not to be more broken up at my father's death. I feel–oh, I don't even know."

"Free," said Uncle Billy. "For the first time in a long time."

Sydney stared at him.

"He was in pain, my dear. And he hated being waited on. It frustrated the hell out of him to have you wait on him. He once told me he'd always wanted to take care of you, and couldn't understand why you wouldn't let anyone do that. It was a bitter pill that it became the other way around. He was ready to die, Sydney. I really think he was."

Sydney leaned back and closed her eyes.

"Well, it's all yours, to do with as you want now, my dear."

After a few minutes, her eyes still closed, she said, "I hired a new managing editor today."

She heard Billy get up and go over to pour himself another drink. She opened her eyes and looked at him. "We've been so damn highfalutin, so naive, so out of touch." She wondered if Billy even knew what she was talking about.

He was all those things.

"I think we should cater to a variety of tastes. We need someone like a Walter Winchell, a Dorothy Kilgallen, someone to report to the masses what the supposedly beautiful people are doing."

Billy laughed. "I hope you're not going to become a scandal sheet, Sydney. You do have more taste than that."

"I may have more taste than that, and I don't want to make money off the peccadilloes of the rich and famous, but people are interested in...in us." She smiled wryly. "Who has been where, not who's having an affair with someone else's wife. Not that kind of thing. Only facts that won't hurt people, but give the common man some inside view of...of the kind of people you hang out with, Billy."

"So, you'd like my opinion of who could do a good job?"

"Not at all. I want you to do it."

It lay there, curling in the air as Billy stared at his niece with a look of utter amazement. "I beg your pardon?" And then, "You can't mean that."

Sydney giggled. Maybe it was the gin. Maybe it was the power she felt, that she'd felt all day. That she'd felt ever since it had sunk in that *The New York Chronicle* was hers to do with as she wished.

"I mean it with all my heart. It's something I've wanted to add for years, but Daddy and Adam thought it would cheapen the paper. I don't want it to be cheap, but I do want it to be delicious. How about three times a week? And maybe once in a while an article in *Focus* about someone, the private side, the unknown part. We haven't had anything like that since Miranda gave it up to be the evening anchor on CBC."

"But, my dear! You don't even know if I can write! A job at my age? Good heavens!"

"Not a job, darling. A career. They're quite different."

"Mmm." He was obviously thinking. He stood up and walked over to the windows on one wall of the living room, then gazed out over the city he so loved. "It would give some discipline to my life, wouldn't it?"

Uncle Billy was a creature of habit and order. His socks lay in neat rows in his bureau, his shoes were polished every night, and nothing had changed in his bedroom for all the years he'd lived here. The only spur of the moment events of his life were when he flew to the rescue of a family member. Uncle Billy was a disciplined person.

He turned to face her, and he was smiling. Sydney realized he didn't have a wrinkle. His face was as smooth as a baby's. His only concession to age were his glasses, which were rimless and thus, he thought, nearly invisible. He looked rather like Noel Coward. He had that same elegance, too, but he was more masculine. She wondered if he had women. Some nights he didn't come home until very late. She hoped that some of that time was spent in bed, though she could hardly imagine Billy uninhibited.

She wondered if he'd ever kissed a woman with such passion that he forgot how he looked, wondered if he ever threw caution to the winds.

"Sydney, I think it might be great fun to try. I hope I won't disappoint you."

Then he said, "Funny, I remember when you were born," as if that had anything to do with the conversation. "Mama brought me down to Oberon, and I brought Silvie a dozen long-stemmed roses that I'd bought with my allowance. She's made me an uncle."

After another minute he said, "I want my picture next to a byline," he said.

Sydney laughed.

Forty Seven

From her hospital window Juliet could see the tall arches over-looking the Mississippi. At the counseling session this afternoon, she'd realized she'd been here five months.

For the first time in that period, she thought she might be ready to face the world again. Might be ready to leave the cocoon. Thought maybe she could do it now.

One step at a time. That's what they told her. The enticements would still be there. Phone if you were even tempted. Don't have long-range goals. Just a day at a time. Should she go to Nashville? Would Johnny pass through there? What would she do if he crooked his finger again?

"Jesus Christ!" she said aloud. Where were her brains? Return to a man who had treated her as he had?

She'd better have a talk with herself. Wasn't it time she began to face what had led to all this? Or at least the Johnny

Mars part of it?

But Nashville was where it was at. She'd been heading for the big time with people like Willie and Patsy and Hank singing her songs. That's what had been wrong. If she'd just remained second-rate, written a song now and then for Johnny, and only Johnny, she'd have been all right. Or would she? Did she want any of that old lifestyle? Awake all-night and sleeping all day?

Sex. Maybe she was through with that as well as dope. Any sex she'd ever had had been degrading—men using her, not caring about her, about her feelings. Only Johnny had cared about pleasing her, but it always seemed more like an ego trip with him. Doing things to her that made her feel dirty, even if she had come to enjoy much of it.

Into her mind stole the memory of her first sexual experience. She hadn't even known what sex was, only knew that his touching her made her feel dirty at the same time she reveled in the sensations.

It had always been thus. A mixture of thrill and revulsion, a combination of peaks and abysses, of pleasure unlike any other and a feeling of evil. She realized her parents had never given her a puritanical attitude toward it. Her mother had always been willing to talk about sex openly, as though it were nothing to be ashamed of. Sydney had always answered any questions Ashley asked, and Juliet had listened, never asking any of her own.

Yet for her, for so long; sex had been a way of life. As had drugs. They'd seemed a part of each other. Where did one leave off and the other begin, or had they always intermingled? She couldn't remember, as she couldn't remember so much of the last couple of years. Couldn't remember all the towns. The only time she'd been clean was those few months she'd batted out the songs everyone had clamored for, when she couldn't seem to spend a day without a new song popping into her head and out through her fingers. Then Johnny had put an end to that. As he'd almost put an end to her.

She took a deep breath. Maybe she'd go out for a run around the grounds. It was late winter, gray and damp along America's longest river. She pulled out her sweats and crawled into a shirt. Where were her running shoes? Ah, there they were, high up in the closet. She wanted exercise, wanted to feel cold air inhaled into her lungs until it hurt, wanted to run against the wind, fight for something.

> Around the curve I saw
> beyond yesterday,
> between the sky and my breath
> all the songs of my childhood.

She flung her arms in the air and laughed.

A new beginning. She could feel it. Feel it in every pore and every bone and in her heart.

What, she wondered, was the difference between your heart and your soul? Maybe she could write a song about that. Maybe she could write songs about all the things other than love that were so important in the world. Did songs always have to be about love? Well, there were "The Star Spangled Banner" and "America." But maybe they were about love, too.

She opened the door and jogged down the hallway, the dreary hallway covered with scuffed linoleum, thinking of all the things concerning love that didn't include a man, that didn't have sex and romance in them. She thought of blades of grass, and the green-gold, of spring leaves, of rushing brooks, of mountains that danced. She thought of sailing a skipjack in the Chesapeake as the sun glinted on whitecaps. She thought of Martha's Forest and of taxis honking on Manhattan's streets, of her sister Ashley, and of sun-drenched beaches fringed with palm trees and she could hardly wait to start writing again.

In the back of her mind, as she jogged around the grounds, looking out through the iron railing that surrounded the hospital grounds, a theme began to play. It was a slow melody-with an erratic drumbeat, soft at first but increasing in volume until she heard and saw nothing else as she began to run fast, her balled fists unclenching.

That night she phoned Ashley, as she did every Sunday night.

Ashley was waiting for the call, but was unprepared for Juliet's news.

"I'm thinking of releasing myself."

There was just a moment's pause, but Juliet was aware of it.

"What are you thinking of doing?"

"Going to Nashville."

A longer pause this time'. "Do you think that's wise?"

"I can't hide, Lee. I can't try to escape life."

"But, Nashville?"

"Well, I've been doing a lot of thinking."

Sometimes, Ashley thought, Juliet had a twang as though she'd been born and bred a Southerner.

"I want to go on writing music, Country and Western music. And my best chance of getting it sung is in Nashville. Besides, I like that town."

What she could remember of it.

"It's not Nashville that's to blame for what happened to me. It's me. And I've grown some smarts. I'm not about to let men like Johnny Mars run my life anymore. I'm not letting any man lead me, not ever again. I'm not getting near any white powder, even if it's only sugar. I was letting myself go right down the drain. I've a heap of living I want to do, Lee. I want to show everyone I can climb to the top. I want to get someplace because of me, not because I'm Jordan Eliot's daughter or a Hamilton descendant or Johnny Mars's ex-wife, or...

"You know, I'm just beginning to understand Mom."

Ashley laughed. "I was hoping one day you'd get around to that."

Juliet asked, "Well, what do you think?" She could tell Ashley was thinking.

"I think you should try it, if you really feel that good about it. I wish I could fly out there and go to Nashville with you, get you settled, but I just can't."

"No, no, I don't want that. But I think I'll set the wheels in motion. Maybe I'll leave Monday. It's not that far, and I'll take a bus." What she wouldn't give for her old motorcycle. Buses were so slow, so claustrophobic. No wind to blow in her face, no thrill on the open road, just sitting looking through dusty windows at scenery passing by. On a bike she felt part of it all. In a bus she'd just be an observer. Oh, well, patience.

"Have you told Mom?"

Juliet shook her head. "Do I have to?"

"She'll be worried if she calls and you've checked out."

"You tell her, will you?"

* * * *

Monday morning, as Juliet was packing her few belongings, her phone rang. The woman at the desk downstairs said, "You have a caller."

Damn! Who? Juliet glanced at her watch. She had just an hour and a half before the bus left, and she had to get downtown.

"I'll be right there," she said, and dashed down the stairs instead of waiting for the elevator.

Standing at the desk, looking out of place because of his impeccable attire, cane looped over his arm, was Uncle Billy.

"Ah, there you are," he said, reaching out to kiss the air next to Juliet's cheek.

"Uncle Billy! What in the world are you doing here?"

"I hadn't anything in particular on my calendar until Friday so I thought I'd drive you to Nashville. Rented a car at the airport, and it's waiting for us. Though God knows, I hope you remember how to drive. I had a man drive me here from the rental agency and he's waiting outside for us, but I hope you can drive to Tennessee."

Dear Uncle Billy! He'd never once failed any member of the family. He was here to make sure she was all right.

"Did Mom send you?"

He drew himself up with an air of haughtiness. "No one sent me. I thought you might like company for a few days of your, er, transition period, shall we call it? If you don't want…"

Juliet threw her arms around her great-uncle. "I'd love your company. I always do. You're a sweetheart. I have been a bit nervous. It's just that I'm always so surprised to see you out of New York. You hate leaving the city."

He looked embarrassed. "Well, there are some things more important, you know. Family…"

"Let me get my suitcases. I'll be right back."

"Can't you send someone for them?"

Juliet laughed. "Uncle Billy, 'you live in such a rarefied world. I'll be back in a sec."

He lit a cigarette. The woman behind the desk glared at him.

"No smoking, dear," Juliet said. Nor in any car I'm in, either. Better go outside and have a last drag."

"You give up smoking, too?"

"I've given up anything addictive. Nothing's ever going to control me again. At least, nothing I can help."

"Oh, my," he said in that funny way of his. "Hm, there must be rest stops between here and … my God, Juliet, country music. It figures. You would never choose anything acceptable, would you? Maybe it's one of your charms, my dear."

He was such a stuffed shirt, Juliet thought as she took the elevator to her floor. Yet he was also one of the dearest people in her world. She wondered briefly if Uncle Billy had any life outside the family. Any women? Any men? Anyone except flitting from one nightclub to another, anything other than the theater or the opera, or weekends at Southampton. Funny, he was always eager to go out there but so seldom was willing to spend time at Oberon.

Oberon.

Suddenly she yearned mightily for that island, for that place that always represented safety to her, purity. Maybe someday she'd live there. Someday when she had a reputation and didn't have to be where the action was, she would be so famous people would come to her asking her to write songs for them, and she could live wherever she wanted. Then, she'd live at Oberon. Not just summers, but year-round.

Billy settled Juliet into a much nicer place than she'd have found. He paid the first three months rent. For the first time in his life he could afford to do things for other people. It was a feeling he liked.

She'd have taken a furnished room, but Billy saw to it that she had space and light. It wasn't only a one-bedroom apartment, but it had a skylight that allowed the sun to pour into her living room, which was on the second floor of a Victorian house that had been kept in perfect shape. The long windows overlooked a back garden, where daffodils already swayed in the breeze. The branches of a dogwood tree beat a tattoo against her window, and Juliet knew that next month it would burst into color, just for her.

Uncle Billy bought her a bed and a desk with a high-backed chair for her bedroom. He suggested she choose a sofa and a comfortable chair for the small living room, and insisted on buying a TV, though Juliet claimed she really didn't need one.

"I'd prefer a hi-fi and a radio," she said.

He bought those, too.

In the kitchen-dining area there was already a small Formica table and four mismatched chairs. She insisted ' she could get along with them. The apartment had been freshly painted; the small refrigerator was new, the stove passable.

"After all, I don't really cook."

Uncle Billy raised his eyebrows. "Can you afford not to?"

She'd never heard him talk about money.

After he'd bought sheets and pillows and blankets, he asked how she thought she was going to write music.

"What do you mean?"

"On a piano?"

Juliet laughed. "That'd be nice. But I'll settle for a guitar.""

Billy bought her one of those, too:

When he left her, five days later, she was relieved to see him go so she could get on with her life. And she was panicked.

Forty Eight

Ashley spent the summer motoring over from Oberon to St. Michael's and driving into Easton, a twenty-minute drive, where she searched for a place that would make a good office. She wanted a place for an infirmary and a kennel, too.

Though there were two other veterinarians in Easton, Ashley liked it so much she decided that's where she wanted to be. She'd considered St. Michael's, one of the most charming towns she'd ever seen, but it was too small. Easton was a town of three-story antebellum houses, lending an air of graciousness to the village of well-kept, even elegant, homes with beautiful gardens. Easton had been a town since before the Revolution.

Her mother had suggested building a place where she could be happy-have a dog run, set up a hospital for herself-but Ashley didn't want to seem ostentatious. She wanted to be accepted in the community, to become part of the town. She was glad her name wasn't Hamilton, so no one would know her connection with Oberon. Funny, she bad to hide her connection with the place she loved most if she was going to be taken seriously.

She drove up and down the streets of Easton a dozen times. Yet each week she looked again, and on the second of August she found it on the last street east of downtown.

Ashley had passed it half a dozen times but hadn't noticed it, because there had been no "For Sale" sign on it. It was a brick house with black shutters and a polished brass knocker on the purple front door. She had to laugh out loud. No other house she'd ever seen had a door that color. She couldn't imagine why she hadn't noticed it before. ,

Flowers trailed from window boxes, and a wrought-iron fence surrounded the front yard, a neatly tended lawn with a border of marigolds and petunias and a tall maple standing alone in the center. A wide covered porch ran the length of the house.

She parked her car and got out. A sign read "Carlton Realty," but she knocked at the door before walking around the side yard to the back. The covered porch made an el, and she continued around to the backyard to discover a dogwood tree, two lilacs, three fruit trees, and a bam that could be converted to a kennel and an infirmary. The bam had window boxes filled with flowers. She peered in a window and saw that it contained a large room with an open stairway that led upstairs, where they must have kept hay at one time.

A magnolia shaded the bay windows of the commodious kitchen, with blue cupboards arid tiled counter space.

She walked back down the side of the porch and peered into the dining room, which could be transformed into an operating room. Wherever the living room was could be her office and consulting room. The house was big enough that there would be space to use as a waiting room. Her adrenaline began to flow.

She stood back and observed the square lines of the house, quite like the other homes that lined Easton's streets. It must have four or five bedrooms upstairs, depending on their size. She could use that whole level as a living area.

She wondered if the street was restricted to residences. She could feel in every part of her that she wanted this house. Oh, God, she wanted it.

She jotted down the address of Carlton Realty and set out to find it, which wasn't difficult. There was no way to get lost in Easton.

A rather colorless young woman smiled as Ashley entered the small office. "I've come about that house on..." She didn't even know the name of the street. "Well, it has a purple door."

"We just put up the sign this morning. Would you like to see it?"

"That won't be necessary," Ashley said. "I need to know about zoning."

The young woman raised her eyebrows.

"I thought," said Ashley, "that since it's not right in the midst of town, maybe I could have a business there."

"I better have you talk to Mrs. Carlton," the young woman said, and she smiled. So sweetly that Ashley suddenly thought her quite pretty.

Mrs. Carlton was a gray-haired woman in her late forties, with a brisk handshake and an open face. "Oh, the Tremblyn place," she said when Ashley described it. Ashley told her what she wanted to do, and Mrs. Carlton shrugged. "I can't imagine why you couldn't have that there."

"How much are they asking?"

"Since it's just come on the market they aren't ready to dicker. They're asking sixty thousand."

Ashley sat down, took out her purse, extracted her checkbook, and said, "To whom do I make out the check?"

Mrs. Carlton sat down. "You have to make an offer that they'll accept first. I suggest you get a lawyer to handle the details and read the small print. Check with him about zoning, but I'm sure it's all right."

Ashley said, "I want that house. I'll pay the asking price, and I don't know any lawyers."

"I'll have to talk with the owner."

"Can you call him now?'" asked Ashley. "No. He's on his way to Virginia. He left this morning for Richmond."

"I'm making out a check for the full amount, which you may hold until you talk with him, and I'll talk to a lawyer. Can you recommend one?"

"Noah Butler's a nice young man and needs some business. He should be able to handle this. He's upstairs here." Mrs. Carlton pointed to the stairway that ran up the outside of the building.

Ashley said, "I'm making this check out to you." She placed it on Mrs. Carlton's desk and started for the door.

"Don't you even want to see the house?"

"I've seen enough," Ashley said. "I'll be back." She walked out into the hot day. It wasn't noon yet, but it was sweltering. She climbed the stairs to the second floor and went into the law office, which was air-conditioned. The August humidity drained her.

The reception room was light and cheerful. Behind a cream colored desk that matched the other furniture and the book cases sat a very attractive, tailored young woman who was talking on the phone. She waved at Ashley, indicating she should take a seat. She finished her conversation and, turning to Ashley, smiled brightly and asked, "May I help you?"

"I'd like to see Mr. Butler."

"He'll be back in about fifteen minutes, if you care to wait. He hasn't another appointment until three."

"I'll wait." Ashley didn't even riffle through the magazines that covered a low table. She sat and thought of the house and what she could do with it. She was so excited she could hardly contain herself. She was probably silly not to look at it before buying it. She would go see it, after all. She could think about it, plan how to decorate it, decide what she had to order. Find a carpenter. She shivered with the excitement.

Noah Butler arrived twenty minutes later, bursting into his office like a cyclone, his blond hair falling across his forehead, his dark glasses looking like pilot's goggles, his shirt tieless and open-necked. He wore carefully pressed denim pants and a short-sleeved navy cotton shirt. A white jacket was slung over his left shoulder.

Before he'd even closed the door his secretary was pointing at Ashley. He grinned, nodding an invitation to follow him, and headed toward the inner room. "C'mon," he said. His office had floor-to-ceiling bookcases. That was what Ashley noticed first. But, like the outer office, anything that could be painted was in cream color, making the place light and cheerful, except for his massive oak desk, which was old and scuffed but polished to a sheen. Ashley surmised it was a family heirloom.

"I want to buy a house and the lady downstairs told me I should have a lawyer."

He tossed a briefcase on his desk and turned to her, extending his hand, saying, "I'm Noah Butler."

"Ashley Eliot."

"Coffee?" he asked, walking over to a machine sitting on the sideboard.

She might as well. "Sure, thanks." The air-conditioning had cooled her off. She sat down in the chair across from his desk. She noticed that the burgundy-and-navy rug was an old Persian, which had once cost a lot of money. The glass in the paned windows was antique, like the rest of the house. Like many of the buildings in Easton.

He handed her a coffee mug, asking, "Want anything in it?"

She shook her head. "No, thanks."

He sipped his coffee a minute and then focused his attention on her. "Well, I can do a title search. What's the address?" Ashley laughed. "I don't even know. I just saw it this morning. It's on the edge of town, and you'll think me foolish but I haven't even been inside." She told him what she wanted. "I need to know about zoning. May I have a business in my home there?"

"In the area you're interested in, all you need is a waiver from the immediate neighbors. Stricter zoning is coming, but it's not here yet." He sipped his coffee and then asked, "Are you new to the area?"

"Yes and no."

He raised an eyebrow.

"Actually, I'm from New York, but I spent summers around here when I was growing up."

"Lucky you," the lawyer said. "I just discovered it two years ago."

"I've recently graduated from veterinarian school and I want to set up a practice here. I thought I could use the downstairs for offices, the barn for a kennel, and upstairs for living quarters. "

"And you haven't even seen the inside?"

"I peeked through the windows and fell in love."

"You want to dicker on price?"

Ashley shook her head. "No, I made a check out for the full amount, but Mrs. Carlton can't get in touch with the owner yet."

He grinned. "You don't know the address? Well, let's go on down and see Mrs. Carlton. Then, let's get a key and go look it over. You don't even want to finance it?"

"No."

* * * *

They drove over in his black Fairlane. Ashley was so excited she was hardly aware of Noah Butler.

There were five large and airy rooms downstairs. From the main parlor a long staircase stretched to the upstairs. It was more than Ashley had hoped for. She decided she'd make the largest her living room. Then there was one she'd convert into a kitchen, for as much as she loved the big old-fashioned one downstairs she wasn't about to run up and down just to cook. A small kitchen upstairs would suffice. She might knock down the wall between that and the room and the one next to it and make one large kitchen-dining area. The large room at the back overlooked the garden, and Ashley decided that would be her bedroom. The branches of the magnolia danced against the windowpanes. The rooms had wainscoting and wallpaper she loved. She'd have no need or desire to redecorate.

Looking at the bathroom, she decided she might modernize it, though. The house was too perfect for words. "I want it," she said, more to herself than to the lawyer.

As they drove back to his office he told her, "I've lived here two years. Gave up the rat race in Chicago and decided I'd rather be a small-town lawyer than get rich and short-tempered."

"Why here?"

"I like birds," he said.

She jerked her head around to study him for the first time.

"I know, I know, you think I'm nuts," he grinned. "Well, I like boating, too. Is that more socially acceptable?"

"No, I don't think you're nuts at all," Ashley said as they walked down the driveway toward his car. "I'm a bird lover myself. And I've sailed all my life. Right here, in the Chesapeake."

"We'll get you this house. But you might negotiate about the price. You're going to have to invest a lot more money to do what you want. The asking price is a lot of money for Easton."

"I want it, Mr. Butler."

He cocked his head and said, "Okay, if that's what you want. And the name's Noah."

When they returned the key to Mrs. Carlton she said she thought she could reach the owner at his son's tonight or tomorrow morning. She asked Ashley how she could get in touch with her.

Ashley decided it might be better to stay in Easton overnight.

"I'll stay at the inn," she said. She went back upstairs with Noah. "Do you want a retainer?" she asked.

"Nah." He smiled at her. "This'll be easy. Bet it won't cost you a hundred dollars."

"Then I'll see you in the morning," Ashley said, holding out her hand.

"My pleasure," he said, giving her a firm handshake.

As she started out the door he asked, "Need to be shown the town's sights?"

"Can't I see everything in five minutes?"

He nodded. "Of course."

She walked down the stairs, thinking that tonight she'd phone her mother and tell her.

She was starting life on her own. Dr. Ashley Eliot. Starting in a place where no one knew her, where she'd have to make it on her own, where she'd found the most wonderful house in the world, next to Oberon. Of course.

She could hardly wait to get out her catalogues and decide what supplies she'd need. She'd ask Noah or Mrs. Carlton if they knew of a good carpenter. She'd need electricity and plumbing in the barn. There was much to be done.

Charmed with Easton, she walked along the street, thinking if she were going to stay overnight she'd better buy something to sleep in and a change of underwear and a toothbrush. Better let Walt know that she was okay and would leave the boat at the marina overnight. She'd drive back to· St. Michael's this afternoon and tell him, though if she wasn't back to leave the car in his garage he'd know the boat would stay in its slip. But she liked checking in with him.

She turned into the first woman's shop she came to and found underwear and a short, tailored nightgown, hardly worthy of the name. It barely covered her, but it was lilac satin and Ashley was surprised to find a shop in so small a town that had such nice quality. In fact, it was downright expensive. Somehow, that reassured her.

She left her car in the parking lot by Carlton's and walked to the inn, where she took a room for the night. Her room overlooked the street, its window open to the afternoon sounds of the village. She realized she was starving and went down to the dining room, where she had a Caesar salad and the most delicious home-baked bread she'd had in a long time. The dining room faced the street. It was dark and cool.

The couple at the table near the window smiled at her, and Ashley felt exorbitantly happy. She knew this was the right step, the right town. She thought of how she would arrange furniture and what she wanted the cupboards in her office to look like, and where she'd place file cabinets, and how she could make her office look professional yet comfortable at the same time. After lunch, she walked back to the parking lot and got her car, wishing it were a convertible on such a glorious day. She drove down to St. Michael's, told Walt she'd be back tomorrow, then drove south on the spit of land that jutted out into the bay, to Tilghman's Island. She couldn't imagine a prettier locale. She silently thanked her ancestor, Martha, for having the first Hamilton baby in this part of the world. She had no doubt at all that she'd find contentment, something that had escaped her and Juliet all their lives, though certainly Juliet more than her. She'd never been driven as her sister had, never felt a need to take the risks Juliet had taken, never needed to question her own ability or ask whether or not she was loved.

The only time she ever questioned that was when a man was in her life. And from now on, there weren't going to be any, t least not for a long time. There hadn't been a man in her life since Jonathan two years ago. It was the one realm where she'd had no success.

She wasn't like her mother, Ashley thought, in that she didn't have to prove anything to herself. Her mother had grown up in a time when women were considered second-class citizens, and had to prove to the world that they were as capable as any man. Ashley could understand that. Juliet said she couldn't, yet she kept trying to prove something to herself. But she, Ashley, thought she didn't have to verify herself to anyone, including herself. She liked herself.

Now all she yearned for was to belong some place, and she thought that place was here. She yearned to become a part of the town. And she knew she could find happiness if she did.

When she returned to the inn, the hot afternoon sounds floated up to her room and she lay down on the bed, hugging herself. I am the most fortunate of people, she thought, and fell asleep before she even knew she was sleepy.

It was after five when the phone awakened her. It was Noah Butler.

"How about dinner?" he asked.

Why not? She had nothing else to do. No one to do it with, either.

Noah arrived at seven. "I thought since it's such a lovely evening you might like to see some of the scenery around here," he said. "We'll drive over to Oxford. It's not far, and they have one of the world's great seafood restaurants. They also have the oldest continuous running ferry in the hemisphere, as well as one of the shortest."

"Where does it go?"

"No place. It's just about a ten-minute ride."

Although the evening was still hot, Noah's air-conditioning made the drive pleasant. He was a delightful and easy conversationalist, pointing out sights and telling little stories about various places. She had never been over this road.

The evening was golden.

The hotel in Oxford also had the best roast beef, which Ashley preferred to the crab that delighted Noah.

He asked her endless questions about herself, about vet school, about why she had chosen that career. Her answers were guarded. She thought carefully before answering his questions. She told him next to nothing about her mother, nothing at all about Jordan, a little bit about her sister.

He told her, "When I can afford the luxury of not worrying about an income, what I really want is to be an environmental lawyer."

"I didn't know there was such a thing."

He nodded. "It's a coming thing, but you have to care more about ideals than money. My passion is seeing that this part of the world's never urbanized. I don't want the birds here to become extinct."

Ashley laughed. "That can never happen."

He shook his head, waving his fork in the air. "I know that's what everyone says. Just like no one wants to think the ecology of the bay is being jeopardized. But wait and see, and I hope I'm wrong, but I predict that within fifteen years there won't even be any oysters left."

"Come on! The Chesapeake Bay has more oysters than anyplace else in the world."

"I want to be wrong," he said, "but I don't think I am."

"So, you want to protect it? A one-man crusade to preserve ' oysters?'"

"I think you think I'm crazy," he said, "but once you've lived here awhile you'll understand what I'm talking about. Every year the bay is more polluted, thanks to' oil spills from the thousands of boats, from sewers, from septic tanks. I want to do something to keep it from getting worse."

Ashley sat back 'and studied him. She liked his dark blue eyes, so dark they almost looked purple. Blond people seldom had eyes of such deep color. She liked the intensity with which he spoke when he obviously cared deeply about something.

"Okay," he smiled, "I'll get off my soapbox. What would you like to talk about?"

"Tell me something about you. Like why did you leave Chicago?"

"Oh, that," he said, finishing the food on his plate. "See, didn't I tell you this was a great restaurant? I'm thirty-two and gave up a lucrative law practice in Oak Park, which isn't Chicago really, but close enough. I'm divorced, no kids."

Ashley leaned forward, her elbows on the table, telling the waiter she'd like coffee but no dessert. "Divorced? How long were you married?"

Noah folded his arms on the table and looked at her. "Six years."

"And?"

"I suspect my wife married me in anticipation of a life of ease and luxury. When I decided to give all that social life and money up and move to a small town, that was the end. Looking back, I should have foreseen the end had been on its way for almost four years. It was an amicable parting. We still send each other birthday presents and Christmas cards. She's remarried. "

"I've never lived in a small town. Do you get lonely?"

Noah laughed, a sound that Ashley thought sounded like a running river. "I'm busier here than I ever was in a city. Maybe not practicing law, but I have more friends, more things to do than I ever did in Chicago. I'm on the planning commission, and I teach classes in Adult Ed one night a week, a different class each term.

"I have a little launch. When the weather's nice I take off weekends, exploring all the waterways I can. I like to go alone, and I never feel lonely. I have a dog, and he goes wherever I go weekends. I can't live without a dog. My wife thought they cluttered up the house with their hair and that I loved whatever dog I had more than her." He grinned. "Maybe I did."

"So, you've found yourself here?"

Noah nodded. "You will, too. I feel it. This place isn't for everyone. For some, it's just nice weekends, but for those of us who choose to live here, well, I've come to the conclusion we're a breed apart. When I was a kid I wondered why I wasn't like the others, and tried to fit in. It wasn't until I was in my mid-twenties that I realized it was something to be proud of. I don't think I'm an iconoclast, but I like independence. Not having to conform, I can be whatever it is I want to be here."

When he left her off at the inn, she told him, "I had a lovely evening. Thanks for such a friendly welcome to my new hometown."

"See you in the morning. And you're right. You are welcome. We'll see more of each other. You see more of everyone in this town."

He waved.

She looked up and the stars were as bright as she'd ever seen them.

Forty Nine

Three months after buying the house, Ashley hung out her shingle. "Dr. Ashley Eliot, D.V.M." It had been a busy time. A carpenter, electrician, and plumber had practically lived at her house.

Ashley was as excited as a child at Christmas when medicines and veterinary supplies began to arrive, putting them in the varnished cherry wood cabinets that the carpenter had so precisely and carefully built. She filled the cabinets with surgery equipment, its bright stainless steel shining, and stood back to admire it. Small things amuse small minds, she smiled to herself.

She furnished the upstairs with a sofa and a comfortable pillowed chair in shades of her favorite colors: lilacs, pastels of rose and green with hints of blues. The color theme was carried through the living room into her bedroom. The hardwood floors were so beautiful she opted for throw rugs instead of carpeting. When she was finished she felt elated; her first real home away from home. She had known her Ithaca apartment was temporary, even though she'd ended up being in it for seven years. She hoped that Easton was where she would stay, a little over an hour from where she was born.

Her mother flew down one October weekend to admire Ashley's new home, to see her set-up, and to ask what she could do to help. But she couldn't imagine staying overnight at Ashley's, even though Ashley volunteered to sleep on the couch. She preferred to stay at Oberon, so she and Ashley motored over after a day of browsing through Easton's few shops.

Sydney couldn't really understand Ashley's desire to settle in a little Maryland town, a little east bay village where–with time, she warned Ashley–you'd know everyone and they'd know you and all your business. There would be no privacy, no chance to do anything scandalous.

Ashley didn't want to do anything scandalous. She wanted to heal animals, study geese and ducks, sail down the Chesapeake's rivers, become part of the pulse of Easton. Quite like Noah Butler felt, she thought with a smile.

A mile out of town, up on the highway that looped outside of town, Ashley found the town's most popular breakfast restaurant. It had been in business since the forties, and was where everyone in town went out for breakfast.

She sat and read the morning paper and discussed the weather with the same waitress every day, and studied the people who came in for waffles piled high with strawberries or little loaves of home-baked bread with their scrambled eggs oozing with onions and red peppers. The owners made their own sausage and cured their own bacon, and the restaurant had the best breakfasts Ashley had ever known.

By sitting at the same table every day, within weeks she had become a fixture and people stopped to introduce themselves or smile at her across the room. Some of them even called her "Doc," but then she imagined every veterinarian, every medical doctor, every pharmacist around was nicknamed that. She didn't object. It implied respect and eventually, she hoped, business. Ashley was never the first one to say hello. She had to wait for someone else to do that, but she gazed around, obviously inviting a personal word.

She had fought shyness for years. Sydney had told her time and again that she thought shyness was vanity, thinking everyone else was concentrating on you, afraid to speak up for fear of making a fool of oneself. She thought perhaps people thought her dull because she had to make such an effort to converse with strangers. In all her undergraduate and graduate years at Cornell she had failed to make a close friend. A number of acquaintances, but very few friends and none that she was close to or would miss.

Her last year there she had practically not spoken to a man, so angry was she with the failures she'd had romantically.

Noah Butler didn't know that, but he should have gotten the message. He stopped by several times as the noise of hammering filled the air. He came, he declared, to inspect the improvements and to invite her to dinner. Each time Ashley refused, she gave him no excuses.

So, on the morning of the day when she hung out her shingle, he brought his Chesapeake Bay retriever, whose big brown eyes practically kissed Ashley.

"He's ready for his annual shots," Noah said, looking not at all like the lawyers Ashley had known. He wore dark green corduroy pants and a hand knit sweater the color of the ocean. "Besides, I thought it was time he met you, and we could claim the honor of being your first patient."

Ashley had hired Gladys Hollwedel, an attractive young woman with bronze hair and enormous brown eyes, as her receptionist. The girl was nervous as could be, even though she knew everyone in town. She smiled brightly at Noah.

"You've a good girl out there," he said as he nodded his head toward the outer room. "Hey, look what you've done here. I'd hardly recognize the place."

Ashley examined the dog, which licked her hands and wagged its tail. "Lovely dog," she said.

Noah nodded, his hands on the dog but his eyes on her. "I once stopped dating a woman because she didn't know his name. We'd gone together about two or three months. We'd go bicycling and I'd take Barney. We'd go out on the boat, even overnight, and Barney would come along. Barney goes nearly every place I do. That woman knew how much I love this dog, but she never seemed to pay any attention to it. One night, after we'd been seeing each other a couple of times a week for months, I asked if she knew what my dog's name was. She shook her head. That was the end. I figured she couldn't care very much about me if she didn't learn the name of this dog."

Ashley had to smile. She gave Barney his triple shots and asked when he'd last had his rabies shot.

"Last year," Noah answered.

"Okay, then he doesn't need one now."

"I see you out mornings, jogging along with your dog," Noah said.

When Ashley didn't respond, Noah said, "Barney's never met another dog he doesn't like."

Ashley said, "You can pay the receptionist."

"Hey," Noah said as Barney jumped down from the examining table, "a word of advice. You're not going to make it big around, here with your bedside manner. You've got to be friendly."

Ashley looked over at him, realizing she'd be more sociable if he were a woman. "Sorry," she said, "but I guess I'm nervous, my first day and all."

"Would you have dinner with me if I weren't a threat?"

"A threat? I don't exactly see you as…"

"Yes, you do. Sometime you got hurt and you're not about to let a man even be a friend, are you?"

"Are you a shrink as well as a lawyer?"

He nodded, smiling. "Yeah, I'm good at reading people."

Ashley held out her hand. "Thanks for bringing me my first patient, Mr. Butler."

"I figure you'll remember me then. I remember my first client."

She had three patients that first day.

The next morning, at dawn, as she and Boo Boo ran along the street that led out of town, Noah appeared suddenly, with Barney. Immediately the two dogs began sniffing each other, running in circles in the crisp morning air.

"Not going to be many days like this before winter sets in," he said, his stride easy next to hers. "Well, were you a roaring success your first day?"

"I wouldn't say roaring." They jogged along easily, not talking, Noah obviously slowing his pace to keep in line with Ashley. The dogs barked and jumped, cavorting with each other.

Ashley was surprised to find herself enjoying his quiet company. As they reached her house and slowed down, she smiled at Noah.

"Maybe you'll join me again."

In the fields behind her house, early morning mists rose from the tall, golden grasses. The geese and ducks had arrived and the air was filled with their honkings.

"I have to drive up to Chestertown on business late Thursday afternoon. It's only an hour away. Pretty town. I know a great little restaurant there. Could I talk you into driving up with me?"

When Ashley hesitated, he quickly added, "We'd be home before nine."

"That sounds nice," Ashley said. "I'd like that."

He grinned, and she thought he had quite the nicest smile. He might not be handsome, but he certainly was attractive, and she liked his openness.

"See?" he said. "Perseverance pays off."

Ashley watched him as he trotted away, his big, good-looking dog running beside him. She could use a friend, she thought, male or female. She leaned down to run a hand through Boo Boo's fur and realized the dog was quivering, watching as Noah and Barney disappeared around a comer.

The drive to Chestertown and dinner in the restaurant overlooking the Chester River was a delight. The restaurant's whole south side, facing the river, was glassed-in. It was dark by the time they dined, and candles lit the tables, giving a cozy feeling to the spacious room decked with blue and white-checkered tablecloths.

While they sipped wine and looked out the window at the reflection of the moon on the river, Noah said, "Gives a romantic aura, moonlight."

But, aside from that, there was no romance about the day.

They had talked, though there had been comfortable silences.

He hadn't asked anything too personal. She had responded with what he already knew, that she was from New York City and she'd gone to Cornell. She said she had a sister, and that her parents were divorced. They talked, rather, of other things ... of Noah's thinking he might run for councilman. Local politics interested him. He thought it would give him a chance to make a difference. It was one reason he'd moved to a small town, to get involved.

"I love it when I'm but on Tilghman's Island and see the skipjack fleet sail out mornings. You know they have an annual skipjack race? I'm thinking of making one, spending the, winter building a skipjack and entering the race next year."

Ashley laughed. "Are you a carpenter?"

Noah shook his head and grinned. "To a minor extent. I like puttering, and I'd like to build a boat. There's not one much prettier to me than a skipjack. I don't want to hunt oysters from it, but I bet I could sell it after I race it. Or at least keep it if my worst fears come into play, and have one of the few remaining ones in my own garage."

When he left Ashley off he did not get out of the car to walk her to her door.

"This is one of the last weekends I'll be taking the boat out before putting it in dry dock," he told her. "I'm going out on the annual bird count for the Audubon Society Saturday. How about coming?"

Ashley reached out a hand to touch his arm. "I had a lovely time, Noah, but..."

"Barney and what's-her-name, Boo Boo—my God, I'd better learn her name right away, hadn't I?-will have a great time. Unless Boo Boo gets seasick."

"Boo Boo's a great sailor," Ashley said. What did she have to do on Saturday anyhow? "Sure, that sounds fine."

"Great," he grinned. "You bring the lunch, and I'll bring a Thermos of coffee."

When he picked her up she'd just had time for a glass of orange juice, half a bagel, and a quick sip of coffee. She'd packed a lunch the night before, something her mother had never taught her to do. She felt quite happy despite the fact that she'd only treated twelve animals all week. Not an auspicious beginning.

She had paid attention to Noah's admonition to be friendlier, to act less diffident.

She forced herself to smile, and before the week was out she found herself doing it naturally, responding to the openness of the local people.

She had looked at her calendar last night, slightly dismayed to find no appointments waiting for her next week.

It was seven minutes of eight when Noah knocked on her door Saturday morning. "Dress warmly," he'd advised. "It's pretty chilly. Out on the water it'll be cold."

She knew that. Though she wore an Irish knit, she carried extra sweaters, heavy mittens, and sturdy boots. "We'll drive down to St. Michael's where I keep my boat. You been there?"

Why didn't she tell him that's where she kept her boat, too?

He didn't wait for an answer but reached down and picked up the picnic basket made of woven ash reeds, which she'd found in an antique store.

"Hey, I like this," he exclaimed, holding it up to admire.

Boo Boo, who sensed an adventure, was panting at the door, wiggling her rear end in excitement. When Noah opened the door, she bounded straight for the car.

Noah's boat was sturdy and· efficient. It did not have the graceful lines of a sailboat or the far more expensive cabin cruisers Ashley had spent her summers on, but he was proud of it and touched it with love, running his hand along the polished wood.

"We're heading out in the open," Noah said. Ashley had known Walt would be out hunting today, as he was every Saturday during the season. One of the young men who worked for him had been at the marina today. He greeted Ashley as though he knew her but couldn't remember her name, which was fine with her.

They motored down the familiar Miles River and, as they came to open water, Ashley had the sudden premonition that Noah was heading to Oberon.

"We're in for a treat, or so I hear. We had to get prior approval for the bird count out here, so they're expecting us. Fancy island, I hear. Megabucks. One of the real old-time places around here, but then there are lots that date pre-Revolutionary. God, the whole area is steeped in history." Noah's voice sounded reverential. "Do you know anything about it?"

Why didn't she say yes, I know a lot about it: I was born there.

"I never fail to feel in awe of that great house," Noah said as they rounded the southern point and Oberon came into view. "Do you know the central part of that was built in the 1600s? Look at it, will you? Isn't it an architectural delight? Can you imagine having all that money? Wow!"

For the last ten minutes Ashley had been weighing whether or not to tell him. He was the only friend she had here so far. Wouldn't he be furious if he found out later, and from someone else? There was no way she could keep it hidden forever.

She took a deep breath and touched his arm. He turned to glance at her questioningly.

"Noah. That's my family's house."

He looked at her, back at the house, and said, "Huh?"

"I've spent all the summers of my life there and all my Christmases. It's why I moved to Easton, because the happiest times of my life have been spent here."

He kept on staring at her. "Holy shit!" Then he looked back at the house, which they passed as he took the channel out into the bay, heading to the marsh at the northern end of the island where the geese would be gathered at this time of year. Even with the motor sputtering the noise of the wildfowl could be heard.

"Here I thought I was giving you a treat."

"You are," Ashley stood next to him, their arms touching.

She was almost as tall as he was. "I spent summers and Christmases here, but I'd never been out here at this time of year. I've come out every weekend since I moved to Easton, but I haven't been up to the marshes and seen the geese and ducks."

Noah didn't say anything. He looked at the map and studied the island, searching for a cove, aware of the currents. He headed inland, up the creek that wound toward the center of the island, puttering the boat to a stop by the shore. He jumped overboard and, in his high rubber boots, pulled the boat onto a sand bar. "Maybe you better show me around."

She nodded. "I know every square inch of this place."

"Well, you could have told me."

She reached for the picnic basket. "Would it have made a difference?"

He picked her up and carried her to the shore, continuing to hold her hand even when he'd set her down and she'd found firm footing.

"No." He looked into her eyes. "I wanted your company. It's just a shock to think you must have a helluva lot of money."

The sound of the geese was so loud it was deafening.

"Before we get going," Noah said, reaching into the boat and taking out a Thermos and two plastic cups, "let's have some coffee and decide what our plan of action is."

"You know, we've never allowed hunting on the island," Ashley reached for the cup of steaming coffee.

He nodded. "Yeah. Everyone knows Oberon is sacred ground."

"You're right," she said, sitting on a log and staring out at mist rising off the water. "Sacred is the right word. What's that Emily Dickinson poem? *Some keep the Sabbath going to church, I keep it staying at home…*"

Noah smiled and interrupted, "*…with a bobolink for a chorister, ana an…*"

In unison, they said, "*orchara for a dome.*"

They smiled at each other as each waited for the other to continue. When they realized neither knew, the next stanza they burst into laughter.

Ashley said, "Well, it has something to do with church-goers doing so in order to eventually get into heaven, but she's been in heaven all along, in the midst of nature."

Noah nodded, his eyes appreciating her.

"That's how I've always felt about Oberon. My sister Juliet's always said it's the only place she's ever felt truly safe. I wouldn't go that far, but it's always represented purity to me. I think it's meant that to my whole family. My grandfather came down to hunt every fall, but he'd cross over to the mainland. I've never been able to understand how someone who loves nature can kill parts of it."

"Nor I." Noah sipped his coffee and asked, "Do you know a good place to observe from? Where we could get a rough count?"

"Sure."

"Well, I guess I asked just the right person to spend this day with me." He observed his surroundings, but he couldn't see much with the thick marsh grass.

"Christ," he said, looking over at her, "why a veterinarian? Why anything? You must have so much money you never have to work a day."

"Do you think people work just for money?"

He gave her a long look and then grinned. "Okay, you tell me. Why do people work?"

"You're a prime example. Not just for money, or you'd be back in Chicago earning megabucks. Sure, the majority of people work just to put a roof over their heads, feed themselves and their families, and then maybe buy a few luxuries. But one works, ideally, for the satisfaction one receives." She laughed.

"Of course my Puritan background preaches that work keeps one out of trouble."

"So, why do I work?" She mulled that over. "A feeling of self-worth. You like thinking you help people. Your mind enjoys challenges."

"Not all people who like their work enjoy helping people. What about the wheelers and dealers of the world?"

Ashley shrugged. "I don't know why all people work. They probably thrive on challenges, on risks. They have their own private agendas. And it seldom has to do with money."

Noah finished his coffee and put the top back on his Thermos. Slinging a pack over his shoulder, he reached out for the picnic basket. "Here, I'll carry that."

Ashley handed it to him. "Well, do you agree not everyone works for money?"

"Some days I really have to hustle to make ends meet, but yeah."

"I don't believe you know how to hustle."

He grinned, reaching a hand to help her up from the log. "You should have seen me in Chicago. I could have made the floor of the stock market look like tranquility."

"Are you serious?"

"Come on," he said, continuing to hold her hand; "lead on."

Fifty

Walt was at the marina when they returned. No, he hadn't gotten a single bird; no one in his party had. But they had had a grand morning anyway. He raised his eyebrows when he observed Ashley and Noah together, but made no comment.

"Better dry dock her," Noah told him.

They were chilled. Noah said, "We may look like hell after a day in the wilds, but how about dinner? Rolfe's won't mind how we look."

"I've a better idea. I'll cook dinner if you'll build a fire in the fireplace. I'll make hot mulled wine, and I have a ham and I'll fix new potatoes in garlic. I even baked an apple pie yesterday I had so much time between patients."

"Sold." His voice sounded happy. "And I've got an idea how you could do a public service and build up P.R."

"What?"

"Uh-uh. Wait 'til you've seduced me with hot cider and I'm feeling lazy and comfortable in front of a fire."

While he built a fire, Ashley puttered around in the kitchen, putting the ham in the oven to warm it, mulling the cider. Noah huddled in front of the fire, his shoes off and his feet absorbing the heat.

When she came into the living room, dressed in the same ivory Irish knit sweater she'd worn all day, but dry gray flannel slacks, Noah looked up at her from the pillows he'd taken from the sofa. Her golden earrings reflected the dancing firelight.

"Tell me, what's somebody with so much money doing baking her own pies?"

"Trying to be real," she said, pulling the hassock from in front of the chair to sit next to him.

He accepted the glass of hot cider and gulped it, murmuring, "Oh, boy, this is the life.'" He glanced around the room, "'Maybe when you're born with so much money you just automatically inherit good taste. What you've done with this house is terrific, Ashley."

"I'm a nester," she murmured, staring into the hypnotic fire. "I like to be domestic and surrounded with things that please me."

When the buzzer sounded, Ashley got up to take the ham out of the oven.

After dinner Noah put more logs on the fire and sprawled out on the couch. He'd picked up the pillows and scrunched one under him, putting his hands under his head and looking at Ashley, who'd seated herself in the large chair.

"Want to hear my P.R. idea? Of course you do. It's a way to get people to know of you. Choose some morning — a Wednesday, for instance — and advertise free spaying and neutering."

Ashley considered this. "Won't that aggravate the other vets?"

Noah raised an eyebrow. "Probably, but there are many people who own animals who can't afford to neuter them. You'll be performing a public service and then, when these people have sick animals, they'll remember you."

When Ashley didn't say anything, Noah went on, "It's a competitive world."

A trace of a smile fluttered across Ashley's face. "I like the idea."

"You're welcome."

They stared into the fire, listening to its crackle. After a while, Noah said, "Okay, I want to hear about you."

"You want to hear what?"

About her family and how they got their money and what they did and a whole history of America?

"Why you close yourself off to men."

She cocked her head to the side. "Maybe I don't to all men."

He shook his head. "I know better."

Looking at him, she knew he was right. And she knew that if she was going to open herself up to someone, it should be to him. "If we get to a point where I think it's important for you to know, I'll tell you. How's that?"

"Not good enough. I'm at a point where I have to know why you don't trust. I want to know what I have to do to make you feel safe with me."

Ashley curled her feet under her and hugged her knees. "Today was a good start." He stood up, in his stockinged feet, and walked over to her, sitting on the arm of the chair and looking down at her.

"I don't have a great track record, either. I've wondered if I'd tried harder if the marriage would have worked. If I'd been willing to compromise, to flow with the tide, to settle for financial success, would it have worked? But I'll tell you what, Ashley. I can't compromise. I have to be me. I have to do what I feel I have to do. No woman, no nothing, can come between me and whatever it is I feel I have to do."

"When you walked up those stairs into my office three months ago, and I took one look at you, I knew you'd never compromise, either. You'd never be fake and you'd never operate without integrity and I wanted to kiss you then. You talked of a title search and I wanted to get up and cross the room and take you in my arms."

Maybe, she thought, he was what she'd been waiting for. Maybe all those others hadn't worked out because Noah was waiting for her on the eastern shore of Chesapeake Bay.

He leaned down and his mouth met hers. She closed her eyes and savored the stroking of his tongue as it brushed along her lips, as it parted her mouth, as it touched hers.

She let herself melt into him, held in his arms, warmed by the fire, by his touch. It had been such a long time.

"That was worth waiting for," she murmured.

He laughed as he stood up, reaching for her. "That's the damnedest position. Here, stand up and let's kiss properly."

Properly was hardly the word for it.

"Well," his voice was low, "I might be willing to compromise on some small things."

Shortly after their visit to the marsh at Oberon, Noah invited Ashley to his house for dinner. "I'd like you to meet a couple of friends of mine," he said. "Get to know people."

So, Wednesday after she'd finished work — well, her last patient left at eleven A.M., but she kept hoping — Ashley and Boo Boo walked over to Noah's, six blocks toward downtown. It was getting dark by five, and the streetlights were already lit. She'd brought a bottle of Vouvray and carried it carefully.

Noah met her at the door in a muslin apron decorated with quilted geese. "Do I or do I not look domestic?" He hesitated just a second and then brushed his lips across her cheek. "Brr, you're cold."

He pulled her into the house and accepted the wine. He bent down and patted Boo Boo, saying to her, "Barney's out in the kitchen. We're having spaghetti, as it's one of the few entrees I'm capable of."

"It should be red wine then."

"We'll have this first and Chianti with dinner. How's that?"

He hung Ashley's coat in the closet and looked appreciatively at her red wool dress. She wore small pearl earrings, no other jewelry. He reached out for her hand and invited her to follow him to the kitchen. As they passed through his living room, where a fire was roaring, she was aware of what a cozy room it was. Handmade rag rugs accentuated the shining wooden floors. A cherry rocker was in front of the fireplace and heavy plaid furniture, the kind only men bought, brought cheer and warmth to the room. Ashley didn't know what she'd expected–she didn't think she'd even thought about it-but this looked more like a Vermont farm than a young lawyer's home.

"I like your house," she said.

"I knew you would." He turned to smile at her as she followed him through the compact dining room with its beautiful oak table and captain's chairs. "I finished these myself," Noah said.

"I'm impressed."

"Good. I hoped you would be. I'd like to impress you."

He'd been in the midst of making a salad, chopping lettuce, spinach, onions, peppers; and tomatoes on a wooden cutting board. The doorbell rang.

"Will you get it?" Noah asked. "They're nice and don't bite and are anxious to meet you."

"Why anxious? They don't know a thing about me."

He reached out and took her arm, leaning over to kiss heron the mouth this time. "They know what I know."

"Ah, so you've been talking about me?"

"And thinking of you even more."

Bill O'Rourke taught history at the local high school and Briana Carey, who was called Bree, was one of the pharmacists at the local drugstore. Ashley figured they were about her age, Bill maybe a couple of years older. He was perhaps six-two with an athletic build, dark hair cut short, and brown eyes that warmed you the minute you looked into them.

Bree was red-haired and attractive, though not someone you'd stop to look at twice. She was almost but not quite plump, and she dressed with what Ashley could only call casual abandon. Her eyes were the greenest Ashley had ever seen, and she wondered if the woman wore contacts.

They hung their coats in the closet and followed Ashley to the kitchen. She could tell they'd been here before and felt at home. Bill was from Webster, an upstate New York town near Rochester, and Bree had come from Willoughby-on-the-Lake, a Cleveland suburb. They'd each wanted to get away from suburbia, and had somehow ended up in Easton.

Bill and Noah had arrived at about the same time.

"Tell me about Oberon," Bill said to Ashley. "I've heard stories about it, as who hasn't, but I haven't seen it. Is it true it was an underground railroad where runaway slaves were welcomed and saved, then sent on further north when it was safe?"

Ashley nodded. "My mother used to tell us stories about what she imagined our history was like. I think she pored through diaries and histories of the region when she was young."

Noah poured her a glass of wine and looked at her, but she couldn't tell what he was thinking. She'd felt differently about him ever since he'd kissed her.

"You'll have to come over to Oberon some time," Ashley said to Bill. "I'd love to show it off."

"Great," Noah said and clapped his hands. "Why don't we all go over there this next weekend, before we get frozen out?" Then he stopped and looked at Ashley again. "Sorry. It's not my place to invite people to your family home."

"Oh, that'd be great," Ashley reassured him. "It usually stands empty all winter, except when the family descends for Christmas. We have horses so you can ride, and we can walk on the trails. I'll do some shopping and maybe we could take off before dark on Friday, after you're finished school. I'll phone the housekeeper." She turned to Bree. "It would be marvelous if we could make a weekend of it. I have no patients scheduled for Saturday."

Bree nodded. "I don't work weekends so it sounds great to me. I'll get out my winter underwear."

Ashley felt warmth flowing through her veins. Was it the Vouvray or the idea of making friends, reaching out to invite people into her world so that she could become part of theirs.

Fifty One

Noah had gotten himself elected to the city council and told Ashley his particular area of expertise was going to be zoning.

"It's getting to be so only people with money can live around here. And they don't care about anything but their own immediate pleasure."

Ashley feared he was right. The Bay Bridge, though it had opened over twenty years ago, was responsible for much of the crowding. Now, cars didn't all race across the state to Ocean City and the Atlantic's beaches. Washingtonians wanted to buy second homes, so they could get away from the rat race to a place where they could invite friends and entertain constituents.

They wanted a place where they could dress casually, a roost where they could have a small outboard, a clubby sailboat, or even a modest cabin cruiser. A place where they could jump in a boat and run across the bay or down the spit of land to a seafood restaurant and devour crab cakes while gazing out the window. A place where they could tell their urban children, "See, that's a town like your mommy and daddy grew up in," and the children would laugh at the quaintness. The eastern shore of Maryland would not only satisfy the acquisitive instincts of Washingtonians but lend a shot of nostalgia, too.

The countryside was already littered with trash from those who zoomed through it, but the refuse that was absorbed into the bay and into the marshes and into the bird habitats was not as obvious. And Noah worried about it.

When Ashley volunteered or, as she told him, was coerced into helping his campaign the spring, she became aware of how popular he was, even though he was a relative newcomer.

By that time, they had spent several weekends at Oberon, to Noah's delight. When they did motor out to the island, usually at noon on Saturdays after they'd finished work, they walked through the fields, frozen grasses crunching loudly, pointing at a rabbit or a deer bounding through the woods. They brought skates and danced across the frozen pond.

Ashley invited Noah to spend Christmas at Oberon with the family. Uncle Billy agreed to fly down with Sydney the afternoon of the twenty-fourth, only if he could fly back the twenty-sixth. Sydney had decided to spend the week until New Year's at Oberon, commuting into Washington twice. It was such a task, expensive as well as uncomfortable, to bring Adam down. Nevertheless, she hired an ambulance for the purpose.

Nothing was going to keep her from Oberon at Christmas. The only time she'd missed it was those first two years in California.

For four years she had not dined out in New York or spent summer weekends at the place she loved so well. She made sure she was home from work by six to dine with Adam and talk to him even if she wasn't sure he heard or understood. If it was necessary to have meetings at night, she insisted they be in her apartment.

The one fortunate aspect was that Adam never knew what she and Brock Thomas were doing to the *Chronicle*. He did not know, since he was never even aware of Watergate, that Kay Graham and Sydney Eliot were the two bravest publishers in the whole country.

Gutsy was how Brock put it. Though Ben Bradlee beat him to the punch with his investigative reporters, Woodward and

Bernstein, Brock-with Sydney's total approval-followed *The Washington Post's* lead, confirming and loudly decrying Ehrlichman and Haldeman and the arrogancy of the Nixon White House. Sydney, along with the rest of the nation had spent hours glued to her television that summer, having bought one for her office so she could follow the Senate hearings.

She wished she could say I told you so to her father and Adam about Nixon. It seemed that every day there were more scandalous allegations. How, she wondered, could any democracy spawn such contempt for the people who elected them to office?

Noah arranged to take the days before and after Christmas off, too. Ashley thought he was as joyful as a kid about the prospect of spending Christmas with her family.

Her mother phoned on Sunday to say, "I've some orphans I'm bringing. I hope you won't mind."

"Of course not. I'm bringing one myself." She hadn't told Sydney about Noah yet. She knew her mother would be most interested, and she had to ask herself why she hadn't mentioned him. "Mary and the baby-my heavens he's nearly four-he's not a baby, is he? Well, they're coming and Monday says he has no place to go this year, but I really think he's trying to woo Mary and wants her to see how cozy a family can be. And, to my surprise, my hard-bitten managing editor, Brock, looks like a hangdog when I mention Christmas."

Ashley wondered if he and her mother were having a romance. It would be nice if they did. Her mother wasn't told. What was she now? Forty-six? Well, she guessed she needed companionship, even if forty-six was a bit past passion.

"Don't suspect anything," her mother said as though reading her mind. "We're smarter than that. He loves his job and the paper's never had such a reputation. Not only that, at last we're making money. I want him in that job forever. He likes that idea, too. Nope. No romance, because it might be the end of a beautiful relationship. Besides, I'm too tired all the time, what with the paper and Adam. What about you? Who's this person you're bringing?"

"Well," Ashley admitted, "I'm bringing someone I've become friends with here."

"Well, well. And you haven't told me anything about him?" Ashley knew her mother well enough to know she was hurt not to have been told.

"He's a lawyer, and we've sort of been seeing each other."

"What does sort of mean?"

"Well, there's no grand, glorious passion, but it's awfully nice. He's one of the nicest men I've ever dated. Maybe one of the nicest people I've ever known."

"So, I'd better like him!"

"Oh, Mom, you'll love him."

"Do you?"

Ashley ran her hands through Boo Boo's fur as the dog licked her. "I'm afraid to even think the word out loud."

"Okay, honey. I'll look forward to meeting him."

To Noah, Ashley said, "Don't let my mother intimidate you. She won't try to, but she comes on strong, always so sure of herself."

"Tell me something about her."

"I better tell you about my father first."

"You haven't said much about him except he lives in California. I gather you don't have much contact."

"Not true at all," Ashley said, wondering how Noah would react. He'd been pretty low key about Oberon. He hadn't mentioned her family's money and status again. But she'd never told him who her father was. "I talk with' him several times a month. We're always in touch, except when he's out of the country, and then he calls if he can get through, though the countries he goes to always seem to have terrible phone systems."

"Traveling salesman? State department?"

"No. He's in the movies."

"Eliot? Oh, my God. Jordan Eliot?"

Ashley nodded.

Noah broke into laughter. "Well, no one can say I don't have good taste, even if I don't know it."

* * * *

The family's great regret was that Juliet wasn't with them again. She'd made no overtures to come east in years. But, aside from that, the holidays were lovely. The night before Christmas, when everyone had arrived, they trimmed the tree and sang Christmas carols. Ashley was delighted to see Monday, whom she hadn't seen in years. He'd grown distinguished looking, she thought, gray at his temples, his horn-rimmed glasses perched at the end of his nose. He'd gained some weight and looked fit. When she mentioned that he told her he'd taken up jogging, though he didn't really like it. He'd seen her father in September, when he'd flown out to the coast. They had spent time at Jordan's Malibu beach house. Jordan promised to come east for the opening of Monday's new play in March, but of course, who knew where he'd be then. He had told Monday he was only going to do one picture a year from now on, pick and choose, and learn to relax a bit more.

Monday looked across the room at Sydney, stunning in a mauve wool shift, and said, "I don't know how Juliet escaped. You certainly inherited it."

"Inherited what?"

"The Puritan work ethic. Both your parents are workaholics. It's a sin, you know, or at least a crime."

"I heard that," Sydney called out, walking toward them. "Cure me. I've always wished I could have a beachcomber's mentality, at least now and then."

"Sydney, my dear," Monday said as he reached to grab her hand, "you hardly know what the word relax means. You don't even take vacations."

"What do you call this? A whole week."

"I'm learning to relax. Noah's good for me that way," said Ashley.

"I like him," Monday said.

"You were right," Sydney added, stooping down beside them, "He's a wonderful young man, darling."

"I know." Ashley looked across the room where Noah and Brock were in deep conversation.

Uncle Billy sat down on the sofa next to Monday. "I've been eavesdropping. Am I to expect an in-law at last who isn't also a workaholic? He seems able to relax. That would be an attractive trait in this family. I think I'm the only one who knows how."

"Relaxed and famous, aren't you, Uncle Billy? You've become quite the celebrity, with your witticisms." '

"I think even Brock likes me," he said proudly. "I do take to it, you know. I quite like this fame bit. If I'd known it would happen, I might have gone to work before."

"Well," Ashley grinned, "I seem to be getting total approval. Do you think it's time I seduced him?"

They all broke into raucous laughter.

Brock and Noah looked over at them. Noah asked, "What are you all laughing about?"

Monday answered. "Your destiny, young man, your incredibly good fortune."

Just then Mary returned. She'd disappeared for half an hour and, as soon as she entered the room, Monday stood up and walked over to her.

"He's not used to playing second fiddle," Sydney said. "He never quite got over her ditching him for Denton. Maybe the way to a man's heart is making it ache."

"Daddy's never seriously had another woman, you know. That's what you did to him. I think he's still aching," Ashley said .

Sydney stood up and gazed down at her daughter. "Honey, that was over twenty years ago. I don't think, from all I read in the papers, that your father has been pining away!' But her eyes took on a faraway look. She squeezed her daughter's hand "I've never found anyone like him. That's the ache. I just couldn't have my cake and eat it, too."

Ashley thought she'd wait until everyone had left and bring Noah back over here, to the island. She'd like to make love with him at Oberon the first time.

But when the time came, Noah initiated it on the floor of his living room, on a red and navy blue rag rug, in front of a crackling fire, with Barney and Boo Boo watching.

In fact, they were all in prone positions when the clock struck midnight to usher in 1974.

At the very minute that Ashley and Noah were in the process of committing themselves, Adam left this life, though Sydney did not know it until the next morning. He hadn't spoken in four years, though she knew he recognized her.

After the doctor and the undertaker had come, she said to her uncle, "I haven't eaten dinner out in so long I forget what it's like. Will you come out to dinner with me tonight? I don't want to dine alone, but I do want to dine in a wonderful restaurant. I want to dress to the nines, and if anyone looks at me and wonders why I'm not in mourning, it's none of their business. I am in mourning. But I'm also infinitely relieved."

They ordered champagne, and Uncle Billy made the toast. "To the future, my dear. To our future. To the future of the world. And to happiness."

But the next morning, the newspaper strike that would go down in infamy began.

Fifty Two

Uncle Billy left her after dinner, and Sydney returned to the apartment alone. The funeral wouldn't be until the day after tomorrow. Ashley would come up from Easton, of course, and Adam's sons would arrive tomorrow, but they'd stay with their mother, she imagined. One of the boys was in San Francisco and the other in Boston.

She lay in bed, taking stock of her life. She was forty-six years old and had had two marriages, neither of which had been a roaring success. She had married Adam, and been married to him for fourteen years, to please her father, though she thought they'd had a decent relationship.

Well, it was over. Her immediate reaction had been one of relief, so she was surprised to find sadness overwhelming her. It had really been over for at least four years, of course, but now there was a final, definite ending.

She had a daughter who'd been in an institution for addiction. Perhaps if she'd been content to stay home and be a wife ... even if she hadn't been content, if she'd done it anyhow, if she'd been there every day, if she hadn't had needs and drives of her own, would they all be better people? Could she and Jordan have been happy?

Jordan. She had tried so often not to think of him. Yet, how could she escape? His photographs were on magazine covers, his movies—at least one blockbuster a year. And, of course, she saw them all. Age had been kind to him. She sat in darkened theaters, sometimes sitting through the film two and three times, staring at him, listening to his voice, watching his eyes as he told the heroine he loved her. She remembered that tone of voice, that seductive look, that sense of fun. Once she had had to run from the theater, weeping uncontrollably. How could she have left him? She knew she could never love anyone as she had loved him. Did she still?

Oh, what the hell. What was she doing thinking of Jordan when Adam had just died. When she awoke in the morning, there was no paper at the table. She phoned Brock.

"Strike, Sydney. It began at midnight. I didn't want to bother you when I know..."

"Well, nothing I can do anyhow. How long is it likely to last this time?"

"We're not members of the Publishers Association, you know," Brock said, which was not an answer to her question.

"Then why on earth are we shut down?"

"Well, we and the *Trib* and the *Mirror* have suspended publication to keep a united front."

"Oh, damn. What's the issue? The usual?" She could almost see Brock nodding.

"Wages and hours, of course."

"I thought you told me we pay above scale."

"We do," said her managing editor, "which doesn't endear us to the rest of the publishers. So shutting down is the only way they'll have anything to do with us."

Sydney couldn't quite understand why it mattered if other publishers had anything to do with them. Wasn't competition what it was all about, anyhow?

"On the other hand," Brock said, "with all the others shut down, we could make a killing right now. Stores have no place to advertise. We could have everyone who reads a newspaper reading us."

"And get some of them hooked so that when the strike's over, they'll stay."

"Yup."

They were both silent. Then Sydney said, "I'll see you in the office," which was where Brock already was. "Half an hour, if Carlos can fight the traffic."

It was snowing, big, wet flakes, making the streets slippery and slick.

"You okay, Sydney?"

"Sure," she answered.

"At least you have something to keep your mind off... off..."

"Yes, thanks, Brock. See you soon."

When she walked into her office, Brock arrived within a minute. They stared at each other as Sydney took off her coat, wet with snow, and hung it in her closet. Then she sat down, buzzed for Dominique, and ordered two coffees.

Neither of them said anything for a moment, though they stared at each other, and finally Sydney smiled grimly. "We can't do that, can we? Publish, when the rest of New York isn't."

"It wouldn't be kosher," Brock agreed. "In fact, the *News* has already called. They'd like to have you on the mediation board."

Sydney laughed. "Make sure we don't break the pattern?"

Brock nodded, accepting the coffee Sydney's secretary handed him. "How long is this likely to last?"

Brock shrugged. "I don't know. Last one went forty days."

"Oh, God," Sydney said, thinking of the financial loss.

"We've got to pay our help, too, don't we, since they're not striking. "

"You got it." Brock said, standing up. "Let them know I have a funeral in two days, but aside from that, I'm at their disposal."

"They know that. You can wait until next week. There's not going to be any real negotiation this week or until one side or the other gets desperate."

Sydney nodded, just as the phone rang.

"Sydney, there's someone I want you to meet."

It was Evan's voice.

"What on earth for?" Evan and Kitty and their two children lived in New Y ark all the time now, but she so disliked Kitty, and they lived such different lives, that she seldom saw them. About twice a year, they got together for dinner, sans his wife. She knew he wouldn't bother to come to the funeral.

Evan's children by previous marriages, on the other hand, always seemed to be in the papers. Two years ago his youngest son, whom Sydney scarcely knew, had been involved in a fraternity hazing that had killed a freshman. Evan's money couldn't keep what was his name? Gregory? In Bucknell, and the boy had drifted out of sight. Sydney heard he had gone to Tahiti, but she had no confirmation of that. And though Evan claimed he saw each of his seven children annually, Sydney wondered if it was true. But twice a year, though never consistently, Evan phoned her and they got together for dinner.

She told him about Adam. "Well," he said, "of course I'll come to the funeral, Syd. But, in the meantime, I want you to meet someone."

This time he had an agenda other than brotherly love.

"What's this about?" she asked him.

He shook his head. "I want him to tell you. Please, Syd. How often do I ask anything of you?"

That was true. But Evan made this sound mysterious and Sydney felt a sense of discomfort.

"All right, brother dear. When?"

"This afternoon?"

Sydney pulled out her appointment book and said, "Make it four-thirty, all right?"

Evan brought Peter Pryce, a squat, elegantly dressed man with coal black hair combed back straight from his forehead, a thin mustache, swarthy skin, and eyes that glittered like obsidian. Sydney thought for a moment he was going to kiss her hand, but then realized it was just his old-fashioned, chivalrous manner. Evan explained he was the developer of *Charlemagne*, "a development with heart," though Evan didn't reveal where it was. A development that kept houses in small town clusters yet provided open land never to be developed. At the center was a large enclosed mall of shops and restaurants, with offices included, but the houses were surrounded by natural clearings and woods and streams. Bicycle paths stretched throughout, and an artificial lake was stocked with trout and there was a beach for swimmers. Tons of white sand had been brought in. It was perfect. Too perfect, Sydney thought.

"I believe," Pryce told her, "that people of different races and backgrounds can live together in harmony. Well over ten percent of Charlemagne is black, of which I'm proud, but my dream of including people of low and moderate means collapsed when the federal housing subsidies were cut out by the Nixon administration." He said *Nixon* as though it were a dirty word. Sydney agreed with him there.

"I want to do even more with the Chesapeake Bay," he said. Suddenly Sydney understood. Evan wanted tp invest in the project, and he wanted Sydney to participate.

"I want to protect the surroundings. I think too much development has a negative impact on the natural environment," Pryce continued. "They cut down forests, and I think that's sinful. I've sent naturalists into the area and we've studied it carefully, at all seasons." His eyes took on an intensity and his excitement communicated itself to Sydney. Evan obviously felt the same, for he was leaning forward, listening to every word Pryce said, though Sydney suspected he'd already heard it.

"We found warblers and orioles, finches, bobwhite quail, and towhees in the interior and osprey nests along the shoreline. I want to protect them. I want hunting restricted on the island."

Island?

"I favor a private refuge, where hunting is permitted only by residents and their guests, where we can establish new marshlands, where endangered species can be studied and propagated."

With a jolt, Sydney suspected he was referring to Oberon.

She turned to Pryce, interrupting his spiel. "Just what do you think you're doing?"

He glanced at Evan and then back at her. "Mrs. Yarborough, we've been working on these plans for over six months. We've brought scientists in to study the terrain and the wildlife, the water levels, the density that would make sure this treasure would not be eroded..."

"The bay itself is eroding it each year," Sydney said. "Winter storms always eat away some of the land. Boating is destroying the ecology of the whole area. In 1962, not long after the bridge was built, there were fewer than sixty thousand boats on the bay. Now there are over a hundred and twenty-five thousand. The wash from summer boats, as well as from winter storms, causes erosion. This is a fragile area, Mr. Pryce. Aside from that, Oberon is not for sale."

Pryce looked at Evan, who sat with a stone face.

There was silence. Evan turned to Sydney and said, "Maybe you can afford the annual upkeep at Oberon, but I can't. You must know it takes a million a year. I can't continue to pay half of that. I'm running out of money. "

"I'll pay it all." Sydney's voice was ice.

"Mrs. Yarborough, you can make a fortune here. You don't have to sell it. Let us develop it and we'll all share equally. Or, we'll buy it for fifty million."

"Fifty million?"

"You'll make more than that, much more, if you don't sell it all at once, but become partners in a joint venture where we sell land to the individuals who will buy our homes. Pryce Construction is willing to build a school, finance all the buildings, subdivide the property, and build marinas. You must know this whole area is going to be developed gradually anyhow. It's inevitable. It can either be developed by greedy men who don't give a damn about ecology and the environment, or it can be developed by people like us, who think this is the greatest place in the world and want to keep it that way."

"Why Oberon?" asked Sydney. "There's so much open space. Why Oberon?"

Pryce smiled, and Sydney realized his eyes were depthless. She couldn't see beyond the inky jet of their color to the person behind. He didn't answer her.

She stood up. "Oberon is not for sale. Oberon will never be for sale.'"

Evan reached out to put a hand on Pryce's arm. "It may take time."

Sydney, with no inflection in her voice, said, "Get out."

Pryce glanced at Evan, gathered his black hat from the table by the door, and closed the door gently behind him.

Sydney turned to her brother. "Evan, you must have lost your mind. Even if you're desperate for money, you know I will never sell Oberon."

"It's not just yours. It's mine, too. Christ, do you know what we could each do with fifty or sixty million if we stay in for the development?"

"You'd spend it, I'm sure."

"What the hell is money for, if not to spend?" Sydney didn't respond, but looked out the window, not seeing anything. She didn't think she'd ever been more furious in her life.

Evan pounded his fist on her desk. "Oberon's not just yours, Sydney. I'll sue you if I have to. You're not the only one who has a say about that place. Christ, I haven't even spent time there in over twenty years. I'm paying half a million a year to keep up a place I don't even visit."

She turned to him with fury in her eyes. "I said I'll pay for all of   it."

"We'll decide in court what's to be done with it."

"Evan, for heaven's sake, it's been in our family since 1672!"

"So, who gives a shit?"

Fifty Three

Juliet had holed up in Oberon for three weeks after she'd first arrived. Her dream had come true: she was rich enough and famous enough that she could live wherever she wanted. SO, she'd left Nashville and come here.

She got up every morning whenever she wanted, and the new housekeeper, Cora, would fix her breakfast. And then Juliet would saddle up one of the three horses and ride around the bridle paths, through the woods and past the old landmarks. She'd stop sometimes about eleven and dip in one of the island's ponds, watching ducks and swans swim in the shade of the overhanging oaks. It was like being a child again, only Ashley was missing. Juliet felt a serenity she had never known as a youngster, certainly never as a teenager. She'd always been driven then. Always. As though she'd been running away from something.

She returned to the house for a light lunch, and by two o'clock was in the library, in front of the baby grand that was so out of tune. She would have to go over to the mainland and find a piano tuner so she could stand to listen to her own songs. She'd been told there was a piano tuner in Logan's Point, an old man who might or might not be willing to motor over to the island.

On the first Saturday of June, a day more like spring than a usual Chesapeake Bay humid summer's day, Juliet sailed across the bay and docked the boat at Walt's Marina to pick up her motorcycle. The marina had grown into a big business, especially on weekends, its marina expanded to include docks that housed hundreds of boats. When Juliet arrived there in May, Walt greeted her as though he'd seen her last summer instead of about a decade ago. Though he did say, "I'd have recognized you anyplace. Got real proud when I saw you on the TV getting one of them Grammies."

Taking her cycle out of storage, she headed to Logan's Point. She didn't even know the piano tuner's name, but since the town boasted only four hundred year-round souls, she figured somebody would know of him.

It was a perfect day for a ride. The bike created its own breeze, which felt good blowing into her face even though it was hot. Juliet was never happier than when riding along country roads, at peace with the world, a part of nature, the rest of the world blocked out.

She was at a satisfying time in life, and she knew it. The last four years had been good to her, and she had been good to herself.

She hadn't had a drop of booze, a sniff of coke, or a night of sex in all that time. She worked out at a gym, had bought a small house on the outskirts of Nashville, where she had chickens and a cow and an organic vegetable garden. And whenever any of the big stars were in town, they usually dropped by to see if she had anything they might be able to sing. She was turning out a dozen songs a year, sometimes more. Always, at least three or four made it to the charts.

She'd begun, in the last year, to cross over, go from pure country to pop. And that's how come Darrell Hotchkiss had called her. She'd refused to fly out to Hollywood so he flew to Tennessee to talk with her, outlining the plot of the film he planned to direct, telling her what kind of music he wanted. He gave her a script and asked her to read it and see what she'd think about writing the score. She could have six months, if she'd accept.

How could she say no? It was a wonderful script and Lorna Percy was interested if she liked the music. Darrell would give his eye teeth, he said, to get Lorna for the part of Jemmy. Write him one song, he begged, and let him show it to Lorna.

Juliet read the script three times and then one night, about eleven o'clock, sat down and wrote a song in less than three hours. She knew as sure as she knew anything that Lorna Percy would love it so much that she'd sign on.

Which is exactly what had happened. But Lorna had commitments for another eight months, so that gave Juliet some leeway. She had to write seven songs, and a background theme. One that would be hummed by everyone coming out of the theater, Darrell hoped.

The thing to do, she'd decided, was get away so that all she had to think about was the music. Someplace where there were no distractions, where — Oberon! No one would even be there this summer.

She'd been happy every single minute she'd been here. She felt at peace with the world in a way she never had before. But after three weeks it was not only time to find the piano tuner but she needed to get on her bike, ride through the soft countryside, feel the road fly by under her powerful cycle, get her hands on the wheel again.

Not stopping to visit Ashley, whom she'd seen twice, she passed through Easton, still the sleepy yet charming town that she'd always liked. She rode on to Logan's Point, another three-quarters of an hour beyond, sitting astraddle a point of land, the bay on one side and an inlet on the other. The Stratford House, which had been there longer than Juliet had been alive and catered to duck hunters in the fall and fishermen from April until hunting season began, spread out along a curve of the inlet. She sped past, down the road to what there was of a town in Logan's Point. The post office and the library shared a house that must have been built around the time of the Revolutionary War. Each side was small, but the residents insisted on a library. There was nothing to do but read in the long winter evenings. There were no hunters and no fishermen, and there wasn't even a real store, though up the road there was a Methodist church and a school that went through the sixth grade.

In the living room of the house across from the one gas station, Mrs. Metalius sold milk, coffee, Coke and beer, Twinkies, Hostess Cupcakes, pretzels, Ritz Crackers, Jif peanut butter, Kraft American cheese and Purina dog food. In the spring her porch was lined with newly potted seedlings.

Juliet roared to a stop at the lone gas pump. No one came out of the garage to wait on her. She took off her goggles and her helmet and tore off one of her leather gloves. God, what a beautiful day. She couldn't remember ever feeling this good. She walked through the open door of the gas station and entered a dark little room with a cash register on a tall wooden table and a phone on the wall. Beyond that was the garage where repairs were done. Two cars were in there.

But what caught her attention was the most beautiful cycle she'd ever seen, a silver Kawasaki that had everything possible on it. She walked over to it as though drawn by a magnet. The bike was new, she thought. The owner had made it his own. The polished aluminum shock tubes, brake calipers, and all fittings had been removed, plated with nickel and polished and finished with chrome. The good-enough stock seat had been replaced with a custom saddle. The factory exhaust had been replaced by two-thousand-dollars worth of specially shaped tubing, which ended in brief mufflers, which were tunable by the addition or removal of baffles. It was what a bike should be a statement about the rider. She had certainly never expected to see such a thing of beauty in a little town like this. She ran her hands across the seat, touched the handlebars, and peered through the windshield.

A voice from behind her said, "Need help?"

"It's only gone forty-eight miles," she breathed as though in worship.

"Going to take it out for its initial trial tomorrow," the voice said. "Wanted to do it today, but it's already after noon and I still got work to do."

She turned and saw the man lying on a dolly, his feet nearest her. He was wiping his hands on a cloth and gracefully to stand from that prone position. He was about an inch taller than she was, a sandy-haired, nondescript-looking man with grease-stained fingers and blue eyes that looked like he'd been staring into the sun too long.

She started to tell him she needed gas, but somehow no words came out. She leaned against his Kawasaki and stared at him.

He had a friendly looking face but no sign of a smile. Their eyes locked for a minute. Or maybe it was an hour, Juliet never knew. He finally shook his head and walked through the garage, out to the gas pump.

She followed him in time to see him turn toward her and smile. "Ah, you too. This is a pretty big bike for a girl like you."

He loosened the gas nozzle and stuck it in her gas tank. "I'm leaving here for a trip into Delaware tomorrow morning, if you want to come along. Be back by late afternoon."

Juliet just looked at him..

"You staying at the Stratford? I could pick you up at eight," he said. "You can just sit on that back seat there. I never had a bike christened before. You could do that, if you like."

"Yes," she said. "I'm staying at the Stratford."

He said, "That'll be five dollars, even."

"Eight o'clock," she said. .

He stood there until she pumped her bike into action, heading for the Stratford, where she booked a room for the night.

Juliet discovered the piano-tuner was one Homer Crandall, and she found him, carving a violin out of a big piece of wood. He said he'd drive over sometime next week, if she could wait that long. No, he'd get a boat to take him over. Yeah, he'd tuned that piano a couple times, but not for years.

In the Stratford's dining room, she ate crab cakes and wondered what he was eating, where he lived, what his name was. Vaguely she recalled that over the garage door, in peeling paint, was the name *Mathews*. Was that his name? *Who* Mathews? Back in her room she stared out at moonlight on the water. A flute's notes haunted her. And the words came:

While winter's heat sinks deep beyond the columbine's remembrance,

I, too, shall color all beautiful.

Fifty Four

"You're just more woman than Logan's Point or I ever expected to meet up with," Bart Mathews told Juliet.

Juliet, sitting barefoot in the lotus position on the bed smiled serenely, her eyes shining. "It took you long enough to do something about it."

Bart nodded. He was a thin man of medium height, muscular, with grease always under his fingernails no matter how often or how long he washed his hands. His sandy hair, parted on the left, was cut short, and his eyes were a bleached blue. "We still have dragons to slay," he said.

Juliet knew that. She leaned forward, reaching down to kiss him. He was sitting on the floor beside the motel bed, stretched out, leaning back on his elbows.

"I like the we," she grinned at him.

"Lookit you," he marveled. "Shit, when you blew into my gas station on that Harley Sportster, before you even took your helmet off I was blown away. A woman roaring into town like you did, covered up with all them black leathers ... my, my. That's before I even saw all that black hair." He reached up to gently pull a lock of it around his hand, stroking it as if it were silk. He stretched his neck, puckering his lips. Juliet leaned down again and kissed him, a long, tender kiss.

"You took that helmet off, and I damn near pissed in my pants when you walked over to my new Kawasaki and ran your hands over it like it was a lover. Not," his grin was shy, "that I'd ever done that with Ellen or she with me, but I'd had many a fantasy about what it would be like."

"I can hardly believe you've never been with any other woman in all your thirty-one years, and that one didn't even like making love. Specially with you." Juliet sprawled from her sitting position, lying on her stomach, her legs kicking in the air. She reached her left hand out and ran it down the neck of Bart's collar. "I like touching you."

"Which is still a miracle to me." He took her hand and kissed it, running his tongue over the palm of her hand. "I've never met a woman who was into bikes. All I've ever got from Ellen was why did I spend money on a death trap, why didn't I stay home Sundays instead of going out on the open road, which is the only place I've ever felt free. Until you took me to bed, that is."

"I took you?" Juliet whooped. "I'd say it was pretty mutual."

"I wanted you from the minute you turned from my Kawasaki and said, 'It's only got forty-eight miles on it. New, huh?' "

"So that's what you liked about me?"

"No," he said, his voice filled with the twang of those born and bred on Maryland's eastern shore. "It was the way your fingers caressed my bike, it was your hair, it was the way you ran your tongue over your lips, looking like you were ready for kissing, it was the way you stood with your hands on your hips and your legs wide apart, looking free and like you were someone I knew, had known deep down in my guts and was just waiting for. Didn't you feel it, too?"

Juliet swung her head from side to side, her long hair cascading across her face. She brushed it back and laughed. "I thought you sort of looked like nothing much to have such a bike. Such a big, beautiful bike and you looked like the runt of the litter."

"I always felt that way, too. Maybe that's why I like bikes. Feel big and powerful on them."

"You are big," Juliet said in a soft voice. "You just don't look it. I never met a man who makes me feel like you do. And what? It's been five weeks?"

"Five weeks, two days, and..." Bart glanced at his watch. "...Seventeen hours." He raised his arm and cupped her left breast. "You've got the most beautiful body in the world."

"Seems like every time some man wants to get me in bed he says that."

"I want to get you in bed, too, but you have got the most gorgeous body I ever saw. Ever even imagined. In fact, bed's where I want to spend most of my time with you, except I like talking with you. I never talked with a woman before. Ellen screams at me that I never talk."

"Funny. I never had a man I communicated' with as well.-Even when we're not talking."

"Take off your clothes. And stand up, let me just look at you with no clothes on."

Juliet stood up, sliding gracefully out of her skin-tight jeans, kicking her bikinis across the room. Deftly she snapped her bra and took it off in one motion with her T-shirt.

Bart stared up at her. "You are one spectacular woman."

Juliet pirouetted and then leaped upon him, winding her legs around his waist, unbuttoning his khaki work shirt, peeling it off, rubbing her breasts back and forth against his chest. His mouth covered hers and she felt his tongue run along her lips. Every fiber of her being came alive. She yanked at his belt, unbuckling it and murmuring, "For heaven's sake, help me. I want to feel all of you against me. Over me. Under me. In me."

When he was undressed she smiled at him. "Talking of spectacular bodies."

"It isn't and you know it."

She ran her tongue across his belly, her hand feathering itself down the inside of his thighs. She smiled as he moaned softly.

"No woman's ever done these things to me."

"Poor baby," she said, stroking him. "I'll make it up to you. If you think I ride a bike, you ain't seen nothing! I'm going to ride you to the moon. "She moved on top of him. "Now don't hurt, but bite me," she whispered, her breasts above his mouth.

And she began to move on him, tightening herself against him as his hands pressed her buttocks to him.

"Oh, God Almighty," he whispered.

When they were spent, lying silently next to each other, holding hands, Bart leaned on an elbow and looked at Juliet.

"I want to live with you, spend my life with you."

"How can you do that? You're married. You've got kids."

"I know," he said, his eyes not leaving hers. "But people get divorced all the time. I've known Ellen since I was fourteen years old. I married her when I was three weeks short of eighteen."

"Because you had to, right? See, that's one of the things I don't understand. You had sex with her once, she got pregnant, and you had to marry her. So, why don't you believe in abortion rather than fifteen years of unhappiness for one little roll in the hay?"

"Hey, I'm not trying to talk politics, but about you and me."

"You and me has to do with your being married. Look, it's an old chestnut. If I weren't married, but, Bart, for now at least, it doesn't matter. You don't have to marry me to have me. It's okay as it is."

"It won't be. Someday you'll up and away. You're not a woman who'll be content to be second fiddle in some man's life. Mine. I want to live with you, spend every day and night with you. I've come alive and I don't want to go on living in that prison."

"How can you leave your kids?"

"People do, all the time. I'll see 'em. I'm not about to move to the moon. Trouble is money. That station of mine barely makes us enough as it is. Ellen's always griping about how we can't afford new curtains, a dishwasher. She nearly had a shitfit about the bike. Hey, I do fine in summer when the fishermen come down the point, but there's next to no business winters. I been thinkin'. I get divorced we couldn't live at Logan's Point anyhow. Not one of the four hundred population would even speak to you, and I'd be the town bad boy.

"What if I try to sell and we move? I'll send Ellen and the kids half my pay wherever we go, whatever I do. In a bigger town with year-round business, maybe like Chestertown, I ought to make it. I'm hard to beat as a mechanic. Give me a motor, any motor, and I can make it sing."

Juliet was staring at him, her mouth half open. He was serious about getting divorced. "You're the best mechanic I've seen. Take a bit long, but that's because you're careful as well as just slow by nature. It's one of the things I like about you. You're not in a hurry."

He grinned. "It's the way of life down here." He looked into her eyes. "Well, what d'you think? Will you marry me if I can work this out?"

Juliet sat up and hung her legs over the side of the bed, her back to 'him. She stood up and walked into the bathroom. Bart heard the shower running.

When she finished, he could see her toweling herself dry before she came and stood in the doorway, one elbow resting on the door jamb. "You don't know a thing about me," she said. "I'm flattered. And I've fallen head over heels for you, too. But you don't know enough about me to commit your life to me."

Bart sat up, pulling the sheet over him. "Turn that damned air-conditioning off, will you?"

Juliet walked over to the thermostat and flicked the switch. Then she leaned down and pulled on her panties, her bra, and her jeans. She sat cross-legged on the end of the bed and stared at Bart.

"I come ramming into little old Logan's Point one fine Saturday afternoon, just as you're thinking of taking your new Kawasaki out on the road, and so the next day we had a fine day together.

"The only time we talked was when we had lunch. Only you thought I didn't eat much. That's because you had brought ham sandwiches."

He raised his eyebrows as she continued. "Something that's important to me and you can laugh at it like everyone else does, but if you're thinking of living with me you ought to know. I'm a vegetarian. I don't eat anything that's ever been alive."

He was silent for a minute. "I don't think I've ever met a vegetarian before. But then I never met anyone like you before."

"Well, it's important to me. Kind of like a religion."

He looked solemn and then shook his head. "What else is important for me to know about you?"

"I don't know. We've been out biking every weekend since, and last weekend we ended up in a motel, just like today. I never had a man treat me so tender and care so much about my feelings. I must tell you, sir, sex with you is great."

"That's an understatement," he said. "But it's not just sex that makes me want to live with you. My glands got me into my first marriage, but it was never good, sex or the marriage. It was like at seventeen I had an urge and Ellen was the girl I was dating sorta steady so we shacked up and that one thing led me into a prison. But you…"

"Me? You don't know anything important about me. You don't even know where I'm from or if I have a job or even if I'm married."

He bolted upright. "Jesus. I never even thought. Are you?"

"Not anymore, but I have not lived what you'd call an exemplary life."

"I don't care what you did before five weeks ago. All I know is I'm bewitched by you. When I'm with you I feel like I do on a bike. Free. Pure. Something to live for."

Juliet studied him and then reached down on the floor for her T-shirt and wriggled into it.

He said, "I've probably talked more with you than I have anyone else in all my life. Certainly more than I have with Ellen."

"Do you love your kids?" Juliet asked.

He had to think on that one. "I imagine I do, hut they represent prison to me. They're what tie me to Ellen. She tells them all the things that are wrong with me. She makes fun of my tinkering in the garage at night instead of sitting with all of them and looking at TV. She says I don't listen. And I don't. She says I don't talk. I don't. She's let herself go to flab. She never has anything interesting to say but that never stops her. She prattles on all the time. She doesn't like sex. At least with me she doesn't."

"Maybe," Juliet said, "it represents how she got imprisoned, too."

Bart stared at her. "Never thought of it that way. She wanted to get married."

"Sure, because an abortion wasn't an alternative in those days. And sure, because she was seventeen and in love with love. But it didn't turn out so rosy for her either. Maybe she'd be glad to get out of the marriage, too."

"Except she's never had a job. How's she going to support herself and two kids? And on half what I make at the station? Sounds like you're trying to talk me out of marrying you."

Juliet crawled up the bed and kissed him hard. "You've hung the moon for me. But before we figure out how to do this gigantic step, I want to make sure you're not going to be disillusioned." She paused. "I used to take drugs. I mean a lot."

He took her hand in his. "That's the past."

"I just want you to know about me. I'm a rebel. I fight authority of any kind. I'm the black sheep of the family. I love my father almost without question though he's seldom been there for me or my sister. I love and hate my mother."

"Why?"

She thought a minute. "Mainly because she left my wonderful father. And because her work is as important to her as I am."

"How old were you when your daddy left?"

"I was two. But he didn't leave. She kicked him out."

Bart pressed her hand tight. "You couldn't have known him that much when you were two."

"I don't know him well even now. He lit up-still lights up-my life when he enters a room. But he's had other women who're more important than I've been. And Mother, well, it seems what interests her is power and money."

"So she bugs your stepfather?"

Juliet looked at him and laughed. "What makes you think I have a stepfather?"

"How else is she going to get power and money?"

"Are you ready for this? My mother owns *The New York Chronicle*."

Bart looked blank.

Juliet laughed and clapped her hands. "And me. I write songs."

Bart smiled. "Well, you can go on writing songs."

"You don't even know my last name."

He shrugged. "It doesn't matter. All that matters is I love you."

"I'm Juliet Eliot."

His blank look returned.

Juliet began to sing, "When the flame bums out..."

He grinned and began to hum it. Then gradually the expression on his face changed. "That's you? You wrote that?"

She nodded and named three others. "Now, Willie and Dolly sing them, and I'm working on a whole score for a movie."

His jaw dropped open. "You funning me?" But he could tell she wasn't.

"I'm holed up at my family's home alone this summer so I can write music. But you're screwing me up. I'm not getting much done because all I think about is you."

He stared at her and then asked, "Where do you live?"

"All sorts of places. My family's mainly in New York, but I've spent the last four years on a little farm about four miles outside Nashville. Right now I'm staying at Oberon. We've owned it for hundreds of years."

"Oberon? Oh, my God.'"

"Maybe we could live out there."

Bart stood up and walked around the room, running his hand through his hair. He paced up and down and then turned to Juliet. "I got to take a walk. By myself. I'll be back."

He pulled on his clothes and slammed the door behind him.

When he came back, all he said was, "Let's go."

When Juliet came across the bay the next Saturday and cycled to Logan's Point, Bart met her with. "I'm busy this weekend." His eyes did not meet hers.

Juliet, still straddling her Sportster, felt pain sear across her chest. "If I were a waitress, or was broke, would you be busy?"

His face was rigid. "I'm not in your league. I know it. You know it."

"What's a league?" she asked, trying to hold back tears.

"Whatever it is, I've never been in that one." '

"Me neither. I've never fit in."

Bart looked at her, then said, "Need gas? Help yourself."

She'd be damned if she'd let a tear slide down her cheek. "This is a lousy goodbye."

 Bart lay down on a trolley and slid under a mud-spattered car until all Juliet could see was his feet.

She walked over to the counter and found paper and pencil, writing a number on the torn paper. She knelt down beside his protruding feet and stuck the paper in his right sock. "This is my phone number if you change your mind. I'll be at Oberon at least another month."

He didn't answer but she saw a flickering light moving under the car.

"Damn you," she said. She got on her motorcycle and roared the engine into life. "Goddamn you," she shouted over the noise.

Fifty Five

All she'd needed to get on with it, to do the score quickly and surely was a broken heart. It was, she thought, the first time she'd suffered so since Johnny Mars left her stranded nearly six years ago.

In the last three weeks, in the time since she'd last seen Bart, she had composed virtually all the background music for the movie. She knew it was good.

She'd been at the piano daily from three in the afternoon until well after midnight. She looked at the clock on the mantel. Exactly four. Although it was hot and humid, she refused to turn on the air-conditioning. Might as well be winter as be cooped up in summer. In this humidity her hair frizzled and she'd piled it on top of her head. She hadn't put makeup on since the last time she'd been on the mainland. After a swim in the pool before starting to compose, she had left her wet bathing suit on, the better to be cool in this weather. She'd thought she might go out again for a dip to cool off; it didn't matter to her that the piano stool cushion got wet, though she'd placed a big towel on it, hoping her dripping wouldn't ruin the wooden bench.

This was the first she'd ever spent time at Oberon alone and she relished it, even in the midst of her misery. Of course, she hadn't been back east in years. And wouldn't you know, by the end of the first month she'd met the man who now loomed all important to her. The first time in seven years she'd even been tempted by a man. And now, she had lost the first man ever to touch her in any way other than just sexually because she had too rich and too famous a family and because she herself was so successful. She'd give up her success in a minute to have him. She'd never write another song if it could mean having Bart.

The bell down at the dock clanged. After a few minutes it tolled again. Was there no one to answer it?

She rose and walked over to the long, mullioned window, the sash open, the lower half of the window pushed up so that there was a cross-breeze in the music room.

A Boston Whaler was tied up at the dock, and a man was pulling the clapper again. Juliet could tell he was slim and of medium height, wearing jeans and an open-necked light blue shirt< His eyes were shaded with dark glasses and a visored cap. Juliet could see that much from the house. He raised both hands, waving to anyone who might be looking. Her hand stole to her throat as she let out a small moan before flying across the wide hall, through the great front door, and across the lawn in her bare feet.

When he saw her bounding toward him, he began to run, too. She propelled herself into his outstretched arms, and he held her as though he would never let her go.

"I thought I might never see you again," she whispered as a tear rolled down her cheek. He kissed her and she thought, I'll do anything, anything at all to have this man. "

"Seems like I can't live without you," he said in that twang of his. "I've been miserable."

"I have, too," she said, her arms wound around him.

He was looking up at the house. "I've been here before, you know.'"

She looked at him. "Yup, in high school, my history teacher brought us over in a skipjack, I think it was her husband's-he was a water man and we brought picnic lunches and came over and toured this house and the barns. It was supposed to be a history lesson but I never remembered anything except wondering who could afford to live in a place like this."

"How'd you get away on a Tuesday? Who's minding the station?"

"I closed it. First time in the eight years I've owned it. Never been sick a day. I figure anyone who wants gas in Logan's Point will have to go someplace else or wait 'til tomorrow. My priority today isn't selling gas. I stayed open to noon, though, and then couldn't stand it another minute."

"What did you tell your wife?"

"Nothing. I just took off on my Kawasaki and found a boat for charter and hired it. Guy's gonna wait."

"No," Juliet said. "Pay him and 'let him go and I'll motor you back. Tomorrow."

Bart looked at her, then took her hand and walked toward the dock. Juliet recognized the owner of the boat, though she'd forgotten his name, and they talked for a few minutes. She hadn't seen him in years. He nodded and puttered his engine back to life and took off. She and Bart stood on the dock and watched him become a speck.

"I'm going to phone my wife and tell her I won't be home tonight. First time in fifteen years. I feel like shit but I feel worse without you in my life."

Juliet reached over to kiss him and his arm stayed around her when they broke the kiss.

"We've a heap of talking to do," he said.

"I wish you'd waited another week or ten days," she laughed. "I've just about got the score done, but if I'm happy I may never finish it."

"I'm hungry," he said as they walked, arms around each other, across the lawn. "Got a peanut butter sandwich?"

"Well, if not that, something. Cora will be delighted to fix it. She thinks I've been eating like a bird. I've lost nearly ten pounds."

He stopped and held her at arm's length. "You mean on account of me?"

She sighed, so happy to see him that nothing else mattered. "On account of you. Maybe I didn't get around to telling you, but I've never really been in love before. Not so's I thought I couldn't live without the guy. But nothing else has mattered without you."

"You've been writing music." They continued walking.

"That's true. It just sort of poured out of me. I'm not sure I wrote it. I just sat down at the piano and it came out. I've never felt so much in all my life, and my feelings just flew from my fingers onto the piano keys."

They entered the house and Bart halted, looking around. "Jesus, I'd forgotten. This is pretty impressive, you know."

Juliet shook her head, and her hair, piled on top of her head, came tumbling down. "Yes, I know. As a child I took it for granted, but I've lived in enough places since 'to appreciate the beauty of this place I love more than any other in the world.

"Come on, let's go out to the kitchen and see what Cora can whip up for you."

Cora was delighted to have someone to feed. She cut thick slabs of homemade bread, slathering mayonnaise and mustard on it and thick slices of cream-colored sharp cheese.

"You staying for dinner?" she asked.

"I guess so." He smiled at Cora, and Juliet thought it the most beautiful smile she'd ever seen. His eyes crinkled at the corners.

"Good, I'll gather berries and bake a pie. She hasn't been eating anything I've cooked."

"I will tonight," Juliet promised.

"I guessed as much." Cora opened the refrigerator and took out a jar of homemade dill pickles, placing a large one next to the cheese sandwich. "Take it out on the patio," she said, "and I'll bring you a glass of lemonade."

Then she had a second thought. "Or would you like a beer?"

"No," Bart said, "lemonade will be just fine."

Hand in hand he and Juliet walked back through the house and out onto the patio, overlooking the pool. He stopped in the doorway to survey the scene. "Wow."

"Don't go getting so impressed that you throw me away again.",

His hold on her hand tightened as he followed her to the table under the blue and white flowered umbrella.

"No chance," he said, sitting down, still holding her hand. "I had to have some serious talks with myself, and I figure it's false pride that makes a man feel he's got to be the breadwinner, got to support the helpless female. If that attitude, and I'm having trouble overcoming it, is what is going to keep us apart, I figure it's up to me to make some changes. I guess I'm not too old to grow."

He bit into the sandwich and murmured, "Mm. How can one sandwich be so much better than another?"

Cora appeared with two tall iced glasses of lemonade. "Trouble with her," she nodded her head at Juliet, "is she won't eat any meat. What about you? I can fix something special. I have a freezer full of stuff. Would you like roast beef? Lamb? Virginia baked ham?"

It all sounded good, the way she said it, but Bart shook his head and said, "No. I'll try whatever she's having."

Juliet smiled.

When Cora had gone, Bart said, "Might just as well start changing today."

"You don't have to be a vegetarian," Juliet said. "There's nothing I can do about my family, but I don't insist on your eating like I do. Though I'll tell you what. I'll give up writing music if it'll make you feel better."

Bart finished his sandwich, downed his lemonade, and finally spoke, though he had looked at her the whole time.

"What kind of man would I be if I asked you to do that? I don't aim to restrict either one of us. I'm ready to change. I've been one kind of person for nearly thirty-two years. And I've never very much liked me or my life. I figure it's time to live dangerously."

"How come Ellen doesn't think you talk much?"

He laughed. "I never had anything to say. I find now I have so many things I want to say, I wonder how I'll ever get to sleep.'"

"Maybe sleep won't come easy tonight," Juliet put a hand on his leg, running her fingers up his thigh. "I don't expect I'm going to let you go to sleep early."

Bart sighed with obvious contentment. "Julie, you don't even have a glimmer of an idea what you do to me. I don't just mean to my body, but to all of me. You know what? I want you so bad I can't think of anything else. I can't talk sensibly, despite rehearsing all the things I wanted to say, for you."

"Well, let's shock Cora and disappear until dinnertime."

She took his hand again and led him up the curving stairway, down the long hall into the wing she had appropriated for the summer. She could hardly wait to feel his hands on her body, could scarcely think straight for wanting him next to her, to feel his flesh, to have his arms around her.

She slipped out of her bathing suit.

"Do you know what a turn-on it is to have a woman want me?"

"A woman? Any woman?" Juliet teased.

"I don't know," he grinned. "You're the first one. Maybe if there are others like you, I shouldn't limit myself yet."

She could hear her blood begin to pound. Suddenly he picked her up and carried her to the bed, saying, "I want to kiss every square inch of you," but before he was a quarter of the way done they had reached such a frenzy of de   sire that he moved onto her, and they created a rhythm as forceful as her music, moving together and against each other with hurricane force.

Afterward, as they lay entwined, he whispered, "God Almighty."

"I can never get enough of you," Juliet said, "not if we live to be a hundred." They lay there for a long time, and then finally, he said, "That's what we have to talk about. Forever."

They got dressed, Juliet donning a flowing flowered challis dress, with nothing under it.

"Let's go sit where we can look out at the bay," he said.

"Down by the water's edge."

"I'll go to the moon if that's what you want."

"You know what?" he said as they walked back across the lawn, down to the dock. "All this love doesn't scare me. I think you ought to know that."

"Me, either. For the first time in my life, love doesn't scare me. Losing you does. You say you're willing to change. I am, too. You want me to give up every cent I own? I will."

He laughed. "That's not quite what I had in mind. But then, I don't even know how much you own."

"Maybe not as much as you think."

"Whatever it is, it's more than I have. But I, or we, do have some problems."

"Do they all have to be solved tonight?"

"Don't make me lose momentum. You're all I've thought of since I last saw you. At first my pride kept me away. A wife who's richer than I am, who wouldn't have to depend on me for a living? That's a bit hard to adjust to.

"But I got to thinking, it doesn't seem as bad as losing you." He put an arm around her and held her close, looking out over the calm water, at the trees on the mainland, at the little boats skimming along. The fleet had long gone in.

The sun was still high in the sky even though it was nearly seven. Juliet loved long summer' evenings. She felt exquisitely happy.

"I want to show you Martha's Forest. I want to take you swimming in the lakes here. I want you to see the deer coming to drink at sunset. I want to take you horseback…"

He sat down and pulled her to the ground beside him. "That has to wait until we sort some things out. I've lain awake nights thinking this all out. Of course, I don't know how you feel, but I've got to say what's inside me before I can think about anything else."

She leaned back against the big trunk of an oak tree, putting her hands around her bent knee, and looked at him.

"I'm not the kind of man who can just go along for the ride," he said. "I've got to work, no matter how much money you have. I have to feel I'm doing something. Also, if I'm away from motors for long, I get itchy. I need to respect myself."

When Juliet didn't respond, he said, "That's important."

"I know it." Her voice was soft. She had never felt such inexpressible love before. She looked at this man and listened to what he said and she thought she must be the most fortunate woman alive.

"But I can't stay in Logan's Point. No one would speak to me, and I'd be uncomfortable being near Ellen and knowing what she's thinking and probably saying to people. So, I thought I'd sell the garage, and give it all to her. Give her every cent. She'll think she's rich, practically."

Juliet doubted that. That garage couldn't bring enough to live on for very long.

"She can have every cent of everything I own, including the house. If that doesn't satisfy her, maybe I can give her part of what I'll earn each year. Certainly I'll find a way to earn enough that I can support the kids."

Juliet continued to listen.

"Next, I'm not a Nashville or a Hollywood or a New York City guy. I'll go visit those places with you if you *have* to go, but I need to live around here. I want to be near my kids, watch them grow. Not that I won't try someplace else if you can't bear to do it, but I'd really like to live around here."

"That's okay with me."

He leaned over and patted her hand, intent on things he still had to share with her.

"I don't mind your continuing to write songs. I rather like the idea. I like thinking I'd be the first to hear what's playing around in your head. I don't mind your being famous, but I'd just as soon not be known as Mr. Eliot. I don't even know how to talk with people like you must hang around with."

"I don't really hang around with them."

"I'd sort of like you to take my name. Be Juliet Mathews. I'm that old-fashioned. I don't care whether or not we have kids. That'd be up to you." He grinned at her. "Or fate."

Juliet continued looking at him until he finally said, "Well?"

"Well."

"How do you feel about all I've just said?"

"It's the easiest thing I ever heard in my life. I thought you were going to make it tough. But whatever it is you want, that's okay with me."

"No," he said. "That's not how I want it. I want you to be yourself. I don't want you to be scared that if you disagree I'll leave. I see, a whole new way of life opening up. One that's going to give me excitement like I never had. I hope we argue–fight, even–sometimes, because I want to *feel* everything in this relationship. I don't want you to want what I want because I do. I want you to want something and me to want something and us to talk it over until we're both happy. I don't want you to resent me. I don't want to run you. And just because you have the money I don't want you to run me."

Juliet stared at him until he said, "Say something about what I've just told you."

She leaned over and kissed him. "I think I love you more than I ever loved anyone in the whole world. I'd like to be Juliet Mathews. I'd like to live here. I mean I'd like to live at Oberon.

"Could you hack that? You could motor over from the mainland each night, from wherever you'll work. It only takes about twenty, thirty minutes. I'd like us to live on our own island, away from the world, secure here together. I've yearned to do that all my life–live at Oberon."

"Christ, here?" Bart waved his arm. "I don't know. I've never lived like this before."

"You could get used to it real easily. And I've another idea, but I don't know I fit could work out. We can talk about that tomorrow"

The other idea was Walt's Marina.

"How about our buying it? Together, I mean. You put in some from selling your garage-don't give it all to Ellen at once-and I'll put in some." She didn't suggest buying it herself. She thought he needed to feel the project would be theirs. And she also knew he could never afford it on his own.

"You know motors. And it's far enough away from Logan's Point that you don't have to see anyone from there, but it's close to your kids. It would only take you twenty minutes to motor over there to work each day. You can earn enough from that place to give Ellen and the kids plenty to live on."

"I don't know much about boats."

"You know everything about motors. And thirty-one isn't exactly too old to learn something new. I know lots about boats. And we would be partners!"

He looked at her for a long while and then he grinned.

She'd have been happy to offer Ellen all of the half a million Big Mommy had left her, but she knew better than to even suggest that.

She told Bart she'd talk to Walt, and that afternoon Bart took off to confront his Wire.

"Sell?" Walt scratched his head. "I been thinkin' of it, oh I told you that already, didn't I? It's got to be too much for an old man. But I don't even know what it's worth."

"Have it appraised," Juliet suggested.

The bank said one hundred and eighty thousand.

"Tell you what," Juliet told him. "I want to marry this guy, but he's got too much pride to take all of the money from me. So, I have to fool him a little."

Walt raised an eyebrow.

"I'll give you a hundred and twenty thousand that you never even tell Bart about, okay? And then tell him you'll sell it to us for sixty. Is that a deal?" -

Walt thought about that. "Let me meet him first—see what he knows about motors and boats. See what I think of him."

"What he knows about boats you can put on the head of a pin," Juliet said, "But what he knows about motors will impress even you."

It did.

Fifty Six

Sydney was exasperated. "For heaven's sake," she stormed at Brock, "we're in the hundredth day of this strike. We're losing a fortune."

"Just as we'd gotten rather consistently into the black."

"Not only in the black. For the last three years we've been *making* money." Sydney's voice was filled with pride. "I couldn't have done it without you."

"Oh, yes, you could," he smiled.

"Nope," she shook her head. "Now let's us, you and me, figure how the hell to stop going down the drain financially. This damn publishers' association, not one of them, respects me. They just have me on that board to keep me under their thumb. They haven't paid attention to one single suggestion I've made. They smile politely and totally ignore me. I know before I even open my mouth that they're not listening, or if they are, they do so with amusement, as though I'm not someone to be reckoned with. I'm a woman, and I'm publisher sole owner, not that that matters to any of them, of a paper that's really not known outside of New York. Not like the *Times* or the *News*."

"Everyone who rides the subway reads the *News*."

"Nevertheless, we are making money. Or rather we were until three months ago. You know, Brock, I actually side with the union."

"Shh," he smiled. "Don't let anyone else hear that."

"We pay above union scale. Why can't the larger papers?"

"Because they don't believe in workers telling bosses what to do. Because then they couldn't rack up the same profits. They're run by corporations, Sydney, you know that. And corporations are only interested in bottom lines."

Sydney glanced at her watch. "Well, it may be early for lunch, it's only eleven-thirty, but I'm starved. And I need a drink. Join me?"

"Your treat?" His eyes reflected amusement.

"Chivalrous, aren't you? Of course, my treat. Come on." She stood up and said, "Just let me wash my hands and I'm ready."

"I'll meet you in the lobby," he said. "Give me ten."

They crossed the street to Columbo's, where nearly everyone from the paper ate lunch. It was almost empty.

"When you gonna end this strike? I'm goin' broke," said Columbo, whose real name was Ross Smith. "Twenty-eight years in the same location and suddenly I'm going down the tube."

Yes, Sydney thought, everything we've worked for the last twenty years is going down the drain.

She and Brock continued their conversation when Columbo brought their drinks. Brock, who made it a habit not to drink in the middle of the day, allowed himself to break his own rule. After all, there wasn't any work waiting for him back at the office.

"I keep my cool at the meetings, but I'm seething underneath," Sydney told her managing editor. "I'm so damned mad at them. Stores are losing money, some businesses have already gone under. I want to get back on the street!"

Brock nursed his Heineken. "You know, boss lady, at times like this I'm ready to do battle for you. I couldn't live with you, but I sure as hell wonder why we've never jumped in the sack together."

Sydney looked at him with surprise and then she laughed. "I guess the idea's crossed my mind several times. And then what happens when it's all over? I'm sure as hell not going to be married again to someone I work with. But it's wonderful to have a friend to talk all this over with."

Brock didn't pursue the matter. He agreed with her to a large extent, but he didn't think he'd ever worked for or with anyone he admired more.

"So, you want revenge?"

Columbo himself brought them the hamburgers for which he was famed. "I had to let four of the waiters go," he moaned. "Good ones, too. They'll probably have jobs by the time this frigging strike's over. I'll have to train new guys all over again."

When he retreated, Sydney said, "That's the way the other publishers treat me. Don't even really listen. What the hell are we doing supporting them and going broke when they don't give a damn about a woman's opinion?"

"If we go back on the street, will advertisers punish us? I don't want to take responsibility for that."

"You don't have to take any responsibility at all, except to get us in motion again."

He munched on his hamburger as he thought. "Well, if you're really going to try it, I suggest you hold a press conference to get the most you can out of your break with the association.

"Press conference?" Sydney's voice cracked. "There's no press."

"Oh, yes, there is. Television. The other publishers are going to be furious."

Sydney nodded, finishing her hamburger before answering. "I expect censure. They'll think I'm greedy. And I am. If not greedy, at least wanting to survive. If this goes on much longer we're going to be in dire straits."

"I think we already are."

She sat back in the chair and waved at Columbo. "Coffee," she ordered. "You want some?"

"I guess so if I'm going to gear up for action."

"You are." She waited while Brock ate his last few potato chips and then asked, "How do you feel about it?"

"My money's not involved. But I'm all for it. They've been behaving like idiots. And if we can afford to pay above union scale, they can, too. We're not the wealthiest of the city papers, I know that. And I'm so bored I'm going out of my skull. I'm ready to work again."

Sydney reached across the table and put a hand on his. "Okay, gear up, Contact the TV stations, get the ad department to notify the advertisers, including those who've never advertised with us, and let's aim for Sunday. Gives us four days. Can we get the machinery in action that quickly?"

"Of course."

She picked up her purse and stood. She was smiling.

"Boss lady, smartest move I ever made was to come to work for you."

"I know," she said; leading the way out of Columbo's. He'd put the bill on her tab.

"If I were a man, half the city would think me heroic," she said. "As it is, they'll probably call me a bitch."

"It shouldn't matter," Brock said as they crossed the street, "what anyone else thinks. It's how you feel about yourself. And you know what they'll think? They'll think you've got balls. It'll surprise them."

As they rode up in the elevator, Sydney asked, "What do you think of me? That matters, somehow."

"Would it stop you from going back on the street if I disapproved?"

She thought for a minute. "It might. It just might."

"I think ... I think you're terrific."

She smiled and grasped his hand. "That matters to me. It matters a lot."

* * * *

"The damnedest thing happened at the council meeting tonight," Noah announced, tossing his jacket on a chair. "You'll never believe it."

Ashley looked up from watching "M*A*S*H*." It was the one program she was devoted to, and hated being interrupted.

"Wait just five minutes, will you?" she asked, not taking her eyes from the screen. .

Noah looked at her and muttered, "You don't know how important this is," and went out into the kitchen to fix instant decaf.

Just as he'd taken his first sip Ashley walked into the kitchen, smiling. "Sorry, it's just once a week that Hawkeye Pierce and BJ are more important than you."

She sat down opposite him at the oak table he'd finished a decade ago. Its shine was still beautiful.

"Some guy named Peter Pryce has entered a petition requesting zoning variance for, are you ready for this? Oberon!"

Ashley stared at him, her mouth open.

"Mother would never sell Oberon." It was a flat statement, allowing for no debate whatsoever.

"I know that. You know that. But Mr. Pryce doesn't seem to know it."

Ashley walked over to the phone and dialed her mother's number. Sydney answered on the first ring.

"Mother, Noah heard some distressing news tonight. You know, he's one of the people who helps make this county run?"

Sydney never remembered all the things Noah and Ashley were involved with. "Well, at the monthly meeting, he heard ... wait, let me put him on so I don't get it all mixed up."

She stretched the phone cord to the table and handed the phone to Noah. "I'll speak to you after he's through."

"Oh, my heavens," Sydney exclaimed when Noah told her. "How can he do that about something he doesn't own and never will? Yes, I met him, and I told him I'd never sell one inch of the property. What the hell kind of nerve does he have to petition for a zoning variance when he has no right to that land?"

"I guess he wants to know whether it's worth a fight. If he can get a variance, he'll be willing to pay a lot."

"He's already offered forty million in cash and a lot more if Evan and I'll go into business with him."

"Jesus," whistled Noah.

"I haven't mentioned it because I thought it was settled. I wouldn't even listen to his plans. I just told him to forget it."

"Of course," Noah nodded. "Well, we thought you ought to know."

"I don't know what I can do about it except just tell everyone I refuse to sell." "Thank God," her son-in-law exclaimed. "Here, I'll give you back to my darling wife."

"And my darling daughter." When Ashley was back on the phone, Sydney said, "This irritates the hell out of me, but don't worry. I'll never sell."

Ashley thought of all the stories her mother had told over the years, all the history of that island, until it was as much an entity to her as her great-grandmother, as Martha of long ago, as the ancestors who had owned that island for three hundred and thirty-eight years, longer by far than a United States had even existed.

It was a part of her, Oberon flowed through her. As Ashley hung up, the front doorbell rang. Noah looked at his watch and at Ashley, shrugged his shoulders, and went to the front door.

Upon opening it, he found a young girl, perhaps twelve or thirteen, and a man who was obviously her father. Wrapped in a towel that she held close to her was a bird, its wing broken. It lay limply in the terrycloth, making no attempt to escape.

"I'm George Burnham," the man said. "This here's Nina, my daughter. We live down the road a piece, past St. Michael's. Found this bird and Nina's got a bee in her bonnet about saving it. Deryck and Katie Berry said you'd be the one who could if anyone could."

Noah opened the door wider and invited them in.

They'd bought the land next to Ashley's original office and built a house there, a large house which they confidently expected to be filled with children that hadn't come yet. Ashley kept postponing pregnancy, saying she wanted to do some other things first, but when she was thirty, which would be next year... She came in from the kitchen and immediately went over to Nina, taking the bird from her. She smiled, "Oh, this is easy., Come on over to the infirmary with me, if you'd like to watch."

"Well, I dunno," said George. "It's pretty late, and there's school tomorrow."

Ashley glanced at him. "I'm sure your daughter will learn more watching this than she'll learn in school tomorrow morning. Why don't you come, too?"

The little girl watched without blinking an eye, so fascinated was she. She didn't say a word, but Ashley could tell her heart was in her mouth. "It was my love for birds that made me become a vet," she told Nina.

The girl glanced at her with wide brown eyes.

"Let me keep it here for a couple of days," Ashley suggested, "and then I'll show you how to gradually let it back into the wild. You may have to take care of it for a few weeks."

"Oh, I will, I will."

When they left, Mr. Burnham thanked Ashley. "Thanks. That was a good idea. We'll probably be back tomorrow, if you don't mind. I know Nina won't be able to stand not knowing for sure if it's all right."

Ashley watched them go. Nothing pleased her more than when she could make a child happy. She wondered where she got that trait. No one that she knew on either side of the family had exhibited that characteristic. Maybe she should think of having a child now.

She walked back across the lawn to the house. Yet, if she had a baby, wouldn't she have to sacrifice much of the work that gave her a feeling of doing good in the world? Would she have to give up too much if she became a mother? Maybe she and Noah should talk about that. They'd been married almost five years.

How had she lucked out? Even after these years together, she didn't take him for granted. If anything, she loved him more all the time, maybe more each day. Not only was he the kindest, most thoughtful, interesting man she'd ever known, but each day held some new delight, thanks to him. And their lovemaking had not, even for an instant, lost any of its excitement. He was not threatened when she made overtures, and they were able to fall off the bed, as they did once, and keep right on going, laughing as they made love. He made her feel she had the most beautiful body in the world. She loved to look at him, study him … watch the pulse at his temple. She loved it when his hair got long, probably too long from the viewpoint of Eastonians, but she loved it when it began to curl over his ears.

She loved to watch him dress in the morning, thought his muscular, lean legs beautiful, appreciated every part of him. There wasn't a spot she didn't know intimately. And maybe what she loved most was what he did to her, both to her body and to her mind. She smiled. And to her heart. There wasn't a day when he didn't, in some way, touch her heart, even though it might just be the way shadows fell across his face, or when he reached across the dining table and took her hand, kissing it. Or when he had to share an idea, or a new case, or called her to come look at the sunset.

He cared. His passion thrilled her, and it wasn't just his physical ardor. He cared deeply about so many things, and he wasn't content to sit on his duff and just talk about them. He did things about them. In this part of Maryland there was talk about his running for Congress, but he pooh-poohed it. "What, go to Congress and get locked in? Get nothing done that I care about?

"Besides," he had said, "I have a philosophy: Certainly idealists get elected. Men who think they'll change the world, or at least their small part of it, men who care deeply. Yet once they get in power, staying there gets to mean more than their ideals. Power corrupts. One hundred percent of the time, power corrupts."

Ashley shook her head. "I can't be that cynical. Look at my mother. She's acquired more and more power and I think she grows…"

"I suppose there are exceptions," Noah acknowledged. "So, maybe it's just ninety-eight point four percent that become corrupted. I don't want to cross the Bay Bridge and go to Washington. I want to remain free, to fight for what I feel I need to. No politics, aside from the local city council. Not for me, thanks."

That did not stem the talk, though.

Noah became a monomaniac. He could think of little else, wondering how to fight Pryce, and how to defeat Evan Hamilton.

"What happens," asked Ashley, "when two people own the same property and one doesn't want to sell?"

"They go to court."

Yes, and could the court force its sale? That was the question. And, if not, how could Sydney come up with enough money to buy Evan out, and another million a year for the island's upkeep?

Sydney admitted she could probably come up with that much money, but she would have to liquidate all her assets, leaving her with no backup money for the paper. She couldn't do that.

Noah said to his wife. "You've got money. Couldn't that help? We can live on what we earn."

Of course it would help. But it was not enough. Not enough to keep Oberon going into perpetuity, to buyout Evan and his greedy children. And Peter Pryce, so convinced that the project was going his way, had already invested half a fortune in exploring all the possibilities.

"It scares me," Ashley said. "He must be awfully sure of himself to invest that much money before even owning the land."

"Well, I think we can tie it up in court for years."

"That's not enough," Sydney had said on the phone. "I don't want to spend so much time worrying about it. What can we do?"

Noah didn't yet have an answer. Ashley walked over to him, sitting at his desk in their den, off the living room, in the big colonial house they loved.

"I don't want to stop working, but let's think about a baby, huh?"

Noah looked up, putting down his pen and taking off his glasses, laying them on the desk. "What brought that on?"

"I've been thinking it's about time. I want kids. I want Hamiltons to have Oberon for hundreds more years. I want hope. It doesn't mean I have to stop working. I'll just cut back a bit. We can afford a live-in nanny. I don't have to give up everything that gives me a sense of self-worth to change diapers. I can do both, with your help. I suddenly want a baby. I want to have your baby, our baby. I want to know that I'm going on. A bid for immortality, don't you think?"

Noah smiled and reached to put an arm around her waist. "Well, one thing's for sure, trying will be more than half the fun."

"Clear off this desk," Ashley grinned, standing up and beginning to wriggle out of her sweater.

Noah went to draw the drapes. He turned to look at his wife undressing, something that always gave him great pleasure. He removed his glasses and pen from the desktop, shoving them and the papers on which he'd been working into a drawer. "On the desk, Lee?"

"Anywhere," she said, "but now."

"On the desk. So be it," he grinned, unbuckling his belt.

Fifty Seven

Of the multitude of plans drawn up for the Oberon project, Peter Pryce ultimately considered only three. One placed a town in the very center of the island, with twenty-two hundred houses, some of them townhouses, sprinkled around the island.

The second plan contained townhouses as well as single-family structures in twelve neighborhoods, gathered around the scenic coves and streams.

The one Pryce favored most had three villages on the island, around the three harbors. The north was left as marshland, but south of it, in the island's center, was a golf course surrounded by condos. This plan had sixteen hundred housing units.

Pryce's architect said that the housing would be strictly zoned. When one bought a lot, and only Pryce would do the construction, plans had to be drawn up by Pryce's architect. If they chose multiple villages, the architect suggested one village look like a Mediterranean village, another resemble an English village, and another could take Sea Pines in Georgia as a model, or a village of Swiss chalets. Each would have an architectural theme.

Pryce frowned. He wanted to hear costs. He had already invested over half a million dollars in geologists, architects, planners, engineers. He would, he was told, have to invest about one and a half million to landscape the island. It would cost at least another million to brace up the shoreline, forever losing ground to the water. Roads would have to be built. It was estimated it would take another million to hook up a sewer system, though someone argued that septic tanks were the only answer. Pryce grimaced. Septic tanks would eventually pollute the bay. They might, at a tremendous cost, develop their own sewage treatment system. Wherever that would be located it would be an eyesore and sometimes it would smell. Then there were wells to be sunk and a water treatment plant to be built, plus an elevated water storage tank and pumping stations.

"Bad enough without all these extras," Pryce said, looking at the figures in front of him. "What about storm drains, curbs, sediment control, fire hydrants, land clearing, boundary surveys, paths and trails, docks, a tennis club as well as the golf course? We're going to have to invest at least seventy million in Oberon." That included the forty million to buy the island outright.

He knew it would be expensive. He knew it would be the investment of a lifetime.

"We don't stand," said an engineer, "a snowball's chance in hell of approval if we have more than a thousand homes here. They won't even consider it."

Pryce nodded. Even if they did limit it to a thousand homes, well, at between seven hundred and fifty thousand and a million each that could be close to a billion dollars gross. He didn't like the idea of putting so many houses on the island that it would be despoiled. The fewer houses, the larger the sites, the more expensive the acreage as well as the houses themselves.

"I want those forests kept intact," Pryce said, and permitted no disagreement. "I want this to be as perfect an island as man can create. I want people to look at those chestnut oaks along the rivers, at the willows and the loblolly pines, at the sweetgums and beech and know they have a paradise here, know they're living in the midst of purity, away from the madding crowds of D.C. and Baltimore; and even Philadelphia and Newark. Though," he allowed himself a laugh, "no one in Newark will be able to afford a place here."

He wanted the north marsh kept intact; he wanted birds to winter here, corn to be grown here so that those who lived on Oberon would have the best hunting in the whole area. It would be closed to anyone but residents and their guests.

He'd seen birds along the Chesapeake all his life. Thousands of Canada geese thundering down from the north, spreading out over the water, their wings flapping with such power that the roar was deafening, wheeling down onto the fields and the rivers and the tributaries to which they'd been flying since time immemorial.

He could imagine congressmen and lobbyists and the wealthy of Washington, their adrenaline beginning to pump by Thursday afternoons in October and November, knowing that they would be heading out of town, across the Bay Bridge, south to Oberon, where, Saturday morning, they would be crouched in duck blinds on their own preserve on their own island, and their cooks would serve them duck a l'orange for dinner, or a succulent goose that a month ago had still been in the wilds of northern Canada. Wouldn't that be something, one's own hunting preserve as an automatic fringe benefit to a home on Oberon.

"Let's face it," he'd told his wife. "This part of the country was founded by wealthy people. No reason to change it."

But watermen, natives of the eastern shore, were not wealthy. They would not be able to afford to live here. It was all they could do to eke out a living on land their fathers and grandfathers had worked to the bone to pay for. Tobacco farming and hauling oysters and crabs did not lead to wealth. If you owned the land which grew tobacco, if you owned the big house in the center of that land, if you inherited the big tobacco barn that was often more beautiful and graceful than most of the little houses that dotted the countryside, well, then you might make money. But that was if you already had it, if you'd inherited the land that had been growing it for a couple of centuries. But the small tobacco farmer was lucky to break even each year.'

Battle lines were drawn. Conservationists strangely allied with conservatives.

Conservatives who wanted to keep Maryland the way it had been, who did not want foreigners eating up their land and forcing prices up. People who feared for the well being of those who had lived here for generations, who might lose their land because they couldn't afford what urbanizing would do to prices. The highway would be littered with Wal-Marts, McDonald's, and Kentucky Fried Chickens, motels jammed on weekends, all the kind of business that followed city slickers who moved to the country. Crime would follow, sure as day follows night. Right now you could still leave your door unlocked all day and night.

These conservatives found themselves strange bedfellows with conservationists, who argued that the ecology of the bay was fragile. Motorboats polluted it and scared away birds and foxes and deer. What would happen when the bay was so eroded and so polluted there were no more oysters?

The other side laughed at this. No more oysters in the Chesapeake? Harbingers of doom, that's what the conservationists were. Look what all this would do to the economy. Pryce claimed he'd use local carpenters and painters and electricians and plumbers and back-hoe workers. He promised to hire local help whenever possible. It'd mean that for years, a decade probably, men around here would be assured of work and that would filter into the whole economy. The locals could payoff mortgages, buy new clothes and cars and lawnmowers. New gas stations would be needed, and restaurants would flourish.

Usually it was deserted around here in winter. No income, nothing to do. From the end of hunting season until fishing season began the whole area might as well be dead. Some places pulled in their sidewalks at dark, but the· eastern shore of Maryland pulled them in by Christmas and didn't unroll them again until nearly Memorial Day.

Schools could improve, for taxes would be raised, people would vote for fringe benefits. Maybe their kids could get into top notch colleges, maybe they could even afford to send them. There would be new movie theaters, maybe a shopping center.

Let's not worry about the future, what it'll do to the bay, not now. It means we can live and live better, too. Let the future take care of itself.

There'll always be oysters in Chesapeake Bay. Look at the Susquehanna, every year gathering floodwaters from up north in New York, near Cooperstown, draining in little tributaries running as streams until it became the mighty Susquehanna, rushing each spring southward to spill into the Chesapeake. Think that's ever gonna stop? 'Course not.

Fifty Eight

Sydney looked up from her desk. Her new secretary, Cecelia Hagen, was a whiz but hadn't quite gotten used to her routine.

"Evan, I'm busy. I have no time to talk personal business during office hours."

"Cut the shit, Syd," her brother said, walking across the room to sit in the chair across from her. He crossed his legs, pulled at his mustache, and said, "You refuse to answer my calls. You won't return the messages I leave on your answering machine. I have no choice."

Sydney sighed. When, she wondered, had she begun to dread seeing Evan? When had she stopped loving him? When had the magical times of their youth disappeared, when he and she were the only ones who really understood each other? '

"I won't even discuss Oberon. There's nothing to say about it. I will not sell it. It will not be sold as long as I and my daughters breathe. If you're interested in murder, that's another thing."

"Oh, come off it. And, you may have no choice. I've engaged Lee Atwater and we're going to court about it." Lee Atwater was a name to be reckoned with.

"You can't afford Lee Atwater."

Evan grinned.

"I can at ten percent of what I'll get for that island. And he thinks I can win."

Sydney had been in constant communication with Noah, who felt that if Evan did really sue, they could tie him up in courts for a decade. But he wasn't absolutely sure. It was going to be a headache, a long, drawn-out pain, and it would be expensive. Maybe Evan couldn't hold out. On the other hand, Sydney wondered if Noah was a match for Lee Atwater.

"I'll give you ten million, cash in hand," Sydney said. She'd have to liquidate assets, but it would be worth it to get this off her back.

Evan laughed, a harsh sound. "Dear sister, that would just keep me in gambling money for a couple of years. But that's neither here nor there. I want to buy back my kids. Kitty doesn't even let me see them. I want to screw her to a wall and get custody. I want to be able to prove she's irrational and unstable, not a healthy influence on our children."

Sydney studied him, putting her elbows on the desk and crossing her hands, resting her chin on them. "And you're a stable influence, you mean?"

"I love them. She doesn't. She just wants them in order to bleed me."

"What you can't' stand is that she's the first of your wives to leave you. You've left the others. I don't recall hearing of any paternal love before."

"For Christ's sake, there's not even another man in her life. She had no good reason to leave."

"The only reason you're acting so paternal, and wanting your children, is you're filled with revenge," Sydney said, her voice cool. She tapped her fingers on her faceted glass desk.

Evan lit a cigarette and looked at his sister through hooded eyes. "Why the hell do you say that? Kitty wants to deny me even visiting rights. I've a right to my own children."

Sydney noticed his hairline was receding. That must bother her brother enormously. But he was still aristocratic looking in his bloodless way. His mustache was salt and pepper and the gray at his temples added to his distinguished appearance.

"As I recall, you have other children you never even bother to see, whom I haven't even met,"

He was quiet for a moment. "My dear, you've never approved of anything I've done, have you?" When she didn't respond, Evan went on. "After all, they are scattered around the world."

Sydney wondered if he even remembered all their names.

He partially answered. "I did see Roma in Santorini last year. And Nick may meet me in Phuket in January." He'd call Nick he thought, when he left Sydney's office. Sydney's office. Sometimes he wondered if he hated his sister. "I'm going to fight this in court, of course," he said. "I'm not going to let Kitty get away with it."

"Well, between me and Kitty, you're going to support a lot of lawyers for the next few years, aren't you?"

When he didn't say anything, she added, "Actually, seven years is rather a record for you, don't you think? And what are you now, fifty?"

"Forty-nine," his voice was brittle.

"Four marriages and the record is seven years."

"That has nothing to do with anything. I love these kids and I want them. I'm a far better father than Kitty is a mother."

Sydney leaned forward, her arms flat against the desk's glass surface.

"Between the alimony," Evan's hands were shaking, "and the child support, I don't have nearly enough, not even with the rents from the apartment house, to pay what she's asking."

Sydney shifted back in her comfortable black-cushioned chair. She had often wondered what had attracted Evan to Kitty, a woman who never seemed to find joy in anything. But she was eighteen years younger than Evan, and had a figure, that turned even the heads of strangers.

Evan had told Sydney she was the best of his wives in bed. Though no one knew it, this was proved by the fact that not once in those seven years had Evan been unfaithful. Even after so many years, she still found new ways to excite him and, despite the numerous tiffs, public and private, he had never thought of separation.

It was the first time, too, that he'd stayed in a marriage long enough to get to know his children. To his great surprise, he discovered-where he'd least expected it-love. And his children adored him. He took them riding in Central Park and for long summer weekends at Oberon, the first he'd spent there since his childhood. There he clashed with the current occupants, Juliet and Bart. He brought a motorcycle to the island and buzzed around its dirt paths, sending the birds flocking into the air, cawing with surprise. The deer fled their traditional tranquil pastures, their great brown eyes startled and frightened.

To Juliet and Bart, whose avid interest, of course, was cycles, to see one on Oberon was anathema. They were filled with relief when Evan left, despite the fact they could have lived in separate wings of the house and not met each other except at mealtimes.

Evan was in debt. He had begun to drink heavily as well, not just the two or three he ordinarily drank in an evening but great amounts of vodka. When Kitty formally filed for divorce, he became frantic. He could talk of little else.

Kitty testified that Evan gambled and drank away their money, running up huge bills they couldn't pay, and that he beat' her. For his part, he claimed she was a compulsive shopper, she threw things at him, she'd even tried to push him down the stairs. They charged the other with being an unfit parent, each asking for custody with no visiting rights.

Evan stared out the window, his left hand tightly clenched by his side. "Ah, Sydney," he said, turning to her with a tight-lipped smile. "Dear sister. You've always had everything, haven't you? Even Julie's turned out okay. All you've touched has turned to gold, hasn't it? What's your secret, old girl?"

Old girl? Sydney bristled. Well, maybe she was. Fifty-one. But she didn't feel old.

"You've even aged gracefully." Evan's voice was flat. "Better looking than when you were twenty. Do you have a lover? Brock Thomas? Does Jordie still service you when he breezes into town? Jesus, Syd, I bet you're the best lay any of the men in your life have ever had. You and Julie. I imagine not even Kitty can surpass you and that honky-tonk daughter. But, mostly it's going to waste, isn't it? You probably sleep alone most nights."

Sydney told herself not to be shocked. Evan usually managed to give unpleasant sexual connotations' to any conversation. He revolted her.

She did not let her gaze flicker.

"Shit, without my kids, we don't even have reason to use the island anymore. And certainly I've never used it forty million dollars worth. Christ, we can make much more than forty million. We can make fifty to eighty million each-don't you understand?"

When Sydney still didn't speak, he said, "It's my inheritance and I want something from it."

Sydney tapped her nails on the desk. "What do you want, Evan? I'm busy. I shall never, not ever-do you understand? Sell one inch of Oberon."

He sat in his chair, staring at her. "I've got to admire you, my dear."

"Evan," Sydney said as she stood up, "get out of here."

"See you in court, dear girl. One way or another, you're going to sell Oberon, and I'm going to get my kids back."

"I'll give it to the World Wildlife Federation first. I'd make it a state park first."

He laughed. "Just try. Pryce is working on zoning down there, and those people in that backwater are scared shitless of a state park. Litter, boats jamming the waterways weekends, noise … a state park? They'll rise up and scream. But a nice community of expensive homes, cabin cruisers and sailboats, great tax base? Ah, that's another thing. And jobs for the men there for years? They'll vote their pocketbooks, Syd. And enrich us in the process.

"You can't escape me, sister dear. Neither," a threatening note crept into his voice, "can Kitty. No goddamned woman is going to screw me."

He slammed the door behind him.

Sydney sat for a long time, staring into space. Then she paced around her office. Could he force her to sell? What disgusting things he'd said. '

She thought about his children. He'd never even bothered with his oldest ones, except when it pleased him. Two of Evan's sons had killed or maimed people. Neither had even gone to jail. Evan had bought off the police or the judge or whoever it was who had let them out on bail.

She picked up the phone and dialed Noah's office. She told him about their encounter. "What can he do?" she asked her son-in-law. "Can he win?"

"I don't know. Pryce is taking his time, doing really thorough research. He's putting a fortune into ecologists, chemists, scientists, land-use planners, and architects. He must expect to win or he'd never invest this kind of time and money. He's going about it the right way and he is far superior to other land grabbers, but he's a breed we can do without."

"Noah, I can't be forced to sell Oberon, can I?"

Noah hesitated. "I don't know, Sydney. Not, of course, if I have anything to say about it. I'm keeping on top of it, but it's the unexpected that will throw us a curve ball. Be nice if you had thirty million to throw at your brother, and get rid of him."

"I have, but it's tied up in so many things … the paper, other real estate. I can't give up everything and put it all into Oberon."

"I know. You'd be stripped. Sydney, we can't do anything until they make a move. And they haven't done anything official yet."

Sydney sat staring into the gathering twilight. Was Noah up to it? She'd grown to love and admire him. And she wouldn't turn to another lawyer, she wouldn't hurt him by showing any lack of faith. But it nagged in the back of her mind. Could Noah stand up in court to a Lee Atwater?

Could a judge force her to pay Evan half of what Pryce said he could make from it? What would that be? Pryce claimed they could each make anywhere from fifty to eighty million if they didn't take all the money at once but waited until each lot was sold and each house built, over a ten-year period. Where could she find forty million to buy Evan off? She couldn't. All her assets might add up to that, she wasn't even sure, but then she couldn't back the paper, couldn't pay for Oberon's upkeep, couldn't live as she'd lived all her life. Couldn't preserve a part of Chesapeake Bay in its nearly pristine condition. Oberon was a part of her soul. She didn't want thousands of people running through Martha's Forest, didn't want a thousand boats polluting the waters and the water tables, didn't want hunting on sacred ground.

Yes, sacred ground. That's what it was to her, and to Ashley and to Juliet. She wasn't sure she could put it into words, but she was going to fight Evan and Pryce with everything at her disposal. And she hoped Noah was up to it.

Fifty Nine

Evan had drunk too much, and he knew it. He wandered around the party, listening and observing. In the library he'd tried to join the poker table, but they wouldn't let him. He wondered if it was because they knew he couldn't pay his debts or because he'd drunk too much.

"Christ," he heard Manning Hope murmur as he crossed over to the small group, "all he ever talks about is getting his kids away from that ex-wife of his. He's obsessed." Manning disengaged himself and left a trio for Evan to make into a quartet.

Obsessed, am I, Evan thought. I'll show them. But he lit a cigarette and added nothing to the conversation. For a minute he thought he was going to pass out.

Excusing himself, he tried to find the bathroom but ended up on the terrace. He flopped onto a chaise and closed his eyes. Obsessed? So what if he was? How would they feel to be denied their children?

And they wouldn't let him join the poker game? Not allow him? Not invite him? Evan Hamilton? He thought he must have fallen asleep, for when he next realized anything, he was chilly, but his mind had cleared.

They were laughing at him. Everyone was. Broke. Beaten in court by Kitty. Sydney and all the law that money could buy trying to keep him from his half of Oberon. Well, he had some aces up his sleeve on that one.

Saturday afternoons were the only time he could see his children. He'd taken to standing across the street from their apartment and watching them come out, early mornings, hand in hand with their nanny, who walked them to school.

She met them there afternoons, too. He followed them across the street and half way down the block, the children oblivious to his closeness.

Shit. Once he got that forty-plus million from Oberon he'd open up the case again and that amount of money would change a judge's attitude. Joint custody, at least.

Joint? What had Kitty ever done to deserve them except bear them for nine months? She'd never been much of a mother. She'd never taken them to sail their boats in Central Park, as he had. Never taught them to ride. Hadn't gone to Saturday matinees with them. All things he'd been surprised to find he enjoyed. A family man, at last. His father would have approved.

Ever since Kitty divorced him, in all these months of the trial and living alone, he hadn't turned to other women. Christ, he thought, counting on his fingers, he'd been celibate for six, nearly seven months. He hadn't been seven months without a woman since he'd been sixteen.

It would have been earlier if Sydney hadn't run away from him that day when they'd been swimming in the pond by Martha's Forest. He could still remember it, nearly forty years later. He'd been almost twelve and Sydney a ripe thirteen; her young breasts budding. He'd asked to see what she looked like and, shyly, she'd unhooked the top of her navy and white swimsuit and tossed it on the sand.

"Mother says I'm beginning to be a woman," she laughed.

He thought she looked like the Greek goddesses they'd been reading about in English class.

He'd wanted to reach out to touch her, see if her new curves were soft or hard little knots.

"I'm becoming a man," he bragged.

Sydney sat down, crossing her legs, leaning toward him.

"Mama says men and women look different so they can have babies."

"Shoot. I know that." And he was even younger than she was.

"I'm not sure how."

They gazed at each other.

"I'll let you see me if I can see you."

Sydney hesitated, but curiosity won out. "Promise not to tell?"

Evan nodded.

Sydney stood up and whisked the bottom of her bathing suit off. Even now he could remember how the sun, dappling through the leaves, had danced on her slender body. She stood there, alabaster where the sun had not tanned her.

"Now, you," she said, not seeming at all embarrassed.

Evan slid out of his trunks without taking his eyes from his sister's body.

"Oh," she said.

They stood staring at each other, their eyes not meeting. He walked over and reached out to take a nipple between his fingers.

"Touch me," he'd whispered.

Her hand slid onto him, and she watched, eyes round with surprise, as he grew firm and long in her hand.

"I think." he could hardly talk, "that to have babies, I put that in here." His fingers moved between her legs. Sydney stood stock still as his fingers explored, jerking back with a strange look in her eyes when he slid one finger up inside her.

She pulled back and, looking like a frightened deer, ran into the lake, leaving him standing with a man-size erection, wanting her as he'd never want another woman.

When she came out of the water, her hair slick and hanging down her back, he still hadn't dressed. She didn't look at him but quickly got into her swimsuit.

"Last one back to the house is a rotten egg," she said, and took off running.

They'd never mentioned the incident.

From then on, she always had great power over him, he knew. She studied hard; she knew he wasn't willing to give up fun for schoolwork, and it was her way of showing control.

Dammit, how different their lives might have been if at that moment in Martha's Forest he'd taken her, shown her who called the shots.

His reverie was broken by someone tapping him on the shoulder and asking, "Have a light, old man?"

He lit Richard Kennelworth's cigarette and saw sympathy in the younger man's eyes. "Sorry about your children," Kennelworth said, shaking his head sharply back and forth. "Some day someone ought to show these bitches. Courts always grant custody to the women and try to break us financially."

Someday, Evan thought bitterly, someone ought to show these bitches... Someday, why not now? These bitches. Make a stand against all those women who'd screwed men out of their rights and out of their money. All those women who'd robbed men of their power and their fatherhood—of their manhood. Maybe he could take a stand for every man ... it would serve women right.

He wouldn't wait for the forty million from Oberon. Syd could screw that up for months. Years, maybe. He'd take a stand against women like her, too. Women who emasculated men.

Take a stand?

What kind of stand? How could he get rid of Kitty?

Get rid of?

His breath stopped.

Get rid of?

His breathing came in fast gulps.

He looked around at all the smiling faces. He had to get away from all these people. Have time to think.

He didn't say goodbye to anyone but took a cab home. There he showered, even though it was after two, and brewed a pot of strong coffee. He felt different in a strange way he couldn't define. *Take a stand against women by getting rid of Kitty?*

Naked, only a towel around his waist, he poured the coffee and took it into the living room, sitting down and stretching out on the long sofa.

Get rid of...

For a moment his mind went blank before he said aloud, "Let's face it. Murder." A smile crept across his angular face. "That's what it comes down to, doesn't it?"

Now, how to execute it? Execute. His smile grew wider. Make it seem like a burglary. Or a rape. He'd have to console the children. Any judge would turn them over to him and once Oberon was sold, once he had the kids and all those millions, the world would be his oyster. There'd be no more begging for money, no more women having power over him.

But how? He knew he had to work out a foolproof plan. And soon. Patience was not his strong virtue. Tomorrow. Sunday. He was going to the Metcalfs for the screening of a new movie. It was the nanny's night out. Kitty always stayed home Sundays while the nanny, whoever she was at the time, took off until eleven or even midnight.

He could disappear from the screening and be back before it ended. People would swear he'd been there all the time. Now, how to do it? He glanced at his watch. Nineteen hours to plan and to sleep. Sleep so well all his senses would be sharp and alert. He knew he'd have to plan so well there'd be no slipup. Nineteen hours to change his life, to strike back at women, rid himself of that bitch.

A grin spread across his face. He hadn't felt this powerful in a long time. Maybe not ever. He held the power of life and death in his hands.

And he was choosing death. He was not at all surprised to feel himself growing erect and hard. Very hard.

Sixty

Evan knew what Sunday nights were like at the brownstone on East End Avenue. It was always the same. First there was "Lassie." He'd been surprised to have enjoyed the Sunday evening children's shows. The children clutched at him when Lassie was endangered, crying with fear. Kitty used to sprawl across the other sofa and say, "For Christ's sake, turn it off. They're scared to pieces." But he'd convinced her they had to see Lassie win her way to safety. The ultimate feeling was one of satisfaction and success. And, following that was Disney. The kids particularly loved the real-life animal adventures.

Now Kara and Steve sat in the circle of Kitty's arms. It was not he but that bitch who gave them a sense of safety. His left hand balled into a fist.

Kitty had changed the locks, but when she'd gone to Westport two weekends ago, he'd had a locksmith make a new key to the kitchen door, and he silently entered the dark room, his mackintosh damp from the August drizzle. His rubber-soled L. L. Bean moccasins made no noise.

They'd all be in the upstairs family room. He'd stood outside observing the light while Lassie rescued whoever needed rescuing this week and waited until Disney had begun before entering the house.

At eight-thirty Kitty would send them to bed. Shortly thereafter, before the nine o'clock movie began, she'd come downstairs and fix herself cocoa, piled high with marshmallows. Then she'd zap it two and a half minutes in the microwave, walk back upstairs, add some Kahlua to her hot, sweet drink, and settle back to watch a movie. Kicking off her high-heeled pink slippers, she'd probably fall asleep on the couch before the movie ended.

Evan knew the routine well.

Systematically he unscrewed the overhead kitchen light bulbs, the ones that could be turned on by the wall switch. Kitty wouldn't be able to see when she came for her cocoa.

He smiled. What a surprise. Instead of hot chocolate, he'd be waiting for her.

He'd left the Metcalfs, run the three blocks, changed into dark gray cords and his charcoal mac, and run the seven blocks to East End.

He'd brought a long piece of heavy pipe with him. No gun to trace. He'd read that it took several blows to kill someone this way. That was okay with him. He knew if he had a gun his fury wouldn't let him stop after just one shot.

He stood in the dark and waited. And waited. Sweat trickled from his armpits and he unzipped his mackintosh. He didn't take off his gloves. His mouth was dry but he didn't dare run the water.

Then, finally, he could hear the children's voices. They must have come out of the family room and were heading to their bedrooms.

He waited.

Ten minutes later, a light flickered on in the downstairs hallway. Kitty would have switched it on from the bottom of the stairway. He listened to the sound of her steps down the hallway. She was silhouetted against the hall light. He could see her reach out to the light switch and heard her whisper, "Damn."

With both hands he raised the pipe high over his head, and, with a force that amazed him, brought it down on her head, hitting her squarely so that she sank to the ground with only a low moan. He raised the pipe again and again, hammering her until blood spurted from the darkened kitchen onto the smooth satinwood of the hallway. .

He kept hitting her even after he knew she was dead.

Then he stopped, hearing steps on the stairway, footsteps that halted part way down. He heard his daughter's voice calling, "Susie? Susie, where are you?"

What was she doing up? She mustn't see him, mustn't know he'd been here. Oh, God.

Susie?

And then he heard Kitty's voice, nasal with a cold. "Don't worry, darling. She's just gone to make Mommy tea. Wait right here, I'll go down."

He heard the clattering of high heels on the stairs.

Susie? Jesus God Almighty! He was frozen, unable to move even as the sharp staccato of Kitty's steps moved closer.

"Susie?" she called in that strident voice. And then she stopped. The darkness of the kitchen. The spattered blood upon the parquet floor.

He heard her breath coming in short, frightened spurts. Heard her call, "Go upstairs, honey, don't come down. Tell Steve to call 911. Something's wrong. Hurry! Do you understand? Tell the police..."

He stepped over the bloody body and stood in the doorway, the pipe still tightly gripped in his right hand.

"You," she whispered, backing away as he reached out his left hand and grabbed. her wrist, raising the pipe in his other hand, bringing it down with all his might.

But Kitty jerked her head and the pipe crunched onto her shoulder, sending her sprawling to the floor, her leg kicking high, aimed at his groin. One of her high stiletto-like heels jammed into his balls and he let out a cry, dropping Kitty's wrist to clutch himself but not letting go of the pipe.

He raised the pipe again. Staring at him from the length of the hallway, at the bottom of the stairs, were his wide-eyed children. He heard Kara's voice as though from a million miles away. "Daddy?"

Kitty lay on the floor, clutching her shoulder.

The four of them were frozen in time.

Evan was the first to move. He turned and walked across the nanny's body, through the darkened kitchen, into the drizzly night, beginning to run along in the dark where streetlights reflected circles of phosphorescent red and green from oil slicks shining on the wet streets.

Sixty One

Sydney hadn't seen Jordan in eighteen months. She'd spent the morning finishing up odds and ends in the office so she could take ten days off and fly down to Oberon for a much-needed vacation. In the afternoon she'd sat reading, contemplating fixing herself an omelet for supper. She gave the help Sundays off and enjoyed being alone. Then at five, Jordan's voice surprised her when she picked up the phone.

"I'm at Kennedy," he said, "Just arrived from Buenos Aires."

"Argentina? My heavens." As always, a thrill shot through her when she heard his voice.

"I didn't really expect you to be there but decided to take a chance.'

"It's good to hear your voice."

He spoke in a rush. "Look, I know it's short notice but can we have dinner together? I don't know yet where I'll be staying and don't know how long I'll be in New York, but I'd love to spend the evening with you and have dinner in some nice quiet place. Giorgio's maybe?" She could hear the smile in his voice. The old man's grandson ran it now.

"Giorgio's sounds wonderful but come stay here. I have half a dozen bedrooms going to waste. There's just me and Uncle Billy."

A moments hesitation. "You sure?"

She could tell he liked the idea.

"I'm heading to Oberon tomorrow, if you want to come along and see the girls, though Juliet's in Nashville and won't be back until Thursday."

She showered and ran a brush through her hair, highlighted now to hide the gray. But no wrinkles yet, except for a few crow's feet around her eyes, and she preferred to think that was more from summers in the sun than age. She brushed a mauve lipstick across her mouth and fastened the burnished gold earrings to her ear lobes just as the buzzer sounded.

She'd phoned down to tell Sam, the doorman, to send Mr. Eliot straight up as soon as he arrived.

She cast a last glance in the mirror before running down the hallway and down the stairs, trying not to be out of breath by the time she opened the door. Jordan, bag in hand, stepped out of the elevator.

He stood for a moment, looking at her. Then he put his suitcase down and walked to her, arms outstretched, gathering her in a hug, leaning down to brush his lips across her cheek.

Sydney closed her eyes, engulfed in his arms, thinking she could stay this way forever.

"I haven't eaten all day," he said, backing away to hold her at arm's length, studying her.

Sydney smiled at him, happy to be in his presence.

He picked up his bag and said, "Point me to my room and let me take a shower. Our reservation's for seven-thirty."

"You know where the bedrooms are. Anyone is fine."

His eyes met hers. "Anyone?"

She laughed. He still made her feel desirable.

In twenty-five minutes he reappeared, looking as refreshed as though he'd had a good night's sleep.

Sydney held out a margarita. ,

"Ah," he said. "You never forget."

Giorgio's grandson wasn't at the restaurant and the maitre d' didn't recognize either of them. They settled into a dark corner table, lit only with candlelight, and Jordan did the ordering. Over the years, his tastes had acquired sophistication.

"I recall your liking Vouvray. Is that still a favorite?"

"Mm," she nodded. Though he sat back in his chair, Jordan reached out to take her hand. They smiled at each other.

"Okay, tell me ... talk to me about the family. First of all, can you believe we're going to be grandparents?"

"I suppose it's about time. Ashley's thirty."

"Well, I'm thrilled. I'd love to fly down with you tomorrow, if you're sure I won't be intruding. I want to see the kids. If Julie's not there, who is?"

Sydney began to tell him things she could tell no one else. "Bart will be there, but this time of year he's not home until after dark, almost ten. You know, I can seldom find anything to talk about with him. He's so, well, I don't know if taciturn is the right word."

Jordan smiled. "I haven't seen much of him, but he barely said two words."

"Yet Juliet's happy with him. She's content, perhaps for the first time in her life."

"I noticed that Bart's eyes followed Julie wherever she was. Anyone could tell that everything else in his life pales in comparison to what he feels for her. I suppose that's all I really need to know about him. And Ashley seems to like him."

"When we were all down there together for Christmas-and do you know Uncle Billy's come for the last five years can you believe it? Well, Ashley and Noah seem to have no trouble communicating with Bart. There was much laughter and lively talk."

"I guess we're both still surprised at our daughters' choices, huh? And their lifestyles."

"I've learned, the hard way," Sydney said, choosing her words carefully, "that when they do things that are beyond my comprehension, to keep my mouth shut."

Jordan nodded, finally letting go of her hand. "I long ago learned what you must have learned also. Being a parent is not the easiest thing in the world, but the most rewarding, perhaps."

"I think," Sydney's voice took on a thoughtful tone, "that being a successful and famous woman has created a rift-an abyss sometimes-that would never have been there had I not extended myself. Had I lived my life vicariously through my husband..." she paused to sigh, looking at him, " ... and children, there'd probably always have been the closeness I yearned for."

"But you had to make tracks," Jordan said.

"Funny you should use that term. For Christmas Ashley gave me a slender volume entitled *Tracks,* by some woman who had crossed the Australian desert on a camel. She inscribed it 'To Mom, who's always made tracks of her own.' "

"So how did you feel about that?" Jordan asked.

"I felt inordinately pleased, but now I wonder if I mightn't be closer to, my–our–daughters had I not left tracks anyplace."

"Don't do that to yourself, Sydney." The waiter brought them the best minestrone in the universe.

Jordan talked of being in Argentina, and said, "I'm through traveling." But he thought the film was pretty good. Not his best, perhaps, but okay. He'd liked the director, someone he'd never worked with, a young guy in his thirties.

"Now, what about you? You look stressed, I can see it in your eyes. What's wrong?"

Jordan could always sense what she felt, even after all these years of being apart. Only he had ever looked so deeply into her eyes.

"I'm afraid of losing Oberon."

Jordan raised his eyebrows and reached a hand across the table.

"How in the world can you lose it?"

"Evan. You know we own it jointly, and he wants to sell it for a helluva lot of money."

"What's a helluva lot?"

"'We could each make, somewhere between forty to eighty million. Forty each if we sell it outright. At least twice that much if we participate in a building project, making three towns on the island."

"There are more important things than money, but maybe not to people who don't have it," Jordan said. "Trouble is, Evan just wastes it. He could be a millionaire many times over if he hadn't lived the kind of life he has."

Sydney didn't say anything but sighed an enormous sigh. "I offered him ten million cash. I really can't raise any more than that. It costs about a million a year for the upkeep of the place, and I have to have some assets available for the paper, even though we're making money now. I just can't give every cent to Evan, though I'd do most anything to protect Oberon. Jordan, it just can't be developed. I don't want Martha's Forest cut down to make way for hundreds of new homes. I don't want those marshes filled with duck blinds and hunters. Those birds have been coming there forever, and they've always been safe on Oberon."

"I imagine Evan doesn't think their safety is as important for the future of the world as his having what did you say, forty million?"

Sydney's smile was grim. "It's good to be able to talk with you, Jordan. You do understand."

"So, what's he doing? He can't sell it without your approval, can he?"

"And apparently I can't keep it without his. It's half and half. So, since we can't agree, it's going to court. And Evan has Lee Atwater as counsel."

"Oh, damn. Well, at least you can afford the best lawyer around."

"I have Noah." They looked at each other. "Well," Sydney said, "he is our son-in-law. I'm very fond of him. I wouldn't hurt him or Ashley for the world by having another lawyer."

"I understand your loyalty, but is he up to Lee Atwater?"

"I don't know. But, I've got to have faith. He says at least we can tie this up in court for years."

"What can I do to help?"

Sydney shrugged. "Nothing that I know of."

"What would it take to buy Evan out?"

"Forty million at the least. Maybe more."

"I can let you have some. Maybe a million or two."

She laughed. "What a long way we've come since those days when we lived in that cold-water flat on Bleecker. Thanks anyhow, darling, but one or two won't make a dent."

"Imagine one or two million not making a dent in anything. I suppose Evan and this developer think everything has a price."

"At least I'm fortunate enough to be in a position to fight this. If it gets down to it, maybe I'll have the courage to liquidate everything I own, give up the paper, give up everything."

"He can't win, can he?"

"Noah thinks he has a chance. I've been going nearly insane with the land development studies, with the board of selectmen and the developer both investigating. I don't know what the hell they have to do with it.

Seems simple to me. It's half mine. But nothing involving that much money is ever easy, I guess. Lawyers make it complicated Noah recommends getting a real hot-shot famous lawyer who's used to dealing with millions so that if we lose I don't blame my own son-in-law. But I like him. I want to work with him. But it makes him very nervous."

When it was time for dessert, Sydney shook her head. "Just coffee. I couldn't eat another thing." They were in no rush. She leaned over and brushed a finger across his cheek, resting her hand on his arm. "God, it is so good to see you and talk about family things."

"Are you sure you can stand me for a week or two at Oberon?" She couldn't tell if he was teasing her.

"I'd love it, Jordan. We never see enough of you."

"That can always be rectified, you know."

On their way home in the cab, they held hands. When they arrived back in the apartment he noticed the *Chronicle* spread across the coffee table in the living room. He reached down to pick it up. "I even read it voluntarily now."

"I'm proud of it."

"I'm proud of you."

She looked at him. "You know, no one's ever said that to me before. I thought you'd be the last person to say it."

He shook his head. "I'm as proud of your achievements as if ... as though you're still a part of me."

She didn't know what to say to that.

It had been nearly a quarter of a century since they'd made love. For her there had been Adam. For Jordan, there had been numerous alliances. Yet tonight Sydney wanted Jordan as much as she had thirty years ago, more than she'd ever desired any man. But after he'd held her in his arms and kissed her, he disappeared down the hall into his room.

"Plane will be ready at seven," she called after him.

She sat at her dressing table, brushing her hair, not even seeing the reflection in the mirror, filled with longing, wondering whether she had the courage to walk down the hall and invite herself into his bed. The touch of his tongue against hers lingered.

In the mirror she saw the door open. Jordan stood in the doorway, dressed in gray silk pajamas. He stood there watching her before he crossed the room, and she was aware that he always walked with leonine grace. A smile danced in his eyes as he reached out and took the brush from her hand, brushing her hair in long, slow strokes, their eyes locked in the mirror.

She reached up to touch his hand as he leaned down to kiss her neck, his left hand sliding across her neck, down her chest, brushing her breast.

"I've never stopped loving you," he whispered in her ear.

"Nor I you," she breathed, her whole body alive with yearning.

"Come here," he said, pulling her to her feet, turning her to face him.

One hand cupping her face as he searched her eyes for the answer he'd always wanted, he put an arm around her waist, pulling her close, his mouth meeting hers with a soft urgency.

The buzzer rang.

"Don't answer," Jordan murmured against her lips.

"I wouldn't if it were the phone."

"Tell whoever's there to go away."

Sydney slipped out of Jordan's arms and pushed the button.

The doorman said, "Sorry to bother you at this hour, Mrs. Yarborough, but your brother's here."

Evan, at this hour?

"All right, Sam." She looked helplessly at Jordan. "Evan?"

She reached for the rose satin robe that matched her nightgown. "I'll get rid of him. Unless he's drunk, I don't know why he's here. I haven't even seen him since he started this litigation."

Jordan pulled her to him again. "Don't be long." He kissed her lightly, his eyes smiling tenderly. "I've been waiting too long."

Jordan watched her glide down the stairway. She opened the great door at the end and Evan entered in a rain-soaked jacket, his hair plastered against his head. Even from the top of the stairs, Jordan could see his wild-eyed look.

Evan hardly glanced at Sydney, but walked past her and across the room to the cabinet where he knew there was whiskey. He poured himself a stiff one, carried it to the chair beside the fireplace, swallowed a large gulp, and, staring at the rug, said, "I killed a woman."

Sydney still had her hand on the doorknob, her eyes riveted on Evan. She didn't move.

Evan took another large swallow and turned to look at his sister. "Didn't you hear me?"

Sydney closed the door and walked toward him. From his vantage point above, Jordan thought she'd never looked lovelier.

She sat in the chair across from Evan.

"Was this an accident in your car?"

When he shook his head, she asked, "How?"

Evan finished his drink and lit a cigarette. "With a lead pipe. With malice aforethought. Murder."

"God in heaven," Sydney said, her voice faint.

"Except it was the wrong woman."

Jesus, thought Jordan. Am I hearing right?

Evan explained what he'd planned to do and what he'd actually done.

When he finished, there was silence. Finally, Sydney leaned back in her chair, crossed her legs, and asked, "What do you want of me?"

"Christ, Syd, I want you to help me."

When she didn't say anything, he stood up and walked over to pour himself another drink.

"This is not a good time to have your mind clouded by drink." She thought she might be ill. Evan had killed his children's nanny. And had meant to kill their mother.

Evan placed his glass next to the bottle but did not pour another drink.

"What do you intend to do?"

He shook his head. "I hoped you might have an idea."

"Kitty and the children saw you. They must have already called the police."

Evan glanced at his watch. It had barely been an hour. His shoulders sagged.

"Do something!" He pleaded, his frightened eyes imploring Sydney.

"Why me, Evan?"

"Jesus, Sydney, you're my sister. My family. We're blood."

"That hasn't seemed to matter when you tried to take our heritage from me." Her voice was cold. She thought she might be in shock.

"Syd, it's my life!"

"It seems to me…" Jordan's voice reverberated through the room. Evan's head jerked up to see his ex-brother-in-law walking toward him. He shot a look of panic at Sydney.

"It seems to me you just took a life."

The resentment he always felt when he saw Jordan Eliot surged through Evan. So, even now, Sydney and Jordan were screwing. He felt like striking out at that Hollywood handsome face. Maybe he should have killed Sydney instead. Then he'd have had all of Oberon, and she could never look at him again the way she was looking at him now. Pityingly. Such superiority. Such righteousness.

Jordan walked over to the sofa and sat down, spreading his arms along the back as he leaned into the cushions.

"Are you asking me to help you get away with murder?" Sydney's voice was ragged.

Evan's eyes met his sister's again. "I can't go to jail. I couldn't stand that." He dug into his pocket and pulled out another cigarette, barely able to light it with his shaking hands.

"I won't help you," said Sydney. "It's time you took responsibility for your actions. You've killed someone, Evan."

"Not jail," his voice cracked. "It'd kill me."

"It's that or the electric chair," Jordan said. "Or perhaps a lethal injection." He hadn't known before that there was this sadistic streak in him.

"You keep out of this," Evan snapped, his eyes blazing.

"Too late now," Jordan said mildly.

Sydney leaned forward, frowning. "Evan, you have to call the police and give yourself up."

"No!"

"I'm not going to help you," she said.

"It's Oberon, isn't it?" His voice was a snarl. "It's that goddamned place you love more than anything else in the world."

Was it? She wondered. If he'd never tried to take Oberon from the family, would she have helped him?

"No," she said more to herself than to her brother. "That may be part of it, but I'd never help you get away with murder."

The silence hung heavy.

"I've an idea," Jordan said.

They both turned to look at him.

Sixty Two

"You don't stand a chance, you know. Lifetime imprisonment. Who knows, maybe parole after twenty, thirty years? I'm not up on the law. While you're waiting, rape, sodomy, all sorts of things." Jordan's voice was like steel, with not an ounce of emotion.

"An expensive trial for the taxpayers. Where are you going to get money for a top-notch lawyer, Evan? And you'll need the best. Kitty and the kids as witnesses. Years in jail costing what did I read it costs the government for each prisoner, forty thousand a year? Something like that. What a burden you'll put on society, Evan, just to make sure you'll never take another life."

Evan stared at Jordan. "You're enjoying this, aren't you?"

Jordan was astonished to find that he *was* experiencing a sadistic pleasure. "What I'm thinking of is Sydney and our daughters. They're going to have a lot to live down. So are their children. And your children. The Hamilton name's been besmirched, Evan, but that's not the worst. Don't you believe in the Old Testament? An eye for an eye... "

"Get off your fucking high horse," Evan snapped. Jordan's mouth curved into a smile that did not match the icy blue of his eyes.

"How much is your life worth?" Sydney looked at Jordan, wondering where he was heading. Jordan looked at his watch. "Can't get you on a commercial flight out of the country. The police must already be looking for you." He turned to Sydney. "Can your plane get as far as the Pacific coast of Mexico?"

She nodded. "Given stops for gas."

"I've just come back from Rio," Jordan said, his level gaze meeting Evan's. "You'll like it there. Cheap living. A hundred thousand will go a long way, if you're careful, at least until you find a job."

"A job?"

Jordan let silence hang in the air, giving his ex-brother-in-law a pitying look. Then he said, bringing his hands between his knees, clasping them and leaning forward, "Evan, you're so out of touch with reality. Tell you what I'll do. I'll buy your half of Oberon for a hundred thousand bucks and see that you get out of the country alive."

Like a light bulb turning on, Sydney suddenly understood where Jordan was heading.

While Evan stared at him, hatred blazing in his eyes, Jordan turned to Sydney. "We can get Evan to Teterboro and into your plane now and take off as scheduled, at dawn. We'll call Noah and tell him..."

He turned to Evan. "Well, is it a deal? You haven't a minute to lose."

"Jordan! What are you suggesting?" she asked, knowing full well. "You're going to help Evan escape? Help him get away with murder?"

Jordan turned to her. "Sydney, I don't think what I'm suggesting is *that* immoral. Someday he'll have to go to work. A hundred thousand won't last long. He can *never* return to the United States, *never* see his children again. He'll have to hide out, under a different name. He'll lose his money, his identity, his children.

"We'll help save the taxpayers forty thousand a year and a long, expensive trial. I think what I'm suggesting is punishment as severe as jail. You know they're not going to award the death penalty. If I thought there was a chance of that..."

He looked at her and walked over to put a hand on her arm. She gazed up into his eyes.

"You're the one who taught me morality," she whispered.

"If this goes against your conscience," Jordan said, "call the police."

Sydney turned and walked over to the window, gazing out into the darkness.

When she made no move and said nothing, Jordan again turned to Evan. "Well?"

Evan knew he had no choice.

"A hundred thousand dollars," he whispered. "Shit, Jordan, you know what Oberon's worth."

"I do, indeed. What you have to decide is if it's worth your life. You get sent to prison, you'll never see a cent of it."

He studied Evan for a minute before rising and walking over to the phone. Sydney knew exactly what he was doing. She wondered what fate had sent her Jordan tonight.

Jordan picked up the phone and dialed.

"Ashley, hon, it's Dad. Yes, I'm in New York." He looked over at Sydney. "I'm with your mother. I'm flying down with her in the morning. But right now I need to speak to Noah."

He waited while Sydney and Evan stared at him.

"Noah. Yes, good to hear yours, too. I'll see you tomorrow and we can catch up on each other's lives, but right now I can't waste time. You won't get much sleep tonight, I'm afraid. Here's what I want you to do. First of all, any details can be taken care of in the morning. And don't tell me it's impossible. I'm buying Evan's share of Oberon."

He paused to react to whatever Noah said. He laughed. "Yes, it's true. You'll get all the details tomorrow. What I want tonight is the title, deed, whatever's necessary, for him to sign when we arrive early in the morning. Get whatever you need from the courthouse or wherever first thing in the morning. We'll leave here a bit before dawn, I hope. This has to be done as soon as possible. Evan will sign whatever needs to be signed, then has to take off directly. Don't listen to the radio or TV so you can deny knowing anything. Meet us...

"Yes, this morning. And then I want the deed or bill of sale or whatever's necessary put into Ashley's and Juliet's names and I want it pre-dated, legal or not. Five days ago. Just don't tell me you can't do it. See you in the morning." He hung up before Noah could respond.

Jordan glanced at his watch, picked up the phone again, and dialed Los Angeles. "Carl, this is Jordan. No, I'm in New York. Don't know when I'll be back. I need you to do something for me. Tomorrow, first thing, I want you to withdraw a hundred thousand dollars in cash ... yes, cash. Send it by special courier to that little private airport, I can't remember its name, outside San Diego. Sometime in the late afternoon, I imagine. I'll have more specific details tomorrow. A tall," he looked over at Evan, "balding man about fifty will arrive."

Evan winced.

"I'll give him directions. All he has to do is give the courier my name. The courier is to hire a cab and drive him to the Tijuana bridge, walk him across, and then give him the money, no bills larger than fifty, okay? And then get the hell back to LA. I don't want a word of this to get out.

"I'll call you in the morning, ten your time, to see if there are any problems. I hope there won't be. Don't let there be.

"Yeah, thanks, old buddy."

Jordan hung up the phone and explained to Sydney, "My, accountant."

He looked down at his pajamas and said, "How about we change our clothes, drink coffee, and get ready?"

Evan sat as though in a trance. How the hell long could a hundred thousand last? What was he going to do? He didn't know *how* to do anything.

"Evan, don't you feel any remorse? You killed a woman?" She turned to Jordan. "All he's thinking' about is himself. It doesn't even matter, does it, that someone's dead? That you took a life?"

Evan stared at his sister. "I'm never going to see my kids again."

She would never have to see Evan again. Sydney felt guilty to experience such an enormous sense of relief.

Sixty Three

Sydney realized she was shaking.

She thought she'd remained calm all through the night until now. Noah and Ashley had met them at the little Easton airport with questions in their eyes but neither asked anything.

Jordan and Noah huddled while Evan stayed in the plane.

Noah didn't want to intimidate Sydney's regular pilot. "I don't want anyone to think of tracing your plane," he said. "Let's hire the guy from here who takes charters and send him to Nashville, then transfer Evan to another plane to go as far as Phoenix, then get him a charter to San Diego. I want your plane right here so if the police think of looking for it, it's right where it should be."

"What if Evan escapes at any of those transfer points?" Jordan asked.

"I'll get my clerk, a totally trustworthy young man who'll keep his mouth shut, to go with Evan. Pete knows how to handle a gun. If Evan doesn't cooperate we'll know within five minutes. He'd be an idiot not to cooperate. You're giving him his life, Jordan. He must know that."

"My accountant will send the money via courier to a private airfield near San Diego, where he'll meet Evan's plane, and from there they'll drive to the border, where my contact will walk with Evan across the bridge to Tijuana and then hand him a hundred thousand in small bills. We'll have someone meet him there and get him on a plane to Costa Rica or Guatemala and from there, if he wants, to Buenos Aires. Of course, he'll have no passport. From there on he'll be on his own, but I told him I thought it would be smart to find some way to get to Argentina quickly and leave no traces."

Sydney had asked Jordan over and over again, "Isn't this immoral?"

Jordan didn't know. "It's illegal, I know that. But it seems the simplest solution. It will pain Evan as much as jail would, and will cost the taxpayers less. He'll have to find work and, since he doesn't know how to do anything, chances are he'll spend the rest of his life barely living on the fringe. The money I'm giving him won't last long. He can never see his children or his country again. He can never live the life he's always known. There'll never be anyone to bail him out again. Sydney, I don't know how the world would judge this, but I don't feel I'm acting immorally. I can live with myself. I think this punishment is as severe as prison would be. If you don't feel this way, too, stop me. You're a part of it."

He looked deep into her eyes.

Sydney wondered why she questioned it. She thought it was harsh punishment, indeed. And she knew it would save the family from it long court trial.

She wondered how his children would live with the knowledge that their father was a murderer. She was glad Oliver wasn't here to see this.

And, she felt guilty to feel such great relief at knowing that the worry about Oberon was over. Jordan had been clever about that.

When the chartered plane had taken off for Nashville, they drove to Ashley and Noah's house. Ashley was seven months pregnant. They sat around the kitchen table, and she fixed them homemade granola and yogurt for breakfast.

Granola and yogurt? Sydney didn't know how she felt about that. She wasn't hungry for anything, didn't even know if she could, swallow. But she did drink the orange juice and three cups of freshly ground hazelnut coffee.

It was then that Jordan told his daughter and son-in-law the whole story. Ashley listened wide-eyed, her mouth agape, obviously in shock. Noah shook his head the entire time.

Sydney excused herself, though she didn't want to miss any of the telling, even though she knew all that Jordan was going to say before he said it. She went into the bathroom and vomited. Her whole insides felt knotted

When she didn't come out of the bathroom after nearly fifteen minutes, Ashley tapped on the door and called out, "Mom, are you okay?"

Sydney didn't answer, so Ashley pushed the door open and peeked in. Sydney was sitting on the edge of the tub, unable to move.

Ashley sat beside her and put her arms around her mother. . Sydney couldn't stop shaking.

"It's okay, Mom," Ashley whispered into her hair. "It's okay."

Noah appeared in the doorway. "Sydney, it's illegal, it's immoral, and it's wonderful. Not the murder, I don't mean that. That's tragic, terrible, awful, but I've got to admire Jordan's thinking. I couldn't have done it."

Jordan's voice came from the kitchen. "You'd have been hung up on legalese."

"We've got to keep our stories straight," Noah said.

Sydney stood up, Ashley's hand under her arm, and they walked back to the kitchen table. Ashley went to the refrigerator and poured a Coca-Cola for Sydney.

"Here, Mom."

Sydney accepted it, holding the cold glass against her forehead before drinking.

"All hell can break loose if the authorities ever find out," Noah said, sitting down opposite Jordan. "I, of course, can be disbarred. We'd all be jailed for aiding and abetting. So, let's coordinate our stories. Are you sure your pilot is never going to tell there was another passenger with you?"

Sydney nodded. "I'm sure. He's been with me for over twenty years."

Noah cocked his head in question, but if Sydney was sure...

"Okay. They're not going to check charters out of here headed for Nashville. At least I don't think they are. We all have to lie." And then he laughed. "I suppose this serves us right. If any family believes in integrity and prides themselves on such, it's us. And here we're all going to have to lie through our teeth."

"It won't be the first time for any of us," Ashley said, her hand still on her mother's arm. "And I imagine not the last."

"Maybe not. We may be able to tell the truth, the lies being only through omission," Jordan said. "Sydney's pilot had already filed a flight plan for here this morning. She hasn't had contact with Evan in months, thanks to his suing her for Oberon."

"Yeah, but once the press or lawyers get hold of the transfer of Oberon to Ashley and Juliet dated last week," said Noah, "they're going to want to know who handled it, how the fee was paid, all that sort of thing. We'll face those questions when they come, but let's agree on a story."

They sat around the table ironing but details just in case they were questioned.

Sydney stopped shaking though her stomach remained queasy. Jordan's eyes were bloodshot and there was a pallor to his skin. She could tell he wasn't comfortable about what they were doing, but neither did he regret it.

Sydney kept thinking, my brother's a murderer. Evan had maliciously, willfully killed a woman. The only remorse he had shown was that it had not been Kitty. Should he have been jailed, been forced to spend the rest of his life in a tiny jail cell? Wasn't that a more fitting punishment for taking a life than helping him to go free, even if the rest of his life would be downhill? Might he have been given the death sentence? Might a smart lawyer have gotten him off, with his life, with a brief jail sentence? If that would have happened, then theirs was a more just punishment.

Was it really enough of a penalty, what Jordan was allowing him, Sydney wondered. To get away with his life but never see the children again. Probably never be able to communicate with them. They would never know, all their lives, if he were alive or dead. She tried to imagine Evan at work, and she couldn't. She tried to envision him living on what he could earn, and she couldn't.

The *Chronicle* would have to cover the story, the murder, and his disappearance in some way, wouldn't it? Well, she wouldn't think of that today. She'd wait until Brock broached the subject and together they'd face that. What she had to concentrate on right now was getting through the day.

Sydney looked around the table. This was the first, time they'd sat around a table together as a family since Ashley was a child. Despite her queasy stomach and the fact of a terrible murder, Sydney couldn't help feeling a sense of comfort. Jordan reached out to grasp her hand, holding it tightly.

"It's ironic," Sydney said.

They all looked at her.

"What is?" Jordan asked

"Maybe poetic justice is more like it. Daddy was so worried I'd thrown myself away on a waiter and two-bit actor who was marrying me for my money, wanting to make sure you didn't take Oberon away from the family. And now you're the one who has saved it."

His knee touched hers. "Ultimately you haven't needed my money. You could easily have come up with that amount." She shook her head. "That plan would never have entered my mind." She squeezed his hand

"It's nice to be needed once in awhile." Their eyes locked.

Ashley observed it all.

"You two want to stay here tonight? I've got a freezer full of food. I'll make up the beds in the guest rooms."

"No," Sydney said. "Maybe your father wants to stay, but I need to go over to the island. Is Bart there?"

"He's probably staying over at the marina while Juliet's gone. In fact, how about my giving him a ring and…"

"Don't tell him a thing," Noah warned. "Let's keep him and Juliet out of this. All they ever have to know is that the worry about the island's over, and we don't even need to tell them that yet."

"I'll just say Mom and Dad would like some alone time, or," she turned to Jordan, "would you like to stay here even if Mom's…"

"No," Jordan interrupted "We do need some alone time. Alone together." He looked at Sydney. "Do you agree?"

"Indeed," she sighed

"Okay," Noah stood up. "We'll drive you down to St. Michael's. We can see Bart at the marina, rather than call him. All he has to know is you want the boat and Ashley can hint it would be nice to leave you alone one night anyhow."

"We'll invite him to dinner," Ashley said, "and if he wants, he can stay here. We'll talk about everything but Evan's disappearance, unless he's heard it on the radio."

"Someday," Sydney said to Ashley, "you have to tell Juliet. She has to be included in this family skeleton."

"No, Mom, someday *you* should tell her."

Sydney sighed again, and then nodded. She felt so tired she could hardly stand.

It was twilight by the time she awakened, having slept the entire afternoon away. Jordan had napped on one of the chaises down by the pool. Noah had suggested they not answer the phone at all. Just unplug it, he'd said. If any press or police called, they'd have to try Noah and he'd find ways to head them off. Cora had said she'd fix a light supper. Sydney suggested Cora take the evening off; they'd fend for themselves. She didn't want anyone around.

Cora and her husband, Earl, lived over what used to be the stable, in a four-room apartment that overlooked the bay. It was out of sight of the main house, near the outbuildings about a five-minute walk away.

When Sydney awoke, she lay for a long time, listening to the silence, watching the shadows lengthen on the wall. She felt as though she'd been tossed around in a dryer.

She was suddenly starving, realizing she hadn't eaten in twenty-two hours.

She didn't even comb her hair, but came downstairs, looking for Jordan, seeing him asleep on the chaise. She went to the kitchen and mixed margaritas, always his favorite drink. In the refrigerator she found slices of baked Virginia ham, Cora's incomparable potato salad, pickles, a tossed salad, and iced tea. A berry pie was on another shelf.

She took the drinks out to the patio and sat next to Jordan, deliberately making enough noise to awaken him. He reached over for her hand, but she handed him the drink instead. He shook his head to clear it.

"Well, this has been some homecoming," he said. Sydney didn't say anything as she sipped her margarita.

"Are you all right?" he asked, his forehead furrowed with worry.

Yes," she answered. "I'm all right. It's just been a lot to absorb."

After a while she got up and said, "I'll bring supper out here."

She found a red and white-checkered tablecloth and two hurricane lamps with red candles. Probably something of Juliet's, she thought, but it looked pretty. It was dark enough so that the candles and the lights in the pool cast a gentle glow. The air was soft and the leaves of the trees swished against each other in the gentle breeze.

It seemed impossible that there had been such chaos in one day. Only her still-raw nerves reminded her of the tragedy.

The phone rang insistently as she carried the picnic supper to the patio. Jordan got up and went in to find some tapes to drown out the phone and calm them down. He laughed,

"Frank Sinatra. Eydie Dorme. My kind of music, though it does date us, doesn't it?"

When they sat down, he asked, "Are you up to talking? I have to make some decisions about my life that I'd hoped 'to talk over with you, And I have to make them soon."

Sydney slathered Dijon mustard on the baked ham, which melted in her mouth. She nodded. It was always a pleasure, all too rare, when Jordan discussed his life with her.

"First of all, I have to make a decision. I have two offers, neither of which I want to turn down, but I have to make a choice. I was hoping you'd help me."

Sydney said nothing but raised her eyebrows and sipped iced tea.

"Let me preface this by telling you something you've known since the day I met you." He leaned across the table to put his hand over hers. "I love you. I don't just love you. I'm in love with you. I have never really loved another woman. Never. For thirty-two years I have loved you exclusively."

"You've had other women, lots of them," Sydney blurted.

He nodded. "I've had them, it's true. But no one's ever made me feel as you do. And the thought of you always stopped me from falling in love with anyone else."

Sydney looked at him. "I love you, too."

He nodded. "I know. And that's the most important thing I want us to talk about."

She leaned-forward. "Do you understand at all why I had to leave you?"

"I didn't for years," he said, his fork full of potato salad. He chewed it before he resumed talking. "Damn good food. I've never eaten at Oberon that it hasn't been the best."

Sydney smiled wanly.

"I'm not a total clod," Jordan said. "All the changes of these last twenty years have awakened my consciousness, you know. I do like to think I've also acquired a sensitivity I might have lacked in my youth. And, with you as a model, our daughters have become strong, independent women. Yes, I do understand. Finally."

Sydney sat back and gazed at him. He was still the most beautiful human being she'd ever known.

"If it weren't for you, and women like you, our daughters wouldn't be juggling careers and marriages. But it's been a helluva price to pay."

Sydney agreed. "That it has. I've wondered every day since I left you if it was the right decision."

"I imagined as much. You never really loved Adam, did you? No, don't even answer that. Whatever you felt for him, it wasn't what you and I've always had. And I'm wondering if we can't resume that relationship, Syd. We're at a different time in life than we were thirty years ago. Look at what you've become."

"What have I become?"

"One of the most respected women in the country."

She was able to smile now. "Not as famous as you."

"Look, I've come to realize if you'd stayed with me you'd have begun to resent me. You were in my shadow. Haven't we both achieved enough by now to keep that from happening again? Look, let's stop regretting the past and think of the future.

"Delbert Raines, you know, he's the one who directed me when I won the Oscar? Well, he called me in Argentina and offered me the lead in *Ramparts.*"

It had been the runaway best-seller of the last year. The hero, or anti-hero, was a role younger men would willingly age for. Sydney looked at Jordan. Of course. He'd be wonderful. It would be such a stretch for him to play someone so seedy. And, yet someone who, like all Jordan's characters and Jordan himself, emerged with integrity. Jordan and integrity? Had this situation with Evan compromised him?

"So, where's the dilemma?"

Jordan grinned. "Monday's finally written a play just for me, and he thinks it's the best thing he's ever done."

Sydney looked at him for a long time.

"The one dream you've had that's not happened, a starring role on Broadway."

"It's one of my two dreams that haven't yet come true."

Sydney got up and went in the house, returning with a pitcher of iced tea. He was going to ask something of her, she knew. God, what a weekend. What a twenty-four hours.

"What's that sigh for?"

"I think I'm afraid."

Jordan accepted the drink she poured for him. "Sydney, let's try again. Let's break our routines.

"I used to love New York when I was young, but now, the damn cold winters, the snow, the 'gray skies. The crowds. I have to be close to nature to be happy. But, there *is* an excitement to it, if I thought I wouldn't be imprisoned by concrete. Here's what I've been thinking."

Sydney told herself to relax. She could listen. She loved listening to him. She just wasn't sure she was ready to make a major life change and she suspected that's what he was suggesting.

"You don't have to work as hard as you have been anymore, do you? Isn't it time to let up a little? Smell the daisies?"

Maybe it was.

"This managing editor you've raved about for years. Kick yourself upstairs. Be Chairman of the Board. Let him be publisher. Neither of the girls is interested in the paper. Start training him, or someone."

"But he's such a marvelous editor."

"Give him a choice, then. You'll still be boss. After all, you own it, but start relinquishing some power. Not all, mind you. Do it gradually, over a year, maybe. But give time to us now, to the emotional side of your life. The part we've been denied all these years."

"What are you suggesting?"

"Come be my love. Come away with me and be my love…"

She laughed. "Sounds like a poem or a line of dialogue."

"A poem," he acknowledged. "But try it. Give us a month, a vacation to start with. Come to Kenya with me. Come see my paradise, the place I love so much. It's got one of the best climates in the world. Come see what I do there, what I'm trying to do. Come, let's get to know each other again. Let's make love again, in all ways."

He looked at her and her heart melted.

"Then, we'll come back and rehearsals start in September. I told Monday I wouldn't do the play, I couldn't be in New York, unless you were part of all this."

"Don't put that responsibility on me!"

Jordan went on. "I'll be busy. You'll be busy. But weekends we can come down here. I can get to know our daughters at last. We can be a family here at Oberon. And even when the play opens, we could fly down Sunday morning and not have to go back to the city until Monday afternoons."

"It does sound tempting."

"What about *Ramparts?*"

"Let Newman win his second Oscar."

"I don't know."

"Will you think about it?"

She nodded. "Of course. It's just it seems so late to make such big changes."

He stood up and pulled her with him, his hands on her shoulders. "Is it ever too late for love? I'm not saying let's get married again … at least not right away."

"But you're proposing we try living together?"

"Yes. My life has never been complete since you left me. I want us to try again. We don't have the same needs or desires…"

They both broke into laughter.

"I'm not sure about desires," Jordan said. "One step at a time."

"It's what Juliet's wanted all her life. Her parents together, a family," mused Sydney.

"Don't do it for anyone but yourself," Jordan said. He pulled her close to him, his hands going to either side of her head, gazing deep into her eyes. Then his mouth met hers. He still had the power to make her dizzy, to bring all her nerve ends alive, to inject heat into her blood.

"Jordan, I can't think of it now," Sydney said, pushing him away. "This thing with Evan has me in a turmoil."

"So, let's leave for Africa this week," he urged. "Get away from all the gossip. Have no one in our lives but each other."

"When do you have to let Monday know?"

He shrugged. "Soon. He and Del are both waiting for my answer."

"Let me sleep on it," she asked. "I can't make up my mind this quickly."

"You can't let go of the reins so quickly? Well, don't decide about that. I happen to know you've never taken more than two weeks vacation in all your working years, and you've never gone anyplace other than here. Come be part of the world. Not just my world, as it used to be. Make it our world, darling."

Darling.

"For now let's just sit here and listen to this wonderful music. I'm too tired to think straight."

They held hands as Frank Sinatra took them on a stairway to the stars.

* * * *

When they went up to bed, Jordan drew her close. "I really want to take up where we left off last night, but I can tell you're too tired, aren't you?"

Sydney nodded. She could hardly keep her eyes open. "I've been wondering if that girl, the one Evan killed, had any family. She must have. How terrible." Tears welled in the corners of her eyes.

"Juliet will be thrilled you're here," Sydney said over her shoulder as she headed to her room. She'd taken over Big Mommy's big front room. She'd put Jordan in the guest room down the hall.

She lay in bed, in that dream world between waking and sleeping, and realized she hadn't even thanked Jordan. She hadn't told him that last night, before Evan arrived ... was it only last night? She hadn't told him she'd been ready to go to bed with him, ready to make love, ready to...

There I go again, taking a chance on love...

That's what Sinatra had sung. *There I go again.*

Behind the clouds, in the pale moonlight, she imagined Mt. Kilimanjaro. The stars were brighter there, and in the distance a lion roared. There were roses growing by the front door of Jordan's lodge, and that surprised her. Roses in Africa? She was fifty-one years old and aware of her body, electrified by it. Maybe it was about time for the things that had eluded her, that she had tossed away, kept at bay.

If they lived in New York and spent weekends here at Oberon, while Jordan was in the play at least, and if he was in it and Monday thought it was the best thing he'd written it would undoubtedly have a long run, years maybe ... well, she could still be publisher. She wouldn't have to kick herself upstairs, wouldn't have to relinquish everything. She wasn't ready to give it all up, not after all she'd achieved. She loved her work, but perhaps she could slow down a bit. Do as Jordan suggested, smell the daisies. Take time to enjoy life, not just have the newspaper the only thing in her life.

She could take time-no, *make* time-for love. For a bit of travel, and for the old love to be rekindled and a new love to form, with the only man she'd ever loved in her whole life.

She rose as though sleepwalking and opened her door, walking down the hall, down the carpeted stairway, across the great central hall and out into the night air. Across the lawn she ran, remembering she'd seen wild daisies growing by the dock when they'd landed this afternoon.

She could see them in the moonlight and she gathered so many that she couldn't hold them. She stripped off her nightgown and made a basket of it, filling it with daisies, laughing as she did so.

Carrying them in front of her, she danced back across the lawn, feeling bewitched by the moonlight which was not pale as she'd seen it in her mental image of Kenya. It lit up the world. She ran up the stairs and didn't even knock at Jordan's door, but burst in, crying, "I hope you're not asleep."

He did not turn on a light. "Struggling to keep from walking down the hallway to your room's kept me awake."

She threw the daisies on the bed and her arms high in the air.

"What's this?" he asked, laughter in his voice.

"I've taken your advice and I'm starting to smell the daisies." Her eyes, adjusted now to the dark, found him, sitting up in bed, and she threw her arms around him. "I thought I'd start by running away with you. Not this minute, but maybe later this week, or next. I'll talk first with Brock. But for now, call Monday this minute and tell him you'll take the part."

He suddenly realized she wasn't wearing anything. He glanced at the clock, its hands glowing in the dark. "It's one o'clock," he said as he reached out for her.

"So?" Her fingers found the phone on the bedside table and, as she picked up the receiver, she asked, "Do you know Monday's number?"

"Yeah, but I can't see to dial." She switched on the bedside lamp, but he wasn't looking at the phone.

"I have better things to do than call Monday right now," Jordan said, his hand on her thigh.

"Tell me the number." When he did so she punched it into the handset and handed it over.

Almost immediately, Jordan said, "Monday, it's me. Yeah. No, I'm down here at Oberon, with Sydney. Thought I'd let you know I'm going to do it. No, I don't need to see the script first." He put his hand over the phone as he moaned and grinned at Sydney. "You keep doing that and I'll never get this conversation ... oh, Jesus God!"

Monday said something, and Jordan said, "we're going to be down here all week, and then we're taking off for Kenya. For August, anyhow, but we'll be in New York a week from today." He clutched Sydney's hand and asked, "That okay? Next week?"

She nodded as she kissed his navel.

"I'll see the script then. What?" A pause. "You're going to try your hand at directing it? Well, that may change my mind! No, no, I'm kidding. I think it sounds like a fine idea. We'll see you next week. Dinner, the three of us next Monday, at Giorgio's, okay? Yeah, you, too, old friend." He put the phone back in the cradle and pulled Sydney close.

"I feel," he said, as he gathered her in his arms, "that we've come home. After all these years."

"Welcome back," she whispered. "It feels awfully good."

"Not as good as it's going to feel."

He was right.

Afterward

In two issues of *Vanity Fair* I found articles that were of great help to me.

An article entitled "Treasured Island" by Leslie Bennetts triggered the idea for this book, though that island is off the north east coast of Long Island and my fictional one is in Chesapeake Bay. None of the characters involved has any resemblance to any living people (or any dead ones, for that matter) and are strictly figments of my imagination.

Another article, by Dominick Dunne, entitled "The Gentleman Vanishes," about an English Lord, gave me the idea for Evan's murdering the wrong woman.

I spent the spring of 1993 visiting the Chesapeake Bay region, falling in love with the countryside and its charming towns, as well as being intrigued by the eastern shore people. My great grandparents, my grandparents, and my aunt and uncle are buried not far from there in Smyrna, Delaware.

I am indebted for the song lyrics to my daughter, Lisa Clapp.

As for New York, I grew up there in the years of which I write.

Barbara Bickmore
Ajijic, Mexico
August, 1994

Barbara Bickmore wrote her first short story at seven and has been writing ever since. Her dream to become a published writer came true when **East Of The Sun** was published in 1988. As her heroines grow they become women who make a difference and don't settle for living life the way society dictates. Readers will experience sorrow, pain, happiness, romance, love and will enjoy growing with the heroines as they rise to life's challenges.

Barbara Bickmore relates her writing career to living in a Fairy Tale - her Cinderella story has allowed her to travel all over the world and to experience life in different places and through different cultures.

Barbara Bickmore once said, "Being a writer is the most difficult work I've ever done, because there is absolutely nothing and no one but me and my mind. It's scary, in fact petrifying because I'm always afraid maybe there's nothing there, no thoughts or words to put on a page. Yet the joy, and sometimes ecstasy, is that something comes, a book is created, and I get these marvelous feelings of pride and even astonishment that I wrote what I wrote. I'm still surprised that people pay to read what I write and think. It is a dream come true that all my books are on library shelves!"

Barbara Bickmore books have been translated into 16 languages and have been published in 22 countries. Women all over the world enjoy her stories and her heroines.

Barbara Bickmore heroines are for the thinking woman, they are women who make a difference.

Heroines for the thinking woman, women who make a difference,

Welcome to the world of *Barbara Bickmore.*

Discover other titles by *Barbara Bickmore* at:
Connect with her: www.barbarabickmore.com
Facebook: Barbara-Bickmore
Twitter: BarbaraBickmore
Email: Barbara@barbarabickmore.com

Barbara Bickmore

Made in the USA
Columbia, SC
03 July 2020

13139938R00239